EXTREME DEVOTION

X-TREME LOVE SERIES

BOOK 2

KAY MANIS

ISBN: 978-0-9984930-0-8

This book is dedicated to my beautiful daughter, Kimberly. With four small words, she changed the course of my life forever.
"Just write it, Mom."
Thanks for always believing in me.

CHAPTER 1

HINDLEY

I STOOD at the sink in my hotel room, gripping the counter so hard, my fingers were growing numb. I shook my head in disbelief, willing away my tears. What the hell had Rory done?

First, he'd nearly locked lips with some skank right in the middle of the lobby. Then, he got into a pissing match with a potential endorser. It wasn't like Matt Davis from Sonora Water was putting the moves on me. Or was he? He had been pretty close all evening. Even if it were true, Rory still had no right to act like a jackass.

And as if all that weren't bad enough, he'd ended the evening with the mother of all offenses. He'd basically announced to Axel Pretorius, fellow skateboarder and a potential client, that he and I were dating. Mr. Stedwick, the senior partner at my law firm, was drooling for me to take on Axel as another client.

Why didn't Rory understand, I needed new clients if I was going to be successful in this career and keep my firm happy? Or rather, keep Mr. Stedwick happy. He was heavily invested in my stepfather's real estate business. Paul's potential financial risks always weighed heavily on my mind. And if Mr. Stedwick pulled out, it could ruin Paul, which would ruin me.

I closed my eyes and shook my head as Rory's career-ending words replayed in my mind.

She'll be pretty tied up for a while.

If Axel had half a brain—and I was pretty sure he did—he'd figure out Rory and I were involved in more than just a professional relationship.

How dare Rory! How dare he jeopardize not only my professional, but my personal reputation as well. And for what? For some male testosterone showdown? Some pissing match? Screw that.

The only thing I could do now was go to bed and pray I'd get at least a few hours of sleep.

I unzipped my skirt and let it fall to the floor before tugging off my halter top. Reaching for my toothbrush, I squeezed on a liberal amount of paste and shoved it into my mouth, scrubbing hard. Maybe I could wash this disgusting taste of bitterness and betrayal from my mouth. *Doubtful.*

I laughed as I stared at my reflection in the mirror. Standing in nothing but a pair of Hello Kitty panties Rory had sent me at the office, I looked like the harlot I was becoming. I'd foolishly thought I'd surprise Rory tonight when he undressed me. Looked like the joke was on me.

Well, I definitely wasn't going to sleep in them, that was for damn sure.

I stormed out of the bathroom, toothbrush still in my mouth, and marched toward the closet. I would find the most unattractive pair of underwear I owned, which wouldn't be difficult. I rummaged around the case until I finally found a pair of the ugliest Granny panties I owned. Holding them up, I smiled in triumphant and turned toward the bathroom.

Suddenly movement from the corner of the room caught my eye. Someone was in the room, sitting on my bed.

My skin prickled and I fought down the panic attack threatening to consume me.

I screamed, but my mouth was still full of toothpaste. Only a garbled moan squeaked through the room. Then I remembered I was only wearing my underwear. Shit!

I dropped my toothbrush and clutched my chest to cover myself.

"No," I screamed, toothpaste flying from my mouth.

The man on the bed moved toward me.

"No, no, no...please," I begged, squeezing my eyes closed and curling into a tight ball.

Strong arms encircled me.

I beat and kicked, fighting to break free.

"Hindley," a deep voice said in my ear. "It's me, Rory. You're okay. It's just me."

Rory? My eyes flew open and I stared into Rory's familiar blue eyes.

His expression was one of utter devastation. "Are you okay?" he asked.

I broke free from his hold and stood up. My eyes darted around the room like a trapped animal. "What are you doing here?" Foaming bubbles spewed from my mouth and dripped down my chin. Dammit.

"What did you say?" He bit back a smile.

I glared at him before returning to the bathroom to rinse my mouth. I was in no mood for his crap, not tonight. I rinsed out the toothpaste and wiped my mouth with the hand towel, staring at my reflection in the mirror.

Keep strong, girl. You can do this.

Feeling braver and more in control, I dropped the towel in the sink, vowing to give him a no-holds-barred piece of my mind. How dare he sneak into my hotel room and scare the shit out of me.

I turned off the light and rounded the corner. Quickly snatching up a T-shirt off the floor, I tugged it over my head. Feeling stronger now that my breasts were covered, I marched around the bed to confront him but all my ire left as my stomach clenched and my mouth went dry.

Rory leaned against the headboard, hands behind his head, naked from the waist up. The pose showcased every glorious muscle in his upper body. His full lips were tipped up on the corner in a playful smirk.

I swallowed hard, trying to remember why I'd been mad at him. God, why did he affect me so much? I lost all coherent thought when Rory Gregor was near, and half naked.

"Sorry I scared you," he said softly.

His face looked anything *but* repentant. In fact, I was pretty sure I saw a glimmer of amusement in those beautiful blue eyes.

I crossed my arms over my chest, bolstering my resolve. "You need to leave, Rory. I can't have people seeing you come out of my hotel room late at night."

He didn't move a muscle.

I stood back on my heels, shifting my weight as I narrowed my gaze. "How the hell did you get in here anyway?"

"Magic door." He winked.

I studied him, trying to figure out what game he was playing, but it was pointless. "I don't know what the hell you're up to, but you need to leave."

He remained motionless.

"Now, Rory," I yelled, pointing to the door.

He pushed off the bed, his muscled body moving with grace, a predatory gleam in his eye.

Desire pooled low in my abdomen. Shit. This wasn't good.

He moved past me, his shoulder grazing mine, and I bit back a moan. His proximity and delicious scent had my resolve weakening.

Against my better judgment, I followed his movement, turning to see where he'd gone.

He leaned against the wall, pointing to a door. "We have adjoining rooms," he said, his voice low and seductive.

How the hell had I not noticed a door next to my dresser?

"Did you know that, Hindley?"

I shook my head, unable to speak at the sight of his naked chest so close to me.

He took a step toward me. "I requested it, specifically so I could come," he paused and delivered a wicked smile, "and go, as I pleased."

Everything south of my navel burned with desire.

"With you," he added in a rough tone.

I held my breath, hoping maybe if I didn't inhale his scent, he wouldn't affect me. Screwing my eyes shut tight, visions of his sexy body swirled in my head, making things worse. I was finding it nearly impossible to stay mad at the devilish man.

"I really am sorry, Hindley," he whispered, his breath caressing my face.

I opened my eyes and found him standing only inches away, his hand hovering at my neck. The pad of his thumb brushed my cheek and I exhaled, unaware I'd been holding my breath.

It had been pointless to will him away from my thoughts. There was nowhere I could run, no place safe to hide from the pull Rory Gregor had on me.

"What are you sorry for?" I whispered.

"For embarrassing you." His lips grazed my jaw.

Holy hell.

"For being jealous." His mouth clamped down on my earlobe.

I fought my body's urge to moan and cursed silently as the reminder of my resolve slipped away.

"For coming into your room unannounced." Rory's mouth trailed down my neck, licking and kissing, his touch heating my skin.

A moan escaped and I bit down on my lip to silence myself, but still tilted my neck to give him easier access.

"For being a total jackass." He trailed kisses down to my collarbone, his body pressed against mine, moving us toward the bed.

The bed. Oh, no.

"Stop," I yelled, pushing him away.

His hands dropped to my wrists, his eyes guarded, but barely fazed by my command. He searched my eyes, as if begging me to accept his apology.

I fought the urge to offer my forgiveness so easily.

As if understanding my resistance, his hands slid up my arms and over my shoulders.

Goose bumps prickled across my skin and I fought back a shiver.

He wrapped his fingers around my neck, his thumbs gently caressing my jaw. His eyes were darker tonight, less blue with a hint more brown, but no less mesmerizing. I couldn't break free from their hypnotic spell.

"I really am sorry, Hindley," he said, all trace of sexual innuendo and desire was gone. "I don't know what happened tonight." His eyes searched mine and I could feel myself spiraling.

I held my breath, that hypnotic pull tugging at me again. The man had to be a magician.

"You could have jeopardized everything, Rory," I whispered. "Everything I've been working so hard for. For you."

He sank onto the bed, his head lowered, looking hopeless, helpless, lost. "I knew this would happen," he said, releasing a heavy sigh.

"What would happen?"

He stared up at me, heartache and disappointment etched in his eyes. "I knew I'd fuck this up. I don't deserve you, Hindley."

My remorse quickly faded to annoyance at his continued insistence that I was better than him.

Tell him.

No.

I pushed my own thoughts to the back of my mind. "Why do you do that?"

"Do what?" he asked.

I sat down beside him, tucking my hands under my thighs to avoid the desire to touch him. "Put yourself down. Or rather, hold me up higher than yourself, as if I'm better than you."

"I think you deserve someone who can give you everything. Someone like Dipshit."

I bit back a smirk. "You mean Matt?" Rory was jealous, and the insecure girl inside me was…happy.

"Whatever," he scoffed.

"Look, Rory, you and I are just…" What *were* we? We weren't dating. We weren't even seeing each other, outside of the bedroom and boardroom. I slowly stood, staring down at him.

He tilted his head back, staring up at me.

"Hey, if you don't want to do this," I motioned a finger between us, "that's fine. But don't sit there and act like—"

He bounded up, capturing me in his arms. His hand tugged my hair, tilting my face up as his lips crushed mine.

It was a mistake to continue sleeping with Rory Gregor, logically I knew that, but I'd never felt more alive with anyone than I did with this man.

Pushing down all the reasons I shouldn't be with him, I opened my mouth and allowed him access to more of me than was safe.

His kiss grew greedy, needy, and I felt hot and desired. I met his kiss with a frenzy I'd never experienced.

Suddenly, he pulled away with a groan and threw me onto the bed.

"Well, well, well…" He smirked, his smoldering eyes staring at my mid-section. "Who do we have here?"

My gaze followed his and I realized he was staring at my panties. My Hello Kitty panties. *Oh, crap.* I scrambled back toward the headboard, tugging at the T-shirt to cover myself.

He grabbed both of my ankles and yanked me down the bed. His eyes gleamed with mischief, and something I'd never seen in another man's eyes…desire.

I was suddenly chilled and glanced down at my body, horrified to find my shirt had ridden up over my breasts. I was fully exposed to his predatory gaze. Grabbing my shirt, I tugged at it to cover myself.

Before I could move, Rory was on me, pinning my wrists next to my head. "Oh, no, you don't, Miss Hagen. I want to look at these all night."

Part of me wanted to fight. I shouldn't like this aggressive behavior from a man. But the majority of me loved his sexual prowess, and I couldn't hide my expectant smile.

His bare chest rubbed against mine as his tongue slid over the shell of my ear. Moving slowly, he trailed kisses down my neck to my collarbone, then…lower.

I squirmed and bucked, mostly because his tongue working over my breasts sent sparks of pleasure clawing up my spine.

"Stay still," he growled against my skin.

I moaned and tried to steady my body.

Rory raised his head, his blue eyes piercing me. His lips curled into a victorious grin. "Does Hindley like my tongue?"

I tilted my head, donning the most innocent face I could muster, but my body betrayed me, bucking against his heavy frame.

The glimmer in his eyes said it all. He could feel how much I wanted him.

His mouth returned to its savage assault down south. "Well. Hello. Kitty." He laughed, his words vibrating against my sensitive skin as he kissed every inch of my underwear—the underwear *he'd* bought me.

"Oh, God," I moaned, my head falling onto the mattress. I closed my eyes, absorbing the sensations of his mouth wandering against my skin. "Rory, you can't do this," I panted.

He raised his head, his brows furrowed as he studied me with boyish curiosity.

"I mean, I'm upset," I said, already missing his mouth. "We need to talk about what happened."

"We'll talk." He winked. "Later." Smiling like the devil he was, he lowered his head.

Yes, our conversation was over. For now. But we would talk.

"So you wanted to discuss something?" Rory lay next to me, his head propped on his hand as he leaned on his elbow, staring down at me.

God, he was gorgeous.

"Ummm," was all I could muster. This man was lethal in bed. I couldn't help but smile like an idiot who'd just been thoroughly worked over.

Slowly I rolled away from him, trying to pull my wits about me. I glanced around the room and chuckled at the discarded condom wrapper next to the bed—along with my T-shirt and a shredded pair of Hello Kitty underwear. "You owe me some new panties." I snorted.

His arm wrapped around my waist and he tugged me close to his chest, nuzzling my hair.

Being cradled in Rory's arms felt better than it should have. He obliterated all my thoughts when he was near. I couldn't remember why I'd been upset.

"I think I can arrange a pair of new panties, Miss Hagen," he said, kissing my neck. "I definitely don't want you going panty-less. Unless it's with me." The warm heat of his breath brushed against my skin and I shivered.

"Stop," I laughed, "that tickles."

"God, I love that sound," he moaned.

"What sound?"

"Your laughter." He pressed kisses along my shoulders.

Desire pulsed through my body and I swallowed hard. How could I want him again so soon?

"I'm ready whenever you are, Miss Hagen." He ground his hips into my backside as if answering my silent question.

Our easy connection both excited and scared me. How was it possible to feel safe in the arms of a man, *this* man?

I rolled over in his arms, staring at the hollow of his throat. My finger caressed his skin as I contemplated what I wanted to say.

"Hey." He reached under my chin, raising my face. "What's going on in there?" He tapped my temple. "Come back to me. I miss you." He placed a soft kiss against my lips.

Rory was so attuned to me. It was as simple as that. We were drawn to each other, for reasons I had yet to identify. Instinctively I knew we belonged together, even if it was only for a little while.

"Hey," he admonished. "Stop."

"Stop what?"

"Over-thinking this."

"Over-thinking what?"

"Us," he said.

"You're the one who got heavy earlier."

"I know, I'm sorry."

"Do you really think I want Matt?" I asked.

He shrugged. "He sure as hell wants you."

"That's ridiculous." Wait, did Matt want me? He had been awfully touchy feely tonight.

"He's perfect for you," Rory said.

"What does that mean?"

"He's sophisticated, probably went to Harvard or Yale or some other Ivy League bullshit school. He reeks of old school money. And I sure as shit can guarantee you he knows which fork to use at dinner."

Worry wormed its way into my sated heart. I was losing Rory. I hated hearing him think so little of himself.

I pushed up so we were eye-to-eye, knowing firmness was the only way to handle his insecurities.

"Look at me," I said in a firm, deep voice.

His eyes lifted and he stared up at me.

"Stop this bullshit, Rory Gregor. Now," I growled. "If I wanted someone like Matt, I would be with someone like Matt."

His eyes widened and I knew I had his attention.

"I hate fancy parties and debutant bullshit," I said. "You know that. I went to a crap-ass college and an even crappier-ass law school. I prefer hamburgers to five-course meals, so I couldn't give a rat's ass if there are forks on the table or not. I'm with you, Rory Gregor." I poked his chest to punctuate my point.

He pushed me back onto the mattress as his body hovered over me, his lips finding their seemingly permanent home on mine.

I wrapped my arms around his lean torso, running my fingers up and down his back as our tongues and teeth collided and our bodies intertwined with passionate abandon.

He needed me.

I needed him.

And once again, I was lost in Rory Gregor, consumed by everything about my Skater Boy.

CHAPTER 2

HINDLEY

I STRETCHED out in the passenger seat of the car, my hands raised high over my head as I reached for the sky. Tipping my head back, I lifted my face toward the sun. The rays beaming down invigorated me. Normally, I wasn't a big fan of convertibles, but I had to admit, this was exhilarating. Living in the moment was a foreign concept, but with Rory I had no choice—and I loved it.

I grabbed the sunglasses resting on top of my head and pulled them over my eyes. I turned to stare at the driver, drinking in every delicious feature of the man staring back at me.

Rory looked so damn cool, leaning back in his seat, one arm draped casually over the steering wheel as if he owned the entire west coast of California. He gave me an all-knowing grin before returning his attention back to the road.

"You didn't have to rent a car to drive us back to your house," I said above the noise of the wind whipping through the car. I turned my attention to the long road ahead of us. "We could have taken your motorcycle."

"I didn't have a spare helmet."

I could feel his predatory gaze assessing me, devouring me. Goose bumps raced over my skin amid the heat of the bright afternoon sun.

"Besides, if we had taken my motorcycle," he said, "I couldn't have enjoyed this view."

I shifted my gaze to the cliffs jutting from the Pacific Coast Highway. I had to agree, the scenery along the route was breathtaking. The waves ebbed and flowed, crashing into the jagged rocks below.

"It is breathtaking," I sighed.

"I agree," he said, gently stroking my bare leg.

I turned, staring down at his large fingers pressed against my fair skin. Slowly my gaze travelled along the curves of his muscular body until they met his.

His arresting blue eyes pierced straight through me. His plump lips turned up in a seductive smile that took my breath away. "Very beautiful," he said.

My face flushed crimson when I realized he wasn't talking about the coastline.

"Gorgeous," he said, smiling.

I turned to face the coastline, trying to hide my awkwardness. *If he only knew.*

"Hey." He squeezed my leg.

I didn't turn, I couldn't look at him, not until I got my emotions under check. I wasn't beautiful. I was ugly, I was scarred, I was defective. Sooner or later, Rory would find out. I just hoped it was later.

He slipped his fingers around my wrist and pulled my arm across the console, forcing me to face him.

I sat in silence, wanting to pull away but afraid. Not of him but of losing this moment with him.

He used his thumb to pry open my fingers, pressing my palm to his sensual lips. He pulled my hand back and laid it against his chest before glancing over at me and smiling wide. "Beautiful," he said.

Heat bloomed between my legs and my heart leaped in my chest.

"You hungry?" he asked.

Not for food, I thought.

His face lit up and a single eyebrow arched in amusement.

How could I hide anything from this man?

"I know you, Hindley."

It was a simple answer to a question I hadn't even asked and yet he'd heard it.

I leaned back and closed my eyes, reveling in the knowledge that I'd grown closer to Rory in two weeks than I had to anyone I'd ever known before, except Dana.

He doesn't know everything, a small voice whispered in my ear.

I trusted him though, more and more with each passing day. I reassured myself that no matter what my past held, Rory wouldn't judge me like others had. He gave me confidence and courage, two things that were lacking in my life.

"I didn't bring my motorcycle because Jack loves to ride my Harley," Rory said, interrupting my thoughts. "Kara made him sell his years ago. He'll bring it back to my house today or tomorrow, then fly back to Denver."

"What made you end up in California?" I asked. "Didn't you grow up in Colorado?"

"California has better weather for year-round skating. And it's got tons of boardwalks and empty pools." He laughed.

And beautiful women, I wanted to say.

"What's wrong?" he asked, his brows furrowed.

"Nothing."

"Hindley."

"Let's just say you're not the only one who doubts whether or not you're good enough."

"For what?"

I remained silent, working to keep my tears at bay as I remembered all the beautiful women screaming Rory's name at the competition over the weekend. He could have any one of them, and I feared one wrong move on my part might send him running for his flock of female groupies.

The car slowed and Rory turned into a scenic overlook. I was thankful for the distraction.

"Want to take a look?" he asked.

"Sure." I didn't look at him. I didn't want him to see me like this, so defeated and self-deprecating.

He walked around the car just as I opened my door and took it from me, extending his hand to help me out.

"Thank you."

He nodded once as if sensing I didn't want to talk. Instead, he intertwined our fingers and gently guided me toward the railing.

There was a steep drop off in front of us with jagged cliffs below. I stopped dead in my tracks, almost yanking my hand from his.

"What's wrong?" he asked, looking back at me.

"This is close enough."

"Okay."

He didn't question why I didn't want to get closer.

We stood at a comfortable distance from the railing.

That's what Rory did for me. He let me be...me, no questions, no judgments, no anything.

Quietly, he stepped behind me, wrapping his long, lean arms around my waist and drawing me back against his chest in a warm embrace.

Instinctively, I leaned against him, feeling safe and secure. I drew in deep breaths of the ocean air, feeling lighter than I had in a very long time.

His huge hands splayed across my abdomen, interlacing our fingers, as he rested his chin on my shoulder and sighed into my neck. "This is why I moved to California."

I studied the scenic overlook. It was captivating and magical. I could see why he'd moved.

"Breathtaking," he whispered in my ear above the crashing waves below. "Breathtaking, just like you." Gently he brushed his soft, full lips against my ear. "And all mine, right?"

"What, the ocean?"

He laughed, his breath brushing against the sensitive skin of my neck.

My anxiety began to disappear into the ocean breeze. I melted into his embrace, somewhat secure in his confession that I was the only person he wanted to be with. *For now.*

I was no fool and held no illusions. What we had would never last.

Rory had never been in a long-lasting relationship. It had only been sex for him. Why should I think ours would be different?

I couldn't fight the overwhelming feelings of fear as I realized how much I wanted him. The power he had to completely destroy me nearly crushed me like the breaking waves below.

I knew in time he would grow tired of me, of my damaged soul, a tortured girl unable to give him everything he needed.

I swallowed down the tears, pushing back the dark memories threatening to drown me. I could never survive that kind of pain again. It was too late though. I was already drowning in his beautiful blue waters.

CHAPTER 3

HINDLEY

"HOME SWEET HOME," Rory announced as he pushed the front door to his home open. Standing to the side, he waved a hand in front of him, ushering me inside.

His home was nestled in the hills of Laguna Beach, a gorgeous coastal town.

As I stepped inside, my mouth nearly fell open. Floor-to-ceiling windows offered spectacular views of the Pacific Ocean. I walked through the entryway and stepped down a few stairs into the large sunken living room.

The first thing I noticed was that everything in the massive room was white—the walls, the leather sofa, even the side tables—except for a deep eggplant colored blanket resting on the back of the large sofa. Even the artwork on the walls was limited to a few black and white photos.

His home was modern, yet retro, filled with natural wood and stainless-steel accents, giving it a minimalist feel. Surprisingly, the style seemed to fit Rory's personality.

Rory stepped up behind me. "It's an amazing view, huh?"

"Amazing doesn't do it justice," I answered with awe.

"Come on, I'll take you up to your room."

"Okay."

He bounded up the stairs and I followed.

On the second floor was a loft area that overlooked the main living space below. The room was filled with a couch and several chairs, the colors brighter, and well worn. This was definitely the place where most of the living was done.

Scattered along the white walls were shelves containing all Rory's trophies and medals, along with framed magazine covers, and various photos of competitions he'd been in.

I stood and stared at each item on display, amazed and astounded at all the awards and accolades he'd received. This guy was big time, and I was finally beginning to understand just how much trust he was placing in me.

"Wow, Rory." I ran my fingers over the glass encasement of one of his gold medals, marked with the iconic 'X' of the X Games. I glanced over at him. "This is unbelievable. You're so accomplished, and famous."

"I guess." He shrugged. "Come on."

His humbleness didn't surprise me. He wasn't one to boast of his accolades like many athletes I'd met.

Rory carried our bags down a long hallway and I followed. Stopping in front of one door, he pushed it open with his foot, and nodded for me to enter.

The room was stark white, like the rest of downstairs, except for a bedspread littered with flower appliques of varying sizes and shades of purple. I was starting to see a pattern here, and for a man of extreme sports, decorating with flowers and bright colors was completely unexpected, but beautiful none-the-less.

The far wall was a solid glass, overlooking the ocean, with a sliding door that led out to a large deck. I couldn't help but imagine the view from the bed.

Trying to clear my thoughts, I turned and studied the rest of the room. Black and white photos of oddly shaped objects covered the walls. I stepped closer and realized each photo was actually a different part of a skateboard, artfully taken at close range.

I laughed quietly at the irony. Rory ate, drank, and literally slept skateboarding.

"This is my room," he said.

"Really?" I laughed.

"Yes, why?"

"I don't know, it just doesn't look like something you'd design. Except the skateboard photos."

"What does it look like?" he asked, a bite of defensiveness in his voice.

I ran my fingers over the purple flower appliques. "Actually, it looks more, feminine."

A wave of nausea hit me hard in the gut at the sudden realization that other women had been in this room.

Oh, shit. Had a woman helped him decorate, an old girlfriend? Had she lived with him, had she shared this utopian space?

"I did most of it," he said, "but I had help."

"Of course, you did," I whispered to myself, swallowing down the lump in my throat. Rory Gregor was a player. Why was I surprised.

"Kara helped," he said.

"Who's Kara?" I asked, trying to bite back my jealousy.

"Leif's mom. Jack's wife. My surrogate mother, Kara Jennings. You remember her, right?"

My shoulders slumped in relief. "Oh, yes, Kara, I remember."

"What?" He stepped closer, a playful laugh in his tone. "Did you think I had an ex-girlfriend helping me decorate?"

Well, yeah, the idea had run through my mind but I wasn't going to admit that fact.

He wrapped his arms around my shoulders and brushed his lips over my neck. "No girlfriends, Hindley."

I shivered as his warm breath tickled my skin.

"Although I've had a few crazy *ex*-girlfriends." He chuckled.

I rolled my eyes. "So I've read." I didn't like to think about Rory being with other women. It filled me with uncertainty and insecurity.

"Hey," he whispered, turning me around to face him. "Don't tell me you're jealous?"

"Not jealous. Just..." Just what? I couldn't explain it even to myself. Rory wasn't mine to covet.

"We already agreed that you're mine, right?" he asked, raising his brows.

I nodded.

"If it makes you feel better, I'm jealous too," he said, smirking.

I laughed at the absurdity. "Of who? I don't have any crazy, stalker ex-boyfriends."

"The list is too long to even start."

"Please." I shrugged off his hold but he held me firmly in his grip. "Name one."

"Well, let's see. There was the entire pro skating league this weekend."

"What?"

"Oh, please, Hindley. Every guy on the tour, and half the men in the grand stands, were staring at your ass during the entire competition."

I smiled at his revelation but still didn't believe him.

"It's true," he said, turning me to face him. "I damn near got disqualified."

"How?"

"I was about to beat the shit out of every asshole ogling you."

I smiled, knowing it wasn't good to feed this jealous beast, but loving it just the same.

He gripped my shoulders, massaging them. "And the worst part of the whole damn thing was, I couldn't even tell them to stop, tell them you were mine."

My smile grew wider.

"I couldn't swing my arm over your shoulder and pull you close to me, show them you were already being taken care of, in every way possible." His eyes narrowed as his hands moved up to my neck. "It was pure hell."

"Really?" I bit my lip to keep from giggling.

"Yes, really," he growled. "I was in a shitty mood the entire tournament."

"Was that why Jack was so mad last night?"

"Yeah, mostly."

"Do I want to know the rest of why?"

"He knows we're together."

I jumped back from his hold. "Rory! How could you?"

He scrubbed a hand through his hair. "I didn't tell him. Kara did."

"How does *she* know?"

"Kara and I are…kindred spirits. She knew from my actions that I'd found someone special. She had no idea you were my attorney. Well, not until I told her."

I didn't know whether to be pissed or flattered. "When?" I asked.

Rory's eyes met mine. "When what?"

"When did you tell Kara?"

"I didn't tell her, Hindley. I didn't have to, she just…knew."

"Okay, when did she *know*?"

His head dropped and he stared down at his feet. "That night after I hurt you."

Hurt me?

"What are you talking about?" I asked.

He slowly lifted his head, his blue eyes darker, his fists clenched by his sides.

Oh, no, he was talking about the night I hit my hand—the night I thought he was rejecting me.

"Oh, yeah," I said softly, "*that* night."

He walked to the window, staring out at the ocean.

I hated that he still carried around the guilt of that night.

I stepped up behind him and wrapped my arms around his waist, pressing my body into his. I placed kisses along his back, trying to take away his pain. Flattening my palms against his rock-hard abs, I moved them in slow, soothing circles, willing away the ache of his dark thoughts.

I felt him draw in a deep breath before turning to face me. His hands slid up my arms and over my shoulders until he cradled my face. I gave thanks that his eyes were lighter now, full of hope and promise. The darkness had passed. For now.

"Trust me?" he said in a low voice that had my insides melting.

His wicked smile should have worried me, but it didn't. I drew in a deep breath and nodded.

"Good girl," he whispered, planting a chaste kiss on my forehead. He scooted past me toward his chest of drawers.

I watched as he pulled out what looked like straps from a drawer. Each had metal clip hooks, like carabiners that rock climbers used.

From another drawer, he lifted a thin string of pink rubbery rope. He worked skillfully; he attached the two pieces together then walked toward the bed and laid them on the floor. Yanking the comforter from the mattress in one fell swoop, he laid it gracefully on the floor. Then he removed all the pillows and top sheet, leaving the mattress bare except for the fitted linen.

Oh, God. What was he about to do?

Rory crawled across the bed like a mountain lion, carrying the straps with him. His body was sleek and toned, every part of him gorgeous. I hugged myself knowing he was all mine.

He braced himself with one hand, then stuck the other between the headboard and mattress, reaching underneath for something. The sound of metal snapping against metal echoed through the room.

Oh. My. God.

He sat back on his heels and yanked on the strap, ensuring it was secure before moving across the bed and repeating the process with the other strap.

Then it hit me like a ton of bricks. He's a dominant. And I was about to be Fifty Shades of Grayed.

A myriad of emotions raced through my head. I practiced my deep breathing exercises, trying to stave off a full-blown anxiety attack. How did I feel about being a submissive? Would I run if he tried to tie me up? What if he hit me?

Rory sat in the middle of the bed, his luscious lips curled in a devilish grin. "Come here, Hindley."

I barely heard him above the thunderous beating of my heart.

He held out his hand, and like Eve, I was drawn to him on some metaphysical level.

I wanted to be brave. For Rory. For me. I just had to be sure of one thing.

"You're not going to hit me, are you?" I asked.

He remained silent.

"I don't want you to hit me," I whispered.

"I don't hit women, Hindley," he said as if offended.

"Do you," God, I didn't know the lingo, "do you spank them?"

"Why?" He raised a brow. "Do you want me to spank you?" His eyes twinkled with laughter.

And just like that, my Skater Boy was back.

"Not particularly," I said.

"I might spank you, but not as punishment. This isn't *Fifty Shades of Grey* shit. I'm not gonna tie you up and shove plugs up your ass. I'm not into that." He smirked. "Unless you want me to."

My body stiffened and my eyes bulged like I'd been shocked with a taser. Shove shit up my ass?

Uh, no. That would be a big, fat, fucking hell no.

"Then I'll never do it," he said, seemingly hearing my silent answer.

Feeling reassured, I propped my knee up on the bed and took his proffered hand. I drew in a labored breath, my heart beating in staccato as I shivered with anticipation, and fear. My expression must have shown my apprehension because he brought the straps close so I could touch them.

"These are silicone restraints." He let me hold one of the pink, rubbery ropes in my hand.

It was soft and pliable. I noticed there was a slit in the end.

"This is where you place your wrists or your ankles." He opened the slip, revealing a space barely big enough to wrap around an appendage.

Ah, restraints.

"They don't pull and bite like metal handcuffs."

Metal cuffs? Oh, hell, what was I getting into?

My heart raced and my breath caught in my throat, and yet I still didn't say no. I could tell he was gauging my reaction. When I offered no further resistance, he continued.

"The restraints are attached to these straps, which are tethered to a rail underneath my bed." He yanked on the restraints and I heard the metal rattle underneath us.

Holy, shit. This was a bondage bed. My mouth fell open and I jerked back.

"Wait," he said, slipping a hand around my waist to hold me close. He placed a soft kiss against my open mouth. I moaned, and he smiled against my lips. Pulling back, he studied me, his eyes half-lidded. "You don't have to do any of this, Hindley. Only if you want to."

My mind was racing. What if I freaked out after he tied me up? What if I didn't like this?

What if you do?

I knew all about this kind of play from Regan's store, and I pretty much knew how it all worked...in theory. But to actually use all this bondage equipment was a whole new ball game.

"Is this what you do?" I asked, motioning to the straps. "Bondage? BDSM?"

"Sometimes."

"Do you need it? You know, to get off?"

"I don't *need* it, Hindley. It's just a kink I have. Some people like it, some people don't."

"Are you a dominant?"

He chuckled. "You girls and your erotic novels, I swear."

I remained perfectly still, eyes wide.

"No, I'm not a Dominant in the term of the BDSM world, if that's what you mean. I do like to dominate, but only to a level you're comfortable with."

I swallowed hard, my eyes darting around the room. That was good, I guess.

"Ask me anything," he said.

"How long have you been doing this?" I reached out to touch the pink rope. "Tying people up and stuff?"

He shifted back and somehow, I knew I'd offended him.

"First of all, this is consensual. If you don't want to do it, or you're uncomfortable, we won't do it. I don't *need* it. Second of all, this type of play involves trust. If you don't trust me, if I don't trust you, then it's pointless."

"Why are you getting upset? I'm trying to understand. I never said I didn't like it. I need to make sure I can do this. For you."

"This isn't for me, Hindley." He reached out and stroked my face with the back of his hand. "It's for you. I love that you trust me, and I want to show you how much I trust you too. With everything." His heated gaze traveled the length of me and my body trembled with desire.

"So," I cleared my throat, "you've done all this before?" I nodded to the straps. "I mean, your bed is pretty much designed for it, right?"

He laughed, but stopped when he saw I was offended.

"I'm not laughing at you, Hindley, I'm laughing at myself. To answer your question, yes, I've done this before."

"Oh." I worked to hold back the pang of jealousy threatening to bubble over.

"I don't do it a lot."

"But you have all the stuff."

He shrugged. "I'm adventurous, I guess you'd say."

"Okay." Was that supposed to make me feel better? How many people, I wanted to ask. The question was on the tip of my tongue, but I knew I didn't want to hear the answer.

"But I don't do it very often because I don't trust many people."

"I don't understand. You said this type of play is about trust. How could you have done this with other women if they didn't trust you?"

"I've done it *to* other women, Hindley. But I've never had it done to *me*."

I shook my head, completely confused. "What are you saying?"

"I'm saying these are for me." He yanked on the restraints.

My heart stopped. "Wait, you want me to tie *you* up?"

He nodded, his eyes darting between mine. "Only if you want to."

"So, you've never been tied up with anyone before me?"

He shook his head. "Nope."

I realized in that moment that Rory Gregor was truly mine...and I was his. Surrendering his body to me, giving up control, was his way of showing me.

I'd been able to decipher from his cryptic stories that he'd come from a background of mistrust and abuse. To lay on a bed, completely vulnerable and at my mercy, was huge for him. I got that, big time.

I flung myself into his arms, toppling him over as I covered his mouth with mine. His hands gripped my backside as we tore at one another's clothes.

When we were finally undressed, I sat up, gasping for air with a gleam in my eye. He trusted me enough to be vulnerable with me. It was time for me to do the same.

I dragged my hand along his tattoo on his ribs, tracing the outline of the skateboard.

He fell back onto the bed. "You love my tattoo, don't you?"

"Um hum." I traced a line up his torso, past his shoulder then back down his arm to his wrist. "Are you sure?" I gave him one last chance.

His half smile was my undoing.

I reached out to the rubbery strap and stretched the slit wide as I gently slipped his hand through. "Okay?"

His eyes flashed with a spark of uncertainty, but his face held a trusting smile.

I took my cue and crawled over his body to restrain the other hand, surprised at my nimbleness.

"Wow, you're very good at this." He smirked. "Are you sure you haven't done it before?"

His playfulness was infectious and I wanted to join in.

I tilted my head and raised a brow. "Maybe."

His face went slack with shock.

I giggled sheepishly, leaning down and placing a chaste kiss on his lips. "Only you, Rory Gregor. Only you," I whispered.

Metal clanked underneath the bed, vibrating the mattress, and I looked up.

Rory was reaching for me but couldn't thanks to the restraints.

I studied his beautiful face, intoxicated by his smoldering gaze. "Trying to touch me, are you?"

He waggled his brows. "You are quite the vixen, aren't you, Miss Hagen?"

"Why yes, Mr. Gregor, I am," I said in my best southern drawl.

We both laughed and my anxieties eased.

"Is it okay? Is it too tight?" I asked.

He shook his head. "Nope. I'm fine. So, what do you plan on doing now, Miss Hagen?"

"Oh, you only wish you knew, Mr. Gregor." I straddled his hips, not surprised to find his erection pushing against my backside. "Ready so soon?" I laughed.

He bucked up against me. "I'm always ready for you, Hindley."

His voice was a low growl and I thought I might orgasm right there on top of him, without even touching him.

"That's right," he continued. "I don't even need to touch you to make you come."

Oh, God, how could he read my mind so easily? I swallowed hard and donned my best Dominatrix persona.

"Well, Mr. Gregor, let's see if I can do the same." I rolled off his body and sat next to him, leaning my head down to his chest. I placed my lips as close to his neck as I could without touching and blew a warm breath against his dark skin.

He lifted his head trying to bring his lips to mine.

I pulled away quickly. "Uhnt, uhnt, uhnt," I admonished, shaking my head. "No touching, Mr. Gregor, or I'll stop. And trust me, you don't want me to stop."

His eyes went wide, mouth open. I'd shocked him, and myself.

I was in control, I was in charge, and the feeling was intoxicating. No one could tell me anything. No one could tell me what to do, how to act, or what to say. It was liberating, and addicting.

I reached to the floor and picked up my bra. Wrapping the material around my hand, I held it out so he could see what it was.

His gaze went from the bra to me and a shiver ran up my spine when his blue eyes flickered with desire.

Pushing down my nervousness, I slowly stroked his skin with the lace.

He moaned, the sound vibrating against my skin. Rory had been right. I didn't need his touch to get me off.

I leaned over him, careful not to touch him as my breasts grazed tantalizingly close to his mouth. I stared at his face and I watched with great satisfaction when he closed his lids and licked his dry lips. The chains rattled from below.

"Christ, Hindley."

Feeling empowered, I dragged my bra down his chest, slowly moving the material back and forth over his skin.

He squeezed his eyes closed as he clenched his jaw. Every muscle in his body tensed as he pulled against the restraints.

Fearing he may explode, I stopped and sat back on my heels.

He frowned and opened his eyes. "What's wrong?"

"Are you okay?"

He glanced down at his erection. "You're killing me."

My gaze followed his and a small smile tugged on my lips.

"Proud of yourself, are you, Miss Hagen?"

I turned to face him, leaning down, my lips a breath away from his. "Yes, Mr. Gregor," I whispered, "I'm quite proud of myself." I cut my eyes to his ever-growing erection. "Looks like I can make you come without touching you too."

His chest heaved and his breaths came out in staggered pants as I licked his bottom lip. He raised his head, trying to deepen the kiss but I moved my tongue down his whisker-covered jaw, sucking on his neck as I moved lower.

"Fuck, Hindley." The chains rattled underneath us and I laughed. "This isn't funny."

I tossed my hair behind my shoulder and stared up at him. "I think it's very funny, Mr. Gregor. Now lie back and enjoy or I'll stop."

He groaned but dropped his head to the mattress.

My tongue moved lower to his tattoo, and I traced the outline of "SK8R BOY" as my fingers wrapped around his stiff erection.

"Oh, God," he moaned again, pressing his hips up into my grasp.

I smiled, feeling like a wanton sex goddess, ruler of my seductive domain.

"Hindley," he whimpered.

"Yes, Rory," I answered, kissing his rock-hard abs and moving lower.

"Please."

I laughed against his skin. He was begging me, like I always did him.

The rattling of the clips against the metal railings grew thunderous. If I didn't give him what he wanted soon, he was going to break the whole damn bed apart trying to get to me.

The thought infused me with more confidence and power than I'd ever felt before. I could do this to him—I could do this *for* him.

In this moment I was more alive than I'd ever felt, and for once, in control of my own destiny. It may not last for long, but the feeling was so addicting I couldn't stop. And Rory had given me this chance. I wanted to give him everything.

Slowly I lowered my mouth over him, my tongue swirling around the head. The soft silky feel of him in my mouth was addicting.

He cried out and bucked against me, nearly causing me to gag.

Feeling empowered by his moans of pleasure, I licked and sucked, moving mouth mercilessly. His hips jerked, pressing into me and I matched his movements with the same fervor.

The sounds of the clattering chains below us spurred me on and I took in even more of him. My own arousal grew as I brought him closer to the edge.

"Fuck!" His voice thundered in my ears, driving me on. "Fuck, Hindley!"

With his last exclamation, he released inside me but I didn't let him go. My mouth continued to work him through his final throws of pleasure.

"Please, Hindley," he begged. "Please stop. It's too much."

I smiled, finally pulling away, surprised I could make him come undone.

I was his.

He was mine.

And for the first time in a long time, I truly felt alive.

CHAPTER 4

RORY

I WATCHED in silence as Hindley's chest rose and fell as she slept. A pang of guilt hit my own chest.

It was almost three in the morning. I'd kept her up half the night, ravishing her body. I knew I needed to let her sleep but my constant erection had other ideas.

We were driving to San Diego in the morning to meet Matt, the Dipshit. The thought had my teeth clenching, and my dick softening. Why the hell was I so territorial with this woman?

I stared down at her golden blonde hair scattered across my pillow. Her beautiful face laid nestled against my chest, one arm and leg wrapped around my body as if I were her lifeline. I smiled and sighed deeply, realizing she was mine. In my world filled with constant chaos, this felt right, *she* felt right.

It was beyond me how anyone could have ever told this amazing creature she was lousy in bed. What a dumb fuck. Hindley was the centerfold of *Sex on Wheels* magazine.

She hadn't batted an eye when I pulled out the restraints. Hell, she'd actually looked honored when I asked her to pin me down. I had even shocked myself.

I'd brought out the restraints to use on her, but somewhere in the process of hooking them up, I realized she needed reassurance from me.

Giving up control of my body seemed like the best way to show her. And my God, had she taken advantage of my submission.

Fuck me, but this girl could suck a mean dick. I'd never felt such ecstasy in all my life.

Everything was different with Hindley. From every sexual adventure we had, to our walk on the beach earlier this evening, to just sitting and talking with her on the back deck, there was nothing I didn't love about being with Hindley Hagen.

Love?

Whoa. No, no, no.

Okay, so maybe not love but there was definitely something deeper with Hindley.

My insecurities were fading. Hindley's trust in me was something I never knew I needed in order to feel good about myself. But still, something tugged in my chest, reminding me I had a past that could ruin us both. That dark voice in my head reminded me she deserved better.

Hindley stirred underneath me. As much as I wanted to sink deep inside her again, I remained still, allowing her to reposition.

"Hey," she whispered in a groggy voice, her sleepy gaze meeting mine. "What are you doing awake?"

I twirled a piece of her hair around my finger. "I could ask you the same question."

Her hands rubbed against my chest and moved lower.

I grabbed her wrist. "Hindley."

"Why?" she pouted.

I bit back a laugh. She looked heartbroken…and cute as hell.

"Because you have an early meeting tomorrow, well, today I guess. You need to sleep."

"Please." She batted her eyes, breaking her hand free from my hold.

I couldn't resist. I pulled her body onto mine and sucked on that pouting lip.

She deepened the kiss, her hands raking through my hair.

I tried to pull back but she wouldn't let me. This girl was freakishly strong. "Hindley," I said as her lips pressed against mine.

"Hmmm," she moaned.

That was all it took, hearing her voice, feeling the vibration against my lips. I flipped her over so she was underneath me, and lost myself in her all over again.

Hindley jumped out of bed, her naked little ass walking confidently over to her suitcase.

"What are you doing?" I pushed up on the pillows, drinking in every delectable curve of her body.

She turned around, holding some type of book. Shrugging one shoulder, she batted her eyes.

She was up to no good. But staring at her naked body—she was so fucking hot—it didn't matter what she was doing. She could have been slaughtering a litter of kittens for all I cared.

"Here," she said, jumping back on the bed beside me and holding out the book.

Oh, shit.

A book.

My heart raced with fear, but her excitement was infectious, and I couldn't help but take it from her outstretched hand.

She still sat gloriously naked, and I was having a hard time concentrating on anything other than her perky boobs and delicious mound, which had both been in my mouth only moments ago.

My dick throbbed with an aching need.

Down, boy. This was obviously important to Hindley. My needs could wait.

"What is this?" I asked, studying the book.

She pointed to the word on the cover. "Can you read the title?"

I knew the letters. J-O-U-R-N-A-L, but I didn't know what it spelled. Embarrassed to admit it, I quickly shook my head in shame.

"Hey," she said, slipping a finger beneath my chin and raising my head.

I stared down at the mattress between us.

"Rory," she said quietly.

Slowly, I lifted my gaze.

"I'm just asking you a question, to find out where to start, with your reading, I mean. I want to help you, but I have to know what words you know and what words you don't. I'm not judging. I'll never judge you, Rory. You know that."

She sounded sincere, but I was having a hard time believing her words.

"Rory."

"Hmm."

"You trusted me enough to tie you up and have my way with you, didn't you?"

I lifted my head.

She was smiling, holding back her laughter, I could tell. Unable to stop herself, she burst into laughter and I couldn't help but join her.

I stroked her cheek. "That has to be one of the sweetest sounds I've ever heard."

She leaned her face into my touch.

My heart ached for some unknown reason. Who the hell was I kidding? I knew the reason. Hell, I could even spell it. L-O-V-E. I just didn't want to say it out loud.

"This is a journal," she said. "You know, to write down your thoughts and ideas, your hopes and dreams."

"Um, Hindley, I don't know how to read."

"I know." She shrugged as if the fact were nothing.

"So that means I don't know how to write either."

"I know."

"No offense, but what the hell am I going to do with a journal?"

"You're going to write in it." She smiled with such a look of confidence that I almost believed I *could* write in this damn thing.

Did I even want to? Probably not. I'd found it was always best to keep my thoughts to myself.

"You've survived in a world of words through pictures, right?" she asked.

I studied her, my brows furrowed. Where was she going with this?

"You told me you can tell a can of dog food from a can of soup because of the pictures, right?"

I nodded, still not understanding what she was talking about.

"Then that's how you'll learn to read."

Feelings of inadequacy washed over me as the abusive words of my childhood echoed through my mind.

She placed a hand on my leg. "Rory, stop."

I flinched.

"You can't put yourself down when we're doing this, do you understand?"

"I don't think I can do this, Hindley." I placed the journal to the side, and stared anywhere but at her.

She opened the journal to the first page. "Here." She pushed the journal back toward me. "What does that say?" She pointed to the page.

There were typed and handwritten words.

I stared at the page, unable to read them, I was a fucking idiot.

"Rory," she pushed me.

"I don't know, Hindley. I can't fuckin' read it," I half shouted. "Are you happy? Is that what you wanted to hear me say again? I. Can't. Fucking. Read! Is that clear enough?"

I shoved at the covers, trying to quiet the memories assaulting me, the taunting words of every person who'd called me an idiot, a moron, a half-wit, a dumb-fuck, or worse.

Hindley's arms wrapped around my shoulders and she pulled me back toward the bed with her super-human strength. "Stop," she whispered in my ear. "Just stop it, right now. You're none of those things, all right."

How did she know where my mind was going?

The same way I could hear her thoughts. We were connected on a level neither of us understood.

Maybe she could help me.

She extended her arms from behind me and held the journal open in front of me while her chin rested on my shoulder. "Try to read this," she said. "If you can't, it's fine. I need to know where to start. Eventually, you'll get there. We'll get there."

We'll get there?

What the hell did that mean?

My illiteracy had been a battle I'd fought on my own for so long that the idea of someone else wanting to help was as confusing as my illiteracy itself.

Knowing Hindley would never relent, I grasped the journal from her hands and held it in my lap. I studied the words, surprised that I knew some of them.

"It says, 'To,'" I said.

"Yes," she said triumphantly, squeezing my shoulder.

I studied the rest of the words. "Does that say, My Skater Boy?" I asked in disbelief.

"That's right."

She sounded so excited, it pushed me to go on. "To my Skater Boy," I continued. "From."

"Um hum," she whispered in my ear.

I knew the second word, 'girl', but I wasn't sure what the word before it was.

"Just read what you *can*, Rory. It doesn't matter if it's right or wrong. And if you can't, tell me and we'll work on it. Together." She kissed my cheek softly.

Together. She'd said it before.

I felt infused with a confidence I'd never known before. Hindley believed in me, and that was enough.

"I know that says 'girl'," I said, pointing to the second word.

"Good, yes. It's girl."

I sat quietly, studying the text.

Hindley came to sit beside me on the bed. "Have you ever heard of context clues?" she asked, staring up at me. There was no judgment, only compassion.

I sagged in relief, surprised at how fearful I'd been of her judgment. "No," I said.

"Good."

"Good? How is that good?"

"It's good because you're not judging yourself." She smiled. "You're telling me the truth. You're trusting me to not judge you, and that's where we start."

I let her words sink in. I had to trust her if I wanted her to help me learn to read. I had to stop thinking she would desert me if she knew how stupid I was.

"Stop, Rory," she said softly, admonishing me again.

"Stop what?"

"I can see when you go to the dark side, when you start doubting yourself, thinking that I'm better than you, or that you're beneath me. It's not true. But until you realize that, there won't be much room for success."

I squeezed the back of my neck. "Look, Hindley, I've tried this before. So many people have tried to help me read, but it's never happened."

"I'm not going to teach you to read, Rory," she said confidently.

My brows puckered in confusion as I stared at her. She was so matter-of-fact about this idea of helping me.

"You already can read," she said. "All we're going to do is build your vocabulary through different means."

"What, through flash cards?" I snorted.

"Maybe," she said with defiance. "If that's what it takes."

She *was* serious.

But I couldn't take her seriously. Not when she was sitting next to me, completely nude.

"I'd love to believe you, Hindley, but honestly, I can't hear a word you're saying. All I can think about is how hot you look sitting here butt-naked, and how much I want to throw you down and fuck you into seventh heaven."

She burst out laughing so hard, I thought she was going to fall off the bed. "Okay, I think I understand that." She pushed off the bed.

She tried to walk away but I grabbed her around the waist and pulled her back. Turning her to face me, I pressed my lips to her stomach then lifted my head to stare up at her beautiful face.

She was smiling, the glow from the moon outside illuminating her body, casting her in a magical light. She was a goddess. My goddess.

"Do you have any idea how beautiful you are, Hindley?"

She dug her fingers in my hair, massaging my temples with her thumbs. "With you, I feel beautiful."

I hated that she didn't believe in her own beauty, but I understood her doubts. With her, I felt smart, whether it was true or not.

Without another word, she pushed away and disappeared into my closet. Before I could follow her, she reappeared in the doorway, wearing one of my ratty skateboard T-shirts. The hem hung down to her mid-thigh.

My dick twitched. Naked, micro-mini skirt, shorts, jeans, or one of my raggedy old T-shirts, Hindley Hagen looked delicious in everything she wore—but even better wearing nothing at all.

"I don't think covering up with one of my old T-shirts will help me much, Hindley." I smiled. "You look even hotter now."

She smiled proudly as if unused to being complimented for her sexiness.

How could she *not* see how gorgeous she was?

"May I also suggest you put on some shorts, Mr. Gregor?" She nodded toward my mid-section. "You're very distracting as well. Your dick should be catalogued as a weapon of mass destruction."

I bellowed with laughter. She was becoming so bold, and I loved it.

She smirked and stepped closer. "I'm not sure I can sit next to you naked in all your glory without wanting to fall to my knees to show my appreciation to the maker of the universe for your physical beauty."

Oh, fuck yeah.

Ever since I'd discovered those sassy blue toenails that first night I'd undressed her comatose body, I'd known Hindley Hagen had a kinky side. Today she'd proved it.

I jumped off the bed and grabbed her ass, knowing she was gloriously naked under my shirt. I lifted her off the floor and wrapped her legs around my waist.

My mouth crashed down on hers and desire coiled tight in my body, threatening to explode. Backing her up, I pinned her against the wall with more vigor than I'd intended.

"Ouch," she grimaced, rubbing the back of her head.

"Sorry," I whispered against her neck as I rubbed against her, my dick working its way inside.

"You don't have a condom on, Rory."

I could barely make out her words, my body was throbbing so hard with need.

Condom. Condom. Condom.

"Oh, shit," I muttered. "Condom."

She slid down the wall as I released her.

"Hang on." I rushed back to the bedside table, pulling out a packet and ripping it open. Rolling it on as quickly as possible with my fumbling hands, I turned to recapture the woman who drove me crazy with need.

My heart caught in my throat when I saw her leaning against the wall.

She stared at me, her brown eyes dark with desire as she slowly dragged my T-shirt up and off her body, revealing pure perfection underneath.

She flung the shirt to the side and extended her arms, jutting out one hip in the most alluring pose I'd ever seen. I wanted her more than my next breath.

"Goddamn, Hindley, what you do to me. You're so fucking—" There were no words to describe how beautiful she was, inside and out.

"I'm so *what*, Rory?" she purred.

I rushed to her, scooped her up in my arms, and wrapped her naked legs around me again.

"So fucking delicious I can never get enough of you. I'm addicted." I slammed into her, driving her body into the wall, my desire forced higher by her guttural moans. Our hips moved in unison, lighting up every nerve ending. We were one, made to fit together. Perfectly.

"Oh my God, Rory," she murmured in my ear.

My dick thrust harder with each cry. This woman drove me to climax faster than anyone I'd ever known.

Part of me was disappointed that I couldn't make this experience last longer, for both of us. But I was shallow, a selfish dick to the core. I wanted my release, and with Hindley Hagen it was nearly impossible to stop myself anytime I was inside her.

"Hindley, come on, baby."

"I'm there," she whimpered. "Oh, God, Rory, please."

With one last thrust, our bodies tensed and trembled with release. I clutched her closer as she finally stilled against me.

I'd never experienced joy like this before.

Being buried deep inside Hindley and sharing the ultimate peak in physical connection was unbelievable.

For the first time in my life my world was perfect. I was exactly where I'd always dreamt of being—in the arms of someone I trusted with my life, and my heart.

Hindley calmed me, body, mind, and soul, and I knew in that moment that I would *never* let her go.

CHAPTER 5

RORY

SENSING WE WOULD GET NOWHERE in bed, Hindley pulled her shirt back on. Once I'd found a pair of lounge pants to cover me *properly*, as she'd put it, she dragged me downstairs to the living room

"You're a tactile learner," she said, sitting on the couch. "Do you know what that means?"

"No." I sat beside her, surprised I wasn't embarrassed to admit my ignorance.

"Thank you for being honest and for not judging yourself." She leaned over and kissed my cheek.

"Don't start, Miss Hagen. Just because we're not in bed doesn't mean I won't ravish you like the vixen you are."

"Okay, sorry." She smirked. "I just can't resist you sometimes."

"Believe me, the feeling is very mutual."

"So, anyway." She pushed away from me, crossing her legs and squaring her shoulders. This was teacher Hindley. "A tactile learner means you need to incorporate every sense you have in order to learn new skills. Take skating, for instance. You didn't learn to skate by looking in books, did you?"

I shook my head, thinking back.

"So how did you learn?"

"I don't know, it came naturally, I guess."

"Exactly." She shoved a finger in the air as if she'd discovered a new planet. "That's the way reading is for me. It comes naturally for me. For you, it doesn't, so we have to use everything at our disposal to help you."

"So skating doesn't come natural to you?" I teased.

"Um, no. I'm a natural klutz."

"Have you ever skated?"

"No," she answered flatly. "And I don't plan to."

"Why?"

"Because I'm a major spaz, and it would take a much bigger commitment on your part to see me flat on my ass."

"Are you forgetting how we met?" I cocked a brow.

She smirked and ducked her head. "This is different."

"What does that mean?"

"It means you'd run for the hills if you saw how uncoordinated I was. A sexual relationship would not be strong enough to hold you after you saw me fall on my face."

I laughed then realized what she was saying. "Commitment? What do you mean, like marriage?" I couldn't help but tease her. "So, you're saying I'd have to marry you before I could teach you how to skate?"

Her face flushed bright red.

Oh, God, had I really just said *marry*?

Shit, I had. And my body didn't respond with its usual distaste for the word.

"Anyway," she said, "this isn't about me and skating. It's about you."

"What if I want it to be about you?" I asked, sliding my fingers toward her.

She slapped my hand.

I pulled away and laughed.

"So anyway," she settled into the sofa, "back to tactile. You know sounds of the letters right, and some words?"

"Yes."

"Do you know how to sound out words?"

"Yes." I narrowed my gaze. Where was she headed?

She glanced up at me. "Well, that only works some of the time. Most words in the English language are what we call sight words. That means you basically have to memorize them because there's no way you could sound them out using the rules. Say, for instance, the word aerial. Something you're very good at."

She smiled, seeming almost prouder of me than I was of myself.

My chest swelled with pride. "You like my aerials, Drunk Girl?"

"Rory, your skating is extraordinary."

Extraordinary.

I let the word roll around in my head. Hindley was impressed with my skating. She thought I was *extra*-ordinary.

"Extraordinary isn't a sight word. It's actually two words combined into a bigger one, the word extra and the word ordinary. Once you learn each word, you can put them together into bigger words called compound words."

I heard her talking, but I wasn't concentrating. I was too absorbed in the idea that she thought I was *extraordinary*. I could give a fuck less about how to spell it.

"Are you really that surprised?" she asked.

"At what?"

"That I would be impressed by your skating?"

"Yeah, I guess so," I said.

"Why?"

"I don't know, I guess it's just—" I thought about her question.

"You think I'm so educated and refined that there was nothing you could do to impress me?" she asked with a bit of bite in her voice.

I didn't answer. I didn't have to. She had pinpointed exactly why I was shocked.

"Whatever, Rory." She shook her head. Ignoring me, she pulled out a blue spiral notebook and flipped through the pages. "In this book, I've labeled each page with a letter of the alphabet, starting with 'A.'"

I stared at the folder, a cold sweat breaking out across my forehead. It looked a lot like school supplies.

Apparently not noticing my nervousness, Hindley continued.

"For each letter in this book, I want you to write down all the words you *can* read. Anytime you're out and about and you recognize a word, write it down. Or add it to your phone then put it in this spiral once you get back home. This will become your bible, a way to help you put together words you already know in order to create and learn bigger words. Are you with me so far?"

I swallowed hard, unsure of how to explain my problem without looking like a total imbecile. "Look, Hindley, sometimes what you see and what I see, they're different."

"Doesn't matter," she said with no hesitancy or need for explanation. "As long as *you* know what the word is, that's all that matters."

I sat back on the couch, unsure of what to make of this vixen.

"I'll help show you the correct way to write the letters," she continued, "if that truly is part of your problem with dyslexia. But for now, I just need you to record all the words you do know as they pop into your head. Write them down *exactly* as you see them, misspellings and all. This spiral will help build your confidence. I'm pretty sure you know a lot more words than you think, and can read more than you know."

"What about the journal?"

"That's where the tactile learning comes in." She ignored the journal and instead flipped to the middle of the blue spiral notebook and wrote something down.

"What's that?" I asked, trying to peer over her shoulder.

"This will become your sight word list. As we go, we'll find words along the way that I'll put on this list. You'll need to memorize them."

"I have a bad memory."

"Actually, you have a brilliant memory. *"*

Brilliant? No one had ever called me brilliant, not even for skating.

"It's true." She smiled. "Look at the way you work through your skateboard routines."

"That's easy." I shrugged. "It comes naturally to me."

"Not to most people though. The way you combine your moves and tricks into one amazing run is incredible to watch."

I sat back, allowing her words to sink in. I didn't *feel* amazing. I felt stupid and awkward. Especially now, revealing all my secrets.

"Rory, reading is just like skating. You take letters and create words. You take words and create sentences. You take sentences and create stories."

Was it truly that simple? No one had ever explained it to me that way before.

She scooted closer. "If you can mold your skating skills into a beautiful and technical routine, then I know you can do that with anything, including letters and words and sentences. You *are* brilliant, Rory, in many things." She smirked.

"Oh, yes. Yes, I am, Miss Hagen." I grinned.

"Stop it or we'll never get through this." She giggled.

"Hindley, it's late. We have to leave in like three hours to get you to San Diego in time for your meeting."

"I can sleep on the way home," she said. "This is important."

"What is? Me reading?"

"You, feeling confident in yourself. In all things, Rory. It's the only way…"

"Only way, what?"

She sat still, her eyes unmoving for several seconds. "So anyway, your journal is for your eyes only."

She was a master at moving the topic away from herself.

"If you want to share it with me you can," she said, "but know that I will never look inside it unless you want me to. You can be honest and real in this book, okay?"

I nodded, not sure I would be.

"You've made a lifetime out of memorizing photos, drawings, and pictures to help you comprehend and remember things, right?"

I didn't understand her way of thinking, and the familiar pain of anxiety and fear burned in my chest as I knotted my fingers.

"Stop it, Rory."

My eyes caught hers, the deep dark brown of her gaze penetrating something deep inside me. Breaking free the insecurities I'd held on to for a lifetime. Hindley's ability to bring me back from my disparaging thoughts was truly surprising.

"Your skateboarding tricks, for instance," she said, continuing on as if I hadn't just had an epiphany. "If I were to say, draw the word aerial, not write it, what would you draw?"

She opened the journal to the second page and handed it to me.

I stared down at the blank white page, my heart hammering in my chest.

"Draw it," she instructed.

Fuck it. What did I have to lose, except this girl.

Taking the pen from her, I scribbled a circle with an arrow pointing up.

"See, you know the word aerial, but your picture graphic and the word graphic are different. Once you memorize what the word graphic looks like on paper, you'll be able to read it and draw it like you did this symbol. The letters will become symbols for you, like your picture is now." She scooted closer.

I had no idea what the fuck she was talking about, but she seemed excited…and she was closer to me. Her nearness calmed me.

"All right, next to your graphic," she continued, "I want you to write the word aerial."

"I don't know how." My resolve was fading, and my self-esteem falling even faster.

"That's why I'm here. And Google Translator. Where's your phone?"

"On the charger in my room."

"Go get it."

I loved her air of confidence and authority. I'd only seen it in the conference room during our negotiations. I couldn't help but wonder if maybe it was me, maybe I gave her enough courage to be confident as she did me.

Letting the thought percolate as I ran back to my room to grab the phone, I returned to the sofa, nestling close to her.

"Here." She shoved the journal and pen in my hands. "Write down the word aerial. Open Google Translator and speak the word like you've done in the past."

I did as she instructed.

She pointed to the phone. "Look at the screen. What are the letters?"

"A-E-R-I-A-L." I spelled out.

"Now, write out the word next to the picture you just drew."

My heart raced and my head pounded. My writing had always been atrocious. I hadn't written down much of anything, except my signature, in years.

"Don't be nervous, Rory." She placed a hand gently on my arm. "There are no mistakes during this process. There are only opportunities for us to learn during this journey," she said, smiling. "Understand?"

Journey? She saw my illiteracy as a journey? And she'd included herself in my struggle.

I cut my eyes to hers and saw she was sincere. There was no judgment in her chocolate brown eyes.

She nestled in closer. "Okay, look at the word and study it. Is it possible for you to sound it out?"

I sat in silence, trying to sound out the word in my head.

"Out loud," she said.

I hesitated.

"You can do this, Rory. No mistakes, no judgment. I promise."

I studied the letters on the screen, trying to make out each one. The more I tried, the harder it became. The letters all ran together in a jumbled mess in my head. My mind raced and I couldn't focus above the throbbing pain in my chest. I was going to pass out. "Hindley, I can't do this."

"Why?"

After a long pause, I whispered on a shaky breath. "I'm embarrassed."

"Why are you embarrassed?"

"Because—" I scrubbed a hand through my hair, hoping to slow my thoughts. "My brain doesn't work like yours. All the letters are running together. I don't even know how to sound them out. And the harder I try the more confused I get."

"Good," she said with no apologies. "Now we have a starting point. That's awesome, Rory."

"How the fuck is this awesome, Hindley? The fact that I can't even read one goddamn word? Do you have any idea how fuckin' embarrassing this is?" I shouted.

"All this means is aerial is a sight word and we need to add it to your spiral."

She'd completely ignored my outburst, unphased by my crude language. This girl wasn't going to give into or feed my insecurities.

She cleared her throat and sat up straighter. "You spell aerial A-I-E —" She stopped and broke into a fit of giggles.

My jaw clenched. Was she laughing at me?

"What's so goddamn funny?" I growled. "The fact that I can't read, or the fact I don't know how the fuck to sound out letters?"

"I spelled it wrong." She laughed again, ignoring my outburst. "I forgot how to spell aerial. Actually, I'm not even sure I know how." She turned and glanced up at me. "See, Rory, it takes practice. I never use the word aerial so I would have to look it up. Not so smart, am I?"

She wrapped a hand around my forearm and immediately my pulse slowed.

"Look, Rory, we're both going to mess up here. It's inevitable. What's important is that we recognize it for what it is, correct it, learn from it, and move on. No judgment, no self-condemnation, only determination and perseverance."

Was she talking about reading or a relationship? It didn't matter, both scared the fuck out of me.

"Here." She reached over and flipped to the middle of the notebook. "Add aerial to your sight word list. You better check your phone though because apparently I have no idea how to spell it." She snorted.

I remained silent, sitting in my own pile of Rory-Gregor-Is-An-Ignorant-Asshole.

She held out my notebook. "Will you please spell aerial?"

I laughed at how ironic—and hysterical—and so fucked up this scenario was. She wasn't mocking or disrespectful. She really didn't know how to spell the word and was asking me for help.

"Please." She batted her long lashes and gave me her most coy, innocent look.

We both burst into hysterics and spent the next hour writing down words even *she* didn't know how to spell. And it was that much sweeter knowing she wasn't as perfect as I had once thought.

She talked about truly *experiencing* my words, not just reading and writing them. She wanted me to put things in my journal—photos, scraps of things, blades of grass—anything that expressed how I felt at that particular moment.

She called it word association, or some shit like that. All I knew was it was overwhelming and confusing as fuck. But her energy and excitement were contagious. And her belief that I could actually do this was motivating. For the first time in my life, I felt like I could conquer this huge monster that had chased me all of my life.

She stretched and yawned beside me. I closed both books and stood, scooping her in my arms.

"What are you doing?" she squeaked.

"We have to be up in an hour. I'm driving you down to San Diego for your meeting with Dipshit, remember?"

"Rory."

"Maybe I need to write that in my journal. 'Dipshit'. Do you think Google Translator could spell that?"

She laughed.

My heart ached with an emotion I was unfamiliar with.

L-O-V-E.

I walked her up the stairs and laid her in the bed. "You really believe in me, Hindley, that I can do this?"

"I know you can, Rory. You're one of the smartest people I've ever met."

"Yeah, right," I snorted and slid in beside her.

"We're two peas in a pod, aren't we?"

"What do you mean?"

"We both have so much faith and confidence in each other, but so little in ourselves."

I pulled her close to my chest, nuzzling her neck, inhaling her scent.

"Peas." I laughed.

"Peas," she sighed.

"Good night, Hindley."

She raised my hand up to her mouth and pressed a kiss against my fingers. "Good night, Skater Boy," she whispered.

CHAPTER 6

RORY

I'D DROPPED Hindley off in San Diego at Dipshit's office four hours earlier but still hadn't heard from her. I had no reasonable explanation for my feelings about Matt Davis. The guy just rubbed me the wrong way. It didn't help that Hindley was hopelessly oblivious to the magical charms she wielded over the opposite sex.

I sat outside on my deck, listening to the waves crash below as I recorded all the words I already knew into my spiral. Hindley was right, I was surprised to discover I knew a lot more words than I realized.

When I'd first returned from San Diego, I'd walked up and down the beach, trying to rid my mind of images of her and Dipshit alone in a conference room, talking and laughing and...*reading* my contract together. It had done little to ease my jealous tendencies. But now, as I sat here rubbing on the shells I'd picked up off the beach earlier, I thought of Hindley and her word.

Tactile.

That's the type of learner she said I was. She believed in me, and that one thought resonated within me and brought me hope.

I picked up my phone and pulled up my app. "Tactile," I said into the microphone. The word appeared on my screen and I recorded it in my journal.

T-A-C-T-I-L-E.

I stared at the word, trying to sound it out. It was easier to focus without Hindley's half-naked body sitting next to me.

"Tah-ah-cuh-tah-ih-le-eh." I remembered the sounds of the letters, but it didn't sound like it did when I just said the word, tactile. It must be a sight word.

I pulled out my blue notebook and turned to the back. I surprised myself that I wrote it down almost from memory. Maybe I could do this. I was so jazzed, I wrote it three more times.

"Tactile. Tactile," I repeated out loud. A memory came to the forefront of my thoughts. Something about long vowels and short vowels and shit like that. I needed to remember to ask Hindley about that rule. Maybe it would help me.

I turned back to my journal, thinking about my walk and the emotions that had flooded my mind. I grabbed my phone and spoke into Google Translator.

"I am free in the air." I copied the words in my journal then drew a skateboard beside it with clouds. That symbolized freedom to me. The graphic would remind me of the words associated with the symbol.

I spoke into the phone again. "The ocean is a gentle spirit that soothes me." This sentence was longer, but I wrote it down in my journal as best as I could, surprised to find I knew some of the words. I underlined the words I didn't know and added the others to my blue spiral. Maybe I'd ask Hindley to help me with those.

"Hindley," I said out loud. I realized I wanted to write her name in my journal.

She was in my thoughts right now and I wanted to capture her and record her name forever.

"Tactile," I said, smiling as I thought about her smooth skin, her gorgeous body wrapped around mine.

I pulled her business card out from my wallet and sat it on the glass tabletop.

"H-I-N-D-L-E-Y," I spelled out. "H-A-G-E-N." I memorized every letter before writing her name into my journal.

. . .

Hindley Hagen

I wrote once.

Hindley Hagen

I wrote again.

Hindley Hagen is my air.

I stared at the words on the page and smiled.

It was surreal to be writing down my own thoughts on paper. Partially because I didn't even realize I could write, but mainly because I hadn't ever appreciated how many thoughts and ideas ran through my head every day.

As I reclined in the lounger, enjoying my tall glass of lemonade, I thought back to Hindley's words.

You are one of the smartest people I've ever met.

The words 'Rory Gregor' and 'smart' had never been in the same universe before, let alone the same sentence. Yet Hindley not only put them together, she believed them to be true.

I spoke into Google Translator again. "You are smart." The sentence appeared on my screen and I copied each word in my journal.

You are smart.

I recognized all three words and added them into my spiral.

. . .

You are smart. You are smart.

I stared at the words, absorbing them, letting them sink in, trying to believe them the way Hindley did.

I chuckled at the audacity of my inner-self thinking I was smart. It *was* a complete sentence though, whether I believed it or not.

Throwing caution to the wind, I wrote another sentence.

Rory Gregor is smart.
  Rory Gregor is smart.
  Hindley Hagen is smart.
  Rory Gregor and Hindley Hagen
  Hindley Hagen and Rory Gregor

Combining our two names seemed about as farfetched and impossible as putting mine with the word smart. But looking at our names joined together, I was struck by an odd sense of calmness and peace. They felt right. Our names fit, like two lost pieces of a puzzle.

My cell phone buzzed and I glanced at the screen. Hindley's photo made me smile. It was the one she'd taken of the two of us at her sister's wedding, her face so animated and mine so…infatuated.

I closed the journal. "What's up, Drunk Girl?"

"Oh my God, Rory, you're not going to believe this. I'm so excited." She sounded breathless, like after sex.

"What?" I asked, adjusting myself.

"They want to do a commercial…with *you*."

"What? Are you serious?"

"Totally!" she shouted.

"Why?"

"They feel confident that you'll make it to the X Games, and when you do, they want to run several commercials during the telecast."

"For real?"

"For real. Can you believe this? Oh my God, I'm so excited," she squealed. "Are you?"

"Well, yeah. I've never done a commercial before, even when I was on top."

"I know. They love your comeback story and feel like now that you're clean, you're the perfect spokesperson for their clean water."

"When?"

"I told them I have to check with you, but the sooner the better, I think. I checked your schedule and unless it's changed, you have this coming weekend free."

"Yeah, I think so. Hold on, let me look at my calendar." I walked inside to the calendar hanging on the side of my fridge. I stared at the flags stuck on each date that symbolized the countries I would be in on any given day. Luckily, I had most of the world flags memorized, including all fifty states. That's the only way I kept track of my travels.

In two weeks, I was scheduled to be in France, then in Canada the week after that. If they were serious about the commercial then Hindley was right, the sooner the better.

"I have you in France in two weeks and Canada following that," Hindley said.

Man, did she already have my schedule memorized?

"As long as you place in the top five in both those competitions and get one or two photos in a magazine, that should give you the International exposure you need for an X Games invitation, don't you think?"

"How do you know all the requirements for an X Games invite?"

"Rory, I'm your agent. I've studied the industry inside and out. Trust me, at this point, I know more than you and Jack combined."

I laughed, realizing she was right. Hindley was so fuckin' smart, she'd learned the extreme sports world inside and out just to represent me well. Judging by today's meeting, it had paid off.

"So, this thing is legit?" I asked. "You think they're a good company to work with?" Despite Dipshit, I wanted to add.

"They have the highest growing demographics in the market. Kids and adults alike are flocking to this new type of water infused with vitamins, minerals, and electrolytes," she explained.

"Wow."

"Yeah. And now, with all the gluten free, allergy free, whatever free bullshit diets, no one wants to take on all the extra calories and preservatives of the other sports drinks. I think this water is perfect for you, and your image."

"What about the company?"

"It's a good, solid company as well. They haven't broken through on some key markets, but I think with you as a spokesperson, they could really do that."

"Seriously?" I was stunned to realize someone wanted *me* as a national spokesperson. "You think I could help them sell water?"

"Rory, that's why they want *you*. You're magical. Kids want to be you and love your fresh, clean, come back from the trenches story. You're an amazing athlete and the perfect role model for their brand."

Hindley thought I was "amazing." She thought I was "perfect." I had to remember those two words because I wanted to add them to my journal.

"Hello?" she asked.

"Yeah, I'm here, sorry."

"Why don't you believe me?"

"Same reason you don't believe me when I tell you how beautiful you are."

"Peas, huh?"

I laughed. "Yeah, peas."

"Open your journal," she said with authority.

What the hell was she up to?

"Do you have it with you?" she asked.

She was becoming so bossy, and I loved the confidence she had now. I walked back to the deck and sat down in front of my journal.

"I've got it," I said.

"Do you have something to write with?"

I picked up the pen I'd been using earlier. "Yes, Miss Bossy Pants. Why?"

"Go to a blank page."

I opened the journal to a new sheet. "Okay."

"Write S-O-N-O-R-A."

I wrote the letters as she dictated them. "Okay."

"Do you know how to write the word water?"

"I don't think so," I said, surprised that I wasn't more self-conscious.

"Okay, write W-A-T-E-R."

I wrote the word as she instructed.

"Beside that word, draw a symbol for water, something that will always make you remember that word."

That image came quickly—it was the ocean. I drew squiggly lines next to the word, knowing I would have it memorized in no time.

"Wait, I think I actually *do* know that word, now that I see it written out," I said, surprised at the excitement in my voice.

"Oh, Rory, that's awesome!"

Her praise had me smiling.

"Don't forget to put it in your blue spiral," she said. "Can you read the first word?" she asked.

I stared at the word longer this time.

Sonora.

"See if you can sound it out. If you can't, don't worry, it may become a sight word. I want you to get into the habit of practicing though."

I trailed my finger across the word. "Sah-oh-nah-oh-rah-ah."

"Awesome! That's right. It's Sonora. Sonora Water Company. That's who hired you to be their spokesperson. I figured it would probably be a good idea for us to work on those words first, don't you think?"

She laughed and I joined in her jubilation.

"Yeah, that's probably true," I said.

I'd never known how to spell or write the names of any of my past sponsors, and I'd really never given two flips about it either. I was filled with pride, knowing that not only was I going to represent them, but now I would also be able to read their fuckin' bottle at the store.

"I need you to do one more thing," she said quietly.

"Okay."

"Do you know how to write your name?"

"Yes, Hindley, I know how to write my name," I said, with more offense than I'd intended.

"Don't get pissy," she said. "I have to know where we stand."

"Sorry."

"That's all right, I forgive you because you're so cute and adorable. And because you're about to become a big, famous commercial star." She laughed and slowly I felt my self-doubt and loathing dissipating.

I straightened my back and took on a more studious tone. "So, what is it you want me to do, Miss Hagen?"

"That's better. Now. Turn to a new page in your journal and write out your name."

I did as she told me. "Wait, I thought this was *my* journal to be filled with *my* thoughts."

"That's what I want this sentence to become, eventually. A new belief, in yourself."

"Oh."

"Do you know the word *is*?"

"Yes."

"Write it next to your name."

"Okay."

"Do you know how to spell the word *smart*?"

I froze. It was one thing for me to write it earlier on my own when no one else knew. I wasn't sure if I could when Hindley asked me.

"Rory? Do you know how to write the word *smart*?"

"No," I answered, even though I'd already written it out several times.

She recited, "S-M-A-R-T."

"Okay."

"What's a graphic that makes you think of smart?"

"Your beautiful face." I half expected her to shrug off my statement with a laugh, but instead, all I heard was silence.

"Then draw my face, if you can."

Could I? I had her fuckin' face memorized. I was no Michelangelo so I knew my picture would never do her justice, but it would remind me of what the word meant.

"Now," she said, "put a period at the end and read the sentence back to me."

I didn't want to. I felt awkward, especially because I didn't believe the statement.

"Rory," she said.

"Rory Gregor is smart," I mumbled.

"I'm sorry, I didn't hear that. Would you please read the sentence again, only this time louder?"

Oh, God, she was making me so...what? Strong. Brave. Free.

"Rory Gregor is smart," I said with a bit more confidence. It wasn't a statement I'd ever shout from the rooftops though.

"Much better." I heard the smile in her voice.

How insane was it that I'd written the same sentence myself, not five minutes before she'd called? And now, she had me put it together into her own sentence. But even crazier than that was the fact she believed the statement to be true. And she was teaching me the same lesson.

"I want you to write that sentence down twenty times before you go to bed tonight," she said.

"What?"

"You heard me."

"All right, on one condition." I tucked the pen into the journal then closed it and set it aside.

"What?"

"Do you have something to write with?"

"Yes," she answered. "What are you up to, Rory Gregor?" I could picture her face scrunched with uncertainty.

"I want you to write out the following words, please."

She cleared her throat. "All right. I'm ready."

"Are you ready?"

"Yes."

I smiled, thinking of the sentence I wanted her to write and repeat. "Do you know how to write your name?"

"Yes." She laughed.

God, I loved that sound. I was growing addicted to all of Hindley's joyous moments.

"Write down your name," I said.

"Okay. Now what?"

"Do you know how to write the word *is*?"

"Yes." She chuckled. "What are you up to?"

"Just write it," I said.

"Should I write it next to my name?"

"Yes, please."

"What next, Mr. Gregor?"

I swallowed down a moan when my dick twitched at her sultry voice.

My next word would be hard for her. She didn't believe it anymore than I believed I was smart, but she needed to say it to herself as much as I did.

Our new mantras.

"Write the word, *beautiful*," I said. An awkward silence filled the air, which didn't surprise me. "B-E-A-U-T-I-F-U-L." I spelled out the word.

Still she remained quiet.

"Hindley, did you hear me?"

"Um hmm," she mumbled.

"What's wrong?"

"I'm not sure I believe it."

"Do you believe I'm smart?" I asked.

"Well, of course I do, I wouldn't have had you write it if—"

She'd obviously caught on to my tactic.

"You're right. I am smart," I said, surprised by my own statement. "And you're beautiful. Now, I want you to write out that sentence twenty times before you go to bed tonight. Understand?"

"Yes, sir. Understood." I knew she was scared like me, but there was a tone of playfulness in her voice.

"Good girl."

She laughed again and I felt as if we'd overcome some major obstacle in our relationship, our insecurities dying a little more with each sentence, each word, each letter.

"Listen, I've gotta run," she said. "I'm at the airport waiting to board my plane."

"How did you get to the airport?" There was a long pause and her silence answered my question. Dipshit. But she was in a good mood and I didn't want to ruin it for her. "So where do they want to do this, the commercial, I mean?"

"They said they're flexible, they'll work around your schedule. I suggested Austin. We've got a great film industry there so I know we can secure a good staff for taping the commercial. And it's not far for either you or the company to travel. And…"

I could hear the excitement in her voice.

I rolled the pen back and forth between my fingers, smiling. "But, where on earth would I stay? It's such a busy city. Surely I wouldn't be able to find a room."

"I can think of one place where I would love for you to stay."

Her sultry, southern voice reverberated through the line and my entire body stiffened with need.

"I think Austin sounds like heaven," I said.

"I think spending the weekend with *you* sounds like heaven," she whispered.

"I think spending the weekend *in* you sounds like heaven," I groaned.

"Holy shit, Rory."

Her expletive caught me off guard. "What? What happened?"

"I seriously think I have to go to the restroom and change my panties before my flight. They're soaking wet."

"Hindley Hagen, what am I going to do with you?"

"Oh, I can think of several things I'd like for you to do with me, Mr. Gregor."

I bellowed with laughter. It was still beyond me how any asshat could have ever told her she was bad in bed. Not only was she fan-fucking-tastic in bed, she was pretty fuckin' awesome over the phone too.

"I think I have to go to the bathroom too." I chuckled. "For a cold shower."

"I'll talk to Sonora about the details then call you when I get back home. Maybe you could sneak in a day before the shoot?"

"Oh, I'll sneak in all right, Miss Hagen."

"Bye, Rory. I miss you already."

"Bye, Drunk Girl." There was a pause and I realized she wasn't going to hang up until I gave her the reassurance she needed. "I miss you too, Hindley."

"Bye," she whispered just before the line went dead.

I smiled to myself, knowing it was true. I missed her more than she could possibly know, but surprisingly enough, the thought didn't scare me.

I retrieved my journal and opened it, then began to write.

Rory Gregor is smart.
Rory Gregor is smart.

I continued my new mantra as I captured every sensory detail around me. Tactile learning. That's what Hindley called it.

I seized every minute detail I could—the sight of each wave as it crashed into the shore; the salty taste of the wind; the cold, hard pen in my hand; the seagulls that squawked in the distance. I was in sensory overload, but I understood how it would help me learn.

This moment in time was beautiful, like Hindley.

Reading wasn't about flat words on a piece of paper. They had to come to life if I wanted to comprehend and retain them. And I *had* to believe them if I wanted more with Hindley.

Rory Gregor is smart.
Rory Gregor is smart.

I was doing it. I was reading. And writing. And falling for an incredible woman.

I wasn't exactly sure which fact was the biggest surprise to me. But I was okay living in the moment, believing them all.

CHAPTER 7

HINDLEY

"Look, Mom, I don't know. The shoot is going well, but dinner tonight with you guys may be pushing it."

It wasn't a total lie. Filming Rory's commercial was going perfectly, and we were close to wrapping up two hours ahead of schedule. But the minute my mother told me my stepsister, Geneva, would be at dinner too, everything had changed for me.

"Well, I thought it would be nice for all of us to have a celebratory dinner," she said. "You can even bring your new client with you."

"Nice for who, Mom?"

Caroline Hagen Barton didn't want to congratulate me. She wanted information on Rory. He was a celebrity, and that instantly put him in her inner circle. That, and the fact I was pretty sure my mother still had a small crush on Rory ever since Geneva's wedding. But who could blame her, she was only human.

"What does that mean?" she asked.

"Nice for me, for Geneva, or for you to lust after Rory some more?"

"That's enough, Hindley. If anyone should be upset, it should be me."

"You?" I grimaced. "Why you?"

"Imagine my shock at our Junior League luncheon last week when the wife of the senior partner of my *own* daughter's law firm had to tell me about her promotion."

"It's not a promotion, Mom."

"Well, it certainly was newsworthy to the other women at the luncheon."

"That's because most of their teenage sons and probably half of their teenage daughters know Rory." It was true and it was a demographic I was counting on. Not only could we tap into the purchasing power of these snotty, rich kids, but potentially their whole family.

"At any rate," my mother went on, "it would have been nice to find out from my own daughter that she was representing the rich and famous."

"Whatever," I sighed. "Look, Mom, I have to go. They're calling me back out to the set."

"I'll see you at seven, darling. And don't forget to bring Rory."

Her tone was so giddy, I almost felt sorry for her. There was no way I would ever be able to talk Rory into having dinner with my family. Hell, I didn't even want to go.

"Seven o'clock, Hindley."

"We'll see, Caroline. Bye." Without waiting for her response, I clicked the phone off and shoved it back in my pocket.

Matt Davis stepped through the French doors and stood next to me with a sigh. "Man, I knew it was hot in Texas, but no one ever told me it would be *this* hot." We were standing inside Rory's best friend's home, taking a break from the heat.

Leif Jennings designed skate parks for a living and had graciously offered his gorgeous house, along with his own personal skate park that sat adjacent to his home. The backdrop of the Texas Hill Country made the location a perfect spot for filming. I couldn't have been more thankful to Leif for letting us intrude on his private domain.

Even though the entire creative team of Sonora Water had flown out for the shoot, Matt insisted on coming as well. Rory said it was to look at my "hot little ass," which I thought was untrue, but adorable.

So far, Rory had been a master in front of the camera, hitting every trick the director threw at him and delivering his lines like a seasoned actor. I truly believed there was nothing this tall, dark, brilliantly handsome man couldn't do and I couldn't wait to see the finished product.

But even more impressive was the way he'd kept his jealous tendencies in check when it came to Matt. Especially during times when even I was getting creeped out by the guy. Like now.

"Can I have some of your water?" Matt reached for the bottle of water in my hands that I'd been drinking from.

I froze. I didn't know what to do. Sharing a bottle of water was an intimate act, or it was to me anyway. I didn't want to give him the wrong message. I mean, we needed him, we needed to keep the company happy, and for all intents and purposes, he *was* the company as far as Rory and I were concerned.

Okay, so maybe one bottle wouldn't hurt.

Rory swooped in next to me, all sweaty, and stinky, and irresistibly delicious. "Oh, thanks, Hindley." He grabbed the bottle from my hand and gulped down its contents, his lips never touching the rim.

The seemingly innocent act sent tingles of need straight to my best parts. How the hell could this guy make the simple act of drinking water so damn sexy?

Over the edge of the bottle he winked at me. I reminded myself that with Rory Gregor, nothing was as innocent as it seemed.

Rory knocked Matt's shoulder with his elbow and nodded toward me. "Isn't she the best agent ever, Matty?" He gave a half-hearted grin that didn't reach his eyes as he held up the empty bottle. "She's always thinking of me."

I swallowed hard at the truth. I was always thinking of him, and I feared that may not be the best thing right now.

Matt stared down at his freshly pressed shirt where Rory had just touched it, as if a skunk had sprayed him.

"She always puts my needs first," Rory continued.

Oh, shit. I knew exactly what Rory was doing. He was marking his territory. I gave him a warning glare. We could not do this in front of the sponsor.

"Listen, Hindley," Matt said. "I've been meaning to ask you. Would you like to have dinner with me tonight, to celebrate our first project together?"

I glanced at Rory, surprised to see him still sporting the same smirk. He knew something, but he wasn't going to let me in on the secret.

"Actually, Matt, she can't tonight," Rory answered for me. "Her mother asked us over for a family dinner, to celebrate Hindley and me. You know, now that she's my agent and I'm her client and we're committed to each other and all."

Matt narrowed his eyes as he glanced between me and Rory. This was not going to end well.

"Well," Rory continued, "we're committed for at least the next twelve months, or so the contract says, right, boss?" He bumped my hip and his bellowing laughter echoed through the home.

I grimaced. Why was he doing this? He was jeopardizing everything. Again.

Matt smiled as he ran a hand down his sleeves and tugged at the cuffs. "Well, maybe some other time then."

"Yes, we'll try again another time," I said, trying to sound both excited and disappointed, praying I wasn't leading him on.

"Tomorrow for lunch, perhaps?" he asked. "My flight doesn't leave until the early evening."

I glanced at Rory from the corner of my eye, not surprised to find his once smug face now morphed into an expression of annoyance.

"Um, sure," I said, "I'll, uh, call you tomorrow."

"Sounds good." He reached out and stroked my arm up and down before grasping my shoulder and squeezing it several times.

I held my breath, willing him to remove his hands, fearing a panic attack might overtake me. Or worse, Rory's fist would meet Matt's face.

"Man, you feel tense," Matt said, continuing to knead my shoulders. "You could use a massage. Maybe I should book us a couple's massage tomorrow morning at the hotel where I'm staying. They have a world-class spa."

Oh, shit.

Rory was going to kill this guy, and I couldn't say I'd stand in his way. Matt was being completely inappropriate and unprofessional.

A crunching noise had me turning to find Rory crushing his water bottle in his hand. Every muscle in his arm was flexed, his eyes narrowed with that look that ultimate fighters got right before they went in for the kill.

"Oh my goodness, Rory," I said, stepping in front of him. "I almost forgot. I need your signature on one more document."

Rory was fuming, his jaw clenched, eyes glassed over with fury. It took all my strength to turn him away from the scene.

"Please excuse us, Matt." I grabbed Rory's arm and yanked him hard, dragging him down the hallway. "Stop, Rory," I said in a hushed tone as we moved further away.

His gaze remained fixed behind him on Matt.

I found an open door and pushed Rory into the room, closing and locking the door behind us. Slowly I turned to face Rory, bracing for his wrath. Instead, I was surprised to find him sitting quietly in a chair, gazing out the window.

I crept up beside him and squatted down, resting my hand on his thigh. "Hey," I whispered.

He turned and stared down at my hand before finally meeting my gaze. His eyes were a darker blue than normal.

"Hi," I said, smiling.

"Hi," he answered softly.

I didn't know what to say next. He had already done such a great job of calming himself down, I feared if I broached the subject with Matt, it might set him off.

"So, dinner? Tonight?" I asked, my brows lifted. "With my family? You really want to go?"

He sat quietly with his lips in a firm line, showing no emotion.

"You know, it's with my mom, the one who—what does Dana call it —eye fucked you at her own stepdaughter's wedding."

A hint of a smile tugged at his mouth and I blew out a sigh of relief.

"And my stepfather," I continued, "who I think told you to keep your dick in your pants because I didn't even know your last name."

He smiled, wide and broad, and my heart nearly stopped beating. He was the most captivating, beautiful person I'd ever met.

My Skater Boy was back.

I stood and sat in his lap, wrapping my arms around his neck. "You're amazing," I said, "you know that, right?"

He stared down at his fingers that were tracing an unknown pattern on my thigh.

Okay, so maybe he wasn't completely back but at least he was here with me.

I lifted his chin with my finger until he finally met my gaze. "You are perfect to me, Rory. Perfect *for* me. There's no one else I want more than you." No one else I've ever wanted more, I wanted to add.

My eyes studied his and I held my breath as he sat in silence. I needed him to believe me. "I'm all yours," I said. "Remember?" I leaned in and slowly placed my lips against his.

I moved to pull back but before I could, he snagged the back of my head with his hand and drew me closer, deepening the kiss. Suddenly we were all over each other like an inferno—hands and mouth and tongues—reaching for whatever we could. In less than thirty seconds, Rory had me almost naked and on the desk behind us.

I wanted to protest but couldn't. He needed this, he needed to claim me. And in some strange way, I needed his possession too.

The timing was inappropriate, the location less than ideal to share our coming together, but I didn't stop him. And he didn't try.

I fell back onto the hard wood as he sunk deep inside me. The sounds of our lovemaking echoed in the room, sending me closer to the edge. In the abyss of our release, we found the commonality that had brought us together in the first place. We were better together than we ever had been apart.

"After you." Rory smirked as he held the door open. His deviant smile and crystal blue eyes had my insides melting again, even though we'd just got our clothes back on less than five minutes ago. I couldn't get enough of my Skater Boy and he knew it.

I glanced down at my clothing, ensuring I hadn't put anything on backward or inside out.

"You're perfect," he whispered in my ear, his breath wafting across my skin. "To me."

A shiver ran up and down my spine, and I knew if I didn't get out of his reach soon, he was going to grab me, throw me back on that desk, and devour me all over again.

I skipped out of his reach but not before he swatted me hard on the butt.

"Hey." I rubbed at my bottom. "I thought you said no spanking."

"Well, I think you were very bad in there, Miss Hagen, and I needed to discipline you."

I cocked a brow and he laughed. My Skater Boy was so mercurial, and hot.

"So seriously, dinner?" I asked. "Tonight? With my family?" I knew the subject of my family would extinguish our sexual appetite. "You really want to go?"

"Why? You don't want to take me to your family's house for dinner?" From his tone I couldn't tell if he was offended or joking.

"You know my stepsister and her new husband will be there."

"Did she ever find the spider you put in her cake?"

I smiled at the memory. "I don't think so."

"Well, I can bring another one with us, if you want."

I burst into laughter at the shared memory and Rory joined in. I found myself lost in his charms all over again.

I was slowly learning there was very little I didn't love about Rory Gregor. Okay, so maybe that was a lie. I'd already realized some time ago that I didn't just love everything *about* Rory, I loved him. Period. I didn't know how to tell him, or if I even should.

For now, I would wait, and pretend for a little while longer that he loved me too.

CHAPTER 8
HINDLEY

"So, RORY," Paul purposely paused for effect, "Gregor, right?" He winked at me.

I bit back a smile at my stepfather's wedding reference.

"Yes, sir. Gregor."

"Please, tell us about yourself," Paul said.

Rory wiped his mouth. "There's not much to tell, Mr. Barton."

"Call me Paul. I'm sorry about my comment at the wedding, by the way."

"What did you say?" my mom asked.

We looked at my mother then back to Paul who shook his head slightly, signaling that we should keep our mouths shut.

"Paul," my mother said. "What did you say to Rory?"

"I told him we were delighted to have him at Geneva's wedding."

Paul and my mother looked at each other and smiled, an all-knowing expression that said eventually she would find out what my stepfather had said. I didn't even want to think about her tactics.

"So, are you two a couple or what?" Geneva asked, glaring at both of us.

"No," I said, a little too quickly.

Geneva stared at Rory like he was a tasty treat. "So, you're available?"

I wasn't surprised by her question, but I was appalled that she was doing it right in front of her husband of like three weeks.

"Actually," Rory said, ignoring Geneva's question, "when we met, I didn't know Hindley would be my attorney."

"So, at the wedding, you didn't know Hindley was your agent?" Paul asked, scrutinizing Rory in disbelief.

"No, sir. Once we found out, we both agreed it would be better to keep our relationship purely professional."

As if on cue, every set of eyes at the table rolled toward the ceiling.

"It's true," I said, feeling a little desperate. I hated lying, to anyone, but especially to Paul. "My job is important to me." I stared at my stepfather. "To you."

"To me?" He pointed to himself.

I stared in confusion.

"Why me?" he asked.

Surely Paul realized the need to keep things on the up-and-up to protect my job, and his own company. If the senior partner, Mr. Stedwick, pulled his investment, it could possibly ruin Paul's investment company.

"Well, I thought Mr. Stedwick was a client of yours, an investor," I said.

"He is, but that has nothing to do with you and the firm, Hindley."

I sat in silence, trying to think back. There was no way I'd misunderstood Paul's comments three months ago when I'd taken the job at Stedwick and Nigh.

"Keep Aston Stedwick happy, Hindley, or it could cost us all."

"Hindley." My mother interrupted my thoughts.

"Oh, yes," I said. "Sorry. Well, anyway. This job is very important to me, and these deals we're working on are very important to Rory."

I stared directly at Paul, knowing he was the one I had to convince that Rory and my relationship was strictly professional.

He nodded.

"Rory and I are both professionals," I said.

At least that wasn't a lie.

"We are committed to each other, but only through our legal contract, right, Rory?" I turned to him for confirmation.

He stared down at his plate as he pushed the food around. Everyone stared at him, awaiting his answer.

"Rory," I said softly.

Slowly he lifted his face and stared at me. His bright blue eyes seemingly lost, covered with a veil of darkness.

"Right," he said quietly.

Oh, no. I'd hurt him with my words.

"Hindley tells us you're from Denver, Rory," my mom said.

I wanted to kiss my mom for the change of subject.

He gave a quick nod. "Yes, ma'am, that's right."

She smiled warmly. "I've never been to Denver. I'm sure it's beautiful there. Paul, have you ever been to Denver?"

My mother and her small talk. Bless her, she was relentless, but tonight, I loved her for it.

"What do your folks do, Rory?" Geneva's husband, Stan asked.

I was surprised to hear from Third, my nickname for Stanley Winston III. He'd been so quiet, I'd almost forgotten he was there.

"I'm not close with my parents," Rory said curtly, letting everyone at the table know this was *not* a subject to be brought up again.

"Rory's manager, Jack and his wife, Kara have been surrogate parents to Rory for most of his life," I said.

Geneva tossed her white-blonde hair over her shoulder and placed both forearms on the table, cocking her head. "What's up with that?"

Rory glanced at me.

"Because," I said, taking my cue, "they saw potential in Rory and made a commitment to work with him, train him, and raise him." I turned and smiled at Rory. "And they've done a great job."

Geneva's face contorted with condescension. "So you, what, just like, left your parents?"

"Yes," Rory said, glaring at her.

Geneva held his gaze but only for a few seconds before dropping her head and staring at her fingernails.

I'd never seen someone shut Geneva Barton up like Rory just did. It was an amazing moment in my life and I had to fight to keep from smiling.

"Where are you headed off to next, Rory?" Paul asked.

"I'll be in France next weekend, sir."

Paul looked at me. "Are you going with him, Hindley?"

Oh, shit. I didn't want to bring this up now, not in front of people.

"I'm not sure yet," I answered quietly.

Rory's eyes narrowed as he stared at me

"Why not?" he asked.

"Who wants coffee with dessert?" my mom asked.

Once again, Caroline Hagen Barton saves the day. Well, at least she saved the moment. I knew I'd have to talk Rory down off this ledge as soon as dinner was over.

"The magazines say you've had a lot of women over the years," Geneva said, staring at me instead of Rory. Her medically plumped lips were curled in an evil half-smile.

"I've definitely played the field, that's no lie," Rory said with no hesitation. "My mom always told my sister she had to kiss a lot of frogs to find her prince. Guess that's what I was doing. Trying to find my princess."

Wait, sister? Rory had never told me he had a sister. Then it struck me, I didn't really know this man at all.

"Have you found one yet?" Geneva asked, her voice sensual as if she were auditioning for the part.

Rory laughed her off. "No, not yet."

Part of me was disappointed by his quick answer. God, had I really been dumb enough to think he'd say I was his princess? I understood his answer though. He couldn't divulge anything about our relationship, least of all to Geneva.

"Did you go to college in Colorado?" Paul asked.

My hand fisted around my napkin under the table. God, could this night get anymore stressful?

"I didn't go to college, sir," Rory answered.

Paul looked as if he'd heard the Federal Stock Exchange had been taken over by the Russian Mafia.

My stepfather had always been a stickler for education. No matter what the degree, he wanted a college education behind someone. It made absolutely no sense, considering his wife never even graduated high school, and his daughter wasn't doing a damn thing with her expensive ass diploma in Interior Design except living off her new husband's wealth.

"Rory was pro by the age of eighteen," I said. "It's quite impressive to be signed that young."

"Don't worry, darling." My mother reached out and touched Rory's arm. "I didn't even graduate high school and I turned out all right." Her face warmed with motherly affection.

For the first time in a long time, I truly felt like she was on my side.

"You've got a ton of awards, that's for sure," Third piped in. "He's one of the best skateboarders ever, Paul."

"Thanks," Rory said quietly.

Oh, shit. I was losing him. I knew this dinner was a mistake. Everyone was badgering him, making him relive things he didn't want to remember, and things I didn't even know about.

"Well, if you ever need any investment advice, feel free to give me a call," Paul said.

"From what I've read, you've pretty much gone through all your money, haven't you?" Geneva smirked.

That fucking bitch.

That was the last straw. I hadn't even wanted to come tonight, especially when I found out Geneva would be here. But I hadn't declined because I didn't want Rory to think I was embarrassed of him.

The truth was, I was embarrassed by my own family. I was so over Geneva's bullshit tonight, and I wasn't going to sit back and take it. It was one thing for her to demean me, but I'd be damned if I would sit here and let her make Rory feel like shit.

"Well, Rory made his money the old-fashioned way," I said through gritted teeth. "He earned it on his own. So I guess it was his money to run through. Unlike some people who piss away money that's not even theirs while they sit back and don't do shit."

Geneva's face reddened and I watched as her fake lips puckered with fury.

I was shaking, seething, and I'd had enough from this pompous bitch to last me a lifetime.

"Well, wait, Geneva, I guess that's not entirely true," I went on. "What is it you do again? Oh, yeah, that's right, nothing. Nothing except get your hair and nails done and drink Cosmos by the country club pool all day while your husband works his ass off."

If she wanted to play this game, I could too. Fuck her.

"Oh, and if I were you," I said, nearly reaching across the table to slap her, "I'd go back to that plastic surgeon who botched up your lips and face and get my money back."

"Hindley!" my mother shouted.

"What?" I yelled back.

Paul hit the table. "That's enough."

The room fell silent, the only sound that of my ragged breathing.

"You're right, Geneva," Rory said in a quiet tone. "I wasted most of my money on booze, drugs, and women."

I stared at Paul.

His eyes were cold and narrowed as he studied Rory. He was not happy with the declaration.

Shit. This had been a huge mistake to bring him here.

Rory drew in a breath and continued despite everyone's stunned expressions.

"But you see, it's not about the money, not anymore," Rory said. "It's about the feeling I get from doing something I love, every day of my life. Fortunately, I get paid to do what I love and I don't want to screw that up again. I *won't* screw it up." He stared down at me. "I think I finally have an agent and an attorney who won't let me screw it up either."

God, that was good, poetic even.

Rory smiled, not the broad one like I was used to, but enough to let me know that my Skater Boy wasn't completely gone.

"You're very lucky, Rory," Paul said. "Most people don't get the opportunity to do what they love in life."

I knew I didn't love what I did for a living. Honestly, I didn't even know what I did love to do in life. But I did know one person I was growing to love more every day.

"I don't think it's luck, sir," Rory said. "I've worked hard for what I've earned."

Ut oh, what was happening? I didn't think Paul's comment was offensive, but somehow Rory had taken it that way.

"Rory, would you like a slice of my homemade chocolate cake?" My mother intervened.

"Actually, Mom, it's late and I think Rory and I need to get going."

My mom left the table as if she hadn't even heard my refusal.

Being belittled by Geneva wasn't the only reason I'd had enough of this circus called a family dinner.

No one tonight had congratulated me on signing Rory as a new client. Not once had they said, 'Way to go' for getting him signed with a major sponsor and a commercial deal.

And now, they were offending Rory.

I should have known better than to count on my family for support. Tears burned the back of my eyes and I realized I needed to get the hell out of here before I totally broke down.

Suddenly, the lights went off and a soft glow approached from the kitchen door. As it came closer, I noticed my mother was carrying a cake filled with sparklers. It wasn't anyone's birthday, was it?

I turned and looked at Paul.

He had the biggest shit-eating grin on his face.

I turned back to my mom and watched as she wandered around the table, placing the cake directly in front of me. One simple word was written across the top of my mother's famous chocolate cake.

Congratulations.

Well, hell. What could I say to that? They'd gotten me.

"It's for all of you," my mom said, gazing around the table. "To Stan and Geneva, congratulations on your new lives together."

Geneva gave a half-hearted smile that seemed polar opposite for someone who'd just returned from her honeymoon. She never liked sharing the spotlight with anyone, least of all me.

"To you, Rory," my mother continued, "for hiring the most amazing attorney in the world." She reached down and stroked my cheek, gently wiping away a tear rolling down my face. "And for you, my darling Hindley."

"For what, Mom?" I whispered.

"For Rory."

"What?" I practically shrieked.

Did she know Rory and I were together?

"For starting this new section in your law firm," she smiled, "and for getting Rory two major deals. You're amazing, darling."

"Thank you, Mom," I whispered against her palm, covering her hand with mine.

The lights came back on and Paul stood beside my mother. "You didn't think we'd forget, did you, Hinny Bin?"

I shrugged, laughing at Paul's nickname for me.

My mother cut the cake and passed around the pieces. I was still in shock from the unusual display of affection, and pride from my mom.

Then I realized that Rory had been quiet during this exchange. I watched as he ate the last bit of cake on his plate.

"Hey," I said, gently touching his arm. "Are you all right?"

His eyes met mine and he smiled, but it wasn't a real one. He was only pacifying me. Somewhere during the evening I'd lost my Skater Boy. Fear gripped me hard as I realized how desperate my need for him was becoming.

"You about ready to go?" I whispered.

He nodded once and I knew. I just knew. As hard as I would try, tonight, I may not get him back.

CHAPTER 9

HINDLEY

SITTING at a stoplight in Leif's convertible 1966 Mustang, I gazed up at the stars littering the night sky. Rory had insisted we take the car instead of his motorcycle, claiming helmet hair wouldn't look good. I'd warned him that convertible hair wouldn't look much better. And it didn't.

"Thanks for going to dinner with me tonight," I said. "I'm sorry about my family."

He turned and stared at me, his expression void of emotion. Rory was lost to me, and that realization scared me the most.

"Why are you sorry?" he finally asked.

"For my family. They pretty much raked you over the coals back there."

"You're their daughter, Hindley. Of course they're going to protect you." He turned his attention back to the light and sped off as soon as it turned green.

"Come back to me," I whispered, placing my hand lightly on his thigh. It was the comment he always used with me when I was absorbed in my own dark thoughts. I prayed my words would bring him back as well.

He glanced down at my hand for the briefest second before staring out at the road again. He didn't acknowledge my plea or my touch.

I slid my hand away as if I'd been burned.

We sat in silence the rest of the way to my house, and with every passing mile, I knew he was moving further and further away from me.

Slowly he pulled up to the curb in front of my house, and I wondered if he'd follow me in. When he didn't turn off the engine, I had my answer.

I reached for the door handle, turning my back on him. "Thanks again for coming."

"You're welcome."

I glanced over my shoulder but found he wasn't looking at me at all.

Something in my heart broke and I fought to hold back tears.

This thing between us had come to an end, like I always knew it would. I only hoped I could still work with Rory in the future without completely breaking down every time I saw him.

I stepped out of the car, never looking back. I couldn't.

"I'll see you later, Rory," I said quietly, trying to control my shaky voice. If I could just make it inside then I could break down.

I closed the car door, not surprised when he didn't say anything or come after me. Why would a man like Rory want a broken girl like me?

"Are you coming to France with me?" he asked.

I turned and stared at him. "No. I can't."

His head snapped up and his narrowed eyes met mine. "Why not?"

"I'll be in Miami."

"Miami?" He sounded disgusted by my revelation. "What for?"

"The Baltimore Ravens are starting their summer training camp in a few weeks."

He arched his brows and glared. "And?"

"And," I said, mocking him, "they have a quarterback who may be looking for a new agent. I'm going down to talk with his manager."

"When were you going to tell me?"

"I only found out today so stop being all," I waved my hand in the air, "whatever it is you're being right now."

"I thought Stedwick wanted you with me, touring with me all the time."

"Our contract doesn't bind me to you exclusively, Rory." There, I'd said it, and as soon as I did, I was sorry I had.

His expression morphed into pure anger.

I straightened and glared right back. "What's wrong with you tonight?"

He turned his attention back to the road, shaking his head.

"Rory, please," I begged. "Just, just look at me." I leaned over the door. It was taking everything I had not to climb over it, crawl into his lap and force him to talk to me.

"Your parents are right," he said, never meeting my gaze.

"Right about what?"

"You deserve better."

"What the hell are you talking about? My parents never said that."

"They didn't have to."

"Are we really starting this bullshit again, Rory, because it's getting kind of old."

He whipped his head to stare at me, his eyes narrowed. "What bullshit?"

"This whole, 'I'm not good enough for Hindley', bullshit you like to sling at me."

"It's not bullshit, it's true."

"Says who?"

He remained silent.

"Don't pin this on my parents," I said. "This is your bullshit drama and you need to deal with it, not them."

"I think you deserve better," he said so quietly, I almost didn't hear him. "Someone better than me."

Now I was pissed. Even if I did want a relationship with this man, I couldn't carry both of our insecurities.

Fisting my hands on my hips, I stared down at him. "You know what, Rory, maybe you're right. Nothing in my past would lead me to believe that I deserve a man who's kind, caring, compassionate, funny, smart, talented, and gorgeous. And yet here he sits, right in front of me, casting me off. So why would I be surprised that he doesn't want me? According to you, that's exactly what I deserve."

"That's not what I meant, Hindley."

"Then, please, tell me what the fuck you mean because I am about to lose my shit out here."

He stared up at me, his eyes wide. "You deserve someone better suited for you and your family. Someone like Matt."

And finally, there it was. Everything we'd done together, everything we'd been through, everything we'd fought for, slowly slipped away, all because of his inability to believe in me, to believe in himself, to believe in us.

As much as I loved Rory Gregor, I realized in that moment that I would never be able to make a difference in his life, in the way he thought about himself.

His self-deprecating thoughts had been ingrained in his mind for far too long. There was nothing more I could do to convince him otherwise. I'd been foolish to even try.

"You're right, Rory," I said, backing away. "I do deserve someone like Matt. But not for the reasons you think." I bit back my tears, knowing I couldn't break down in front of him. "Good night," I whispered before turning and walking toward my front door.

I fumbled with the keys, pissed that I'd let him talk me into locking my door tonight.

Suddenly I felt his body behind me. Drawing in a deep breath to steady my fingers, I slid the key in the lock and opened the door, walking inside. Never turning, I pushed on the door but it caught on something. Glancing down I noticed it was Rory's foot.

I turned and stared up at him. His eyes were huge, frightened, frantic, like a wild animal fighting for his life. He raked his hands through his hair several times, his mouth opening and closing but no words came out.

I waited, praying he'd talk, hoping we could move forward. Instead, he remained silent.

I studied his face, committing every detail to memory—his blue eyes, his slightly crooked nose, his well-defined cheekbones, his mouth. Oh, God, that mouth. This was the last time I'd probably see him as anything more than his agent.

"Goodbye, Rory," I said through choked tears.

He finally moved his foot, and I shut the door, locking it behind me before dropping to the floor. Clutching my knees to my chest, I sat in silence as hot tears streamed down my face.

I laid on the floor on my side, curling into a tight ball to protect myself like I always did. The tears continued to fall, and I allowed the pain of my broken heart to permeate every part of my body. The pain was a reminder of all the choices that had been taken away from me in life.

Slowly I drifted off to oblivion, drowning in a sea of sorrow that I feared would swallow me whole.

CHAPTER 10

HINDLEY

I GLANCED at my phone as the coffee brewed, willing it to ring with some type of call or message from Rory, but it remained silent.

I was surprised I hadn't spent half the night crying. Instead, I'd been seething mad, and that one emotion had kept me up half the night, not tears.

With no call from Rory, the hard fact had hit me this morning as I'd laid in bed—this was the end for us. I'd always expected it, yet I still wasn't anymore prepared for it today than I had been the first moment I'd realized our relationship was doomed.

I turned the coffee pot off halfway through its cycle and dragged my body down the hall, tumbling into my bed as the tears finally fell.

I'd experienced heartbreak and devastating loss before in my life, but this was nothing compared to the absolute total abyss Rory's absence had pushed me into. As I tugged the covers over my head to block out the world, I clutched the phone to my chest, praying he would call and end my agony, knowing it wouldn't happen.

I jumped at the sound of a cell phone ringing and popped up from my bed, staring down at the screen. Nothing.

The ringing continued and I realized it was coming from the work phone sitting on my nightstand. I tossed Rory's phone aside and picked up my work one, not surprised to see Matt's number on the screen.

I had no desire to talk to him, or anyone, but he was our sponsor and I couldn't afford to piss him off. I looked at the time on the phone, surprised I'd slept a few hours.

"Hello," I said.

"Oh, hey there, Hindley. I didn't wake you, did I?"

"No, I've been awake for a while." It wasn't a total lie. I'd been up half the night already.

"Oh, good. I was calling to see if you'd like to have a late lunch with me, say maybe one o'clock?"

The only thing I felt like doing was throwing up and shaving off all my hair, but I had to pull out of this funk, and fast. My career, and Rory's, depended on it.

"Sure," I said, knowing the outing would at least get me out of bed. "One o'clock sounds good."

"Great, I'll pick you up from your house."

"Actually, I'm going into the office soon." I hadn't really planned to go in today but maybe a few hours in the office would help clear my mind. "Why don't you pick me up there?"

"That sounds great. I've heard there are a ton of good Mexican restaurants here in Austin. Feel like Mexican?"

"Yeah, that sounds good."

"Any suggestions?"

I didn't even have the energy to shower, much less pick a restaurant. I wouldn't be able to eat anyway. "Why don't you pick."

"Okay, I'll think of a place. See you at one."

"See ya."

"I'm looking forward to it, Hindley."

Suddenly his voice changed and I felt a familiar pang of unease burn in my gut. I reminded myself that Matt was safe, he was a sponsor. And today he was a good distraction.

Two hours later, I was sitting at my desk in my office, trying to concentrate on my next potential client

Humberto Sullivan was a quarterback, two years out of college, who was making a name for himself in the big leagues. I read page after page about him, but I still couldn't quote one single fact about the guy. The only image floating around my mind was Rory Gregor.

Before I knew what time it was, Matt had arrived and we'd headed off to a local restaurant. We sat on the patio and I watched Matt consume his second lethal margarita of the afternoon.

"Those are really strong, Matt," I said. "You should go easy. Especially if you're driving to the airport."

"I'll be fine," he said. "I have a high tolerance when it comes to alcohol."

I didn't, and I sure as hell wasn't going to sit in a car with someone who, in the span of thirty minutes, had consumed two margaritas. The drinks at this restaurant were legendary for not only containing tequila, but Everclear too. I'd seen many a friend fall down fast, literally, after consuming more than they should have.

Another two hours later, I was sitting in the driver's seat of Matt's rented car, waiting curbside at the Austin airport.

Just as expected, the power of the lethal margaritas had proven too much for Matt. I'd insisted on driving and he'd willingly obliged. Staring at his limp body in the passenger seat, I wondered how I was going to get him inside the airport. And even worse, how the hell would he ever get through security and find his gate?

Rory's words rang through my mind. 'You deserve someone like Matt.'

I laughed to myself. If he could only see Matt right now, I didn't think he would agree.

Didn't Rory understand? We were all broken in some way. No one was perfect. Well, no one singularly.

On our own, Rory and I were damaged and abused. But together, we were perfect in our imperfections. He was the missing piece of my broken soul that made me whole. I had to convince him of that.

"Thanks for taking care of me," Matt said, his words a bit slurred as he reached out for a hug.

"Whoa, Matt." I pushed on his chest. "I think you're a little too drunk."

"I like you, Hindley," he said softly, his breath reeking of tequila.

"I like you too, Matt, but in a professional way. Not personally."

"Oh. So, what, you only get personal with him?"

"Him who?"

He laughed sarcastically. "Him, your client."

Oh, shit. He knew. Which probably meant others did as well.

I straightened my shoulders and donned my most professional voice. "I don't know what you're talking about."

Matt snorted. "Please, Hindley, I may be buzzed but I'm not a fool. Anyone can see the guy's crazy about you."

"Who?"

"Who?" He laughed. "You sound like an owl." He sat back against his door, studying me, his head cocked. "And you like him too. Don't you?"

I cleared my throat and squirmed in my seat. "Matt, I don't know what you're talking about."

"Okay, Hindley. If that's the way you want to play it."

"Play what?"

"Hindley, you're not fooling anyone. You and Rory Gregor are involved in more than a professional relationship."

I sucked in a breath as a wave of nausea and panic raced through my body. I was going to lose everything.

"No, we're not," I half shouted.

"Hey," he held up a hand, "don't get me wrong. I think it's great. In fact, I'm jealous as hell of the S.O.B."

I had no response, no words. I was paralyzed with fear. If Matt knew, then other people must know as well. Even my family seemed to ignore our insistence that Rory and I weren't a couple.

"Don't worry," he said. "I'm not going to say anything to anyone. I like you too much."

His words should have assured me but they didn't. My head was pounding and I was breaking out in a cold sweat.

"Just be careful," he said. "It's not like you can't be involved with him. It's just that…" He thought hard about his next words.

"Just what?"

"You're new in the industry, Hindley. I would hate to see you get a reputation, you know?"

I swallowed down the urge to vomit. "What kind of reputation?"

"You're smart, you're talented and creative. Those are the things you want to be known for in this business."

"As opposed to what?"

"As opposed to the agent who sleeps with her clients to sign them."

Shit. I'd completely fucked this up, for me and for Rory.

"Don't get me wrong. I think Rory's great," Matt said. "I think you're great too. Together, I think you're unstoppable. I'm not saying I don't think it's a good idea for you and Rory to be together, personally."

"Well, what are you saying?"

"Sneaking around doesn't always give people the best impression."

"So, you're saying if we are together, personally, it's better to go public?"

"That's your decision. All I know is, there is no way you two can hide your feelings for one another and think you're getting away with it."

I sagged against the door, releasing a heavy sigh. How stupid had we been, thinking we could hide our feelings from everyone around us.

"If you really do want to be together then it is probably better to confess and get it over with. Hiding only makes things worse."

And wasn't that truth, not only about me and Rory, but about life.

"The press loves secrets," he said. "They love *exposing* secrets. That's what ruins reputations, not the actual relationship. Rumors will destroy you in this industry. If there are rumors about Rory, that he's secretly screwing his attorney, I'm not sure Sonora would want to keep him."

I covered my mouth with my hand, fighting back the tears.

"I'm sorry, Hindley, but I don't want you to be blindsided."

I nodded. Matt was being cool and I knew he truly did have my best interest at heart.

"Thank you for talking to me," I said. "For being brutally honest."

He smiled reassuringly. "I don't want to give you the wrong impression. I love working for Sonora Water, I really do. And I do care about their reputation. It's a good, solid company. But the reason I'm sharing this with you is because of *you*. I care about you and your reputation more."

I felt the emotions welling up inside and fought to control myself. "I know," I said, touching his arm gently. "And I appreciate your concern more than you know."

"You're smart, Hindley. Very smart. You'll be fine. Just be careful, that's all. Thanks for the ride. Sorry about getting sloshed."

I laughed. "I tried to warn you."

"That you did." He chuckled. "Thanks again." He leaned over and gave me a kiss on the cheek that felt more innocent today than offensive. "I'll talk to you soon."

He shut the door but leaned in through the open window. "I was a fool to think I ever had a chance with you."

"Why do you say that? I think you're a very attractive man."

"I was a fool to think that Rory Gregor would ever let someone steal you away. The man's completely in love with you, Hindley." He searched my face as if he recognized something within me. "It's not hard to see why."

My mouth fell open at his revelation. Did Rory really love me? I knew I loved him.

"I'll call you as soon as the commercial's done," he said. Stepping back, he waved goodbye and disappeared into the airport.

I sat in stunned silence. Did Rory Gregor love me? Could he love me? Why was that fact so unfathomable?

A banging noise jarred me from my thoughts as I jumped in my seat.

"Hey, lady." A man stood next to my window, dressed in some type of uniform. "You can't park here. Move it or I'll have it towed."

"Do you know where the rental car counter is?" I asked.

"All rental car drop-offs are down below in Terminal A."

"Thanks," I said, rolling up the window. Shoving the car into drive I slowly pulled away from the curb.

Rory Gregor loved me—whether he knew it or not. I had no doubt

Matt's words were true. That's why Rory was so possessive of me, why he didn't feel worthy.

A smile bigger than Kim Kardashian's ass spread across my face. Rory Gregor loved me. And I had a plan to show him.

Dana pulled up to the curb at the rental car facility in her BMW convertible and I slipped inside. "Thanks for picking me up."

"No problem. Glad I was awake."

I gazed over at my best friend. Her normally tan complexion was ashen and her eyes were bloodshot with dark circles underneath. She looked like death warmed over. "Rough night?" I asked.

"Oh, yeah." She laughed. "I'm surprised I didn't see you there. I kept expecting you to walk through the door any minute."

"Where?"

"At Leif's."

"Why would I have been at Leif's?"

"Because Rory was there."

Oh, God. Rory had gone to a party after their fight. Suddenly she had an urgent need to find him.

"What were you doing at Leif's?"

"It was Rory's wrap party," Dana said.

"What wrap party?"

"The one Leif threw him last night, to celebrate the end of filming his first commercial."

Images of Rory at a party flashed through my head. What if he'd gotten drunk or high? What if he'd buried his anger with me inside another woman? Bile rose in my throat and I was about to ask Dana to pull over.

"Calm down, Cinderella," Dana said. "Prince Charming didn't do anything. He came in, looked around, said hi to everyone then locked himself in Leif's back bedroom the rest of the night."

"Really?" I asked, still unsure of his commitment to me.

"Yes," she sighed. "What the hell happened between you two

anyway? He was so pissed off when he came in, storming around with his hands fisted like he was going to punch a wall."

"We had dinner with my family."

"Oh, lovely. I bet that went over like shit on a birthday cake." Dana laughed. "Was Geneva there?"

"Oh, yeah. Stan too."

She shook her head. "Poor Stan."

"It was sad. Geneva has no shame. She was all flirty with Rory with no regard to her husband."

"That bitch is a skank. I bet she fucked five different guys on her honeymoon. And Stan wasn't one of them."

We both burst out into peals of laugher. The sad thing was, Dana was probably right.

I sunk back into my seat with a heavy sigh.

"What's wrong?" Dana asked.

"I'm gonna tell him."

"Tell who what?"

"Rory. I'm going to tell him everything. About my past. About what happened."

She pulled over to the side of the road and shoved the car into park. Turning in her seat she sat directly facing me, her eyes wide. "Are you serious?"

"Yes."

She held her hands up to the sky. "Well, thank the Lord, Buddha, Mohammad, and any other savior of the world." She reached across the console and squeezed my leg. "It's about fuckin' time. The guy was a mess last night, Hindley. No one could reach him."

"I don't know why he thinks he's beneath me."

"He had a shit stepfather who beat his ass on a daily basis."

"Really?" Rory had never told me that. I knew he'd had a bad childhood, but he never told me he'd been physically abused.

"One day," Dana said, "he fought back and beat the shit out of his dad. The cops arrested Rory and his mom didn't do jack shit to bail him out of jail."

I sucked in a breath, covering my mouth. "Oh my God."

"Leif said he spent almost six months in juvie."

"Why hasn't he told me any of this?" I wondered out loud.

"Same reason you haven't told him any of your shit story. It's not something that gives people the warm fuzzies. Especially someone you've fallen in love with."

I gasped, my eyes widening as my body stiffened. Did everyone know? "Is it that obvious?"

She laughed. "You two have been in love since that first kiss back at Geneva's wedding. You're both just too damn stupid, stubborn, and hard-headed to see it."

I couldn't contain my joy any longer. I reached across the car and hugged Dana tight. "Thank you."

"Why?"

"For always being my voice of reason." I released her and sat back in my seat. "For always being there. Especially when I thought I'd go over the deep end."

"I love you, Hindley. You know that. I'll always be there."

I nodded, unable to speak.

"And trust me," she said, smiling, her deep dimples drilling into her cheeks. "There is nothing you can say about your past that will make Rory stop loving you. He'll probably love you even more once he finds out how strong and brave you are."

"Can you drop me off at my house?"

"You don't want to go straight to your boy?"

"No, not yet. I have an idea. But I need your help." I just hoped against hope that Dana was right. I prayed Rory would still love me in spite of my past. Maybe even because of it.

CHAPTER 11

RORY

I SURVEYED Leif's living room, convinced I'd done as much good as I could to clean up from the party last night. It had been quite the celebration, supposedly in my honor, only celebrating last night was the least thing I'd wanted to do.

I couldn't remember feeling lower in my life. Had I really pushed away the only woman who gave two shits about me, the real me, and not my fame, or money, or anything else?

Afraid to answer my own question, I fell into the plush leather couch, not surprised that, once again, I'd fucked up a good thing.

Hindley had been nothing but kind and caring, completely genuine in her feelings for me. Something about watching her parents interact in a gentle, loving way had pushed deep-seated buttons within me. Their exchanges of love and adoration for Hindley only reiterated how far apart our worlds were.

Her parents loved each other, cared for one another, cared for *her*. My parents despised each other and hated the fuck out of me.

Hindley's mother supported her and nurtured her. My mom had let her own asshole of a husband beat the shit out of both of us on a daily basis. And she'd never contacted me since she'd had the police cart me off to jail ten years ago. Well, that wasn't entirely true. She found me shortly after I went pro. Apparently, she was drawn more to my money. When I refused to give her a dime, she'd left as fast as she'd come.

It wasn't just Hindley's family dynamic that screwed with my head. It was also painfully clear that Paul valued education more than anything. I was pretty sure there was no way he'd ever accept me as worthy of his daughter's love after he found out I was a fucking high school dropout.

What worried me most of all though was her family's obvious denial of our 'professional' relationship. Who were we kidding? Everyone knew we were together. Everyone except Dipshit Matt Davis from Sonora Water. *Dick.*

Why was I so jealous of him? I didn't know where this rage came from inside of me. Actually, I did know. It was born from my childhood, the need to protect those who couldn't protect themselves.

But I couldn't understand this situation.

Hindley reassured me that I was all she needed, all she wanted. Yet, I still let old insecurities cloud my judgment. I could have spent the night holding her, caressing her, making love to her. Instead, I had let my shitbag ego get in the way.

Suddenly, I had an urgent need to see her. I had to tell her how sorry I was. I had to make her understand, make her forgive me, and tell her how much I loved her. Loved her. I smiled at the thought. I loved Hindley.

I jumped up from the sofa and reached for my phone but stopped short when I became acutely aware of her presence. I always felt Hindley before I saw her. I had the first night I'd met her. It was a sixth sense for me. She was inside of me, a part of me.

Slowly I turned and held my breath as I saw her standing in the entry-way, looking as beautiful as ever.

Her lips curled up into a soft smile, an expression I wasn't expecting, considering what a douche bag I'd been last night.

"It seems as though I'm not the only one who keeps their door unlocked," she said.

My heart ached at the sight of her. I'd never seen anything so welcoming in all my life. I raced toward her, arms outstretched, but before I reached her, she held up her hand to stop me.

Oh, shit. Here it comes. But I couldn't be mad or upset. I deserved any ass beating she wanted to give me. Whatever she said, whatever she did next, I'd take it, as long as in the end I was left holding her in my arms.

"I'm so sorry, Hindley," I said, so desperate I nearly dropped to my knees.

She raised her eyebrows and shook her head, warning me to stay silent.

I dutifully obeyed, knowing I couldn't risk upsetting her again. She was giving me another chance with no questions asked, and I wasn't going to fuck it up again.

"I need to show you something," she said, her voice and her body completely calm.

I stared at her, perplexed. What was she up to. "All right."

"Come with me." She held out her hand.

Gazing down at her small, pale hand, I marveled at how different we were. Maybe that's why we were drawn together.

Without question, I threaded my fingers around hers. The connection between us was undeniable. No matter how much I fought it, Hindley Hagen fit me perfectly. I followed her like a lamb to slaughter as she led me outside and ushered me into her car.

After making sure I was comfortable, she walked around the car and slid into the driver's seat "Trust me?"

Trust her? "With my life, Hindley."

A smile bigger than I deserved spread across her beautiful face and I knew in that moment I was forgiven for being a total dick last night.

"Turn around," she said.

I furrowed my brows, not quite understanding what she was asking.

"Turn." She made a circular motion with her finger.

I did as she asked, sliding around in my seat and looking out the passenger side window. A soft scarf covered my eyes.

She tied it tightly around my head, yanking on the knot to make sure it was secure. "Can you see anything?"

Her voice was a step higher and I could hear the apprehension in her tone. My stomach knotted as I tried to imagine what she was going to do with me.

"No, I can't see anything."

"Are you okay with this? Not knowing, I mean?" she asked. "I know how much you like control."

She was right, I was a control freak, had been since adolescence. Apparently, control was a coping mechanism kids from abusive homes used, or so a counselor in juvie told me. But with Hindley, I was finding it easier and easier to relinquish my need to be in charge. In fact, I welcomed it. It was nice to let her make the decisions.

"I'm fine, Hindley. I trust you."

I could hear her breath even out. She'd been nervous and the thought somehow eased my own anxiety. How could I have been so stupid to believe anyone else would suit her better than me?

"Good," she said. The car roared to life as she put it in gear and pulled away from the curb.

We drove in silence. I was completely shocked at how peaceful I felt. I had no idea what lay ahead of me, but I didn't care.

Hindley had come and extended an offering of forgiveness when I didn't deserve it. There was no place I'd rather be than in her presence, no matter where we were headed.

After driving for an eternity, the car finally came to a stop. Hindley's door creaked opened, then closed with a bang.

I waited patiently, trying to curb my anxiety. My door opened, and her hands slid into mine as she pulled me from the car.

"Watch out, there's a step here," she said.

Where were we?

I shuffled my foot along the ground until I felt the obstacle then raised my leg to step up.

"Still trust me?" She was inches away from my face and I could smell her intoxicating aroma. The scent that was uniquely her own.

I nodded, unable to say more.

"Just follow me, I'll tell you when to step, okay?"

"Okay."

She tugged on my hand and wrapped it in the crook of her elbow.

I followed behind her, not giving a rat's ass where we were going. As long as it was with Hindley, I'd follow her anywhere.

A door squeaked open and a bell rang above us as the scent of roses assaulted me. Every sensory organ I had was on high alert.

"Hey, girl," a woman's voice echoed. "Oh, sorry," she whispered. Hindley must have instructed her to stay quiet. "Room three," she whispered.

Room three? Where were we, a hotel? Oh, hell yeah.

Another door opened and Hindley tugged on my hand. "Watch your step here, there's a threshold."

I felt for the ridge with my foot then cautiously stepped over it.

"You doing all right?" she asked.

Better than all right, I wanted to say. I nodded and we continued on.

The floor beneath us creaked every so often, the sounds echoing through the large, and obviously empty room.

"Sit here." She pushed me and I fell into a huge chair.

My hands rubbed along the soft material. It felt like velvet. I was praying Hindley would join me, naked. The thought of having Hindley nude and wrapped around me had my head spinning, and my dick halfway to hard.

Before I could conjure up anymore images of what she and I could do in this lush seat, Hindley leaned over and pressed her lips against my ear.

"Wait here. I'll be right back." I was fairly certain she'd just purred. Fuck.

I inhaled deeply, her scent washing over me. I wanted to reach out and grab her, but her fading footsteps indicated she was leaving me.

A door in the distance shut with a bang and I was more than half tempted to remove my blindfold. But this was important to Hindley and I wasn't about to do anything to jeopardize her trust.

I surveyed my surroundings with my remaining senses. The scarf around my eyes was thick and Hindley had tied it so tight, I couldn't make out anything with my eyes. I drew in another deep breath but all I smelled was her lingering scent. Muffled voices outside of the room caught my attention. Females?

I nervously rubbed the velvety material of the chair, seriously thinking of running, but that would be futile. I was completely blinded by the scarf.

Where the hell were we?

A door opened in the distance and the clicking of heels echoed through the room. The sound grew louder as the person approached me.

"Hindley?" I asked, sitting up straighter.

"Nope," a female voice with a rich Texas twang said.

My senses became hyper-aware of everything—the soft material of the chair, the light hissing noise of a stereo system that had just clicked on, the floral aroma of the woman in front of me, and the sour taste of fear and anxiety in my mouth.

The knot of the scarf slowly loosened and the material fell away. I blinked several times, adjusting to the dim lighting in the room.

Sitting on the edge of the seat, I stared up into bright green eyes so different than Hindley's. The crimson haired woman standing in front of me was unfamiliar, but her smile indicated she knew me. She was wearing leggings and a loose-fitting shirt that hung off one shoulder.

"Welcome to Miss Understood, darlin'. Enjoy the show." Her breathy and sensual voice left no doubt in my mind we were definitely somewhere naughty. I smiled at the thought.

Turning on her high heels, she sauntered away, dimming the lights even more before disappearing through a velvet curtain on the far wall.

I surveyed the room, with my eyes this time. The far wall was covered with mirrors and three steel poles stood in front of the wall. I noticed the center pole was on a raised platform.

The lights dimmed even more and two spotlights appeared from the ceiling, one on the center pole and platform and the other on a mirror covered disco ball hanging from the ceiling. Specks of light rotated around the large room, giving it a hypnotic effect as music started to blast from the surround sound system.

There was an electric guitar solo and a deep beat to the music I recognized instantly. It was one of the songs I'd downloaded onto Hindley's phone, *Pour Some Sugar on Me* by Def Leppard.

I was an 80's rock music junkie and she'd always given me shit about it. I'd felt it only fitting that I introduce her to it by creating a playlist. I wasn't sure she totally appreciated the songs, until now.

From the far corner of the room, a single shoe emerged from behind the velvet curtain. The heels were at least six inches tall with spiked heels and a black strap wrapped around slender ankles. Slowly the next leg appeared and I stared in fascination. Her legs were long and lean, the most beautiful legs I'd ever seen.

My gaze travelled up her gorgeous body as she walked toward me. No, she wasn't walking, she was stalking, like a lioness about to pounce.

Her outfit was outrageous, and seriously hot. A barely-there black leather bra and bikini bottoms that left little to the imagination clung to her like a second skin. A thin strip of material connecting the two pieces making a man want to rip through it to see her entire mid-section.

The entire outfit was covered with rhinestones that reflected the rotating sparkles of light from the mirrored ball overhead. A small chain was draped from one side of her hip to the other and swayed with every step she took. It was the most exotic, erotic, alluring outfit I'd ever seen.

Willing my gaze higher, I saw my temptress's face. Her makeup was heavier than usual but sultry and sexy. Her eyes were outlined with smoky black and dark eyeshadow covered her lids. The makeup set off her brown eyes and made them appear even larger.

Her long hair was full and luscious and fell in golden waves over her shoulders. The flaxen locks caressed the swells of her breasts and my hands grew damp wanting to do the same.

This woman standing before me was the hottest person I'd ever seen. My mouth was dry and my dick was harder than it ever had been in my life.

This wasn't Hindley Hagen, the Drunk Girl. This wasn't Hindley Hagen, the attorney, or Hindley Hagen, the sports agent. This wasn't even Hindley Hagen, the rich, cultured debutant.

This was Hindley Hagen…the stripper.

CHAPTER 12

RORY

CHILLS RAN up and down my spine and my hands grew damp. Had Hindley really been a stripper? Even worse, was she still a stripper?

She stopped in front of the center pole, her hips swaying to the beat of the music. Slowly she extended her arms and grabbed the pole behind her head. The motion tugged her outfit to dangerous levels. Her breasts nearly popped free from her top, and I didn't know if I was excited or pissed as hell.

I wanted to stop her, ask her questions, find out if she truly was or had been a stripper, but my body betrayed me, and the animal inside took over.

I reclined back into the soft velvety chair and prepared for the show.

Her body moved in perfect time to the beat of the music as she slid down the pole. Her thighs spread wide as she sank down, her ass on the back of her sky-high pumps. Her new position gave me access to parts of her I prayed few had seen.

She turned and grabbed the pole, climbing almost to the ceiling before inverting herself, her long blonde hair hanging below her head. She spread her long legs into a horizontal split while simultaneously spinning around the pole.

Shit, how the hell was she doing that without falling on her face?

Her body slid down the pole and plunged toward the floor. I almost lunged out of my chair to catch her, fearing she actually would smash her face.

Before I could move, her legs flexed and wrapped around the pole to slow her movement. The momentum of her fall had her entire body swinging around to an upright position.

What the hell? She'd definitely done this before.

Hindley continued her dance, performing acrobatics I'd never seen or even known were possible. All the while, her thick mane of golden hair swung with the smooth movements of her body, wrapping around her neck and framing her face like a work of art.

She twisted around to a standing position, one hand above her head to steady herself. I had no idea how she wasn't dizzy as fuck after twirling around that damn pole.

Her gaze held mine as she shoved off the pole and stalked toward me like a predator, every step choreographed to the beat of Def Leppard's song.

She was a siren, and I was caught in her trap.

As she drew nearer, her eyes narrowed and sparkled with a look of hunger I'd never seen. One side of her plump lips tilted up with an evil smirk. I feared this she-devil in front of me may eat me alive. Her expression left no doubt in my mind what she wanted.

Me.

And right now, I was totally okay with that.

She stopped a few feet away from me and sank down to her hands and knees. Flipping her hair back over her shoulders, she crawled toward me, that some predatory look in her eyes.

My mouth grew dry and my dick stiffened to a painful level.

She stopped between my legs, leaning back on her ass as her hands skimmed over my thighs. Using my body as leverage she lifted herself and rolled her entire body against mine like a snake.

Fuck, I was gonna blow a load all over this place if she kept this up.

Oblivious to my pain, she rocked her hips and chest against me, moving in perfect rhythm to the beat of the music. Suddenly she flipped around, gripping the arms of the chair as she ground her ass into my dick.

Fuck.

I held my breath, counting backward from one hundred to keep myself under control.

Her head fell back, her hair splaying across my face, blinding me. Her body was unreal and she smelled so fucking amazing, I had to have her. Just like this. Now.

I reached around her small waist and moved my hand further down, but was stopped by the sting of her slap.

She fell back against me, her body melting into mine as she twisted her head to whisper in my ear.

"Don't touch the dancer."

I didn't think it was possible to come without someone actually touching you, but I was pretty sure that's what I'd done as soon as her hot little breath had caressed my skin. I closed my eyes and gripped the chair with all my might, afraid that if I touched her, my private dance may come to an end. And I did *not* want that to happen.

The song came to an end and my mind screamed, "No!" But my dick said, "Thank God."

She flipped around to face me, her brown eyes holding my gaze. Before I could reach out and touch her, she pushed up into a standing position, then turned and stalked back to the pole.

For the first time, I was able to get a good look at the back of her outfit.

Holy fuck-bags. I always knew Hindley was hot with a killer body, but this chick in front of me was like molten lava.

I'd expected a G-string or a thong of some kind, the kind of outfit you see most strippers wear. Instead, she wore low-rise leather bottoms that revealed only a portion of ass, thank God.

The design was even better than most I'd seen. With half of her back-side covered, a man's mind begged to see more. It was perfect. She was perfect.

Hindley grabbed the pole and hoisted herself up again, swinging around two full revolutions before turning herself upside down. With one leg wrapped around the pole, she let the other fall down and touch the floor in a perpendicular split.

Who knew she was so limber?

Upside down, the outfit barely held in her breasts. All I could think of was ripping that damn costume off her body.

Slowly her other leg lowered to the floor and she lifted herself to a standing position as the music came to an end. In the silence, she stared at me with doe eyes, her shoulders slightly slumped. The confident woman who had stood before me just minutes ago was gone, replaced by my shy Drunk Girl.

My gut burned with the realization that Hindley had definitely been a stripper at one time in her life. She'd danced on a stage while dirty old men ogled her, and pined after her. Like I'd just done.

I sank back into my chair, wondering what to say to this revelation.

Her eyes grew wider and shimmered with tears. Terror struck me as I realized I might not be able to get past the fact that she may have been, or may *still* be a stripper.

Hindley walked slowly toward me, sinking down to her knees at my feet as if I were her master.

I gazed down at her beautiful face, now covered with more makeup than I'd seen her wear before. Her true beauty underneath still shone through.

Her expression was apprehensive but innocent.

My anxiety eased a fraction.

"So, what did you think?" She raised her brows in mild amusement, but we both knew she was nervous.

I sat in silence, unprepared to speak.

Her eyes darted back and forth as she stared at me, seeming to be searching for something I couldn't seem to give her.

"Rory," she whispered, putting her hands on my thighs. Her long false eyelashes splayed across her lids like fans and I wondered how many times she'd donned this costume and batted her lashes for money. How many acts had she performed in the course of her life? How long had she been dancing half naked for men?

"Rory," she called again.

"Yes?"

"What did you think?" She swallowed hard. "Of my dance? My dance for you," she added.

"You've done this before, haven't you? For other people?" My tone was more accusatory than I'd intended.

She pulled back as if I'd slapped her. "Why? Would that bother you?"

I sat up straight. "Hell yes, it would."

She reared back, a snarl curling her lips.

"What?" I asked in shock. She couldn't possibly think this wouldn't bother me.

She remained silent, her brows knitted as she glared at me.

"Hindley, come on. Are you seriously asking me *why* it would bother me to find out that perverted old men have pawed at your naked body for money?"

Her jaw fell lax.

I wanted to feel bad for my harsh words but I didn't. All I felt was a sick type of fury burning in my stomach at the thought of other men in dark, seedy places touching her.

She cocked her head and raised a brow. "So, have *you* ever been to a strip club before?"

"What the fuck does that have to do with anything?"

She pushed against my legs and rose to her feet, glaring at me with disgust. "It has *everything* to do with it. Answer my question, Rory." She slammed her clenched fists to her hips as her eyes narrowed.

Fuck. I was totally screwed.

"Yes." I finally answered.

"So what's the difference between *that* woman dancing on your lap, and *you* being one of the perverted old men lusting after her?"

Sometimes I hated that she was such an attorney. I would never win against her arguments, she was too damn smart. Her reasoning was right though, I had been a dirty old perv.

"You think you're better than that stripper, don't you?" Her voice was louder now, echoing through the small space.

I jumped to my feet and approached her. "What the fuck do you expect me to say, Hindley? That I'm okay with this?" I waved my hand toward the pole. "With you being a stripper?"

"You're just like everyone else." She swept a hand through the air. "So judgmental."

"*Me*, judgmental?" I cocked my head and stared at her in disbelief.

"Yes, you." She poked my chest. "What you're saying is, it's disgusting for a woman to dance around naked for a man, but it's perfectly fine for a man to let her?" She shook her head, her blonde hair falling over her shoulders. "God, you're so hypocritical."

"I'm not hypocritical or judgmental."

"Oh, yeah?" she spat. "When you were in one of these clubs, did you pay a woman to sit on your lap and dance for you?"

Oh, shit. I knew where she was going with this, and I hated it. It was true, she was right. I had paid for women to do exactly what she'd done and had never thought twice about it. It had always been in fun, during a bachelor party or some other stupid shit like that.

"That's what I thought." She turned on her six-inch 'Come Fuck Me' pumps and stalked toward the velvet curtains.

I chased after her, grabbing her elbow and turning her to face me. "This is different, Hindley."

She crossed her arms over her chest, pushing her breasts higher. "How?"

I fought the urge to stare at her chest, which would only prove how much of a dick I was.

"It's you." I pointed to the pole. "It's *you*. Up there." I scrubbed my hands through my hair wanting to yank it out by the roots.

"So?"

"So. You don't know what those fuckers are like in those clubs, Hindley."

"It's just dancing."

"Maybe to you, but not to them."

"You mean, not to *you*? Don't forget, you're one of those perverted old men, remember?"

I bit down so hard, I was afraid I might actually break a tooth. How was this girl getting the best of me?

She shifted her weight on her feet, jutting out a hip. "Just be honest with me, Rory."

I steeled my features, wanting to argue but the truth was, she was right. It was a double standard, no matter which way you looked at it.

I had been hypocritical and judgmental. But the girl didn't understand the way men's minds worked.

It may have been a job to her, but to us sick fuckers, these women were dream girls, an image perpetually stuck in our mind as we whacked off later at home, or worse yet, in the bathroom stall of the fuckin' strip club. I swallowed down the bile rising in my throat at the image.

"Do you think differently of me now because—" She swallowed hard.

How could she seriously expect me to be okay with her being a stripper if she couldn't even say the word?

I stared up at the ceiling, trying to erase the image of her, bare ass naked on a stage as sick, perverted men licked their lips in anticipation of touching her milky white skin. I was seriously going to hurl.

"That's what I thought," she said in disgust. She yanked her elbow from my grasp as her heels clicked on the wooden floor.

"Wait, Hindley!"

She stopped but didn't turn around.

I slid in behind her, my body only inches away from hers, careful not to touch her in any way. "It's not what you think."

She turned to face me, the height of her shoes placing her gorgeous eyes directly across from mine. "What is it then?" she asked, her eyes softening.

"You're right. I am a hypocritical, judgmental dick. It's a double standard, and I've participated in it. It's just..." I didn't know how to articulate all the things that were racing through my mind. "Look, Hindley, you don't understand how men think about shit like this. To you, it may be just dancing, but for them..." I had no idea how to express what I was feeling.

"For them, it's more?" she finished.

"For some of them, it's a lot more."

"You think I don't know that?"

"Some girls take it further."

"Like prostitution?"

I nodded. I'd never done it but I knew guys who had.

"Yes, some of them do," she said, "but not all dancers. In fact, most of them are extremely smart women who know how to take advantage of men who are dumb enough to pay money to see something they could probably get for free."

"You're asking me to completely change my way of thinking in one afternoon, change beliefs I've had for years. I'm sorry, you're right. It's wrong to think that way. I'm sure a lot of you are smart. I mean, look at you, you're an attorney. It's just. It's *you,* Hindley."

"I was never a stripper, Rory."

It took several seconds for her words to register. "What?"

"I said I was never a stripper."

"But, you just danced. And then, you were defensive of the lifestyle, and—"

"It's not a lifestyle. It's a profession, a means to an end."

"Not a great means," I added.

She shook her head.

"So, if you weren't a stripper, how do you know about all of this?" I waved my hand around the vast room.

"I worked with them."

"Doing what?"

"I designed their costumes and they taught me how to dance. It's good exercise."

"Seriously?"

She nodded.

My shoulders slumped in relief. She hadn't been a stripper. Well, thank fuck for that.

"There you go again," she huffed.

"What?"

"Your body language says you're relieved to find out I wasn't a stripper."

"Well, I'm sorry, Hindley, but I am. Call me crazy, but the thought of men trying to touch you kind of sickens me. Just thinking of those bastards jerkin' off to images of you in their mind makes me want to puke."

She shook her head and stared at the floor.

"I know it may seem wrong to you but…" How could I explain it to her without causing her to get angry again?

She lifted her head and stared at me. I had to get this right.

"How would you feel if you found out that I used to dance around on a table, completely naked and let women touch and fondle me?"

Her eyes widened with what I hoped was understanding. At least she was willing to see it from my point of view for once.

"But it doesn't mean anything to the girls," she said.

"But it *does* to the men, Hindley. We're all sick motherfuckers. And trust me, if someone as hot as you shakes her ass in a guy's face, he's gonna dream about fuckin' you for weeks. Hell, he'll probably jack off to your image in the parking lot."

Her head fell and she played with the chain of her outfit.

I reached out and lifted her chin until our eyes met. "You're right. It wasn't fair to judge. But men and women are different. I wouldn't think any less of you if you told me you were a stripper."

She yanked her chin from my grasp. "Sure," she huffed.

"I mean it, Hindley. I couldn't care less what's happened in your past or what you've done. But you can't expect me not to be affected in some way, not have a feeling about it one way or the other." I waited for her to return my gaze, but she didn't. Panic flooded me. Was I going to lose her over this?

I moved to stand in front of her again. "Hey," I whispered.

She lifted her head.

"I'm sorry."

"Why?" she asked, her brown eyes wide.

"For judging you, for judging these women. I'll never look at the profession the same again, I can promise you that."

"But?"

"But it doesn't mean it would be any easier to know that other assholes drooled over you and fantasized about you—knowing they went to bed at night jackin' off to images of your naked ass running through their demented minds."

"What?" she half laughed.

"I'm serious, Hindley. That's the way guys are. We're sick fuck bags. If you put eye candy in front of us, we're gonna want a lick."

"That's a visual." She giggled.

Oh, thank fuck. My girl was back. I grasped her in my arms but leaned back so I could see her.

"I meant what I said, Hindley. There's nothing in your past that would make me love you any less."

"Love me?"

Oh, shit. Had I just said *love*? Yeah, I had.

"Yes," I answered honestly.

I did love her. I'd known it for a long time, I was just too scared to say it out loud, afraid to give her that kind of power over me. But after I watched her dance, and listened to her defend a profession that I'd judged so harshly, I realized she had a fire and a passion in her that I was addicted to.

She leaned in and kissed my cheek before pulling away to stare at me. She smirked, her eyes softer now, like she held a secret that could change the world.

"Give me a second to clean up then I want to take you to dinner."

"Okay," I said, thankful she wasn't running for the door.

She turned and walked away, disappearing behind the curtains she'd entered through earlier.

I made my way back to the chair and collapsed with a huge sigh.

She wasn't a stripper, thank fuck for that. But she was right. It was hypocritical to think that way. I had ogled strippers before. Was it all in fun? Did it matter? No, it didn't. I'd taken advantage of them and you know what? Hindley was right. They were smart enough to charge me for it. Who was the dumbass now?

I closed my eyes, unable to stop the visions of Hindley dancing around that pole, splitting her legs, rubbing her little ass on my crotch had my soldier standing at attention, again. Shit. There was no way I was going to be able to walk anywhere or eat with this rod between my legs.

"What's wrong?" Hindley said.

I opened my eyes and saw her standing in the doorway, holding a bag. God, how long had I been sitting here fantasizing of her?

She wore shorts and a T-shirt now. Her face was void of any makeup and her hair was slicked back in a ponytail. Whether she was dressed for the stage or a day at the beach, Hindley Hagen was gorgeous.

And I loved her.

But my dick was rock hard and desiring nothing more than to bury itself deep inside her. I prayed my face didn't give away how weak I was. That was the last thing I wanted her to know, what a typical man I was.

She walked toward me and dropped her bag by the side of my chair. Kneeling down in front of me, she spread my knees apart.

Oh, fuck.

"Is something wrong, Rory?" she asked, one eyebrow arched high. "Is there something that we need to take care of before we eat?"

Holy shit.

"I'm really hungry," she said softly, a spark of desire in her eyes. "But not for food. Not yet." She licked her lips. "I could eat now *and* later."

Holy motherfucker. What was she saying?

Before I could even ask, she raised up on her knees. Leaning into me, she reached for the button on my jeans and popped it open.

I sucked in a breath at the sound of my zipper giving way.

Against my better judgment, I stared down at her face.

"Okay?" she asked, biting her bottom lip.

Okay? Her lips on my dick was pretty much a necessity at this point.

She placed a small hand on my chest and gently pushed me back in the chair. "Show's not over yet," she whispered.

I fell back into my seat, watching as her head lowered, thinking how much I loved my Drunk Girl.

CHAPTER 13

RORY

I STRETCHED out in the passenger seat of Hindley's car as we drove away from what she'd declared, the best barbeque restaurant in Texas. I had to agree, the food was amazing.

"Thank you for dinner," I said, rubbing my stomach.

"My pleasure."

"Where are you taking me now?"

"Another surprise."

"If it's anything like my last one, I don't know if I'll survive." I reached over and grabbed her hand but was surprised to see my sassy comment received no reaction from her. "Hey." I drew her hand to my mouth and lightly kissed each finger.

Finally, she turned to look at me, her brow furrowed.

"Everything all right?"

"Umm." Her gaze returned to the road.

"So, you really made that much money designing stripper clothes?"

She cut her eyes toward me, raising her brow.

I'd been derogatory. "Sorry, exotic-wear. Isn't that what you called it?"

"Uh huh."

"So how in the world does a girl go from law school to designing naughty clothes?"

"Actually, I went from designing naughty clothes to law school, if you want to be specific." She drew in a deep breath and held it for several seconds.

I squeezed her hand. "Hey, what's wrong?"

She shook her head.

"I swear I won't judge, Hindley, I promise."

"My friend, Regan, the one I told you about that owns the sex shop in Dallas?"

"Oh, yeah, I'd like to meet her." I laughed.

"Well, she always told me I should be a stripper."

I couldn't argue with that logic, although I'd only want Hindley dancing for me.

"I knew I wanted to go to law school," she said, oblivious to my thoughts, thankfully. "But Paul was having a difficult time financially and I didn't want him to struggle anymore than he had to. And there was no way I was going to strap myself down with two hundred thousand dollars' worth of student loans."

"You made two hundred thousand dollars making these clothes?" I sat straight up, giving her my full attention.

"No." She laughed. "If I had made that much money, I never would have gone to law school. I got grants and scholarships and stuff, but some of it I made by sewing. Then my business grew."

"Grew how?"

"Regan sold the outfits at her store. They caught on in the dancing world and it went from there. Then regular women wanted to dress naughty for their partners, so orders started coming in faster than I could keep up."

"I could see that."

"I'd design them and create a pattern then send it to Regan. She'd have them manufactured and altered in Dallas then ship them out to the customers, or sell them in her store. We worked our business together. I think she gave me most of the money, even though she did a lot of the work. She wanted to see me succeed, see me graduate from law school."

"Do you still make them?" I asked. "These naughty clothes."

"Why? Do you want to buy some to put in another Naughty Box and send it to my work?" She winked.

My Drunk Girl was becoming braver.

"Maybe." I held up the barely-there outfit she'd worn earlier tonight. "Why didn't you tell me this earlier?"

"I don't know. It just never came up."

"So, why now?"

"Honestly?"

I turned to face her, giving her my undivided attention. This was serious. "Of course, honestly. Always honest."

She looked at me, her face riddled with an unspoken anxiety.

"I told you from the start not to put me on a pedestal, Rory," she said. "You kept beating yourself up, thinking you were so far beneath me, like I was some perfect little rich girl from a lofty mansion high on an unattainable hill."

I leaned over and kissed her cheek. "I still think you're perfect."

She smiled and something in my chest tightened. I loved making this amazing girl happy. For the first time in twenty-four hours, the tension in my body seemed to ease.

She pulled into a dead-end driveway. "We're here."

I glanced out from the windshield. Overgrown weeds surrounded the car and a dilapidated chain-link fence stood a few yards away on a hill. The place looked deserted and desolate. I was definitely not excited about *this* surprise.

"Where are we?" I asked.

"Come with me." She opened the door.

I watched her get out and walk around the hood of the car. Her movements were different now—she shuffled with hunched shoulders instead of holding her head high and prancing like she once had.

A knot of fear burned in the pit of my stomach. Something wasn't right. It felt like the beginning of the end. I wanted to grab her, run away, and never look back.

She leaned against the hood of the car, wrapping her arms around her mid-section as she stared blankly at the fence in front of us.

I got out of the car and stood beside her. "What's this?" I pointed toward the hill. "Where are we?"

"This used to be the old airport in Austin."

I swallowed down my anxiety, trying to keep my tone steady. "Why are we here?"

"My mom got pregnant with me in high school."

This was her story, and something inside said I wasn't going to like it, but I needed to remain calm.

"Her parents kicked us out when I was only two months old," she said.

"Who the fuck does that?"

She turned and stared at me. "I know, right?" Slowly she returned her gaze to the fence, drawing in a deep breath.

I could sense this was difficult for her, like disclosing the fact that I couldn't read had been for me. I thought about moving closer but decided I needed to give her space.

"We didn't have much money growing up," she continued. "My mom didn't meet Paul until I was thirteen."

That was news. I'd assumed she'd grown up with money her whole life.

"I'm not who you think I am, Rory," she said, her voice flat.

The words cut me like a knife and I could almost feel the blood pouring out of me. What horrible memory was she about to relive?

I didn't care. I loved her, no matter what. But something in my gut told me to brace for the worst.

She leaned her head back and stared up at the night sky. "My mom used to bring us out here and we'd lay back on the hood of her beat-up car and watch the planes take off and land. It was deafening but I loved it. We'd dream of being on a plane one day, jetting up into the sky and flying far, far away."

I watched as her mind travelled back in time, her face carefree and hopeful like I'm sure she was as a young child.

"Since we couldn't afford much, this was entertainment for us, I guess you'd say." She laughed, but it wasn't the same bubbly sound she usually made.

Shit.

She took a deep breath and closed her eyes.

Instinctively, I knew better than to interrupt her.

"You told me earlier that you love me," she said. "I mean, I think that's what you said."

I was about to answer but she continued on.

"You need to know everything about me, Rory. It may change the way you feel about me. I'm not sure you'll love me after you know."

Fuck me, what had happened to this girl?

I heard the tiny hiccup of a sob and scooted closer but she slid out of my reaching, shaking her head.

"Hindley, I love you. Nothing that you've done or been through will change that."

Her eyes cut to mine. They were pooled with tears.

I swallowed down my emotions, my need to protect her almost primitive. "I mean it, Hindley. Nothing will change how I feel. Nothing."

She stood motionless, silent, staring past me.

"Talk to me," I whispered. "Just tell me what happened. It doesn't matter." And it wouldn't.

She stared up at the dark night sky again, as if the stars held all the answers.

Dread washed over my entire body and I feared I might be sick.

"When I was in college, I had a roommate," she said quietly. "Felicia Graston. It was our junior year and we moved into a new apartment before the semester started."

I didn't like where this was headed. My heart nearly beat out of my chest with fear. I clenched my hands to keep from reaching out for her.

"She and I were really excited." She smiled. "It was our first apartment. We'd been in the dorms for two years, so being on our own was a big deal for both of us."

I could only imagine. The thrill of being on your own was intoxicating.

"Anyway," she said, "the complex was small, maybe only fifty units, but fairly new. Paul's investment company had purchased the complex a few months before with the intent that Felicia and I would rent one of the units." She paused.

I held my breath, feeling like I was watching a horrific car accident about happen.

"Shortly after we moved in, it seemed like something in our apartment was breaking all the time. A showerhead one week, the stove the next week, maybe a fan motor, whatever that is."

She gave a short laugh but I couldn't find anything humorous about this story.

"There were no major repairs, just enough for the maintenance team to always come out. It seemed odd, especially because the property was fairly new. We teased Paul and told him he should buy stock in a maintenance company to break even."

She laughed again but the sound did little to settle the bile rising up in my throat.

I moved to reach for her but her body went still, rigid, her eyes glazed over as if she'd entered some sort of trance.

"His name was Donald Lee Westbank," she whispered.

Fuck.

I drew air through my nose and willed my body not to punch something or vomit. She didn't need to say another goddamn thing. In fact, I didn't want her to. I could tell by her voice, by her body, by her entire demeanor what happened. I wanted to scream for her not to continue but I knew she had to. If not for me, for herself.

"It's not what you think, Rory."

Fuck if it wasn't. Without realizing it, I leaned in for her.

She held up a hand to stop me. "Please let me finish. You need to know everything before you say you love me."

I turned her to face me, staring into her brown eyes. They appeared so empty and desolate, void of the life and passion that usually shone back at me. Silently I willed her all the strength I had and prayed she knew in her heart I'd love her no matter what her story was.

"It was just before Halloween," she said, her expression still blank and void of emotion. "Felicia and I were at home studying for midterms when Paul showed up at our door unannounced. He and my mom lived in

Austin so for him to travel to Dallas without warning, I knew something was wrong."

The beating in my head was relentless. I wasn't sure I could take much more.

"At first, I feared it was my mother, that maybe she'd been in a car accident, but Paul assured me she was all right. He asked the two of us to sit down on the couch. There was something strange in his tone of voice and I got a sinking feeling in the pit of my stomach. Instinctively I knew something was very wrong."

And I knew it too, but I shoved down my own fears and mentally prepared myself for her story.

She walked toward the tall blades of grass, plucking one out of the ground, running the weed back and forth through her fingers.

"Paul told us the police had called him the day before. They'd found video footage of our apartment in one of Paul's rented apartments."

My entire body burned and I thought I might pass out. I watched helplessly as Hindley meandered through the grass.

"Donald's apartment," she said quietly. "He was the maintenance man. Paul thought it would be better to have him live onsite. As more and more things started breaking in our apartment, we all agreed." She dropped the weed on the ground and drew in a deep breath.

I stood still, fighting the urge to rush to her side.

"The footage was from hidden surveillance cameras," she said. "It took the police a little while to figure out who Donald was filming, but once they realized it was from a unit within the complex, they contacted Paul because he was the owner. He immediately drove to Dallas to verify what the police already knew."

She turned to face me, her once vibrant eyes now as dark and desolate as our surroundings.

"They found hours and hours of footage of me." She touched her chest. "Donald had installed cameras everywhere in our apartment, in my bathroom, in my bedroom, in the shower, in my closet."

What. The fuck.

She stared off into the darkness, her body tense. "There wasn't an inch of our apartment that wasn't completely captured on tape. Everywhere except Felicia's room. The police were convinced Donald was stalking me."

Fuck. Fuck. Fuck! What could I say to this? How could I help her?

She remained stoic, not trembling, not crying, just standing before me, telling a story like it wasn't the worst thing she'd ever lived through. The most horrific crime I'd ever heard of if this was going where I thought it was.

"I never looked at any of the footage," she said, stepping closer, "but Paul assured me it was me. I could only assume what all I'd done in that apartment. Changing clothes, showering, bathing, sleeping. I pretty much went over the edge and flunked out of school that semester."

I wanted to take her in my arms, to tell her it would be all right, but my body was numb, and at this point I wasn't sure it would be.

She grabbed at another blade of grass and threaded it around her finger. "I did all right until his trial. Then I kind of went over the edge."

Well fuck, who wouldn't, I wanted to yell, but she was in the middle of her story and I didn't want to interrupt.

"The prosecutor insisted on showing the recorded footage in court, but no one had warned me."

"Who does that?" I asked.

She glanced up and I was pissed I'd broken her trance. I only hoped she could finish, find the closure with me she needed.

"I don't know," she said quietly. "I had to sit there with my family and friends and watch myself on video, undressing, bathing, washing my body." Her body shook and for the first time, real emotion overtook her. "They showed me taking a fucking shit right in front of the whole goddamn courtroom," she yelled. "All the while, that motherfucker sat there and smiled." Tears trailed down her cheeks and she stumbled forward, her body wrecked, having relived it all.

I rushed toward her and scooped her into my arms. She folded into me, cocooning her body into my chest, folding her arms tightly between us as she cried.

I held her close, kissing her on the head. "Shh," I whispered, trying to comfort her. "I've got you, baby. You don't have to say more."

As if not hearing me, she continued on. "It was the most humiliating thing ever, Rory," she stuttered through her muffled sobs.

I held her tight, trying to absorb her pain as I rocked her back and forth.

Finally, she pushed me away and took an unsteady step back, wiping at her eyes and nose. "My mom didn't want the story to go public, mostly because of me, but I knew she didn't want it to taint the high society world she was a part of."

"You can't be serious?" I asked.

She shrugged. "I don't know, she never really said. Paul paid so much money to have the tapes sealed. It was an obscene amount, but I'd be lying if I didn't say I wasn't thankful he had. I wanted to burn them all, but the district attorney said they had to be held for evidence in case he ever tried to file an appeal. Eventually, Donald was convicted and sentenced to fifteen years and I went on with my life."

"Fifteen years. That's it?" I studied her face, something in her blank expression told me there was more. "Hindley, you couldn't have just gone on with your life. What happened next?"

"It was a rough year. I basically had a nervous breakdown after the trial. I spent a lot of time with therapists and doctors. They tried anti-depressants and anti-anxiety drugs, sedatives."

Oh, shit, was she an addict too?

"I didn't get addicted, don't worry." She smiled, a real smile this time that broke through the darkness.

"How did you make it out, what pulled you through?" I asked.

"Dana, sewing, school. Diversions."

"Hindley, I'm so sorry." I grabbed her and pulled her in close. "You know none of that changes how I feel about you, right?"

She nodded and released a heavy sigh. "I'm tired. Do you mind driving home?"

"Of course not." I kissed her head then walked her around to the passenger side, and helped her into the car.

As I walked around the hood, I glanced up and saw her head slumped into her hands, her shoulders shaking.

Fuck it all, there was more. Had this guy raped her?

I clenched my hands into fists as if readying for a fight.

If he did, I swore to God I'd drive to whatever fuckin' prison he was in and kick the shit out of him, then cut off his dick and shove it down his throat until he choked to death. I wasn't sure I wasn't going to do it right now. But I had to calm down, for Hindley. I had to get her home and take care of her.

The drive to her house was short and silent. I led her straight to the bedroom. Pulling open the top drawer of her dresser, I removed a set of pajamas and held them out to her. When she made no move to take them, I tossed them on the bed then walked toward her, about to undress her. I stopped mid-stride. Was this okay now?

"Stop," she whispered, placing her hand over mine.

"Stop what? What's wrong? I can leave."

She shook her head. "I don't want you to leave."

"Then I won't."

"There's more," she said so quietly I almost didn't hear her.

And just like that, I knew. This motherfucker had raped her.

Every muscle in my body went rigid, my heart beating wildly in my chest. I feared I might actually explode.

"Will you lay down in bed with me?" She glanced up at me, her eyes pleading.

Didn't she already know? There was nothing I wouldn't do for her. Lying beside her in bed would be an honor, not a chore.

I drew in a deep breath and slowly blew it out, knowing she needed my strength right now, not my anger. I leaned down and scooped her in my arms, making the short walk to the bed. Gently I lowered us down on the mattress, cradling her to me like a small child.

Her body curled into mine and I squeezed her tight as we lay in the dark. I gently kissed her head and stroked her back, knowing she needed the calm as much as I did if she were going to open up and tell me the rest of her story.

She burrowed deeper into me, one hand clutching my arm, the other tucked beneath her head.

She looked so young and innocent, and I couldn't even imagine what she'd been through.

"Two weeks after the trial, the police called me," she said, never looking up. "They'd found additional footage."

Her body trembled and I clutched her tighter, trying to offer comfort. This was going to be bad, very bad, and I needed to keep my shit together.

"Shortly after we had moved into the apartment," she said, "I started waking up with awful headaches. I thought I was getting migraines, and Felicia threatened to take me to the doctor, but I convinced myself it was the stress of school. After Donald was arrested, the headaches disappeared and I never correlated the two. Until…"

My mind raced and my stomach burned, thinking of what was coming next. When she flinched, I realized I was squeezing her too tight and released my grip slightly, even though I wanted to crush her against me.

"Donald had been drugging me." Suddenly she was clutching at me like a wild animal being chased by hunters. Her sobs were loud and heavy, ringing through the room as her body shook against me.

I couldn't hear anymore, but I knew she needed to say the words, for herself if no one else.

As much as I wanted to jump off the bed and punch something, I knew I couldn't. Instead I lay quietly, holding my girl tight to me as she released what was probably years of pent up sorrow and shame.

Hindley had been my rock, my strength during weak times, sharing my secrets in confidence. Now it was my turn to be strong for her.

"I've never told anyone this," she said. "Not my mom, not Paul, not even Dana."

I marveled at her faith in me. "I won't tell anyone, Hindley, I swear to you."

She pushed up on my chest, her eyes darting between mine in disbelief. Her cheeks were stained with tears that I wanted more than anything to kiss away.

"I won't judge you either," I assured her, pushing back a lock of hair. "You're perfect to me. You always will be."

She fell against my chest and sobbed, her sorrow echoing throughout the room.

My heart ached for what she'd been through. All doubt had been erased.

That fucker had drugged her, raped her, and recorded it. She didn't have to tell me or say it out loud. We were connected on a deeper level and sometimes needed no words.

I stroked soothing circles on her back and kissed the side of her face, willing away her pain.

Her sobs turned to whimpers and her breathing slowly evened out.

I drew in a sigh of relief despite my urge to kill that motherfucker, rip him limb from limb.

When her breathing matched my own, I pulled back the comforter and placed her underneath. Kicking off my shoes, I slid in behind her, tucking her body into mine, as much to comfort myself as her.

We lay in silence for an eternity, the seconds painfully ticking by as I waited for sleep to overtake her.

She drew my arm closer to her chest. "The police wanted to bring additional charges against him, for rape," she said. "He'd attacked me so many times, the detectives said he could get life in prison. I would never have to worry about him ever again. But I refused."

I swallowed hard, biting back the vomit. "Why?" I asked.

She rolled over and stared at me. "I couldn't do it, Rory. I couldn't face another trial. I was already broken, and to think of them playing those tapes in front of another jury, having to watch him and me doing…" She tucked her head into me and began to cry all over again.

It felt like I'd been stabbed with a hundred knives to the gut, my insides burned so hot with rage.

"I'm sorry," she whispered against my chest.

"What?" I asked, pushing her away so I could see her. "Baby, why are you sorry?"

"I probably should have told you all of this sooner. Everything. But I was afraid if you knew the truth, you wouldn't want me."

"Hindley." I laughed, shaking my head at the ridiculousness of her comment. "I'll always want you. You're the most desirable woman I've ever met."

She scooted away from me, her eyes wide. "Really?"

I couldn't believe that after all this time she still doubted how extraordinary she was.

I stared at her, my silence giving her the answer she needed. Of course, I wanted her, now more than ever.

Her face broke into a glorious smile that lit up the room. Her joy was like heaven—a saving grace to my tortured heart.

"Of course, Hindley." I stroked a finger down her cheek, wiping away the tears. "I've never wanted anyone as much as I want you."

She slowly climbed on top of me.

My body stiffened.

"Please don't, Rory," she whispered.

"Don't what?"

"I'm still the same person I was yesterday, and the day before that, and the day before that. The woman you have amazingly awesome, kinky, crazy sex with."

I chuckled. She was right.

"I don't ever want that to change." She grasped my hands, clutching them to her chest. "I'm all right. I promise. This is what I want. You're what I want." She brought our joined hands to her mouth and kissed them. "I love you. I just hope you still love me."

"Oh God, Hindley." I wrapped my arms around her and brought her down against my chest. "I love you so much. I told you that would never change. If anything, I love you more. I want to protect you. I never want anything like that to happen to you again, and I'll do everything in my power to keep you safe."

"Will you do something for me?" she asked softly.

"Anything. I'll do anything for you."

"Make love to me. Please."

I rolled her over, mindful that the position may trigger something inside her.

"Please," she repeated. "I'm okay. I want you."

Hindley Hagen was the epitome of pure love and natural beauty, and I couldn't believe she wanted to be with me.

"Are you sure?" I didn't want to hurt her more.

"I'm very sure, Mr. Gregor." She smirked.

The desire in her eyes told me I was her strength, and she needed me. No one had ever needed me. The realization filled me with a joy that I'd never known.

I grinned, cocking a brow. She needed the playful side tonight. "Oh, Miss Hagen, it would be my extreme pleasure to make love to you tonight."

She lifted her head, peppering my neck with feather-light kisses.

Her soft moans and resounding laughter vibrating on my skin sent my heart beating in a hard rhythm, pounding with pure bliss.

I knew without a doubt, good times or bad, I would love this girl forever.

CHAPTER 14
HINDLEY

I BOLTED STRAIGHT UP in the bed, breathing hard like I'd just run a race. There was only one person who could illicit such fear in me. Donald Lee Westbank.

I'd been having nightmares about him ever since I told Rory my story. I wasn't surprised, but now, as I sat in my bed all alone, it affected me more than I wanted.

The idea that he was still a threat was silly. I knew Donald was in prison and would be for at least four more years. He'd had his first parole hearing last year and I begrudgingly went.

Paul had said I owed it to myself, Felicia, and other women to make sure Donald Lee Westbank stayed in jail as long as legally possible. Another hearing was coming up soon, and like last year, I was dreading the whole ordeal, but I knew it had to be done.

The judicial system had screwed me over royally. They'd deemed half the tapes inadmissible, which was total bullshit. The Assistant District Attorney was still able to get Donald the maximum sentence on the videos the jury did see, a whopping fifteen years with possible parole in ten. I hated the Texas Penal System almost as much as I hated Donald Lee Westbank. Maybe I should let the police charge him with rape.

I reminded myself that I'd probably be face down in a gutter with a needle poking out of my vein right now if I did.

Images of the videos raced through my mind and I felt the familiar taste of bile rise up in my throat. I willed myself not to vomit but who was I kidding?

Racing to the bathroom I expelled everything inside me. I quickly stood and brushed my teeth, trying to think of something that would get my mind off those horrible memories. Only one thing came to mind and a smile spread across my face.

Rory Gregor.

I went in search of my phone, well, his phone, the one he'd given me for dirty talk. The clock on the display read 2:47 a.m. Paris was seven hours ahead so it would be a perfect time to call. It only rang once.

"What's my favorite pole dancer doing awake at three in the morning?"

His raspy voice was a soothing balm to my soul. I could listen to it forever.

"I wanted to hear your voice," I said.

"Another bad dream?"

I paused, not wanting to worry him.

"Hindley?"

"Yeah, another dream."

"I'm so sorry, baby. I didn't mean to conjure up old memories for you," he said, his voice filled with despair.

"It's not your fault. It actually felt good to finally tell someone."

"You sure?"

"I'm sure."

"But having these nightmares over and over again can't be good, especially without me there to hold you."

"It comes with the territory."

"God, you have no idea how much I wish I was there."

"What would you do?" I asked, trying to sound seductive but probably failing miserably.

"Oh, Miss Hagen, the things I would do to you." He laughed, his deep voice doing wicked things to my insides.

We spent the next half hour fornicating over the phone. I didn't even know that was possible, but with Rory traveling so much, having phone sex had become a way of life for us, the only way for our growing sexual appetites to be fulfilled.

"You're bad," he said, once releasing a satisfied sigh. I could picture him in his bed, one arm above his head.

"Me?" I chuckled.

"I love to hear you laugh."

I pulled the covers close. "What else do you love?"

"I love your ass. You have the best ass in the world."

I smiled at his confession. "Thanks."

"I love the crook of your neck and the way my face fits into it perfectly."

"What else?" Playing this game with him was fun and kept my mind from wandering. Plus, it was really good for my ego.

"I love the way you're helping me read."

"I'm so proud of you. You're doing an amazing job, you know that, don't you?"

"Well, you're a good incentive."

I laughed at his words. There were many times when I had withheld sexual favors from him unless he'd read something out loud. But I never had to follow through because Rory had made up his mind weeks ago that reading was a goal he wanted to achieve, much like a difficult trick in skateboarding.

I'd been surprised when he showed me his journal the day after I'd told him everything that had happened to me. It was already a third of the way filled up with words and pictures and drawings, anything he could stuff inside.

But what especially filled my heart was the way he scribbled my name on almost every page. Tears had welled up in my eyes when I read his first entry. 'I love Hindley Hagen.' He said he'd written it long before he ever told me. I'd thought it ironic that the first time he declared his love for me was in writing.

Since then, he'd written me small love letters. I knew some of the words were in his vocabulary list and some were translated from the internet, but it didn't matter. He was reading and writing, and thriving.

"I wish you were here," he said softly.

"I wish I was too." I hated waking up alone after these dreams.

"You could have come, you know."

"Rory, I already told you. People know about us, or they at least have a high suspicion. Even Matt knows."

"Good."

Although I'd had no choice but to tell Rory what had happened the afternoon Matt got drunk, I knew Rory still didn't like him.

"Their endorsement is huge. You can't afford to lose it."

"I know, I know."

"It's better if I don't travel with you to every event now, especially to Paris, the romance capital of the world. It brings on more suspicions."

"I know," he said more firmly this time.

"I love you," I whispered. "Does that help?"

"Some. I can't stand having to hide this. I want to shout it from the rooftops. I want to drag you around like a caveman and let everyone know you're mine, and they better keep their fuckin' eyes, and hands, and whatever else off you."

I smiled even though I knew he was being chauvinistic. "You're so bad."

"But you love it."

"Yes, I do." I nodded. "This is serious though, Rory. I could get fired."

"You don't even like that law firm anyway."

"I may not be the biggest fan of Mr. Stedwick's, but I like the people I work with. And besides, I'm under contract. If I get fired, I could lose a lot of money."

"I know," he said, his voice firm.

"Don't yell at me."

"I'm not yelling. I'm sorry. I'm just frustrated."

"I am too."

"How much longer?"

"Until what?" I asked.

"Until I can make this official and tell people you're my woman."

"I'm not sure my hair wants to make it official if you really are a caveman and are going to drag me around."

He laughed, the reverberations ringing through the phone. His joy was infectious and I couldn't help but smile too.

"We have to make it to the X Games," I said.

"Shit, Hindley, that's still six weeks away."

"I know, I'm sorry, but we've got to get the Sonora Water commercials out on the air. You need the exposure, and the money."

"Hindley, I couldn't give a shit less about the money, the exposure, the endorsements, any of it. All I care about is being with you."

My heart swelled and tears pooled in my eyes. I'd never heard anything so loving in my entire life.

"Are you still there?" he asked.

"Yes," I whimpered through my tears.

"Are you crying?"

"Maybe."

"Good tears or bad?"

"Good." I laughed. We sat in silence, enjoying the fact that we were together even though we were thousands of miles apart. "Do you love me?" I asked.

He didn't hesitate. "You know I do."

"Do you love skating?"

"Of course."

"If you want to keep skating then you need the money, Rory. And if you lose the money and can't skate anymore, you'll grow to resent me for it."

"No, I won't."

"It's only six weeks. I'd rather wait six weeks to be with you than take that chance."

"What about what I want?"

I let out an exasperated sigh. He sounded like a four-year-old. "What do you want, Mr. Gregor?"

"I think you know what I want, Miss Hagen."

His light-hearted tone had me smiling, the mischief warming my heart. I knew without a doubt that I would give this man anything he wanted.

I burrowed down in my bed and covered up with my comforter,

anxiously waiting for his familiar raspy voice to bring me the release I was quickly growing addicted to.

CHAPTER 15

HINDLEY

"HINDLEY, will you come into my office?" Mr. Stedwick's voice rang over the intercom on my phone.

Instinctively I knew something was wrong. He never called me directly.

"Yes, sir."

Oh, shit, maybe he knew about Rory and me.

"Let's go, kiddo." I raised my head and saw Michael standing in my door.

"What's going on?"

He shrugged. "Beats me."

"He called you in too?"

"Yep."

"Oh, shit."

Michael and I walked silently to Mr. Stedwick's office.

"He's expecting you," Donna, his assistant said, pointing to the open door.

Michael ushered me in.

"Oh, welcome," Mr. Stedwick said. "Please, have a seat." He pointed to the chairs in front of his desk.

I slipped into one of the winged-back chairs as quietly as I could, trying to hide my fear.

"First, Hindley," he said, "I want to congratulate you on the job you did down in Miami. It seems like you impressed Mr. Sullivan so much that he would like to sign with our firm."

"Really?" I asked.

I'd only met with Humberto Sullivan once last week during the team's training camp. He'd been extremely standoffish during our brief time together, and I felt there was no way I'd impressed him enough to even see me again, let alone sign.

"How did that happen?" I asked. "He seemed disinterested in our offer."

"What can I say?" Mr. Stedwick shrugged. "Apparently, he was interested in what you had to offer."

Mr. Stedwick's insinuation wasn't lost on me. My stomach twisted in knots. Did he believe Humberto signed with our firm because of my sexual prowess? I laughed silently, knowing I had none.

"Well," he continued, "it seems as if you have a knack for nabbing new talent, and now another opportunity has arisen."

I couldn't help but smile. I was actually succeeding in my new job. "Who is it?" I asked anxiously.

"Axel Pretorius."

All the blood drained from my face and I searched for the trash bin, afraid I might vomit.

Mr. Stedwick leaned back in his chair, oblivious of my reaction. "His manager heard about you securing the Sonora Water deal. He was especially impressed that you'd negotiated a commercial. Axel is very interested in capturing that type of national exposure. And because you obviously know the industry inside and out, you're a natural fit for him."

I swallowed down my anxiety, grasping at any reason not to take on Axel. "But won't that be a conflict of interest? I mean, we're already representing an extreme skateboarder. Splitting my time between the two seems like it could rob them both of the exposure they need individually."

"Perhaps, but not in this case. I'm giving Rory over to Luis so you can handle Axel full-time."

I blinked several times, my body going rigid. Rory not my client?

"But he signed with me," I squeaked out.

Michael glanced at me.

I ignored him.

"Actually," Mr. Stedwick said, "Rory signed with our firm, not you personally."

Well, shit. Was this right? It had to be, I'd drafted the damn contract. There was no way Rory would be okay with this situation. I had to figure a way out.

"Sir, with all due respect, I think Rory may not agree to this. He's been very skittish around attorneys and I think he finally feels comfortable with me now."

I bit back a laugh. Oh, yeah, he feels comfortable with me all right.

Mr. Stedwick's eyes narrowed and his lips pressed into a thin line.

"Besides," I continued, knowing I sounded desperate, "I have a really good working relationship with Sonora Water."

He stared out the window and I hoped he was giving my ideas thought.

"Perhaps Luis or Michael could take on Axel," I said.

Michael's brows furrowed and I knew he wasn't onboard with my idea but I didn't care. I couldn't lose Rory, especially not to Axel Pretorius.

Mr. Stedwick turned and stared at me, his forearms resting on his massive desk. "I'm afraid that's impossible, Hindley."

"Why?"

"It seems Axel's team has become," he hesitated, as if searching to find the most appropriate word, "partial to you."

I stared in confusion. "What does partial mean?"

"They've asked for you specifically."

Oh, no. There was no way I was going to get out of this.

"I've already talked to Michael," Mr. Stedwick continued, "and Luis can clear his schedule to take on Mr. Gregor full-time."

I stared at Michael but his gaze remained on Mr. Stedwick. He'd known exactly what this meeting was about all the time, he'd lied to my face earlier.

I turned my attention back to Mr. Stedwick. He was my only chance now. "I don't mean to be disrespectful, sir, but I'm not all together sure that's a good idea."

Mr. Stedwick's eyes widened and he tilted his head. "How so?"

This was my chance. I had to think of some viable reason, and fast.

"Umm," I stumbled, "Rory and Axel are on the same tour. It seems silly to have Luis travel to the same places I'll be. I feel confident that I can handle both Mr. Gregor and Mr. Pretorius. At least through the X Games."

Yes! That sounded plausible.

Mr. Stedwick stared just above my head and I prayed he was considering the option.

"It will save the firm money," I said, trying to throw in more reason. "You'll only have to pay for my travel." It sounded weak, even to me, but I had to try.

He remained quiet and then an idea hit me.

"If I leave Rory now, his team may feel abandoned, especially considering the pending deals I've been negotiating."

"What deals?" he and Michael asked at the same time.

Yeah, what deals?

I cleared my throat and steadied my voice. "I've been, um, looking at other avenues, including the clothing industry."

That wasn't a complete lie. I could sew. And I'd had the idea before. I knew people who knew people in the clothing industry. Of course, designing sexy lingerie and exotic dance outfits was a far cry and about a zillion miles away from the extreme sports industry, but still, it was a start.

"Really?" Mr. Stedwick leaned forward. "That's impressive."

I fought the urge to sag back and sigh. Thank God, I had him. Now, I had to set the hook.

"The clothing market is very lucrative," I said. "If I'm able to break into that industry, as I feel I can, it would be possible to secure not only Rory's own brand, but Axel's as well."

"That's true." Mr. Stedwick nodded. "Michael, you didn't tell me any of this."

It was obvious from Mr. Stedwick's tone, he wasn't pleased with

Michael. I didn't want to get my boss in trouble, but it was his own fault for not warning me about this meeting. Had it been his idea to pull me off of Rory's contract?

Michael stared at me, a brow lifted. "I didn't realize Hindley had been so industrious, sir."

I returned his glare, raising my brows, even though I knew it was a sign of insubordination.

"Well, Hindley," Mr. Stedwick said, "I don't have to tell you how pleased I am with all your hard work. I am concerned however that you're taking on too much. Axel and Humberto added onto Rory Gregor may burn you out before you even get a good start in this division."

I shook my head to the point of dizziness, biting back a smile. "I don't think so, sir. I mean, taking care of Rory and Axel together will be like catering to one client. They're in the same industry."

He remained silent and I felt the need to further justify why I could do this.

"And Humberto's season doesn't start until August so that gives me plenty of time to come up with a game plan for him."

Mr. Stedwick's eyes narrowed. He still wasn't one hundred percent on board. Shit. What else could I offer?

"Why don't we give it until the X Games?" I said. "Rory's commercial will air and we'll have a clear winner in one of them. After that, we can decide who on our team best fits the needs of our clients." That sounded fair.

"When are the X Games?" Mr. Stedwick stared between us.

"Six weeks, sir," Michael answered, a little too quickly.

How the hell did he know that?

"All right, Hindley." Mr. Stedwick pounded his desk. "I'll give you six weeks. But if anything falls through the cracks, Mr. Gregor gets reassigned."

"Yes, sir. I understand completely." I nearly saluted him I was so happy.

"That will be all," he said in a clipped tone.

I pushed out of my chair and walked toward the door, thankful to get out with Rory still as my client.

"You need to meet with Mr. Pretorius as soon as possible," Mr. Stedwick said behind me. "His manager was insistent on sometime this week."

Oh, shit. I'd hoped to spend time with Rory somehow.

I turned to face Mr. Stedwick. "They have another competition this weekend in Calgary. Why don't I fly in a day early and meet with his team, then spend the weekend trying to make contacts with more industry leaders? For Axel and for Rory," I added.

"That sounds good." He nodded once. "But I'd still like Michael or Luis to accompany you."

"Why?" The word was out of my mouth before I could stop it.

"Two heads are always better than one," Michael said behind me.

My gut clenched and everything in me went on high alert. He knew something. Maybe not everything but he had an inkling. I tamped down my fear and anxiety and steadied my voice. "That sounds like a good plan, sir."

"I look forward to hearing the progress notes when you return from Canada." Mr. Stedwick nodded to the door, dismissing us, and that was fine by me.

As I reached his door I glanced over my shoulder. "Sir, I'd like to take Thursday off. I have some personal things I need to take care of before we leave for Canada." What I wanted was very personal, and I bit my cheek to hide the smile threatening to emerge.

"Why are you asking me, Ms. Hagen? I'm not your immediate boss?"

Yeah, why was I? Because right now I was afraid of Michael and what he might know.

"I didn't want you to think I was slacking off, taking time off now that I have three clients."

Mr. Stedwick rose from his chair and walked around his desk, leaning on the chair I'd just vacated. "Hindley, I think we both know it behooves you to stay in my good graces."

What was he talking about?

"Let's say," he tapped the edge of the chair, "I'd hate to see anything happen to your career, or your stepfather's."

Shit.

And there it was. A warning. Not a warning, a threat. If I fucked this up, not only would my ass be on the line, but so would Paul's.

"What are you saying, sir?"

He tilted his head, eyes mocking.

Every hair on my body stood at attention. I did not want to cross this man if I wanted a future working anywhere. Aston Stedwick was rich and powerful and had the potential to destroy not only me, but Paul and his company as well. If Mr. Stedwick pulled his investment, I knew others would too.

I glanced over at Michael who stood expressionless. He understood Mr. Stedwick's power as well, and he would never intervene on my behalf.

"I'm saying that having you here at my law firm is an asset," he said. "Don't make it a liability." Without another word, he turned and sauntered back to his desk.

I quietly slipped from his office, knowing I'd been warned. And if I didn't follow his directive, I could destroy everyone I loved.

CHAPTER 16

HINDLEY

I STEPPED out of the cab into the cool Canadian air, sucking in a deep breath. Man, it was cold.

"Baby, I'm so glad to see you," Rory said, rushing out of the hotel toward me.

I shook my head, nodding behind me.

Rory stopped dead when he saw Michael step out behind me. He stared at Michael then at me, his brows furrowed in confusion.

I hadn't had a chance to tell Rory that Michael would be on this trip with me nor the circumstances surrounding Axel.

"Later," I mouthed. I glanced over my shoulder at Michael. "Hey, I'm pretty tired. I think I'll go lay down for a bit before our meeting." I stared down at my watch then back up to Rory. "You have a skater's meeting at five. Why don't Michael and I meet you afterward for dinner?"

He stared at Michael then at me. "Um, okay, sure. That sounds good." He walked toward the back of the cab where the driver was unloading our luggage. "Why don't I help you with your bags?"

"That's all right." I shoved past him and picked up my things. "I'm going to check in." I stared at him, hoping he could hear my silent question. Had he secured us adjoining rooms? It would make explaining this entire ordeal much easier.

"Oh, um, I already checked you in," he said, removing a key card from his back pocket.

Thank God, for Skater Boy.

He glanced behind me. "I'm sorry, Michael, I didn't know you were going to be here or I would have checked you in too."

"That's all right, Rory."

Michael and I hadn't spoken again after our meeting with Mr. Stedwick, but it had been painfully clear he knew something was going on with Rory and me. I couldn't give him any evidence on this trip. Rory and I had to be hyper-vigilant about all our interactions this weekend.

"Why don't we meet at the restaurant here in the hotel at seven?" I said.

"Sounds good," Rory said.

Michael looked between the two of us as if we were wayward teens he was leaving alone for the weekend. He didn't trust me. But after our meeting with Mr. Stedwick, I realized I didn't trust him either anymore.

"I'll see you at dinner, Rory." I walked inside the hotel and toward the bank of elevators.

"Hindley!" My name echoed across the lobby.

I turned and my body stiffened.

Axel Pretorius.

Rory was going to flip his shit. I hadn't yet told him about our new contract with Axel. I'd wanted to wait until we were face-to-face. Seeing Axel's smug expression now though, I realized that might not have been such a smart strategy.

My plans to take off Thursday and fly to California to be with Rory had been thwarted by Michael. He must have suspected something and called me in for an emergency meeting, claiming it was about Humberto. Since I hadn't wanted to raise any red flags, I'd had no choice but to comply and cancel my trip to see Rory before the tournament.

"I'm so glad you've taken me on as a client," Axel said, his voice louder than necessary as he made his way toward me.

I saw Rory out of the corner of my eye. He'd been headed in the opposite direction but stopped dead in his tracks when he'd heard Axel's declaration. I willed myself not to look at him.

"Um, yes," I said, smiling.

"Why don't we meet for drinks tonight to go over our game plan?" He put his hand on the small of my back and I felt Rory's fury fill the lobby.

Moving to skirt his touch, I wound away from him but he quickly caught up, following my movements like we were seasoned dancers.

"I'll have to get back with you," I said, trying to pacify him. "I'm a little tired and want to get up to my room and rest for a bit."

"Here, let me help you with your bags."

Before I could say no, he had my luggage firmly in his hand.

Against my better judgment, I stole a glance at Rory.

His eyes were narrowed into tiny slits, his jaw clenched hard, every muscle in his body taught. If I didn't get up to the room and pacify him soon, he was going to explode.

The elevator doors opened, and Axel grabbed my hand and tugged me inside.

I tried to pull away but he had me in a vise grip. This was a pissing match, and Axel was purposely trying to incite Rory. I couldn't let it happen.

"You're hurting me," I said quietly.

"Oh, sorry." Axel released my hand. He looked anything but sorry.

This was bad, really bad. I'd had the same sinking feeling in the pit of my stomach, an instinctive warning once before in my life—the day Paul had met us in my apartment during college.

As soon as the elevator doors opened, I wrestled my bags away from Axel and rushed down the hallway, leaving him without a word. Inserting the key card, I pushed the door to my room open and I tossed my luggage to the side before falling onto the bed with a sigh.

I waited for Rory to emerge through our Magic Door, as he called it, but he never came. The burning in my stomach grew more intense.

I rose and pushed on the handle to the connecting door, surprised to find it locked. Rory never locked the door. This was bad. Really bad.

Shuffling back to the bed, I fell on top of the covers and curled into a tight ball, trying to make myself as small as I could so the world would swallow me up.

~

His wet lips pressed against mine. I reached to push him off but my arms wouldn't move.

The sound of a zipper opening echoed through the room just before calloused hands rubbed against my underwear. I flinched but still couldn't push him away. Why couldn't I move?

This was wrong. I opened my mouth to scream but nothing came out.

Cold air brushed against my bare skin as he pulled down my jeans and underwear.

Hot tears trailed down the sides of my face but I couldn't wipe them away.

I was paralyzed. Literally.

The same rough hands pushed my legs apart and something hard entered me. I opened my mouth to scream for help, beg my mother, or Felicia, for anyone to make this stop. Again I heard nothing.

The bed bounced and my stomach lurched. I turned my head, fearing I might vomit and choke to death. Where was I? What was happening to me?

As he continued to shove inside me, something coarse scraped against my bare chest. It felt like sandpaper, scraping my skin with every move. I prayed my thin bra would be enough to protect me. I begged him to stop, pleaded, but my words were silent, only ringing in my own mind.

Cool air wafted across my bare chest. He had removed my bra and was now placing slobbery kisses against my breast.

The springs beneath me squeaked with every thrust of his hips. Tears fell heavy from my eyes and I couldn't reach to wipe them away.

I inhaled deep breaths but the stench of his body odor had my stomach churning, so instead I held my breath.

His hands were all over me now, his calloused fingers grazing the soft skin of my neck, turning my head so he could touch and lick and kiss every inch of me. He groaned as he ripped through me. I felt my body tearing apart and my soul shattered as I realized there was nothing I could do except lie here.

With eyes drilled shut, I willed myself to float away from this horrible place, from this monstrous person now bouncing atop me.

I envisioned a tropical beach, a snow-capped mountain, anywhere but here with this wretched intruder.

I jerked upright with a start, my heart pounding and my entire body drenched in sweat as I blinked to consciousness.

"Baby, what's wrong?" A familiar voice broke through my nightmare.

"Where am I?" I whispered.

"You're in bed, in your hotel room, with me."

I turned and found Rory sitting next to me.

"But," I panted, "you were gone. I was alone. All alone." I fought to keep my tears at bay.

"I'm sorry, baby." He scooped me into his arms and burrowed his face in my neck.

Dark images flooded my mind and I pushed him away. "No," I yelled, trying to escape.

He held me firm to his body.

"Let me go!" I screamed. "Let me go!"

He released me and I shuffled across the bed, staring at him with wild eyes.

"Baby, you had a nightmare," he said. "It's me. Rory. I love you. I won't hurt you." He crawled closer but I pushed him away, nearly falling off the bed. "Hindley. You're safe. No one is going to hurt you. I'll protect you, I promise."

I heard his words, but they made no sense. My eyes darted around the surroundings. I was in a hotel room. Why was I in a hotel room? I blinked several times, staring at the man in front of me. His own eyes were wide, the beat of his heart visible at the base of his neck. He seemed just as petrified as I was.

I focused on his eyes. They were a brilliant blue, like the sky on a cloudless, summer day.

"Rory?" I asked quietly.

"Yes, sweetheart," he said.

It was him. Rory. My safe haven. The one person who could quiet my nightmares when Donald Lee Westbank invaded my dreams.

I bounded off the bed and flew into his arms, clinging to him like the life raft he'd become.

"It's all right, baby," he said, rubbing his hand up and down my back.

I reminded myself that Rory was good, he was safe, he wouldn't hurt me. Well, not physically.

He burrowed his face into my hair, inhaling deeply. "Do you want to tell me about it?"

I shook my head. I didn't want to remember anything except right now, being in Rory's arms. I needed a connection with him, skin to skin. Leaning back, I tore off my shirt and fumbled with my bra.

"Hindley, wait." He covered my hands with his.

"What?"

"Is this a good idea? I mean, now?"

I sat back and stared up at him. "You don't want me?"

He grasped my face between his hands. "Hindley, you know I will always want you, baby. Always. But I'm afraid."

"Why?"

"You just had a nightmare, and I'm assuming it was a flashback. I don't want to take advantage of the situation or cause you more harm."

"The only way you'll harm me is by pushing me away."

His brows drew together, apprehension marring his beautiful face. He was deliberating, deciding whether touching me would do more harm than good. Slowly, he bent down, resting his forehead on mine, sighing deeply.

I pulled my head from his hold. "Don't, Rory."

"What?" His eyes shot wide and his hands dropped from my face as if he'd hurt me.

"Don't treat me like this."

"Like what?"

"You know like what. I'm the same person. I want you. And I don't want you to be gentle because you think I'm fragile or broken."

He stared at me, still a bit frightened. "Are you sure?"

I smiled and nodded, surprised by my request. "Please," I said softly. "Don't let my past change how you feel about me."

"Hindley, that would never happen."

"Then don't let it change how you treat me."

He sat silently, his body tense.

My chest clenched in fear. Maybe he didn't want me because I was a broken woman.

His eyes grew darker and a slow grin spread across his face. He understood what I wanted. What I needed.

Pulling my body against his, we fell onto the mattress, his hands reaching behind my back and unclasping my bra.

I reached for the hem of his T-shirt and yanked it with such force that I whacked his jaw with my fist.

We howled with laughter, and the tension in the room dissolved.

"I fear your sexual desires may be the death of me, Miss Hagen."

"You wish," I said, kissing his neck.

"That would be a good way to go." His lips skimmed over my body, planting kisses along my torso as he inched down to my still fastened jeans. "I believe these are in my way. Do you mind if I remove them?"

My Skater Boy had returned.

I dug my hands through his thick hair. "Not at all, Mr. Gregor. Do you need some help?"

Without saying another word, he had my jeans unzipped and on the floor with lightning speed. He lifted up slightly and stared down at my underwear. "Well, hello Kitty," he said, his breath wafting over my skin.

I laughed, remembering I'd worn the panties he'd given me.

"God, I love this," he said with a raspy voice as his hand slipped beneath the elastic border.

"She loves you too." I laughed.

"She?"

"My kitty."

"Oh, yes." He smirked, tugging my panties down past my ankles and throwing them carelessly behind him. He lowered his head and placed hot kisses against my skin.

"Oh my God, Rory."

"What?" He raised his head, panic in his sky-blue eyes.

"Don't stop," I moaned breathlessly

"Anything you say, Miss Hagen."

His mouth worked me over with great care and diligence. I was on the verge of a major cataclysm that threatened to destroy me. But what a way to go, as Rory had said.

A knock on the door brought me back to the present. I lifted on my elbows, trying to move but Rory didn't stop. His tongue continued its delicious assault. I pushed at his head but he stayed where he was.

"Hindley, are you there?" a familiar voice called at the door.

Oh, God. Michael. I needed to get up and answer.

Rory was relentless as he pushed me higher to the peak. I couldn't have stopped him even if I wanted to, which I didn't.

Another knock came but I dug my fingers into Rory's hair, keeping his head firmly in place.

He laughed, and I felt the vibrations against my sensitive skin.

"Shh," I whispered, my voice broken and breathless.

I fought the screams that threatened as his mouth and hands ravished my body. Knowing I was about to scream, I grabbed a pillow next to me and covered my face, biting into the material to muffle my cries. My body stiffened as the first wave of pleasure rolled over me. Heat shot through my body and my arms and legs tingled to the point of pain as Rory brought me to the edge just before pushing me over.

My body stilled and he slowly pulled away. I groaned from the loss.

Rory crawled up my body and pulled the pillow away, staring down at me. That notorious smirk appeared.

"Proud of yourself?" I whispered.

"Very." He lowered his head and kissed me tenderly. His kisses only made the aftershocks more intense and I moaned.

"Shh," he said, placing a finger against my lips.

I studied him, afraid he was still upset about my earlier interaction with Axel. He smiled, every trace of anger seemingly gone, replaced with joy. "Better?"

I nodded, reaching up to stroke his face. In that moment I knew I'd walk through fire every day of my life to see him happy.

"I better go," he whispered in my ear. "Until next time, baby." He gently pecked my cheek. Before I could gather my wits to say goodbye, he disappeared through our Magic Door.

I stretched out on the mattress, gloriously naked, and completely satisfied.

CHAPTER 17

HINDLEY

By the time I finally pulled myself together and dressed again, Michael had already left, thank goodness.

I glanced down at my watch and realized why he'd been here. It was ten minutes until seven and we were due down in the restaurant for our meeting with Rory soon.

I studied my image in the bathroom mirror. Good Lord, I was a hot mess—hair tangled, makeup smeared, eyes screaming that I'd been thoroughly satisfied. I smiled at my reflection. I looked good with the afterglow of sex on my face.

Although I liked the look, I knew Michael would see straight through me. I needed to shower and change. Being fashionably late was supposed to be a woman's perogative, right?

By the time I reached the restaurant, it was twenty minutes after seven, and Michael and Rory were already deeply engrossed in conversation. I thought it interesting because the two had never socialized before. Perhaps Michael was more interested in the industry than I thought.

Before I reached our table, a hand darted out and grabbed my arm.

"There you are," Axel said.

Shit.

"I've been holding a table for us." He pointed to a booth in the corner that looked private, intimate, and dangerous.

"Oh, I'm sorry, Axel, I already have an appointment with Rory and my boss. Can I get a rain check?"

"Certainly," he said. I was surprised that he'd given up so easily. "Why don't I meet you at the bar later, say around tenish?"

Bar? Rory would never let that happen. But he didn't have a choice. I didn't have a choice. This was my career, and Mr. Stedwick had made it perfectly clear, he expected me to succeed at whatever cost.

"Are you sure you want to stay up that late?" I asked. "Tomorrow's competition schedule is supposed to be pretty grueling and starts early."

"Oh, it's sweet that you're concerned." He reached out and stroked my face.

I pulled away.

He cocked a brow. "I have more stamina than most of these guys on tour." He winked and I thought I'd barf. This guy was a predator. Every cell in my body went on high alert.

"All right then, ten o'clock it is," I said. I didn't have a choice. I just prayed I could make Rory understand between now and ten.

"Looking forward to it, Hindley." His voice was filled with sexual innuendos that had my skin crawling.

Without glancing back I walked away, praying I could get out of this awful mess with as little collateral damage as possible.

Dinner with Rory and Michael wasn't over until almost 9:30 p.m. Apparently, Michael had lots of plans for Rory's future.

Normally, I wouldn't have minded, and part of me was excited to hear how involved Michael wanted to be. But I needed to get Rory out of here so I could explain the situation with Axel.

His eyes had been locked on mine most of the evening, and not in a good way. Michael had to focus Rory's attention back to the item at hand more than once. He was doing nothing to help me convince Michael that our relationship was purely professional.

Rory finally excused himself, feigning his need for rest before tomorrow's competition.

Michael tried to get me to stay behind to discuss business but I convinced him that I still wasn't feeling well. I told him I must have slept through his earlier knocks, but inside, I was smiling at the memories of Rory's face buried between my legs.

By the time I got to my room, Rory was sitting in a chair, one ankle propped on the knee of his other leg. His hands were balled into fists in his lap and his face was taught with what seemed tempered fury. This was not good.

"What's going on, Hindley?" he growled.

I tossed my purse on the bed and walked toward him. "It's not what you think."

"How do you know what I'm thinking?"

"Because I know you." I uncrossed his legs and knelt between them. "I love you. That's how I know." I rubbed my hands up and down his thighs, trying to contain the anger burning in his eyes.

"I'm not going to like what you have to say, am I?"

I shook my head.

"You know I hate him."

I knew who he was talking about. I didn't care for Axel much myself either. I drew in a deep breath, trying to figure out where to start. The beginning seemed like a good idea.

"Apparently, Axel's manager has asked our law firm to represent him."

"Your law firm?" His brows furrowed. "Is that why Michael is here?"

I shook my head. "Not exactly."

"What exactly then, Hindley?" His words shot out like a machine gun and I feared how he may react next.

"Rory, you have to know, I had nothing to do with this. It's completely out of my control."

"Just tell me, Hindley."

"Axel's team has asked for me to personally represent him. Mr. Stedwick thinks it's a good idea and is basically forcing me to."

Rory closed his eyes and drew in a breath.

"There's more," I whispered.

He raked his hands through his hair and let them rest on top of his head as he blew out the breath he'd been holding. "Tell me the more."

"They want Michael to take over your career. They want me to concentrate on Axel and Humberto."

He sat up straight as if he'd been shocked. "Who the fuck is Humberto?"

"Rory, you have to understand. This is my job. I have to seek out new clients for the firm."

"Who. The fuck. Is Humberto?"

"He's the backup quarterback for the Baltimore Ravens, I've told you this. His contract with his current agent is up soon. We've watched the films on him and Luis, Michael and I agree that he's an up and coming player worth our investment." There, I'd said it, let the shit fly where it may.

"Investment? What the fuck does that mean?"

"Rory, please. Mr. Stedwick is forcing my hand. I don't want to do this. I don't like Axel any more than you. You know you're the only person I want to represent."

"Do I?"

My head jerked back as if he'd slapped me, the sting of his accusation burning something deep inside me. "Of course you do. What are you insinuating? That I purposely sought out Axel Pretorius to represent?"

He didn't answer.

Anger welled up inside of me and I jumped to my feet. I would not take a subservient position with him now. "Don't you dare question me, Rory Gregor. I don't like the guy either but this is my job. What part of that do you not understand?"

"So quit."

"I can't quit."

"Why not?"

How could I explain this to him without revealing what Mr. Stedwick had insinuated?

Rory stood and grabbed my arms. "What has happened that would make you agree to take on the one man in this world who I asked you—no, begged you—to stay away from?"

I wiggled, trying to free myself from his hold. "It's complicated."

"Well, uncomplicate it, Hindley."

I loved Rory and I didn't want to screw this up—not because of Axel Pretorius, and certainly not for Aston Stedwick. My stepfather's well-being was the only thing that would make me risk more than I was comfortable with.

"Tell me, Hindley."

I pulled from his hold and stepped back. "Mr. Stedwick sort of black-mailed me."

"How? With what?"

"With Paul."

"What about Paul?"

"Mr. Stedwick and the law firm have substantial investment holdings in Paul's company. If they remove their money, it could financially bank-rupt Paul." I exhaled a long, deep breath I didn't know I'd been holding.

"Did Paul force you to take this job?"

"No, of course not. But he knows I'm aware of his financial situation."

Rory fell back into the chair and scrubbed a hand down his face. "Well, fuck me."

"Tell me," I moaned, falling onto the bed. "Oh, crap. What time is it?"

Rory looked down at his watch. "Ten-o-five. Why?"

Shit. How the hell was I going to explain this one?

He scooted to the edge of his chair. "What is it, Hindley? Just tell me."

"I'm supposed to meet Axel in the bar at ten. To discuss his future with our firm."

"He hasn't signed a contract yet?"

I shook my head.

"Well, fuck him then."

"Rory, you know I can't do that."

"Then I'm coming with you." He marched toward the door. "There's no way that prick is going anywhere near you all alone, especially not in a bar. He's dangerous, Hindley."

"You can't come with me."

He turned and stared at me, his face stern and serious. "There is no way that motherfucker is going to put his hands on you again. Do you understand me? Do you know how fuckin' hard it was to see that shit?"

I did know. I had seen it in Rory's eyes the moment it happened.

"I had to take an hour-long walk in the cold-ass Canadian outdoors just to cool down. I was so afraid I was going to bash his fuckin' head in." His eyes pleaded with me. "He's dangerous, Hindley."

"I know." Rory didn't have to tell me, I already knew Axel Pretorius was a threat.

"This isn't about jealousy, Hindley, I swear." He came closer and took my hands in his. "I'm sorry, I'm worried about you, about your safety, and it's driving me crazy. Axel has assaulted women."

"It's not like I asked to represent him, Rory."

He stared at me for a long time, jaw clenched as he squeezed my hands.

"Look. Why don't you let me go," I said. "I can handle him. Then when I'm done, I'll come back here and we can talk about the future. How to handle this situation going forward."

He rolled his eyes and I feared I was losing him.

"Rory, I've told you everything about my past, my entire life. Things I've never told anyone. I love you and nothing will change that. Not any contract, not any job, not any client. I swear. Please believe me."

His blue eyes searched mine. "I believe you but I worry about you too."

"I know." I lifted up on my toes and kissed his cheek before pulling my hands from his. "I promise to be done by 10:30 p.m., 10:45 p.m. at the latest."

Before he could argue more, I rushed to the door. Stopping to grab my purse, I thought about looking back but thought better of it. The sooner I got this over with, the sooner I could get back to the man I loved.

∼

I slipped onto the barstool next to Axel. "Sorry I'm late."

He swung his legs around, trapping mine as he rubbed against me.

Alarm bells rang in my head but I tamped down my fears.

"No worries," he said. "I knew you'd be down eventually." He took a long drink from his beer. "How's Rory doing?"

"Oh, um, dinner went well." I wanted to give him as little details as possible when it came to Rory.

"Would you like something to drink?" He motioned toward the bartender. The glassy look in his eyes told me he'd had enough for the both of us.

"No, I'm fine. I'm really not feeling well so I'd like to get back upstairs soon."

"That's fine. This won't take long."

Oh, thank God.

The bartender placed another beer next to his half empty one.

Something inside me went on high alert.

He moved his body closer, leaning against the bar for support. "You've done an amazing job for Rory. Getting him that commercial was insane, especially given his past."

"Yes," I cleared my throat and leaned back, "we're very happy about that. Sonora Water really likes him."

"I want a commercial too."

"I'll put that on our list of priorities once our firm has a signed contract."

"I'm not waiting for a fucking contract, Hindley. I want a commercial before the X Games."

Oh, no. This was going to be bad. "Look, Axel, I'm more than happy to work with your team, but technically, we can't do anything for you until we have a signed contract."

"Oh, really?" He let out a humorless laugh and raised an eyebrow. "Wanna make a bet?"

I steeled my resolve and squared my shoulders. "What does that mean?"

"It means," he paused and his face morphed into an evil expression, "I know you're fuckin' Rory."

I gasped.

"And unless you want the owner of your firm and the entire world to find out about you and Fuck Face, then your sweet little ass will get me a commercial. Pronto. Or I talk. Got it?"

I reminded myself I had to stay calm. He had no proof Rory and I were involved.

"My relationship with Rory is purely professional, and none of your business."

"Oh, it's not my business?" He leaned back and laughed. "Well, let's see. Why don't I call one of the media staffers right now? Maybe one of the guys from, oh I don't know, ESPN. I think the networks would have a much different opinion about the affair you're having with one of your clients. A guy who just happens to be an X Games contender, and the spokesperson for the squeaky-clean Sonora Water."

My eyes went wide as saucers and I gripped the bar for support.

He glanced down at my hand and chuckled. "I don't think Sonora Water would be too happy to find out their All-American Comeback Kid is fuckin' yet another faceless bimbo, do you? Only this bimbo is his attorney." He laughed. "Not to mention, how well that would go over with your law firm, and your sweet little stepfather, ya think?"

I gasped. How did he know about Paul? "You wouldn't, Axel."

"I'm a little disappointed in you, Ms. Hagen. Obviously, you haven't done your research on me. I can, and I will, unless I get a commercial to air at the X Games."

"That's only five weeks away."

"Then I suggest you keep your legs closed and your mouth off Rory's dick until you get me a deal."

Oh my God. The blood drained from my face as my dinner churned in my stomach, threatening to make a reappearance. This was my worst nightmare come true. There was no sense denying our relationship now.

"That's not enough time, Axel."

"Is going public with your affair not enough of an incentive for you?"

He held my gaze and I knew in that moment he was completely evil.

"Well," he smirked, "maybe this will light a fire underneath your pretty little ass. Not only will I tell the media you're fuckin' your client,

I'll tell them he's a retard who doesn't even know how to read his own goddamn contract."

Fuck!

This was beyond bad. This was unbearable. How did he know about Rory's illiteracy?

"You can't do that, Axel, please," I begged, but immediately wished I hadn't. I'd just confirmed what may have been just speculation on his part.

"Oh, I can, and I will. I'll humiliate that motherfucker on national television if you don't get me what I want." His eyes burned with an evil I'd seen before in my dreams, only this time I was having to work for the monster.

I didn't doubt for a second that Axel would go to the rag mags and networks with information, true or not. What the hell was I going to do now?

He leaned in even further, his alcohol-infused breath making me even more nauseous. "And don't even think about telling Rory any of this shit or it will get worse. Much worse. For both of you."

His emphasis on the word 'much' made me shiver. All I could think of were Rory's words of warning about Axel, the insinuation that he may be a sexual predator.

"Don't worry, Hindley, this is business, not personal." He ran his forefinger along my jawline as his other hand came to rest on my mid-thigh. "Although I have to tell you, I'd love to make it personal. You're so fuckin' hot, I can honestly say I envy that asshole for being the one who gets to bang you senseless."

I bit back the tears, unwilling to let this monster see me break. How could I have been so careless, putting my affections toward Rory on public display?

"Why do you think I asked for you by name, Hindley?" He grinned. "I hope you give all your clients the same treatment."

I jumped off the stool and slapped his face as hard as I could but quickly regretted it. I'd poked the tiger with a very sharp stick.

"Okay," he whispered, smiling as he rubbed his cheek. "I see you're into the rough stuff. Not a problem, baby." He leaned in as if going for a kiss.

I turned my head and drilled my eyes shut.

His sticky, wet lips landed square on my cheek. I fought to control the familiar images of a similar assault now racing through my head.

He pulled back and I opened my eyes, upset he was still near. I glanced around the bar to ensure no one had seen my assault. Suddenly my eyes met familiar blue ones in the corner. His were narrowed into slits, and growing darker by the second. He pushed off the wall and stormed toward the bank of elevators.

I shoved Axel out of my way and raced toward Rory, trying to catch him before he could leave.

Sliding to a stop, I watched in horror as his beautiful face disappeared behind the elevator doors, leaving me all alone with a monster. I'd been unable to catch him, in more ways than one.

My head fell against the cold steel doors as that familiar feeling of fear hit me in the gut.

Once again, I was lost and out of control. My life was no longer my own. I was being manipulated by men who only wanted to use me. Again. But this time I wasn't sure I would survive.

CHAPTER 18

RORY

I PUNCHED the sixth-floor button on the elevator panel and I watched it light up like the fury inside me. As the elevator ascended, I fumed. What was she thinking? What had I been thinking, letting her go see that fucker on her own?

As soon as the doors opened to the sixth floor, I realized I couldn't go back to the room. That's exactly where Hindley would expect to find me. I couldn't look at her, not now.

Letting the doors close again, I pushed the highest number available on the elevator. Fourteen.

I stepped out and scanned the floor, ensuring Hindley was nowhere in sight. I had to clear my head, and I knew being in her presence would make that nearly impossible.

I paced the empty hallway like a caged tiger.

"She doesn't like him, she doesn't like him," I repeated silently.

"She's being blackmailed, she's being blackmailed."

The words echoed in my mind but did little to soothe the green monster raging inside me. I was fuming as images of that asshole's lips planted on her beautiful ivory skin raced through my mind.

I had to get out of this fucking hotel, go somewhere where I could hit something without being filmed or photographed.

A light at the end of the hall marked an exit. The stairwell might be a good place to escape.

I pushed the exit door open with a bang and waited for it to close before yelling at the top of my lungs. My thundering voice echoed off the walls but I still found no solace.

I raced down all fourteen flights of stairs, nearly losing my balance more than once. As I emerged onto the first floor, a door marked 'Kitchen' stood in front of me. I pushed through the entryway, oblivious to what might lay on the other side.

I burst inside the small room with all the subtly of an elephant.

Several employees jerked their heads up and stared at me.

"Outside?" I grumbled.

They all remained silent but one pointed to a small hallway behind a rack of bread.

I rounded the shelf and raced toward the door on the other side, shoving it open. The door slammed against the brick wall on the other side, nearly shattering the small window but I couldn't find the energy to give a shit.

Cool air hit my face like a wet mop and immediately fanned the flames of rage burning inside me. For once, I was thankful for Canada's cold weather.

I searched up and down the alleyway, not knowing which way to turn. Streetlamps illuminated one end. I didn't want to be seen by anyone, so I turned in the opposite direction, making my way toward the darkest end of the alley.

I walked past a dumpster and kicked it, listening as the sound echoed through the night. That physical exertion wasn't enough to douse the rage burning inside me, so I drew back my fist and punched the metal container with all my might.

Searing pain shot up my arm and I dropped to my knees as the physical pain momentarily eclipsed the ache in my heart. I sat on the cold pavement, my jeans soaking up the rain on the ground from the storms earlier in the evening.

I was pretty sure I'd broken my hand but I didn't care. It was either my hand or Axel's face, and I knew I didn't need the bad publicity. I could explain away my injury, but I wouldn't be able to explain away his.

Axel was up to something. I'd felt it back up in the hotel room as I'd waited for Hindley to return from their meeting. That's what had led me down to the lounge, even though she'd told me to wait for her in the room.

There'd been something inside me, a sixth sense that told me she was in trouble. I couldn't sit by and let it happen. I would protect her at all costs. There was no fuckin' way I would let anyone hurt her ever again.

Panic hit me in the gut when I realized she was still alone. I had to find her, make sure she was safe, make sure that fucker hadn't hurt her. Something wasn't right. I knew it with every fiber of my being.

I raced down the alley, laughing at the two dents in the side of the dumpster. Well, at least I could level the shit out of that asshole if he ever did anything to Hindley.

As my head cleared and my thoughts returned to Hindley, to that desperate look on her face, my heart ached. What had I done, leaving her?

I held my hand to my chest. The thing was throbbing like a mother-fucker but the pain was nothing compared to my fear for Hindley's safety.

I'd fucked this up royally. Not only with Hindley but professionally too.

What if I'd broken my hand? Skating with a fucked-up hand was nearly impossible. How the hell was I going to hold my board?

I didn't care what it took or how much pain I was in, I was going to wipe the course with that motherfucker tomorrow. I may not be able to kick his ass tonight for touching my girl, but I sure as shit would lay him out flat tomorrow during the competition. And I planned an ass-whipping so grand, he'd never forget it. I was going to crush Axel Pretorius.

I didn't want to enter through the main entrance of the hotel for fear someone would see my hand. Instead, I walked back to the kitchen door I'd left through and banged on the glass.

I waited forever before someone finally came to the door. The guy looked out at my face with a menacing glare.

I held up my hand hoping for a sympathy pass. "I need ice!" I shouted. "I'm a guest." I dug in my pocket and yanked out my key card.

Apparently appeased by my credentials, he pushed the door open and let me in.

He glanced down at my already swelling hand. "Dude, you need to go to a hospital. That hand looks bad."

"I'll be fine, I just need some ice."

"You're one of the skaters, aren't you?" the man asked. "Rory Gregor?"

I nodded.

"Hang on, dude, I'll fix you up." He returned shortly with a bag wrapped in a dishtowel. "This is crushed ice so it will mold better to your hand."

"Thanks." I wrapped it around my aching fist.

"You should have that looked at, seriously. Want me to call the house doctor?"

"Nah, I'll be fine. I can move my fingers so I know it's not broken. Thanks, though."

"Hey, my nephew's a huge fan. Do you think I could get an autograph?"

I held up my right hand that was wrapped in the dishtowel and packed ice. "It won't look too good, I'm right handed."

"That's okay, he won't mind. Can I get a photo too?"

"On one condition," I said.

"Anything, man."

"Don't tell anyone what you saw tonight. My hand, I mean."

"You got it." He nodded. Fishing in his pocket, he brought out a scrap of paper and a pen.

I spent the next twenty minutes signing autographs for half the kitchen staff. It worried me to have that many people know about my injury. But luckily, my buddy explained my wound away, claiming I'd caught it in the back door. It sounded like a good excuse so I went with it.

Thankfully he also loaded me up with Ibuprofen and a large bucket filled with crushed ice to take back to my room. This was one of the million reasons I loved skating. The fans. They believed in me, more than

I believed in myself most days. They'd do just about anything for me. I couldn't let them down. Not this time.

I trudged up the six flights of stairs back to my room, feeling more pain in my heart than in my hand. I'd let Hindley down, again. She'd needed me, needed my protection from that fucker, and instead I'd run away.

I knew Hindley, knew she'd never let that asshole take advantage of her. He had something on her though, and I had to find out what it was.

I pulled the key card out of my pocket as I balanced the ice bucket with my injured hand. Stepping onto my floor I glanced down the hallway and flinched.

Hindley leaned against my door, her head lolling to the side. My chest tightened and my soul ached for the pain I'd caused her. I knew I wasn't responsible for all of it, but knowing I had played a part in any of it made me sick to my stomach. I knelt down in front of her and stroked her soft hair.

"Hey," I whispered.

She jerked her head up. Her cheeks were stained with tears and her eyes swollen and red.

Shit.

I felt like such an asshole, having left her alone.

"Let's go inside." I stood and extended my good hand to help her stand.

She stared at my wrapped hand. "Oh my God, Rory, what happened to your hand?"

Knowing the hallway of the hotel was the last place I wanted to explain my injury, I inserted the key into the slot and pushed the door open, ushering her inside.

I set the ice bucket down on the side table and turned to face her, twining the fingers of my good hand through her hair and pressing a hard kiss against her mouth. I just prayed she would forgive me for being such an asshole.

She clutched my shirt and dragged me close to her. "I'm sorry," she said against my lips. "Please forgive me, Rory."

I leaned back and stared down at her beautiful face. "For what?" I wiped away the tears falling freely down her cheeks. Knowing I contributed to her anguish broke my heart.

"I didn't kiss him, I didn't initiate anything, I swear to God."

"Baby, don't apologize. I'm sorry for leaving you. I know you didn't do anything. I just, I don't know…" I tried to articulate my feelings but I couldn't find the right words to express what I wanted to say, how much she meant to me.

"Where's your journal?" She let me go and stepped back.

I didn't like the distance. I wanted to be close to her, needed her close. "Why do you want to know where my journal is?"

"Because now is a good time for you to express your emotions."

I hauled her back against my chest. "I don't really give a flying fuck about my journal or my emotions right now." I pressed another possessive kiss on her swollen lips, relieved that she responded by returning my passion with her own level of desperation. "All I want is you." I threw her onto my bed and crawled on top of her. "Fuck!" I shouted as I tried to put weight on my right hand.

"Rory, what in the world happened?" She looked over at my hand before staring up at me.

I rolled off her and clutched my hand to my chest, half because it hurt like shit and half because I didn't want her to see what a dumbass I'd been.

"Let me see it." She reached across my body, trying to grasp my hand.

I drew it from her reach.

She narrowed her eyes. "Rory."

She sounded like a spinster school teacher reprimanding me. I'd already put her through enough shit tonight.

Relinquishing my hold, I pushed my hand toward her.

She laid my arm gently on her lap and removed the ice pack aside. Unwrapping the dishtowel, she gasped. "Oh my God, Rory! What happened to you?"

I stared up at the ceiling, not wanting to confess how stupid I'd been.

Her hand grasped my chin and tugged it down, turning my face so she could see me.

I searched her eyes, wondering if I could escape this silent inquiry, knowing all the while she'd never let me.

"Tell me," she whispered.

"Tell me what happened with Axel first."

She released my chin. "What do you mean?"

"Whatever he said to you, it's not true."

"What are you talking about?"

"Whatever that asshole said about me, it's in the past. I may have slept around and done some stupid shit, but it's over, I swear. And if he threatened you, I'll fucking kill him."

"I know about your past, Rory. Everyone does." She smirked. "I'm fine. Now, tell me what the hell happened to your hand."

I knew I'd never escape her interrogation, and there was no way I would ever lie to her. I needed her to trust me. "I had a fight with a dumpster in the alley and the dumpster won." I tried to laugh it off, but her stern expression stopped me.

"You might have broken it, Rory." She pulled my hand up to her mouth and pressed feather-light kisses on my knuckles. "Does it hurt?"

"Like hell."

"We've got to get you to the hospital. If those bones set improperly, it could cripple you for life."

"It's not broken." I reassured her.

"How do you know?"

"I've had enough broken bones to know the difference in the pain. Actually, it hurts less when you break a bone. Plus, I can move my fingers, so it's good. Just bruised."

"You did this because of me." It wasn't a question and she sounded more guilty than angry.

"Hey." I cupped her face in my good hand. "Stop. I'm a dumb asshole with a hot head who's jealous and protective and stupid. It doesn't make for a good combo."

"But..." She bit back her words.

There was more going on. I could feel it deep within my soul. That fucker had something on her. "But what, Hindley?"

She didn't answer.

"What did Axel say to you?"

"He's putting a lot of pressure on me."

Shit. "What kind of pressure?"

She hesitated, as if trying to make up a story.

My gut clenched.

"He wants a commercial by the X Games."

"That's like five weeks away."

"I know," she said, nodding. "Plus, my law firm doesn't even have a signed contract with him so if I get him one, the firm could technically be screwed."

"How?"

"Mr. Stedwick wants Axel because of the money. That's all they're concerned with."

I knew what she said was true. For Hindley, it had never been about the money. She wanted me to succeed, and that's what made me love her all the more.

"You have to know, Hindley, if that motherfucker hurts you in any way, especially physically, I will crucify him."

"Please, don't," she whispered, stroking my face.

"It's in me."

"What?"

"My insane need to protect you. It's what brought me to you the first night I saw your drunk little ass on the street."

She smiled at the memory. "Your Drunk Girl?"

"Yes, *my* Drunk Girl." I laughed. "You'll always be mine, Hindley."

She pushed me over and straddled my waist, her eyes full of love and adoration like I'd never seen or felt before.

"Always." She smiled and her lips crushed mine.

I could trust her. I'd always known it, but every day, she gave me new reasons why.

"I trust you with my life," I whispered against her lips.

She pulled back and stared down at me.

"I know you'd never lie to me or hurt me," I said.

Her eyes darted between mine like a caged animal, scared and wild.

I sat up slightly. "What's wrong?"

She planted her palms on my chest and pushed me back down into the mattress.

I had no idea where all her physical strength came from but I wasn't going to complain. Not when she was straddling me on top of a bed.

"I love you," she said. "You know that, right?"

Her words were like a plea, not as confident as they'd once been.

"Of course I know you love me. What's wrong?"

"Nothing." She smiled. "Everything I do, I do for you, you know that too, right?"

"Hindley, what's going on?"

"I want to show you."

"Show me what?"

"How much I'd do for you." She sat up, still straddling me as she tugged at the hem of her shirt, dragging it over her head. She reached behind her back, unhooking her bra, and letting it fall to the side.

She was the most captivating creature I'd ever seen, sinfully delicious in every way. I tried to push Axel's face out of my mind, but it was hard. He'd touched her, and fury burned inside me again.

She leaned over me, her bare breasts pressing firmly against my shirt as she captured my face between her hands. "No one will *ever* change how I feel about you, Rory Gregor. Not Matt, not Axel. No one. It's only you for me."

"And you for me, Drunk Girl," I replied softly, drawing her body into mine, trying to mold us into one.

She covered my lips with hers. Her kiss was different tonight, more possessive and urgent, as if she had a purpose, a message to reveal. Or a secret to hide.

My dick twitched in apprehension and I was lost in everything about her as the memory of Axel Pretorius's smug face disappeared, replaced by the love I had for Hindley. A love she obviously felt as well, judging by her aggressive kisses.

Her words rang through my head. 'No one will ever change how I feel about you.' I tucked the statement away deep in my heart, feeling eerily confident that one day I might have to cling to them for survival.

I settled back into the bed, watching as she slowly and seductively undressed us. Her lips moved over my skin, caressing every inch of me. Thoughts of my throbbing hand evaporated.

She slowly lowered herself onto me, her eyes never leaving mine as I filled her completely.

There was nothing better than being inside my Drunk Girl.

Her chest heaved a deep sigh.

After a lifetime spent in hell, this right here, being with Hindley, was heaven for me.

Her body rocked against mine, rising and falling as we made love. I gripped her hips, driving into her, my need to be closer to her pushing me on.

As our gazes locked and our bodies became one, I felt for the briefest of moments that we were safe. No one or nothing on earth would ever come between us.

But a knot of despair deep in my belly warned me that our time together was fleeting and may not last forever. Eventually I would fuck this up. Like I did most things in my life.

For now, I would enjoy what I had, the feel of her body against mine, and pretend that Hindley would be mine always.

CHAPTER 19

RORY

"So, Rory, your fans and I are all curious. How does it feel to be headed to the X Games in L.A. for the sixth time?"

Jacob Fuller was a sports commentator with ESPN and I knew him better than most journalists. I'd always felt comfortable in his presence and gravitated to him for interviews after competitions.

The camera and the microphone were both shoved in my face. I was never comfortable being interviewed, even when it was with someone like Jake, but I needed the exposure, and my growing confidence with my reading skills made me braver.

"I'm totally excited. For the fans. They deserve this."

"Don't you mean *you* deserve it, Rory?"

"No, I definitely don't deserve all of this. I've been fortunate to have an amazing comeback. It's the fans who deserve this. That's who I'm skating for now."

"But winning the Calgary International Skateboarding Competition with a record-setting score can't feel bad for you personally, can it?"

Jake was right. Not only had I mopped the floor with Pretty Boy's ugly ass, I'd broken an international record by receiving perfect scores from three of the five judges in my final round.

"Yeah, I guess that does feel pretty good personally." I laughed, knowing it wasn't for the reasons he and the rest of the viewing audience thought though.

"Rumor has it you're working on an original trick. Any comment?"

"No comment."

"Do you think you'll debut it at the X Games?"

"Let's just say, it's a possibility."

"Do you think your hand will be healed in time?"

I looked down at my hand, still wrapped in bandages. We'd decided to go with the story that I'd slammed it in the kitchen door and everyone seemed to buy it. Hindley had talked me into going to a minor emergency clinic in the wee hours of the morning and they'd confirmed it wasn't broken, just badly bruised. It still hurt like a motherfucker though.

"Well, it doesn't seem to have affected me today." I laughed.

"Broadcasters and league insiders predict you'll be ranked second in the world after this weekend's big win, possibly even first going into the X Games. Any comment?"

"First or last place, it doesn't matter, Jake, as long as I can still ride." And that was the truth. It wasn't about winning now. It was about competing against myself. Being the best that I could be.

"You have to know that sounds like a line of bull, right, Rory? Everyone wants to be number one."

"You forget, Jake, I was number one. It only lasts for a little while. There's more to my life than being number one." I searched the crowd, looking for my reason. Her name was Hindley Hagen.

"Fair point, Rory. Hey, good luck in Miami."

"Thanks, man." I smacked him on the shoulder and broke through the crowd, making my way to the grandstands in search of my Drunk Girl.

"Nice skating, Rory." I felt a hand on my shoulder and turned toward the voice, disappointed to find it was Michael.

"Oh, thanks. Where's Hindley?" I knew my tone was too possessive, but I couldn't help it. She was the only person I wanted to share this win with and the one person I had yet to find.

"She's with Axel." The look on his face was menacing, as if his words were a warning of some sort.

Fuck. I willed myself to stay calm.

"So, your firm is signing Axel too?" I asked. "I'm not sure I'm comfortable with that."

"Why?" He stared at me.

"Having two athletes in the same sport seems like a conflict of interest."

He laughed smugly.

I realized in that moment that I couldn't stand this asshole.

"That's funny," he said.

"What?"

"That's exactly what Hindley told Mr. Stedwick when he broached the subject of taking on Axel as a client."

That was my girl, standing up for me at any cost. I couldn't help but smile.

"And I assume you all determined you could represent both of us fairly and equally?"

"Of course, Rory. Was that really a doubt?"

"Yes."

"Well, I can assure you, Luis and I will work twice as hard as Hindley did to secure the most endorsements we can."

"And what if I don't want to work with you and Luis?"

"Well, I guess that's your prerogative, although I don't think you'd want to jeopardize Hindley's future by being so selfish, would you?"

"What the fuck does that mean?" I was tired of playing nice with this prick, like I gave a fuck about him or his firm.

"Hindley's a brilliant lawyer, and on her way to being a top-notch agent as well."

"Who better to represent me then?"

"Don't you think you've had enough bad press in the past to last a lifetime?"

"What are you saying, Michael?"

"I'm saying let Hindley go. Let her do her job, a job she's good at. You do yours, let me and Luis represent you, and things will go a lot more smoothly."

And there it was. He knew. Fuck.

"Does Hindley know?" I asked.

"Know what?"

"That you know about us?"

"No. And I'd like to keep it that way."

I would too, but I couldn't lie to Hindley. "I won't go out of my way to tell her, but I'm not going to lie to her if she asks," I said.

"She's a smart girl, I'm sure she already suspects I know something. Let's keep her in the dark."

'Keep her in the dark?' What a douche bag.

I didn't have a choice. I had to suck it up and play along. I could be dangerous if left to my own devices, and the throbbing pain in my hand was a reminder of that fact. I couldn't jeopardize Hindley's reputation.

"What's the deal with Axel? Did they really ask for her?"

"Yes. His manager was impressed with her ability to get you a commercial deal so quickly. They think she can do the same for Axel."

"He's a dick, you know. I don't trust him at all."

"Need I remind you that your reputation isn't so stellar either?"

I may hate the guy, but he was right.

"Need I remind *you* that you work for me?" I said, tilting my head.

His raised eyebrow was all the indication I needed to know he understood I wasn't going to play his dumbass little game.

"Look man, Axel's different," I said. "He's unstable, explosive, dangerous."

Michael's brow furrowed.

I knew what he was thinking. *So are you, my friend.* Maybe. But Axel's fury was fueled by something different than mine. I wanted to protect Hindley. Axel wanted women, at any cost.

"I'll keep an eye on him," he said. "Just let Hindley do her job. She's much smarter than you give her credit for."

"And Axel's much more dangerous than *you* realize."

"Great job, Rory." Hindley yelled behind me.

I turned to face her but tried to hide my excitement. "Thanks," I said coolly.

Her eyes darted between Michael and me as she processed the scene unfolding before her.

"Michael and I are going to discuss some details of the deals you've been working on later tonight after dinner," I said.

"Okay, what time should I be there?" she asked eagerly.

"I think you probably need to concentrate on Axel. Michael's got me." My stomach cramped with dread and fear, knowing I was forcing her in the direction of the one man I despised more than life itself.

But fuck it all if Michael wasn't right. It was Hindley's reputation on the line. I had to last five more weeks and then I could declare my love for her. Until then, I had to let her go, but the expression on her face broke my spirit. I'd hurt her.

Her eyes cut to Michael's.

I felt sorry for the bastard.

"What the hell's going on, Michael? Rory is *my* client. We agreed I could handle him and Axel together until the X Games."

"Rory and I have talked and we both agree that it would be better for him to have the undivided attention of me and Luis to further his career."

'Further my career?' He'd have to come up with something better than that or Hindley would see right through him. She knew I couldn't care less about my career.

"It's all right, Hindley," I said. "I know you're busy with other athletes, but if I need you, you'll be there for me." I gave her a slight smile, hoping she'd understand my underlying message.

Her face showed no signs of acknowledgment. She was pissed.

"Rory! Rory!" People screamed from behind the barricades. Fans. Shit.

"Go. Your fans want you," she said with a slight hint of sarcasm in her voice. Her lips pressed into a thin line and her once glowing eyes were now dulled with apprehension. She knew there was more going on, but she also realized I needed to address my fans. "We'll talk later," she whispered.

My body burned at the thought of having to lie to her. I wouldn't. I'd never lie to Hindley. It was physically impossible. I just hoped she would be all right with the truth.

CHAPTER 20

RORY

"WHAT THE FUCK is going on, Rory Gregor?" Hindley slammed the Magic Door behind her as she barged into my hotel room.

"Nice to see you too, sweetheart."

"Cut the bullshit. What's going on with you and Michael? What did he say to you?"

"He said you're working hard, and you need to concentrate on Axel and your other dude."

"And you just rolled over and accepted that without fighting for me?"

I held up my throbbing hand that was wrapped in a bag of ice. "I think we've seen where my fighting gets me."

"You know what I mean, Rory."

"He said you're a great lawyer, and now an accomplished agent too, so I should let you continue to grow, professionally."

"So you don't want me anymore?" Her huge doe eyes were quickly filling with tears.

"What?" I scooped her into my arms. "Are you kidding me?"

"It's just that, usually, you don't let me go without a fight."

"Hindley, I care about you more than anything in this world. Even skating."

Her eyes grew wide with surprise.

It was the truth. I understood in that moment just how much she truly meant to me. "I guess I've realized that maybe it's me who's putting you in harm's way."

"What the hell does that mean?" She shoved me off.

God, this was going to suck. I was nauseous just thinking about the words rolling off my lips.

"I trust you, with Axel, I mean. I know you're strong and you won't take his shit. I don't want to stress you out. I know the law firm is putting a lot of pressure on you, and then there's the worry you have about Paul's company. I don't want to put more stress on you too, that's all."

She tilted her head and furrowed her brow. "Where's my Rory?"

"What do you mean?" I laughed.

"Where's my caveman Rory, the one who beats his chest and stands on top of me, peeing around me in a vast circle, staking his claim?"

I grabbed her around the waist. "That Neanderthal is still here."

"Neanderthal?" she questioned. "That's an impressive word, Mr. Gregor."

"I have lots of new words, Miss Hagen."

"Read to me," she begged.

"What?"

"I love when you read to me."

"Really?"

"You know I do."

When she'd first asked me to read out loud to her, I'd been so self-conscious I could barely do it. But over the weeks, I found it totally relaxed us both. If I got to a word I didn't know, I'd pause and try to sound it out. If it was still beyond me, I'd either type it into Google Translator or she would help me and we'd add it to my sight word list.

While she walked over to her room, I stacked the pillows against the headboard of the bed and leaned back against them.

She returned with her e-reader, opening a familiar book. *That's What Friends Are For* by Valeri Gorbachev. It was the story of unconditional love between two unlikely friends, a pig and a goat caught in a tidal wave of misunderstandings. They felt like Hindley and me. Even though it was a low-level reading book, I didn't care. It was one I could read without help, and that brought me more joy than almost anything in the world, besides Hindley Hagen herself.

"Come here, baby." I patted my lap.

She handed me the e-reader then she snuggled up to me, laying her head on my lap.

I twirled a strand of her hair around my finger as I read to her. The entire scene felt surreal, something I never pictured myself doing in a million years.

"I love your voice," she said softly.

I moved the e-reader to the side, staring down at her face. It was glorious, glowing with pride for me. "And I love *you*." I smiled down at her.

She took the device from my hand and set it aside, then shifted onto my lap and straddled me. "I love you too, Rory Gregor." She leaned in and placed a gentle kiss against my lips. "Thank you for trusting me."

"It's Axel I don't trust, baby."

"I know. But I can handle him, I promise." She tilted her head the opposite way and placed a kiss high on my cheek next to my ear.

"You'll call me the minute that fucker tries anything, promise?"

"I promise." She placed another kiss along my jaw.

"Thirty-five days," I said.

She drew back, tilting her head in confusion, her eyes narrowing. "What does that mean?"

"Five weeks, thirty-five days until…"

"Until what?"

I flipped her over, crushing her body with mine.

She squealed in delight.

"Until I can tell the whole fuckin' world you're mine," I growled.

"Rory," she admonished.

"Oh, no, you're not backing out now, Miss Hagen. You promised me the X Games would be my finish line, in more ways than one."

She giggled as my lips blew along her neck.

"Thirty-five days," she repeated. "But we have to be careful, Rory. Okay?"

I lifted up, staring into her gorgeous cocoa colored eyes. "Oh, Miss

Hagen, I vow to be anything *but* careful with you." I buried my face in her neck and littered kisses along her jaw.

"You know what I mean," she panted.

"Umm hmm," I hummed in her ear. "I know what you mean, all right."

"Rory," she blew out.

"Yes, Hindley." I smiled against her skin.

"I love you." Her words were desperate and pleading.

I lifted off her completely. "What's wrong, Hindley?"

"Nothing," she said, grabbing my neck and dragging my face to hers. "I want you to always remember, no matter what happens in the next thirty-five days, that I love you."

I pulled her hand away from my neck and broke our embrace, rolling on to my side.

"What's wrong? What are you talking about?"

She pushed on my chest, forcing me onto my back and climbed on top of me again, taking my face in both her hands. Her eyes searched mine, looking for traces of something that I couldn't comprehend.

"I'm talking about the fact that I love you more than anything or anyone on this earth. I'm talking about how I'd do anything to protect you, no matter what it is."

Her words were soft and gentle, but I still felt a tug at my heart that didn't settle well with me. "Are you all right, Hindley? Are you in some type of trouble?"

"No, baby," she whispered against my neck. "But you're going to be in trouble if you don't take me to bed and fuck me thoroughly."

"What?" I laughed.

"You heard me, Rory. Stop with this sappy shit and fuck me already."

"Why, Miss Hagen, you have such a potty mouth."

"Yeah, and I'm about to wrap that mouth all over your dick in a second."

Well, fuck me. Somewhere between the first time I'd found her shit-faced on the street back at that club in Austin, and now, my modest, meek little Drunk Girl had turned into a vicious sex goddess—and I loved it. Not only that, but against all the odds, we'd fallen in love.

The feeling should have comforted me and brought me great peace. But tonight I felt as if Hindley's love for me may be her own undoing, a block around her neck that had the potential to drown her.

No matter how much I loved her, I had to be willing to pull away if my love ever endangered her life. My only problem was, I was a weak motherfucker, a selfish bastard to the core, and I feared I wouldn't be able to walk away from her if that time ever came.

I shook internally, realizing I'd never survive without her, but knowing one day, I might have to in order to keep her safe. Tonight, she was all mine though, and I was going to enjoy her.

She unzipped my pants, freeing my one-eyed soldier who was already standing at full attention.

I wanted inside her so badly it hurt. I helped yank down both my jeans and boxers in one fell swoop, gazing up at her beautiful face. Her golden blonde hair fell in front of her, caressing my thighs as she stared at my dick.

"Is it possible to be in love with a penis?" She giggled.

God, that laugh. My dick swelled even bigger.

"Oh my God, Rory, how did you do that?"

I knew what she was talking about, but I was tired of talking. I spread her legs wide, allowing her to straddle me, pushing up her skirt to reveal her satin thong.

"I believe your exact words were 'Fuck me already', Miss Hagen. Was that correct?" Her temptress smile was my undoing. In one fluid motion, I flipped her over and jerked off her panties then grabbed a condom from the nightstand drawer and rolled it on in record time. Before she even had time to think, I slammed into her, all my emotions pouring out into the one place where I felt safe. Inside Hindley Hagen.

"Oh, God, Rory," she moaned in my ear.

"Say it, baby," I begged as I thrust inside her over and over, hitting every spot I knew lit her on fire.

"Oh, Rory!" she shouted through her heavy breathing, her hands gripping my ass, pushing me in further as her long, lean legs wrapped around my hips.

"What, baby?" I yelled. I wanted to hear her say it, while I was buried deep inside her. I didn't even have to tell her, she knew what I needed to hear her profess.

"I'm yours!" she shouted. "You're mine."

"Always, Hindley?"

"Forever," she panted. "I'll be yours forever, Rory. You're *my* Skater Boy." She let out a moan like I'd never heard as her body shook and spasmed underneath me. She clamped down on my dick, drawing me further inside, sending a shot of sheer ecstasy through my entire body.

I pumped into her several more times, my dick growing thicker with every thrust. Sex had never felt this spectacular, with anyone, ever. I knew the reason why but I wasn't sure I could say it out loud.

"Forever, Drunk Girl!" I exclaimed as I found my own release. I fell on top of her, my panting slowing as I returned back to earth. "I'll love you forever, Hindley," I whispered in her ear. Whether together or apart, it was the truth. I would always love her, even if it meant I had to leave her one day to keep her safe.

CHAPTER 21

HINDLEY

I STRETCHED out in the lounger on the beach, listening to the waves of the Pacific Ocean crash into the shore. The warmth from the sun overhead heated my skin and I let out a relaxing sigh. This place, this time, felt like heaven. "Thanks for inviting me out. It's exactly what I needed."

"You're most welcome," Rory said. "But you better be careful. I don't want you to burn again."

I turned my head, lowering my shades to look into his beautiful blue eyes sparkling in the brilliant California sun. The smirk on his face was unmistakable. I knew the insinuation and memories he was referring to and I couldn't help but smile as I remembered our first intimate night together.

"I'd let you rub lotion on me if I burn, Mr. Gregor."

"Oh, I'm sure you would, Miss Hagen." He laughed, taking my hand in his and bringing it up to his lips, his eyes full of promise.

This felt real. It felt like we were a normal couple doing normal things, and for the first time since I met him, I found myself counting down the days until the X Games when we could finally declare our love for one another, publicly. I didn't care what happened to my professional career, as long as I was with Rory, I knew we could make it work.

"Are you hungry?" He changed the topic before we both stripped down here on the beach and went at it like rabbits.

"I'm always hungry." My voice was low and sultry and sexy. Or, at least I hoped it was.

"Oh, Miss Hagen. Let's get you upstairs and see if we can't feed that never-ending appetite of yours."

Something deep within me tingled at the hint of things to come. I dusted off the sand from my lounger.

Rory easily picked it up and tucked it under his arm, reaching out his empty hand for mine.

This was right. I knew it in my heart. Being with Rory was where I was supposed to be, and damn the rest of the world. But visions of Axel's sinister face surfaced and I remembered how much damage he could cause us.

I'd yet to secure a deal for him. Sponsors alike seemed standoffish, hesitant to come anywhere close to him until the rumors about his sexual assaults were cleared. To date, no one had stepped forward to either charge or acquit him. I tried to assure potential sponsors that the allegations were vicious rumors, but part of me felt guilty and sick to my stomach trying to explain away Axel's crimes.

"Hey." Rory squeezed my hand. "Where'd you go?"

I laughed at his question, knowing it had become his way of bringing me back when my thoughts drifted to the negative. "Nowhere." I smiled.

"Well, in that case, let me take you somewhere."

The promise in his voice was unmistakable and my mouth watered thinking about what he had in store for me.

As we walked into the house, he nodded toward the stairs. "Go take a shower."

His words were commanding but tender, and I was lost in anticipation.

"You're not coming with me?" I pouted like a child.

"I'll be up in a minute." His playful wink and mischievous smile said it all.

God, I loved this man. I was so thankful he'd talked me into coming out to spend a few days with him at his house before we hit the road for his next competition in Miami.

Our new plan was perfect. I was supposed to meet with Humberto and his manager in Miami anyway, so I thought to kill two birds with one stone and be with Rory too. But Axel's threat kept creeping into my mind and my stomach cringed as I thought about the power he had to ruin my future with Rory. I had to work my ass off and find a commercial deal for him, otherwise my fantasy world with Rory would be over sooner than I wanted.

"Go!" He slapped my butt hard.

"Ow!" I rubbed my backside.

"There'll be more where that came from if you don't get your sweet little ass up to my room and shower."

"All right already. I'm going." The predatory gleam in his blue eyes sent chills up and down my spine. I raced up the stairs in lightning speed.

I showered in record time and waited on his bed, wrapped in a plush robe, high on anticipation, dreaming of what lay ahead. I knew it was something kinky and I couldn't wait. Would he tie me up? Would I tie him up? All types of illicit images ran through my head.

"It will be even better than what you're imagining, I can promise you that."

His deep voice ripped through my thoughts. I turned and stared at the delicious man leaning against the doorframe. He stood in pajama pants that hung off his hips, naked from the waist up. God, he was beautiful.

One hand held up a tray, but I couldn't see what was in the containers that lay on top of it. He stalked into the bedroom and set the tray down on the dresser before making his way over to the bed.

"Off."

I jumped off the bed at his deep growl.

He ripped off the pillows, comforter, and top sheet. "Robe off. Face up on the bed," he commanded.

I stood still, afraid to move.

"Now!"

Oh, God! This is gonna be good. I was already dripping with anticipation.

I ripped off the robe and threw it to the floor next to the comforter and sheet. Crawling up on the bed, I stretched out on my back, unsure of what position I should be in. Arms above my head? Out to the sides? Legs closed or spread apart? My heart was beating so fast and loud, I could barely hear the familiar clinking noise of the straps being hooked to the railing below the bed.

"Arms," he commanded.

I'd done this enough to know what he wanted. I stretched my arms toward the edge of the bed. I watched as he took one wrist and cuffed it in a leather restraint, tugging to make sure it was secure. These were new, and rougher than the material he'd used before. Every cell in my body was on fire.

He walked to the other side of the bed and secured my other arm. "These are different," he explained in a gentler tone. "They'll pinch a little more. If it hurts too much, you have to tell me. Okay?"

I nodded, not wanting to stop anything he was doing.

"Good girl." He leaned down to kiss my nose. "Legs," he commanded. "Spread them."

Immediately, I obeyed. I couldn't see them, but it felt like the same type of leather restraints at my ankles that were on my wrists.

He crawled up my naked body, his legs on either side of my hips, hands on the mattress next to my face, but his body made no contact with mine.

I felt empty and deprived.

"Same thing with your ankles. If it bites or hurts, let me know."

I nodded again, a wanting smile spreading across my entire face.

"Someone's excited." He laughed. Just as soon as the words escaped him, he was gone.

Clinking near the dresser garnered my attention. It sounded like he was preparing something, but I knew better than to look. Instead, I lay still on the bed, staring up at the ceiling, wondering at what point in our relationship had I relinquished control to this man. If someone would have told me three months ago that I'd be trussed up like a prisoner on some man's bed, I would have laughed them off the face of the earth. Yet, here I was, spread eagle and loving every minute of it.

The bed dipped with his weight and I strained my neck to find him sitting between my legs, his body never making contact with mine. My insides were throbbing for his touch.

"You called me a tactile learner in the beginning, remember?"

Where's he going with this? I wasn't sure if I should be excited, or scared shitless.

"T-A-C-T-I-L-E." He spelled the word in staccato as his lips curled up in a devious grin. "It's become one of my favorite words, Miss Hagen."

I swallowed hard, realizing I was in trouble. And I loved it.

"Do you know what the word tactile means?"

I shrugged my shoulders, unable to speak, wondering what he would do next.

"It means you use every sensory organ to learn."

Sensory organ? Good Lord, he had me panting like a dog on a hot summer day and he hadn't even touched me.

He stalked up my body until his face came within inches of mine. I realized he was gloriously naked, his hard-on dangerously close to my lady parts. I was burning with desire and he hadn't even touched me yet.

"It occurred to me that as I've been learning how to read," he said, "I've used every sensory organ at my disposal." He leaned in closer and his hard-on grazed my stomach. His lips were just below my ear.

I inhaled his intoxicating aroma, a mixture of his spicy cologne and body wash. He'd showered as well.

"Perhaps you should do the same." His breath blew across my neck.

My mouth went dry and my body heated with desire for this man.

Reaching behind him, he produced a silk mask. "I think it's time I reciprocated."

"For what?" I squeaked out.

"Oh, please, don't tell me you've already forgotten about blindfolding me?"

Goose bumps spread over my skin. What kind of revenge did he have planned?

"That's right. Tit for tat." He leaned down, lapping and sucking one of my nipples.

My body rocked up to meet his mouth, wanting more.

"Oh, not yet, baby."

Knowing he would draw this out and tease me relentlessly, my body fell lax.

His mouth retreated as his large hand slid under my neck. "Up."

I raised my head off the mattress and stared at his face for as long as possible, watching as his eyes burned with mischief.

Slowly, he slipped the silk mask over my head, securing the elastic strap behind my hair as he adjusted the cover over my eyes. "Can you see me?"

"No," I panted.

"Good." He placed a soft kiss on my lips.

Instinct and experience warned me that would be the last gentle act he would perform.

I listened intently, trying to figure out what he was going to do next, but it was futile. Instead, I relaxed back into the mattress as best I could and waited. I heard soft music envelope the room. It sounded like a symphony, something completely opposite to Rory's personality.

"Do you like the music?"

I felt his warm breath against my stomach.

"Yes," I moaned.

His lips caressed my abdomen.

I rocked and yanked on the straps.

"Careful, baby," he admonished. "We haven't even started yet."

His voice was so deep, vibrating across my skin. I could sense the smile on his face even though he wasn't visible through my mask. We were so attuned to one another. That's why it was so easy to lay here, strapped down, completely naked and defenseless. I trusted him. I loved him.

"This is going to be intense," he said. "I need you to tell me if anything hurts or if it gets to be too much, okay?"

I barely registered his words before something hot dripped on my skin. I was startled at the sensation.

"Okay?" he asked.

I nodded, unable to speak. Hot liquid trailed from my belly button up to my chest, skimming between my breasts and falling over my neck. I flinched at the temperature. It was hot but bearable, barely.

"Open your mouth."

I licked my dry lips before parting them as he'd instructed. All of a sudden, the hot liquid was rushing down my chin, spilling over my tongue. It was chocolate, hot chocolate syrup.

"Swallow," he whispered.

As I let the liquid fall down my throat I tasted something so dark and decadent I knew immediately this was an expensive type of chocolate.

"Open."

I did as he told me but instead of more chocolate syrup, small pellets of ice slipped over my tongue, almost choking me.

"Swallow," he whispered again.

As I shut my mouth, the hot chocolate dripped across my lips. I tried to open my mouth again.

"Keep your mouth closed," he commanded.

I puckered my lips to hold in the melting ice.

Suddenly his tongue was rubbing over my lips, licking and lapping up the syrup.

I wanted to open my mouth so badly, to taste him and devour him, but I knew better than to defy Rory Gregor.

He moaned against my lips, making every nerve ending in my body explode with desire.

His tongue trailed down my chin and caressed my neck, following the path of chocolate syrup he'd drizzled down the middle of my body. The sensation was thrilling, irresistible and almost agonizing.

I tried to pull my hands down to touch him, forgetting I was strapped down to the bed. The leather restraints pinched, chafing my skin.

His tongue continued its assault down my stomach to my belly button as he swirled around the sensitive area.

My hips bucked up, trying to press against him. Hot syrup dripped on my nipples and I flinched in surprise. "Oh."

"Are you okay?" His words were genuine and sincere, much different than the commanding presence of before.

"Yes," I whispered. I wanted his mouth back on me. Pain or no pain, I wouldn't yell out again.

His tongue trailed back up my body, making his way to one nipple, sucking away the melted chocolate. As he continued to lap at my breast, something ice cold slipped over my other nipple.

I jerked on the cuffs, unable to free myself.

"Feel it, baby, absorb all the sensations," he whispered against my skin.

The pleasure was so different from the hot syrup, but within seconds, the coolness of the ice felt just as sensual.

He moved his lips over to the cold and puckered nipple.

I thought I might come just from his assault on my breasts alone. Was that even possible? "Oh my God," I panted, lost in the euphoria of it all.

"Patience." He smiled against my skin. "Tactile. T-A-C-T-I-L-E. Remember?"

I was beginning to hate that word. Before I could debate my loathing of the word, my senses were assaulted by the smell of fruit—strawberries, bananas, even cantaloupes, maybe.

"Open."

I opened my mouth and something cool with a rough exterior was placed inside.

"Bite," he whispered, his voice sinfully delicious.

My teeth clamped down on the object. It was a strawberry. The juices ran down my chin.

"Open," he said.

I obeyed and hot syrup filled my mouth, almost choking me.

"Close."

I did as he demanded.

"Chew," he blew in my ear.

God, it tasted so sweet and juicy, like no strawberry I'd ever eaten before in my life.

"Swallow."

His voice become huskier with every instruction. The juncture of my thighs burned. My body quivered uncontrollably as my mind spiraled out of control, lost in his erotic taunting.

The mattress dipped as he straddled my hips, placing cold objects along the mid-line of my body, from my throat down past my belly button.

What was he doing?

Using my body as his canvas, he drizzled more chocolate, artistically swirling the hot liquid around the objects. His lips licked between my breasts. He was eating whatever it was laying on top of me. I was his human dish.

I wanted him so badly. I tugged at the restraints, unable to take the sensual assault.

He moved down to the next morsel, his lips stroking my skin, his tongue pushing the food around on my body before he sucked it in. "You taste so sweet, baby." His breath caressed the heated skin of my abdomen.

My hands and feet jerked on the cuffs and my legs spasmed as my own liquid heat spilled over in a pre-orgasmic rush. I wasn't sure how much longer I could take this. "Rory," I pleaded.

He crawled closer to my face. "Yes, baby?"

I couldn't talk, I couldn't think, I was delirious with desire. It was excruciating pain mixed with mind-blowing pleasure that had me going crazy.

His lips pressed against mine, his tongue probing for entrance.

I opened my mouth, licking and sucking at him, as I lifted my hips off the mattress. I needed something, anything to rub against to relieve the ache between my legs.

"Oh, no, Miss Hagen. Not yet," he admonished, moving off the bed.

Shit!

I was going to spontaneously combust if he didn't touch me down there soon. I had to find something to distract myself.

I concentrated on the music. It was soft and melodic, floating through the room like a lullaby. My over-sensitized nerves subsided for a bit, but as I drew in a deep breath, my nose was overcome by the erotic scent of Rory himself, and I was pulsating with need again.

I yanked on the restraints so hard, I knew I'd have bruises for a week. How would I explain that at my next client meeting? Images of work invaded my mind, especially Axel and his threats.

"Come back to me, Hindley," he murmured in my ear.

How could he tell I was gone when he couldn't even see my eyes?

"I know you." He rubbed his fingers along my nipples then squeezed both so hard I whimpered. As soon as he released them, I felt such exquisite pleasure I almost cried. How was that possible?

"Pleasure from pain," he said, answering my silent question.

"Oh my God, Rory," I panted.

"I know, baby." His mouth worked its way down further.

I held my breath. As he neared the spot where I needed him most, his mouth retreated, replaced by something hard and cool.

"Rory," I begged, not knowing how much more I could take.

He laughed, moving the object slowly back and forth, dipping it between my legs.

"Oh, God," I moaned at the beautiful pressure. It was heaven, and hell. I needed more. I needed *him*.

He continued to tease me with the object, pulling it away just as I was on the cusp of release. "Feel it all, Hindley," he whispered in my ear.

My breathing grew labored and I feared I might pass out. Something slid inside me but it wasn't Rory. I tried to close my legs around the object but the straps held my legs in place, making it impossible to find the relief I so desperately needed.

A loud click echoed through the room and the object within me came to life, pulsating inside me. Oh, God, it was a vibrator. And it was inside me. I'd seen plenty in Regan's shop, but I'd never used one.

The music grew louder, reaching a deep crescendo just as warm syrup dripped on my breasts. He rubbed something cold around my nipples before taking one in his mouth.

I pulled at the restraints, overcome with the sensations.

He slipped something against my lips. "Open," he said.

I complied and he slid something soft and large inside.

"Bite," he commanded.

I did, the taste exploding in my mouth. It was a banana covered in the chocolate syrup.

"Chew."

I groaned, the intensity of the vibrator pushing me further to the edge almost too much to bear. I wanted to complain, tell him I couldn't go on, but the banana kept me from speaking.

"Hold on to it, Hindley," he whispered against my cheek. "Don't come yet. Chew."

I did as he asked, focusing on the taste, the smell, the feel of the fruit.

Something clicked and the vibrator's speed increased. I bucked my hips.

"Swallow," he said.

I did, panting with need.

"Now," he whispered as he tugged the vibrator out then pushed it back in before rotating it several times.

The orgasm hit me so fast, with an intensity I'd never felt before. I cried out, my voice hoarse as my fingers curled and dug into my palms. My body hummed with pleasure as I pulled at my restraints.

Before I could catch my breath, the vibrator was jerked out of me and replaced with Rory.

"Oh, God," I yelled, my body still convulsing from the climax.

"Again," he said, thrusting into me.

I shook my head. There was no way I could come again. I was aching to the point of pain.

His body rocked into mine and I felt the pressure build again.

"Feel it," he said. "Tactile."

Heat spread across my skin as his voice sent chills up and down my spine. A sharp tingle started between my legs and quickly spread through my body.

"Again," he repeated.

One last thrust of his hips and my body was pushed over the edge. Every muscle burned and contracted, pleasure flooding through my veins. I opened my mouth to cry out but Rory fastened his over mine, his tongue thrusting, pushing my orgasm even higher as he pulsated inside me.

Completely spent, I collapsed back into the mattress.

Rory lifted his body from mine as he slipped the blindfold off my face.

I blinked several times, unable to open my eyes.

"Are you in there?" Rory whispered.

"Umm hmm," I moaned.

"Tactile," he whispered against my neck.

"Umm hmm."

"T-A-C-T-I-L-E."

Finding the strength to move again, I turned my head toward his voice, blinking my eyes open as I tried to focus on his beautiful face. "Umm hm," I repeated.

"Is that all you can say?"

"Umm hmm." I giggled.

"Let's get you out of these."

"Okay," I sighed, having no idea what he was talking about. I closed my eyes, still lost in the tingling sparks racing through my body.

"Come on." He scooped me up, tucking me into his warm, hard body.

"Where?" I asked. I rotated my wrists and ankles freely. He'd unhooked me.

"Hot tub. Outside." He opened the sliding door.

A cool breeze rushed over my exposed skin, waking me from my lust-filled haze. "But we're naked."

Without saying a word, he gently sunk down into the deliciously warm water.

At that moment, I didn't care whether I was dressed or as bare as the day I was born.

Rory nestled me between his legs, his hard-on resting against my backside.

"Don't worry," he answered my silent worry. "I only want to rub your muscles. I know you're sore. I was pretty relentless with you. I'm sorry." His fingers wrapped around my shoulders, rubbing deep into my muscles. His touch was heaven.

I sunk back into his chest with a heavy sigh.

The sun was setting, blanketing the sky with a kaleidoscope of blues, magentas, and oranges, their reflective colors dancing across the ocean. I'd never felt more peaceful in all my life. I belonged here.

"Live with me," he whispered.

"What?" I twisted around to face him, afraid he'd heard my thoughts.

"After X Games. Move here. Live with me."

"Are you serious?" I searched his eyes but found no trace of humor.

"Very serious. California's beautiful. You'll love it here."

"Rory, I can't just up and leave my life."

"Why not?"

"You're on the road like forty weeks out of the year."

"You can come with me." His trance-like smile was drawing me in. "We'll come back here when we're not traveling."

"What about my job?"

"Quit."

"You can't be serious."

"I'm very serious," he said. "I love you." His blue eyes shined in the light of the last rays of the setting sun. "I want you with me. Always."

Always? What was he talking about? Was he asking me to marry him?

"Rory, we've known each other like, a hot minute?"

"So?"

I turned around, pressing my back against his chest, drawing in a deep breath, willing away my pending anxiety attack. We hadn't even gone public yet and he already wanted me to move in with him.

"Let's enjoy tonight, okay?" I whispered, letting my head fall back on his shoulder.

He kissed my temple as he continued to massage my shoulders and wrists. "I love you, Hindley," he whispered in my ear.

I trembled when his breath danced across my skin. "I know," I replied. "Just give me tonight, okay?"

His strong hands moved down to my hips, twisting me around to face him.

Instinctively I wrapped my legs around his waist, straddling his body, shackling his shoulders with my arms. This was my favorite place to be in the world, wrapped around my Skater Boy.

His eyes were a sky-blue tonight, brighter and livelier than I'd ever seen them before. He was happy, that was clear.

"You're mine, Hindley."

"I am." I pulled myself toward him so our bodies were molded into one. I felt his heartbeat strum against my chest.

Axel's vicious face popped into my mind again. He held the key that could possibly destroy my life with Rory before it even began. I couldn't let that happen. I squeezed Rory's neck even tighter. All I wanted more than anything in the world was to be with Rory, and there was nothing I wouldn't do to make that happen.

"I *am* yours," I repeated in his ear, more for myself than for him. "Always."

CHAPTER 22

HINDLEY

I SCOOTED CLOSER to Rory on the couch, snuggling into his body. "This is nice."

"What?" he asked, draping his arm over my shoulder, tightening his hold on me.

"Sitting here, on the couch, watching a movie with you. It seems so, regular."

"You like regular?" he asked with a hint of sarcasm.

"Sometimes, I love regular." I knelt up and placed a kiss on his cheek. "Sometimes."

His eyes shined with playfulness. I could get lost in him.

I wanted to live with Rory more than anything in the world, but too much was up in the air right now to commit to him. I sat back down and snuggled into his huge frame, laying my head on his chest and inhaling his delicious scent. Times like these were rare for us.

The ding from the microwave broke our moment. "Popcorn's ready." He set me aside and stood.

"Awe," I whimpered.

"I'll be right back, babe." He reached down and took my face in his hands and gave me a light peck on the lips. It was a small gesture but it meant so much. "What do you want to drink?" he yelled from the kitchen.

"What do you have?" I looked over the sofa, admiring his muscular body. He was wearing the same pajama pants from earlier, but now he had a snug T-shirt covering his torso. I smiled at what lay underneath. I wasn't sure I'd make it through the entire movie without trying to lick every inch of him again.

"Lemonade, tea, milk, or water?"

"Chocolate milk?" I snickered, raising my eyebrows.

He straightened up from the refrigerator and turned to look at me. "That could be arranged, Miss Hagen."

"Better not." I laughed. "I want to watch the movie. How about lemonade, please?"

"One lemonade, coming right up."

I watched as he gracefully moved around the kitchen, piling the popcorn in a bowl, filling our glasses with ice and mixing the lemonade.

A chiming sound echoed through the room.

"It's my cell." He nodded toward the coffee table. "Who is it?"

I picked up the phone but the number said 'Unknown.' "It doesn't say."

"Answer it, please."

"Okay." He was giving me a lot of trust by letting me handle his cell phone. The thought made me smile. "Hello?" No one answered. "Hello?" I repeated.

"Shelly?" a woman asked.

"Who?"

"Is this Shelly?"

"No. I'm sorry, I think you have the wrong number?"

"Is Rory there?"

Oh, no. Then it hit me like a ton of bricks. What if Shelly was an ex-girlfriend, an ex lover? What if this chick was? Who was she and why was she calling him from an unlisted number? And how the fuck did she even have his number? My stomach cramped and my hands broke out with sweat as the green monster of jealousy spread through my veins. I'd never felt this possessive before in all my life.

"Yes," I said flatly. "Hold on please." I stood to take the phone to

Rory, but he was already standing in front of me. He stared at me in confusion.

I held out the phone toward him. "It's for you."

"Who is it?" he asked, setting the bowl and drinks down on the coffee table.

"I don't know, she didn't say."

His fingers folded around mine as he covered the mouthpiece. "Are you all right?"

"She asked if I was Shelly."

His face went ashen. His crystal blue eyes grew darker with every passing second and his fingers twitched as he slowly took the phone from my hand. Turning his back on me, he stalked away from the sofa.

"How the fuck did you get this number?" he seethed.

I shivered as I realized my worst fears were coming true. This was a psycho ex-girlfriend. Maybe he had asked this woman to live with him too. No, he wouldn't have talked to her that way if he had. The battling dialogue in my head was making me nauseous.

"I don't give a fuck what's wrong with you," he growled into the phone. "I told you not to ever call me again." His voice grew louder with every syllable.

There was silence as I stared at his back. Every muscle tensed under his shirt as a small trail of sweat rolled down his neck. It was clear he didn't care for whoever it was on the phone.

"No, she's not Shelly, you psycho bitch. Forget you ever knew me and leave me the fuck alone or I swear to God, I'll kill you and that sorry piece of shit you call a husband with my bare hands."

I gasped in shock, dumbfounded by his words. I'd never heard him talk this way to anyone. Ever.

He turned to face me.

I stood in stunned silence at the image of the man standing before me. This wasn't Rory Gregor, and for the first time in his presence, I was afraid of him.

He still held the phone to his face. "You can tell them whatever the fuck you want to, you crazy-ass bitch, but you're still not going to get a fucking dime from me. Don't ever call me again or I *will* kill you." He drew the phone away from his face, glaring at the screen as if whoever was on the phone was visible.

What was happening?

I jumped when he let out a blood-curdling cry and hurled the phone across the room.

I watched in horror as it crashed into the wall, shattering into a million pieces. I cut my eyes back to his. He was possessed, a completely different man, and I was scared shitless.

He stalked past me, sliding the glass door to the balcony open and disappearing into the night.

I stood silently, paralyzed. How had we gone from a fun-loving domestic moment to this in less than two minutes? And who the hell was that on the phone? He'd threatened to kill her, and his tone seemed like he was telling the truth. I truly feared for the woman's safety. This was bad, really bad, worse than what I was going through with Axel.

I wondered what, if anything I should do next. I was familiar enough with Rory now to know I had to let him cool off. It was never wise to push him.

I went to clean up the mess made by the shattered phone. After I'd picked up the larger pieces by hand, I walked to the kitchen and pillaged through the closet, searching for a broom to sweep up the smaller fragments. As I shut the door, my eyes swept over the living room and I saw Rory standing in the doorway leading out to the patio. His face was still void of color, but his expression at least revealed that my Rory had returned, barely.

I knew that look. He was ready to talk.

I set the broom and dustpan down and made my way across the great expanse of the living room, coming to stand in front of him. The cool night air made me shiver.

He took me in his arms, kissing my head and rubbing my back to warm me. "I'm sorry," he whispered into my hair.

I wrapped my arms around his waist and stroked his back, trying to soothe him as he always did me.

"Come on," he said, dragging me inside and closing the door behind us. "You're cold."

He was right, I was cold, but not from the weather. My Rory was back, but not all of him.

"Let's go to bed."

He didn't want to talk and I didn't know what to do. I didn't want to push him, but I had to know what was going on. "Wait." I pulled him back.

He turned to face me. Some of the color was returning to his beautiful face, but his eyes were as dark as the night sky.

I reached up to stroke his face, caressing his cheek with my thumb. "I love you." I lifted up on my toes and placed a light kiss on his lips.

He grabbed my face and pressed his lips into mine with a painful urgency.

I knew what he was doing. It was how he handled difficult situations. Sex. This time was different though. I couldn't let him escape, not like this. I pushed him away with all my strength and broke our embrace.

He stood back and stared at me with a furrowed brow, stunned by my reaction.

"No, Rory."

"What the fuck?"

"I know what you're doing."

"What?"

"You're trying to soothe yourself with sex. Normally, I'm okay with that. But this time is different."

"Why?" he asked.

"Because you became a different person just now. One I don't know. I don't want to go to bed with that man. You need to talk to me and tell me what's going on. I'm not going to force you, but I'm not going to make love with you until you calm down and explain all this."

He was wounded, but I didn't care. This situation was too important and I couldn't let him escape with no justification, not this time.

"Who's Shelly?"

He looked at me as if I'd slapped him across the face, and just like that, dark Rory returned. He was shutting me out.

"Rory," I pleaded, reaching out to rub his arm.

He yanked it back as if I was the most disgusting person on earth.

"Who is she?" I asked again.

"She's none of your fucking business, that's who she is," he shouted at me.

Okay, I could understand. This was really, really painful for him and I'd pushed him too far. This part was my fault. He needed time. I walked around him, making my way up the stairs.

"Where the fuck are you going?"

I glanced back at him. He was a lost little boy trapped in a grown man's body, but unless he asked for help, there was nothing I could do to reach him.

"I'm going to bed. If you want to talk, you know where I am." I made my way painfully and grudgingly up the stairs, hoping he would follow, but not surprised when I looked down over the balcony and saw he was gone.

The slamming of the front door was the last thing I heard as I dragged myself down the long hallway and threw myself across his massive bed, shedding a lifetime of tears for my lost boy.

CHAPTER 23

HINDLEY

I JUMPED WITH A START, my heart racing. Was Rory back? I stretched my arm across the bed, not surprised to find nothing but cool sheets on the other side. He still wasn't home and I was choked with anxiety and fear. I glanced at the clock beside me. It read 1:33 a.m.

I pushed up, but stilled when I noticed the curtains covering the sliding glass door blowing in the moonlight. When my eyes finally adjusted to the darkness, I recoiled, slamming into the headboard when I saw a silhouette standing next to the window. My heartbeat slowed as I realized it wasn't an intruder. It was Rory. I didn't say anything, I let him stand quietly. When he was ready, I knew he'd talk.

His arms were raised above his head, his fingers combing through his thick hair as he leaned quietly against the glass, staring down at the ocean below.

What could possibly have happened that would make him threaten to kill another human being? I wanted to think I knew Rory Gregor, inside and out, but the man I saw on the phone tonight was foreign, like a split personality. Dark Rory scared me. That was an understatement. He petrified me. I let my head fall back against the headboard, lightly sighing, trying to figure out a way to bring back my Skater Boy.

"Shelly was my sister," he said quietly.

Oh, shit. He had a sister?

He turned slowly, but made no move to come closer. His face was barely visible in the soft light of the moon's glow, but it was still breathtakingly beautiful.

I sat as still, afraid any movement may stop him.

"She was two and I was six when my mom married her current husband."

I remained frozen, afraid to interrupt his story. The silence between us dragged on, but eventually he began to speak again.

"Vic had always beaten my mom, but he never messed with me and Shelly. When I turned twelve all that changed. I decided to stand up against him, try to protect my mother. Instead of beating her that night, he beat the fuck out of me, knocking me out cold. It was pretty much the same story every day after that until I turned sixteen and fought back, beating the shit out of him."

Holy hell.

"I don't remember any of it," he continued. "The police said I beat him unconscious. My mom let the cops take me to jail, never once intervening to protect me or tell them I'd only been protecting her and Shelly."

I wanted to run to Rory, grab him and bring him into my embrace, but just like he'd done with me when I told him my story, I had to let him continue on his own.

He stalked toward the bed and sat down. His shoulders slumped and his head rested in his hands.

I couldn't stand his broken state. I crawled over the covers and gently rubbed his back, caressing him from shoulder to shoulder.

"When the cops took me away, I was petrified for Shelly," he said. "I knew without me there, Vic would probably take out his aggressions on her, and it wouldn't be just physical."

My stomach lurched and rolled with nausea at his insinuation. I physically fought against the need to vomit.

He twisted around and dragged me into his arms. "Oh, God, Hindley, I'm so sorry. I didn't mean to upset you or scare you tonight."

I caressed his face, trying to relieve his anxiety like he always did for me. "I'm fine, Rory. Go on. I want to hear the rest of your story." This was probably the first time he'd ever spoken about the horrors of his childhood and it would take time for him to feel safe in my arms.

"The last thing I remember as they shoved me in the back of the cop car was the look on Shelly's face. She was petrified, and I didn't have a way to protect her from the monster that had lived in our house basically her entire life."

He drew in a ragged breath and reclined us both onto the bed, coming to rest against the headboard. He stared out through the large glass wall in front of him, lost in some type of misery that I couldn't take away.

"The judge sentenced me to six months in a juvenile detention center. When I got out four months later, I tried to go back home to check on Shelly but she wasn't there. My mother answered the door, her face a busted and bruised mess."

"Good God," I whispered.

"It was clear that Vic was still abusing her, and I feared he was hurting Shelly as well. She told me Vic would kill me if he found out I was there and that I should leave and never come back. I told her I wasn't leaving without Shelly. I was nearly seventeen and I'd already worked out in my head how I could make a living and take care of her, just the two of us. She told me if I didn't leave, she'd call the cops and have me arrested again for child molestation."

"What?" I shouted. "I'm sorry," I whispered, covering my mouth. Thinking of Rory as a child sex predator was like calling Mother Theresa an ax murderer.

"It's all right."

His half smile gave me a minute of relief, but it didn't last long.

"You see, I always knew Vic was evil from the first time my mom brought him home," he said. "Something inside me told me he was dangerous in more ways than just physical. Shortly after he moved in, I started sleeping in Shelly's room. I was afraid he would try something with her, and I wanted to make sure I was there, just in case."

He raked his hands through his hair. "When I was six and she was two, it seemed innocent. But when I was fourteen and she was ten, it seemed perverted." He grabbed my shoulders. "It wasn't like that, Hindley, I swear. It wasn't like that at all, you have to believe me. I wanted to protect her."

"It's all right, Rory, I believe you. I know you're a protector." I gave him what I hoped was a reassuring smile as I pulled one hand up and gently stroked his cheek, happy to feel him lean in toward my touch.

"My mother found me in Shelly's bed and was scared. Vic convinced her that I was molesting Shelly, even though Shelly and I vehemently denied it. From that moment on, my mother said I couldn't come anywhere near Shelly. I don't like to think about it, but I'm pretty sure that's when Vic started molesting her." His eyes closed and tears slid down his cheeks.

Oh, no.

I wrapped myself around him, body and soul, and held him as his shoulders shook with sobs. Finally, his breathing calmed and I loosened my grip, thankful when he continued.

"When I beat Victor McKinney unconscious, the judge said I was an irredeemable delinquent. But I wasn't, Hindley." His eyes begged me to understand. "I wanted to kill him so he would never hurt Shelly again. I couldn't give a shit less about me or my mother. It was Shelly I was trying to save. Instead, I pushed her right into the arms of the biggest monster she'd ever known."

"Rory, I know you're not a delinquent and you're anything but irredeemable. I love you." I sat up on my knees and kissed his eyes, trying to dry his tears.

He wrapped his arms around my waist and dragged me into an embrace that was so tight it was almost painful.

"Hey," I whispered in his ear. "I'm here, I'm not going anywhere."

He eased his grip on me but still held me close.

I massaged his neck and shoulders, trying to do anything I could to bring back my Skater Boy. We sat together in silence for a long time before he finally spoke again.

"By the time I went pro, Shelly was fourteen and getting into all kinds of trouble in the neighborhood. She was already drinking, and I feared drugging too. I know I should have stayed back and helped her. I was eighteen by then, an adult. I could have done more, but I didn't."

His shoulders slumped.

I wanted to wipe away the guilt of his pain, but he needed to finish his story first.

"After my first big endorsement check cleared, my mother called and wanted money. I wouldn't give her a dime and told her to never call me again. Until tonight, she never had."

Then it hit me. He worked hard to protect others because he hadn't been able to protect his own sister. That had been his mother on the phone. He'd been talking about killing her and his stepfather.

"So that was your mother on the phone tonight?"

He nodded.

"Why do you think she called? Now, I mean, after all this time?"

He shrugged his shoulders but I knew there was more.

"She thought I was Shelly, your sister," I said.

"I think she's lost it, completely gone off the deep end."

"Why? Has Shelly lived with you in the past? Is she here in California?"

His hands shook as he took in a deep breath. "Shelly's dead."

"Oh my God, Rory. I'm so sorry," I whispered in his ear and wrapped my arms around his broad shoulders, tugging him into my body to shield him from the pain that was crushing him. I wanted to ask the usual question. *How? When? Why?* But I knew better. He would tell me in his own time and in his own way.

I slid off his lap and knelt down in front of him, taking off his shoes. "Come on," I said, drawing back the covers. "Let's go to bed. It's late and I know you're tired." I felt like a mother tucking in her small child. In some way I was. He was my lost boy. I lifted the covers on the other side and slid in behind him, holding him gently against my chest. It felt strangely perfect.

Rory's protective nature was born from his need to shield his sister, yet she was the one person who he hadn't been able to save.

My heart ached for him. He wasn't crazy jealous like I'd once thought. Well, maybe a little. But mostly, he didn't want to lose me like he'd lost Shelly. And given my past, I could only assume how much more urgent his need to protect me was now. He didn't want anything or anyone to hurt me. He was going to protect me no matter what the cost.

I finally understood my Skater Boy on a level I never had before.

"Thank you," he whispered.

I didn't have to ask what for, I knew. "You're welcome."

I thought his story was over and was preparing to close my eyes when the mattress dipped as he rolled over to face me. His large calloused hands caressed my face, smoothing out my hair.

"Kara called me at a competition three years ago to tell me the police had found Shelly's body in a flea-bag motel in the Five Points area of Denver, a place known for drugs and prostitution."

"Oh, Rory." I covered my mouth with my hand. What the hell had happened to her?

"The original report said it was a drug overdose, but we never knew for sure if it was accidental or suicide. In my mind, I like to think of her as taking a nap, the way she did when she was little." His shoulders shook again with quiet sobs. "I should have been there, to protect her," he whispered through his tears. "Instead, I left her there all alone, with that monster."

"Oh, Rory, you did what you could." I tried to draw him in closer, but his broad shoulders made it nearly impossible.

As I lay quietly in the dark, his enormous body wrapped in my arms, my mind did the math. Three years ago was the exact time Rory went off the deep end and hit rock bottom, losing all his endorsements and falling in the national rankings. Shelly's death had been his catalyst for destruction.

Shit. He wasn't the bad boy everyone thought he was. He was the lost boy that society had overlooked.

An overwhelming need to shield him from all the pain he'd endured in life washed over me. No one had ever protected *him*. Until now. He was *my* Skater Boy and I would do everything in my power to make him feel safe.

CHAPTER 24

HINDLEY

"Hey, Hindley, how's it going?" Matt's voice rang through my phone.

I sat behind my desk at work, twisting the phone cord in my fingers, glad he couldn't see me. "Good, Matt, how are you?"

"I'm doing well. Hey, I wanted to apologize again for my actions the last time we were together."

"Please, don't worry about it. I did warn you about the margaritas though." I laughed.

He joined in.

I felt the tension between us ease.

"Yes, you did."

We were reaching a new phase in our relationship, one of platonic friendship. I could hear it in his voice.

"I wanted to let you know the commercial's almost done. I've seen a rough cut and it looks awesome."

"Oh, that's great. I can't wait to see it."

"Rory is amazing."

Yes, he is.

I'd left California two days ago and I was still reeling from the revelation of Rory's story about his childhood and his sister, Shelly. I was committed now more than ever to protect Rory, no matter the cost. There was absolutely no way I could let his secret get out. He'd endured too much. For once in his life, someone was going to protect *him*.

"Hey, listen, Matt, I need a favor."

"Anything."

"I'm trying to get a commercial deal for Axel Pretorius."

"With Sonora Water?"

The doubt in his voice didn't surprise me. "With anyone."

"You haven't found anyone yet?"

"No. And I'm pretty desperate." I fell back in my chair with a sigh.

"Why?"

"His team is hell bent on getting a commercial to air during the X Games."

"That's a little over three weeks away. You couldn't even get the films into editing in that amount of time."

"I know. Tell me I'm not totally screwed?" My voice resounded with the desperation I felt.

"Okay, I won't tell you. But you know you are, right?"

I nodded.

"I can talk to the guys in marketing, if you want me to," he said.

"Really? That would be awesome. You'd do that for me?"

"Of course I would, Hindley."

There was an awkward pause and I feared he'd say that he'd do *anything* for me, but thankfully he said nothing.

"How's Rory?" he asked.

How's Rory? He'd been through the wringer, had a shit childhood, and a pretty fucked up adulthood too. But if I had anything to do with it, the rest of his life would be much happier.

"He's good." Or at least I planned to make him feel good.

"When are you getting into Miami?" Matt's words broke through my thoughts.

"Luis and I will fly in Friday. Our meeting with Humberto is scheduled for Saturday after the skating tournament. Are you still good with that?"

I'd approached Matt with the idea of signing Humberto Sullivan as a possible spokesperson for Sonora Water as well. Matt wanted to meet Humberto in person so I figured why not get them together while we were in Miami for Rory's skateboard tournament?

"Saturday evening sounds good. Do you have a place already picked out?" he asked.

"There's an amazing Cuban restaurant in the hotel we're staying at. Have you ever eaten Cuban food?"

"Nope, can't say that I have. Don't see a lot of Cubans where I'm from," he teased.

I laughed out loud and choked on my drink. "I almost spit water all over my keyboard."

"I hope that's Sonora Water you're spitting out." He chuckled.

Actually, it was. "Of course it is. The entire fridge in my house and the law firm is stocked with it, thanks to my good friends in your PR department."

We both laughed.

"So, I'll call you on Saturday and let you know what time, okay?" I said.

"Actually, I'm coming in Friday evening. I want to see our boy in action."

Our boy. Thoughts of my conversation with Rory before we left California raced through my mind. Somewhere in the midst of our sexcapades over the weekend, I'd agreed to move in with him after the X Games.

"Rory's the new face of Sonora Water and I'm hoping he'll get tagged in a ton of photos while displaying our logo," Matt said, interrupting my thoughts of Rory.

"I can promise you he will."

"I'll see ya in Miami, Hindley."

"Okay, I'll see you then. And let me know about Axel, okay?"

"Sure thing."

"Thanks, Matt."

"Anytime. Bye, Hindley."

"Bye, Matt."

I put the phone back in its cradle, feeling as hopeless and as desperate as I did when Axel first gave me his ultimatum. Commercial or confession? I prayed Matt would be able to pull a miracle out of his ass and get me a deal before my perfect future with Rory came crashing down.

CHAPTER 25

RORY

My hands were unsteady, my tricks were shit, and I was wringing wet with sweat. The heat in Miami was brutal this time of year. Unfortunately, this event was outdoors so there was no escaping the ruthless humidity that invaded every nook and cranny of the city. I was on edge and I had no idea why.

That was a lie.

The call from my mother had rattled my cage. Not only had she wanted money—again, this time she threatened to go to the police with charges that were completely absurd. She threatened to tell the authorities that not only had I molested my own sister, but I'd introduced her to drugs at the young age of twelve. It was classic Marion Gregor, blaming other people for the shit decisions she'd made in her life.

Just when I thought I'd put that part of my life to rest, in came my mother, threatening to fuck up the one good thing I had going in my life.

Hindley Hagen.

I'd been half-skating and half-searching for her the past hour, worried sick.

I hadn't talked to her since yesterday morning, which was unusual for us. I'd texted her several times too but I knew she had a late night at the office, preparing for this weekend's trip.

God, I hoped our lack of communication didn't have anything to do with Axel, but my mind told me it did. He was her job now. Fuck, that tore me up. Almost as much as thinking about my sister.

Images of Shelly had haunted my dreams for days.

In all this time since I'd left Colorado, I'd never forgotten one single detail of my sister—her golden blonde ringlets that bounced every time she moved. Those enormous green eyes that lit up anytime she smiled. Her petite frame that could hide in my shadow. I smiled as I remembered the way she would throw her hair back behind her shoulders when she laughed.

Her laugh.

God, I missed her laughter more than anything, that infectious sound that you couldn't help but join in.

I'd forgotten how much I loved her, how much I missed everything about her. Every time I heard Hindley laugh, it reminded me of Shelly's. I adored them both, but for very different reasons.

I'd tried to protect Shelly as best as I could growing up. I'd been naive to think Victor had started his molestation of my little sister only after I was thrown in jail though.

If I let myself think about it, which I rarely did, I was sure his attacks had started much earlier than that. I hadn't been able to stop him, hadn't been able to do a damn thing about it. That realization was what I'd tried to block out for years through drinking and drugging.

I knew Shelly had turned to drugs as an escape from her fucked up home life like I had. Eventually, it had turned into an addiction at a very young age.

My friends who kept up with her after I left home would give me updates on her from time to time. None of them had been able to stop her. Somedays I would watch her from a distance until I turned pro and started traveling. Every time I returned to Denver, I would try to find her but never did.

My intent had always been to make it big in the skateboarding world, sock away a few bucks, then go back and save her. By the time I had enough money to support her, it was too late. My mother blocked me from seeing her and convinced Shelly I had been the one to molest her.

It broke my heart to know she wanted nothing to do with me. To this day the fact haunted me. My inability to protect my sister was what made me so desperate to guard Hindley so closely. She was the first person I'd let back into my heart since my sister had died. This time I wouldn't let anything happen to her.

It wasn't jealousy that drove me—well, not completely. I was afraid. Afraid something would happen to Hindley, afraid I wouldn't be able to protect her, afraid I would lose her like I'd lost Shelly.

Trying to tamp down my dark thoughts, I studied the course. I always mapped out my routine for hours before a competition but it was useless at this point. My head was fried. I tucked my skateboard inside my bag and grabbed a cab. I would go back to the hotel and take a cold shower.

With the X Games only three weeks away, I had to shake off this feeling and get my head in the game. Something inside me felt off though and I wasn't entirely sure I could blame it on my mother. This weekend would be huge for me but not necessarily in the way I wanted. A sinking feeling sat in my gut like a hot boulder.

I returned to the hotel and rode the elevator up to my room. Opening the door, I tossed my bag onto the floor before pulling out my suitcase. I grabbed the journal I'd packed, opening to the page of my last entry.

I ran my fingers over words covering the page.

Shelly

Shelly

Shelly

Everything about her had been pure and good. Until Victor McKinney had entered our world, taking away her innocence and then eventually her life.

A knock on the door brought me back. My heart raced at the thought of seeing Hindley. Just the anticipation of seeing her again calmed my frazzled nerves.

I flung open the door, thinking how amazing it would be to have Hindley join me in the shower.

"Hey, Rory."

I studied the man in front of me who obviously was not my Drunk Girl.

"Luis?" I glanced around the hallway. "What are you doing here?"

"Did I catch you at a bad time?"

Yes, I wanted to say.

"No, come on in." I opened the door further and ushered him in.

"Expecting someone else?" He laughed.

I ignored him. Denial was the only option I had.

He sprawled out on the sofa, his legs extended beneath the coffee table.

Luis Marquez was a good man. I'd sensed it the first time I'd met him at the law firm when I first signed with Hindley and her team. He'd had a strong handshake and always looked me square in the eye. Even though he was an attorney, he never looked down on me or was condescending like Michael had been a time or two.

Jack had informed the firm a week ago that if I couldn't have Hindley, then I only wanted to deal with Luis, no more Michael. So far, they'd conceded to my wishes.

"So, what's up?" I asked, dropping into the chair next to him.

"Ah, *nada*, just wanted to stop by and touch base with my favorite client."

The man was handsome, suave and sophisticated, but strangely enough I never felt intimidated. He felt like an old friend, someone I could talk to openly.

Hindley told me he was aware of our relationship, and for the most part, he seemed cool. She felt comfortable with Luis, safe, and that always eased my mind.

"So I'm your favorite client." I chuckled.

"Actually, you're my only client, but I won't tell if you won't."

"I'm more of a babysitting project than a client," I said.

"Whatever it is, I'm glad I'm here. Miami feels like home."

"Because of the Latino culture?"

"No, because of the heat. We didn't have air conditioning when I grew up."

We both laughed. Luis could always lighten the mood.

"Matt from Sonora Water is going to be here for the competition," he said. "I've hired a photographer to take some photos then we'll push them through some of the top sports mags to get them published before the X Games. You need the exposure. Word got out about your hand and some people in the social media world aren't so convinced you slammed it in a door."

"Whatever," I said. "I don't give a shit what people think."

"Well, you better start giving a shit because the less the public likes you, the less sponsors like you."

"Fuck," I grumbled. Luis was right but I didn't like to admit it.

"Skating for yourself costs money. These swanky hotel rooms don't come for free, you know." He waved his hand around the large living area.

"Fine. I'll be squeaky clean from here on out. Wouldn't want you staying at a discount chain of motels."

Luis rubbed his nails on his shirt. "Please, like that's ever going to happen."

"So, where's Hindley?" I asked, trying to steady my voice.

"She's at the Ravens' football camp on the other side of town."

"That's right. I forgot."

"Don't worry. She should be here soon."

Not soon enough, I wanted to say. I pushed up from the chair and paced the large room.

"What's going on with you, man?"

I stopped and stared down at him. "What do you mean?"

"You look like a rooster strutting around the hen house."

"What?" I laughed. "Is that some Mexican metaphor bullshit?"

"First of all, I'm from Brazil, not Mexico so that's enough of a reason right there to beat the shit out of you."

I chuckled, knowing that he very well could.

"And second, no. My boyfriend's mother, who's whiter than a KKK rally, introduced me to the saying many years ago when I couldn't make up my mind if I was good enough for him or not."

I stopped dead in my tracks. "Good enough for who?"

"It's whom." He smiled. "Good enough for Teddy, my partner."

I remembered Hindley telling me about Luis and his not-so-stellar past. He'd been a player like me, only with dudes. I tried not to dwell on that image. I mean, I wasn't a homophobe or anything, but still, his story sounded eerily similar to Hindley's and mine.

After years of partying and drugging, Luis had found someone worth changing for. Even though he'd treated his boyfriend like shit in the beginning, apparently Teddy kept coming back and eventually helped Luis deal with his past. That's what Hindley did for me.

I was a nervous wreck because I hadn't seen her. She was my rock, my anchor, and I felt like I was floating out into the open seas without her.

"You deserve her, Rory."

"Who?"

"You know who, dumbass."

I turned in time to catch him rolling his eyes at me.

"She's come alive since she met you," he said, "like I did when I met Teddy. I admit I discouraged her at first."

I glared at him. "Why?"

"Don't get pissy, man. It's not for the reason you think. You're totally worthy of a woman like Hindley. I don't want to see her get hurt, professionally or emotionally."

Luis was right. I had the potential to harm her in both capacities, and the thought sent shivers down my spine.

"Relax, Rory, everything will be fine. She'll be here."

As if on cue, a light knock came from the door.

I nearly tripped over my own feet to answer as quickly as possible. I flung open the door and saw Hindley standing before me, her hair a gorgeous mess from the humidity outside, her cheeks stained red from the sun. Our eyes locked and my breath caught in my throat. She was captivating. And mine.

"Well, I'll be shoving off." Luis pushed by me.

I barely noticed. My eyes were glued to the goddess in front of me.

"See ya in a few, doll face." He bent over and kissed Hindley's cheek.

"Okay," she said, her eyes never leaving mine.

"You two have it bad." I heard Luis mumble just before I pulled Hindley into the room.

My mouth was on hers like a starving man. I had to taste every inch of her.

"Rory," she moaned. "I'm a sweaty mess."

I carried her into the bedroom and tossed her on the bed, tearing off her shoes and skirt within seconds.

"Rory." She laughed, trying to cover herself.

I smiled when I saw Hello Kitty staring up at me. "For me?" I asked.

"Always for you," she whispered.

I crawled on top of her and captured her mouth, claiming every part of her as mine. This was what I needed. She was what I needed, a soothing balm for the anger that raged inside of me, a sedative to calm the horrible memories flooding my mind.

"Come back to me," she whispered against my lips.

I smiled at the words coming back to haunt me. "Sorry." I pulled back and stared into her dark brown eyes. They reminded me of the hot fudge syrup I'd drizzled all over her body only a few days before. How had my mindset changed in such a short amount of time?

She pushed me over so we were both lying on our sides. "What's going on, baby?" she asked.

Her concern baffled me. I still didn't feel worthy. I wanted to shield her from anything bad in this world, especially if it came from me.

"Hey." She tapped my temple. "Right here, with me." She wasn't allowing me to leave her, mentally. "Is it your mom?"

I rolled onto my back, letting out a deep sigh as I cradled the back of my neck with both hands.

She rolled over so that her body was molded to my side as she gently stroked my hair with her hand. She didn't ask more questions, instead she littered my face and neck with soft kisses.

Yes, this was what I needed. Hindley Hagen. And I would be damned if I screwed it up.

I rolled her onto her back as my hand grabbed the bottom of her shirt and slowly dragged it off. Smooth creamy skin lay underneath.

She moaned as my mouth moved over her body, licking, sucking, caressing her. I tucked one finger into her bra and slid it down, exposing her breast for my banquet. My mouth sucked in one nipple and she bucked against me.

"Rory," she cried.

I raised up, afraid I might have moved too fast. "What is it, baby?"

"I want you," she moaned.

I smiled. "I want you too."

Her hands made quick work of my shorts, dragging them down my legs with ease. Her small hand slipped inside my underwear, squeezing and stroking.

"Jesus, Hindley, you're going to end this before we even start."

She giggled and lifted up, kissing my neck. "Sorry."

"No, you're not."

"Get naked," she said, sitting up and removing her bra.

Who was I to argue? I stripped off the rest of my clothes and made my way back to the bed but stopped just before I reached her.

"What?" she asked.

"We need a condom."

"I have an IUD."

"A what? Is that contagious?"

She swatted at my chest. "Not an STD, silly."

Well, thank God.

"It's a contraceptive they put inside of me. I don't need condoms anymore."

"Are you sure?" Contraception was not something either one of us took lightly. Although I wanted to spend my life with Hindley, the thought of kids had never entered my mind. I was too fucked up to ever be anyone's father, and although we'd never talked about it, I hoped she would understand that one day.

"Yes, I'm sure. It's safer than the pill and just as effective." A slow smile spread across her face as she slid her panties off and tossed them at me. "Care to join me, Mr. Gregor?" She patted the space beside her on the bed.

Fuck yeah, I did.

Without another thought I blanketed her body, spreading her thighs and sliding inside. She was more than ready for me. The feeling of being skin on skin was unreal, like nothing I'd ever experienced in my life.

I'd been using condoms since the first time I'd had sex, never once going unprotected. I didn't trust a woman with contraception, especially once I'd started making money. Having a kid was a sure-fire way for them to make off with my cash.

But now here I was, driving into this beautiful woman who trusted me, believed in me, and sacrificed everything for me. Nothing had ever felt more right in my life.

I wanted the moment to last forever and tried to stave off my release but the sensations were too much.

"Hindley," I moaned.

"It's okay, baby. I'm here for you. Just let go."

Her raspy voice was my undoing, and with no trace of thought or reason, I spilled inside of her, letting every emotion I had pour into this woman I adored.

She held me tight, taking in everything—all my self-doubt, my worry, my guilt. She was my safe place, the person who accepted my past and loved me in spite of it. Her arms and legs were wound around me, reassuring me that she was my anchor.

My heart hammered, nearly beating out of my chest, my body pulsating with desire. My need for her overwhelmed me.

I wanted her.

I cherished her.

I loved her.

Clutching her body to mine, I vowed to never to let her go no matter the cost. I couldn't exist without Hindley Hagen. I *didn't* exist without her.

CHAPTER 26

RORY

"How'd your meeting with the quarterback go?" I asked Hindley as we waited in the lobby for Luis.

She rolled her eyes, knowing I couldn't give a shit less. I hated anything or anybody that took her away from me. And right now, Humberto Sullivan was at the top of my list.

I'd done my own research on him. I needed to know who Hindley was dealing with and I refused to let her walk into situations unarmed anymore.

By all accounts, Humberto seemed like a decent guy. His mom was from Guadalajara and had married a man from the Bronx. He'd been a star athlete since high school. He'd never gotten in trouble that I'd found, and had earned a full-ride scholarship to Notre Dame, graduating with honors. He was talented and smart as shit.

The guy was a poster child for the All-American dickhead. Not only that, but he had a clean reputation, was a stand-up guy in the community, doing volunteer work out the ass. According to all the Internet websites, he was one of the most sought-after bachelors in all of sports. And as if that weren't bad enough, the dickhead was insanely good looking too.

At the ripe age of twenty-three, it seemed Humberto Sullivan was ready and poised to make it big. The only reason the Ravens didn't have him at number one was due to a small thumb injury from the previous season.

I glanced down at my hand, which still hurt like a motherfucker. In the skating world, we didn't have a string of guys to back us up. If you were injured, it didn't matter, you played the game regardless.

Old feelings of insecurity and self-loathing flooded my mind as I convinced myself once again why Humberto was a much better match for Hindley than me.

"Do you really want to know?" Hindley asked, breaking my thoughts.

"Know what?"

"You just asked me how my meeting with Humberto went."

"Oh, yeah. Actually, I do."

She spent the next five minutes rambling football stats that, to any other guy, probably would have had his dick rock hard. But for me, it was proof that she was spending her time with another man, a talented man who could offer her a lot more than me.

"Hey." She nudged me in the ribs. "Come back to me."

I stared at her, unsure of how to stop these feelings that always seemed to well up inside.

"If you didn't want to know about my meeting then why did you ask?"

She was right. "I'm sorry. I was just…" Being a dick.

"I love you, Rory."

I nodded. "I know. And I'm sorry about earlier."

"What are you talking about?"

"Upstairs." I nodded toward the elevators. "I didn't exactly um…" How could I politely say that I'd left her hanging sexually? It wasn't like me to get my rocks off without taking a girl with me. Especially Hindley. But she'd felt so fuckin' good, I couldn't last.

"It's all right." She smirked, holding up a plastic card in her hand. "I fully intend for you to make it up to me later tonight."

"Is that my room key?"

"Umm hmm." She stared me up and down and licked her lips.

Well, fuck me. I was rock hard and ready for round two. "I may take you up there right now if you keep licking those pretty little lips like that."

She giggled.

My one-eyed soldier was back on active duty, ready to do battle on the front lines.

One corner of her mouth tipped up in a devious smile. "Promise?"

My Drunk Girl was getting braver, and I loved it. "How the hell did you get my key?"

"Oh, I have my ways, Mr. Gregor, don't you worry about that." She winked.

Indeed, she did have ways, and I loved them all.

Her gaze cut to the front of the lobby. "Shit." All sense of playfulness was suddenly gone.

I instinctively slipped an arm around her waist and pulled her close. "What is it?"

She pushed me away and steeled her features.

A sinking feeling hit me in the pit of my stomach. My gaze followed hers.

"It's my mother," she said. "And Geneva. Great."

"What? Are you serious?" I glanced around the area but couldn't see them.

She pointed toward the terrace at the front of the hotel.

Sure enough, Caroline Hagen-Barton and Geneva Barton-Whatever-the-Fuck-Her-New-Name-Was-Now were traipsing through the sliding glass doors. Caroline pushed her huge shades to her head as she searched the lobby, probably looking for Hindley.

"What the hell are they doing here?" Hindley whispered, more to herself than me.

"You didn't know they were coming?"

She shook her head. "Hell, no. They're the last two people on earth I need here right now."

Something was going on, I could hear it in her voice. There was something she wasn't telling me, and my gut said I needed to find out. Soon.

"Hindley," her mom exclaimed from the middle of the lobby. Caroline's face lit up with genuine excitement when she saw her daughter.

I wondered what it must feel like to have a mom who wanted you, who would protect you, at all costs. I knew there was more going on between Hindley and her mom than she had shared, a tension that lurked underneath. But it was evident that Caroline loved her daughter immensely, and for me, that was enough.

Geneva's face puckered when she saw Hindley and her mother embrace. She looked like she'd swallowed a bug. I would have gladly provided one. Slowly she turned and noticed me. She perused the length of me like she was buying a side of beef. When her gaze finally met mine, her expression morphed into that of a sexual predator. On some women the look was hot, but on Geneva it made her look desperate, and made me want to vomit. There was no denying the fact this chick wanted me.

I'd never slept with or gone after a married woman. Even if Geneva had been single, she never would have turned my head. She was cold, callous, and manipulative. She reminded me of my mother, a self-centered bitch, and there was no bigger turn-off in the world to me.

"Hey, Geneva," Hindley said.

Geneva never turned her attention away from me.

"Geneva," Caroline yelled.

Geneva jumped, and snapped her gaze to Hindley's mother. "What?"

"Say hello to Hindley."

Her eyes cut to Hindley. "Hey," she said before turning her attention back to me.

I was pretty sure she fucking me in her mind. The thought had me nearly falling to the floor on all-fours and puking my guts up. I couldn't think of anything more disgusting than fucking that bitch.

I stepped toward Caroline and kissed her cheek. "It's good to see you, Mrs. Barton."

"Oh, please, darling," she patted my shoulder, "call me Caroline."

I was happy to see that the predatory smile she'd worn when I'd first met her at Geneva's wedding was now replaced with one of motherly affection. Her smile grew wider and she winked like she knew a secret.

Shit. She knew Hindley and I were involved, there was no doubt. If she did, she seemed genuinely happy about it, which surprised me.

"What are you guys doing here?" Hindley asked with a tone of annoyance. She stared between the two nervously like she was hiding something.

"Well," Caroline said, "I've always wanted to come to Miami. They have the most wonderful shops, and a beautiful beach that my friend, Barb says is to die for."

"And she wanted to come check you out," Geneva added, looking me up and down.

"I've heard so many great things about your skating, Rory." Caroline smiled brightly. "I hope you don't mind, but I thought it would be a perfect opportunity to see the sights, watch you skate, and support my daughter." She raised her brows and stared at Hindley, tilting her head.

Hindley remained silent. Something was definitely going on with her.

"I think that's a great plan, Caroline," I said.

Caroline's gaze remained on Hindley.

"Isn't that great, Hindley?" I bumped her arm.

"Oh, um, yes. Great, that's fine, Mom. It's just that, I'm super busy this weekend. I'm taking care of several clients and I probably won't have time to entertain you."

"That's all right, darling."

"In fact," Hindley looked down at her watch, "Rory and I have a team meeting in thirty minutes over at the venue."

We did?

Hindley stared up at me, her eyes pleading.

"Oh, um, yes, we do," I said. "It was good to see you both. Maybe we could have dinner tonight or tomorrow after the competition."

Hindley's eyes went wide.

Oh, shit, I'd said the wrong thing.

"Perhaps tomorrow," Caroline said. "We can celebrate your win."

"You're very confident." I laughed.

"From what I've heard from my daughter and others, you're also very talented," Caroline said.

Caroline's reassuring words were foreign coming from a mother figure. She sounded so confident, as if she really thought I could win just by her faith in me.

"Thank you, Caroline. I appreciate the vote of confidence."

She winked. "Of course, sweetheart. I know you'll do well. It will be a celebratory dinner tomorrow."

"I can't do dinner tomorrow," Hindley said.

"Why not?" I asked, sounding more defensive than I'd meant.

"I have a business meeting tomorrow night with a client."

"With who?"

Hindley glared at me.

Shit, I was being all caveman again. I couldn't help it, I worried about her when she wasn't with me, which seemed like a lot lately.

"Well, don't worry, darling," Caroline said. "We'll get together sometime this weekend."

Hindley grabbed my arm. "We've got to go, Mom."

"We'll get together, Caroline, I promise," I called over my shoulder as Hindley dragged me to the exit.

Caroline smiled, her expression just as beautiful as her daughter's.

Once we made it well past the front entrance and on to the sidewalk, Hindley turned on me, her glare lethal. "What the hell was that?"

"What was what?"

"Promising my mom we'd get together with them," she said through clenched teeth. "Did you forget what happened the last time we had dinner with my family?"

"She's different, Hin."

"Don't call me Hin," she barked.

"What the fuck is wrong with you, *Hindley*?" I hissed.

She cut her eyes around the block as if we were being followed then traipsed down the street without answering.

I yanked her around to face me. "Why didn't you tell me about dinner tomorrow night?"

"It's no big deal, Rory."

"It's a big deal to me."

"Well, it shouldn't be. It's my fucking job." She yanked her arm from my hand and walked away.

I swallowed down my natural response to retaliate with some flippant comment. Something was wrong. I'd never seen this side of her and my heart raced with fear and dread.

I caught up with her in a few strides but didn't touch her. "It's not jealousy, Hindley. When you don't talk to me I get scared. When I don't know what's going on in your life I worry about you. I can't help it, it's who I am."

She stared at me as if I were a stranger and we hadn't just been in bed together an hour ago.

"What's going on with you?" I asked.

"What's going on with me?" She laughed sarcastically. "What's going on with *you*? You've been on edge ever since your mom called, and you've been taking out all your shit on me."

I stopped to think about what she was saying. Was it true? Had I been dumping my emotional baggage at Hindley's doorstep? It sounded like something I'd do.

"Look, I'm sorry, Hindley, I didn't realize what I was doing. Is that why you haven't called lately?"

"What are you talking about?"

"We haven't talked much since you left California."

"I've been busy, Rory."

I told myself she was just stressed, overworked, and I was only making things worse by pushing her.

"I'm sorry," I said.

"For what?"

"For taking my frustrations out on you. For being defensive. For inviting your mom to dinner when obviously, it's the last thing you want. For getting crazy jealous back there when I found out you had a business meeting."

Her phone rang. Ignoring my comment, she stepped away and answered. "Hey, what's up?" There was a short pause. "No, I'm not busy, what's going on?"

Not busy? Me apologizing for treating her like shit was considered "not busy"? What the hell was going on with her?

Her face went slack and her shoulders slumped. "All right," she sighed. "You're sure?"

This obviously wasn't good news.

"Why?" she asked. Still more silence. "I can't make that decision, you know that."

Her eyes cut to mine and she bit her lip. A sickening feeling hit me hard in the gut.

"Hold on just a second," she said, placing her hand over the phone. "I have to take this call, it's important. I'll see you later, okay?" Before I could answer, she turned and walked away from me.

I grabbed her arm. "Who's on the phone?"

"It's work."

"The firm?"

She didn't answer.

"Hindley, who is it?"

She tried to pull away, but I held her tighter. Something was definitely wrong and I needed to know what it was. Now.

"Rory, let go of me," she seethed.

We stood, glaring at each other but I held firm. I was not going to lose her. Not like this.

She put the phone back to her ear. "I'll call you right back, I don't have a good signal." She ended the call and yanked her arm out of my grasp. "What the fuck are you doing?"

"What the fuck am *I* doing?" I stepped closer, my eyes boring into hers as I chuckled sarcastically under my breath. "What the fuck are *you* doing? Or should I say, *who* the fuck are you doing?"

As soon as the words came out of my mouth, I knew they were a mistake. I hadn't physically hit her, but my words had slapped her harder than my hand ever could. What the fuck was wrong with me?

"I'm sorry, Hindley, I didn't mean it." I lunged toward her.

She backed away, her lips pursed, eyes narrowed as she glared at me. "I don't even know who you are right now." Her words were laser sharp and cut straight through to my heart.

Since my mother's phone call, I'd felt like a completely different person and I didn't know how to get my old self back. But I knew the only way I could was with her help.

"Please, Hindley." I stepped toward her but she backed up. "I'm sorry, it's just..." I didn't know what to say, mainly because I didn't know what the fuck was wrong with me.

"Look, it's hot," she said, "we're both tired. Why don't we get some rest and talk later?"

Her suggestion sounded more than ideal. It sounded perfect. Me, wrapped around Hindley's body, lost in in the safety only she could provide, sounded like just what the doctor ordered before my tournament.

"Your room or mine?" I asked.

"For what?"

"Our nap." I smiled.

"I didn't mean us together, Rory."

Was she serious?

"I have a lot of work to do," she said. "I meant that maybe we should give this a rest." She waved her hand back and forth between us.

Give this a rest?

Oh, fuck. This couldn't be happening, not now. Was she leaving me? The city began to spin around me and I couldn't feel my limbs. I drew in a steadying breath to calm my racing heart. "Are you sure everything's okay, Hindley?" I asked. My voice shook, I was so scared.

"No, it's not okay," she said, seemingly unfazed by my emotional breakdown. "I have a shit ton of work to do, my mother and my wicked stepsister are here poking their noses in where they don't belong. And now you're being all..." She waved her hand in the air, circling it above her head.

"All what?" I asked, my voice barely above a whisper. What had I done? Had I pushed her too far? How could I make it right?

Her gaze darted up and down the street like she was on the lookout for someone, or something.

My eyes followed hers, suddenly feeling paranoid. "What is it?"

"Not here," she said. "We can't do this in public."

"Do what? We're just talking."

"Are we?" She arched a single brow. "It feels more like fighting."

"Hindley, we don't exist in a bubble. If we're going to be together, we're going to fight sometimes."

"Look, I don't have time for this right now." She wiped the sweat from her forehead. Perspiration I wasn't altogether sure was from the heat and humidity. "I have to make some calls and pull some stuff together," she said.

"For Axel?"

"Yes, for Axel," she nearly screamed. "Goddammit, Rory, you're not the only fucking athlete on the face of the earth."

And there it was. I was getting nowhere with her. Hindley was going through something, and it was more than just me taking out my past aggressions on her.

"I'll let you get back to it then." I turned and walked back toward the hotel.

"Wait!" She grabbed my arm.

I didn't turn to face her but didn't pull from her grasp. For the first time since I'd met her, she'd lashed out at me in a way I didn't deserve. I was aware I'd done it to her a million times before, but she was tougher than me. She could take my shit. I wasn't convinced I could take hers.

"It's okay, Hindley," I said, staring down at the sidewalk. "I don't want to stress you out. When you have time, call me and we'll talk." I turned, chancing a look at her, afraid of what I might see.

"I'm sorry," she whispered. "I'm just stressed, and freaked out and tired." She stepped closer. "And missing you."

My heart eased and I was able to take in a breath. She wasn't ending things with me. Thank fuck.

"You know where my room is," I said, "and you have the key. Come by when you're done, okay, baby?" I wanted to reach down and take her in my arms and lay a big, fat, wet kiss on her to remind her how much I fuckin' loved her and who she belonged to, but we were in public and I knew that was forbidden.

I had to become something I had no experience in at all. I had to be selfless. And if that wasn't the funniest thing I'd ever heard. I'd always been the most selfish bastard on earth.

"Go," I said, "make your calls, get caught up. Is there anything I can do to help you?"

She shook her head.

I noticed the dark circles under her eyes and the strain on her face. For the first time since she'd taken me on as a client, I was worried about her. Had she taken on too much in representing me, Axel, and the football dude? Was I putting too much pressure on her by acting like a jealous, overprotective dick? Of course I was.

If I didn't let her go, allow her to process this shit on her own, in her own way, I knew she'd never tell me the truth. This time, I had to leave her alone and let her come to me when she was ready.

My one mission in life was to protect Hindley at all costs. Giving up control was foreign to me, and I wasn't comfortable having to do it. The last time I had, my sister had overdosed.

I squeezed her shoulder, the only sign of affection I could show in such a public place. "Go," I said. "I'll wait for you."

Her eyes lit with relief as tears welled inside.

"Always, Hindley." I released her shoulder and walked toward the hotel, never looking back. My chest ached with the realization that she may never come to me. I may have actually lost her.

The glass doors to the hotel spread open and the cool air hit me in the face. It was a welcome relief to the fear coursing through my body. I wove through the maze of people. I just wanted to get to my room and take a cold shower.

A hand reached out from behind one of the large flowery pots near the elevators. I followed the arm, shocked to find Geneva standing there with a shit eating grin on her face.

"Hey," she said with a sexy rasp. "Want a drink?" She held out a fruity cocktail with an umbrella.

"Uh, no thanks. I don't drink."

Her head lurched back. "You don't?"

"Nope." I yanked my arm from her death grip. "Where's your husband?"

Her face wrinkled like she'd sucked a lemon. "He's working."

"That's too bad." I turned to walk away.

"I was going down to the pool to catch some sun. Want to come?"

I turned to say no and watched as she unlatched her floral wrap, revealing a hot pink, barely-there bikini.

This bitch was bold, I'd give her that.

My eyes traveled up and down her body. She was definitely hot. And I was a man who could appreciate that fact.

A huge smile spread across her face when she realized she'd affected me.

"Look, Geneva, you don't need me to tell you you're gorgeous."

Her grin broadened.

It's your personality that makes you ass-ugly, I wanted to add.

"So join me," she said, all breathy.

"I can't. I have some work to do."

She raised one eyebrow and wrapped her lips around her straw, sucking hard before speaking. "Maybe I could help you."

"Maybe you should call your husband."

Her smile fell, replaced by that resting bitch face.

I turned and stepped inside the elevator, praying she would take the hint and leave me alone. I was still reeling from my conversation with Hindley and needed to decompress.

She stood in the doorway, hand on her hip. "Maybe later?"

"Maybe not."

The doors began to close but she leaned forward, stopping them. "All I heard was maybe." She winked and stepped back, letting the doors close.

Well, shit. The bitch obviously didn't know how to take no for an answer. She'd become yet another problem to add to the growing list of complications in my life.

I punched the button to my floor and raked my hands through my hair. Hindley was pulling away, and she was hiding something. There wasn't a damn thing I could do about it.

Today I'd realized something horrible—I may be a source of her pain and anguish. I had to protect her from myself, and the only way I could do that was to leave her alone.

Losing Hindley *wasn't* an option. But it was out of my control, and that realization scared me the most.

CHAPTER 27

HINDLEY

I FELL ONTO MY BED, my body feeling as heavy as my heart. I needed privacy for this call, and the crowded streets of Miami hadn't afforded me that option.

I pulled my phone from my pocket and pushed the 'Call Back' button, listening as the phone rang.

"Hey, Hindley. Better signal now?"

"I'm sorry about earlier, Matt. It was a bad reception."

Bad reception? God, I was scaring myself with how easily the lies rolled off my tongue.

"So, what's the word on Axel?" I held my breath.

"Not good, I'm afraid."

Shit.

"Sonora is into family values and wholesome images," he said. "Axel isn't the epitome of either of those two things, not with the allegations of sexual abuse in his past."

"I don't mean to be rude, but Rory's past isn't that stellar either."

"Well, that's true. But everyone loves a comeback story," he said. "Rory is the underdog. Everyone roots for the long shot, and the PR guys here at Sonora are counting on that. Plus, Rory's an amazing athlete."

What the hell was I going to do now? Tears burned my eyes and I struggled to keep my voice steady.

"There is one option," he said. "But you probably won't like it."

"What is it?" I asked a little too desperately.

"Well, another reason they don't want to take on Axel is the money. Having two athletes would be pretty pricey."

"But we're meeting to discuss a deal for Humberto tomorrow."

"Yeah, but he's in a different sport. It's a whole different beast with completely different demographics."

"So, what's the other option then?"

"Well, maybe I could talk to the execs about taking on Axel *instead* of Rory."

"What?"

"It's not for sure, and I couldn't guarantee it, but it would be a much easier sell if we only sponsored one of them."

Could I actually ask them to drop Rory?

"It's not something I want to do but you sound desperate," he said. "That's the only reason I'm offering up alternatives."

Could I do that? Could I throw Rory under the bus like that?

No way. I loved Rory. If I took this deal away from him, he'd never forgive me. And I would never forgive myself.

I drew in a heavy breath and sighed. Well, shit. What the hell was I going to do now?

"Hindley?"

"Yeah, I'm here."

"Like I said, I don't know if it's even an option. Sonora really loves Rory and his story. But I can try if you want me to."

"No, don't try. I'd never take anything away from Rory." Even though it may cost much more in the end.

"So, what's going on?" Matt asked. "What's got you so hell bent on representing this punk anyway?"

"Who, Rory?"

"No." He laughed. "Axel."

"Oh, him. Well, my firm kind of pushed him on me. Actually, his team asked for me."

"I can see why."

"Why?"

"Hindley, you're good at what you do. I mean, look at you. You're trying your hardest to secure a deal for your client, even knowing it's virtually impossible at this point."

"Yeah, at the expense of another client."

"There's more going on here than you're telling me," he said. "Do you want to talk about it?"

I bit back the tears. Holding all this in was killing me. "Maybe tomorrow after our meeting."

"Okay. You know I'm here if you need me. Not just professionally. I like you, Hindley. As a friend, I mean. You know I wanted more, but I know you love Rory and I'm okay with that."

"Thanks, Matt. I appreciate it. I'll see you tomorrow for dinner?"

"Yeah, I'll see ya then. Bye."

"Bye."

I tossed the phone on the bed and rolled over onto my stomach. I buried my head in my hands as the tears began to flow. What was I going to do now?

There were only three weeks left before the X Games. Even if, beyond some miracle, I was able to secure a deal for Axel, there would be no time to film a commercial and get it approved through all the channels in time for it to air.

I hit the mattress with my fist. "Shit!"

I had to tell Rory. But he'd think I betrayed him. There had to be another option.

My phone chimed with a text message and I reached for it. Turning the phone over, I saw three simple, yet powerful words.

<I love you>

How could I respond? What could I say?

Nothing. I couldn't say anything until I saw Axel. Maybe there was another way out of this mess. There had to be.

As much as it killed me, I ignored Rory's message. If I responded, he'd call. And if he called, I'd invite him to my room. We'd be lost in one another, no closer to a solution than I was right now. Instead, I picked up the hotel phone and dialed Axel's number.

"What's the word on my commercial, sweet cheeks?"

"We need to talk."

"Unless you're giving me a time and a location to show up for the shoot, we really have nothing to talk about."

"Can you meet me downstairs at the bar at 8:00 p.m.?" I tried to sound seductive, knowing this was the only way to lure him into a meeting. God, had I really sunk this low?

"For you, gorgeous, anytime."

I fought the urge to puke.

"Don't worry, Hin."

I gritted my teeth, hating the nickname from anyone except Paul.

"Your secret's safe with me," he said. "For now."

I was thankful that he'd disconnected. I couldn't stand to hear his voice anymore.

Rolling over, I buried my face in my pillow and cried, ignoring the ping of my phone. I knew it was Rory. What could I say to him now?

Sorry, I fucked you over, but I swear I didn't mean to.

I loved this man so much, I'd do anything for him. If he left me or rejected me, especially because of something I'd done, I wasn't sure I'd be able to survive.

No, I couldn't answer. I had to hold him off a little longer until I could meet with Axel. As much as it killed me, I ignored his messages, burrowing my face further into the pillow as I wept.

Axel was perched on a stool as I approached the bar. His eyes raked over my body.

I cringed, nausea rolling in my stomach.

"No offense, Hindley," he said, "but you look like shit."

I felt like it too. "Thanks."

"Can I get you something to drink?"

Ignoring Axel, I spoke directly to the bartender. "Maker's Mark, neat, please." I rarely drank, but tonight I needed some liquid courage.

"Wow. Didn't picture you as a whiskey girl. You're really tying one on tonight, huh?"

"Well, you said you're buying, right?"

He laughed and my skin crawled.

The bartender set the tumbler in front of me.

I picked up the glass and brought it to my mouth, a little apprehensive about what it would taste like. I'd never actually had whiskey before. Taking a tentative sip, I let the alcohol roll over my tongue, trying not to choke. After my body adjusted to the initial burn, I realized it actually tasted pretty good.

"So, how's the commercial coming?" he asked.

"That's why I called you."

He arched a brow. "I'm here."

Axel knew what he'd asked me to do was nearly impossible. He was stringing me along. If he'd wanted to out Rory, he could have done it a long time ago.

This was a bullfight and he was the matador. Every spear he threw at me would cause a slow, painful death and jeopardize the relationship with the one man who'd become everything to me. Axel knew it and reveled in the power he held over me.

I picked up the tumbler and took another swig. Even though I wanted to numb my pain, I knew it would be a mistake to get drunk in front of the enemy.

"So, what's going on, Hindley?"

"There's no way I can get the commercial."

"I know," he said with a wry smile.

"If you knew then why did you ask me to try?"

"I knew if anyone could, it would be you. I believe you've worked hard on my behalf."

Oh, thank God. I sagged in relief. Maybe I could talk him out of this ridiculous idea of going to the media with Rory's secret.

"I really have, Axel, you have no idea."

He nodded.

"So, you'll keep Rory's secret?"

He laughed, an evil sound that sent shivers all over my body.

"Oh, Hindley, that's hysterical. You never told me you were a comedian."

My palms broke out in a cold sweat, and I began to shake when I realized what he was saying.

An evil, sinister expression washed over his face as his mouth curled into a vindictive grin. "There's no way I'm sitting on this bit of information for free."

I swallowed hard, praying the whiskey wouldn't make a reappearance. "What do you want, Axel?" I whispered.

"You. In my bed. Tonight."

The burn in my throat had nothing to do with the alcohol. I stood frozen, fighting my natural urge to flee.

"Axel, I can't do that."

"Can't or won't?"

"Does it matter?"

He let out a spiteful laugh.

My head was spinning and I gripped the bar to keep from falling over. I swallowed down the tears that burned the back of my eyes. "Why do you want to do this, Axel?"

"You can't be serious?"

"I'm totally serious. Why do you want to destroy Rory?'"

"You really don't know?"

I shook my head. "No. Why?"

"That little bitch in Seattle."

I didn't have to ask, I assumed who she was, but I asked anyway. "What woman?"

"She wanted me so bad," he said, lost in his own sordid memories. "She was screaming for it."

Oh, God. I really was going to be sick.

"Then that fucker busted in and broke us up." He pounded the bar. "He tried to convince the bitch that I'd attacked her. Shit. That chick wanted it rough and she knew it. But your dumbass boy put ideas in her head."

Rory had been right. I'd known it all along. Axel had attacked this poor woman and Rory had rescued her.

I stood stock still, knowing this matador may go in for the kill any second.

Rory really had been fearful of Axel, not jealous. Afraid of what he might do to me. Knowing about my own sexual assault, he'd been trying to protect me, not control me. I'd been too naive to realize it.

"Thank God, she didn't listen to him about going to the police," Axel continued.

"Look, Axel, I don't know what happened back then, but how can revealing Rory's secret help you at this point?"

"How can this help?" He threw his head back and laughed like the villain he was.

A chill ran down my spine and I instinctively scooted back.

"That fucker has killed my endorsement deals," he said. "Do you know how many sponsors want to back a guy who has rumors of rape swirling around him?"

My eyes went wide at this revelation.

"I can tell you exactly how many. Zilcho, that's how many. So to answer your question, this can help me. A lot."

Revenge. That's what he wanted.

"There's got to be another way, Axel."

"Oh, there is." He licked his lips, his eyes asking the silent question I didn't want to hear.

I shook my head, abhorred at the thought of sleeping with him.

"No?" he asked.

"No," I said quietly.

"All right then. I have one more alternative. Actually, it may work out better."

"What is it?" I hated the desperation in my voice.

"Throw the X Games."

"What?"

"Tell your boy to throw the X Games. Let me win."

"How could you enjoy a victory you know wasn't won on your own merits?"

"Jesus, get a clue, Hindley." He laughed. "I couldn't give a fuck less about winning fair and square. I need endorsements. I need money. I've got a shit ton of debt and I need cash, fast. If I win the X Games, everyone and their fuckin' brother will want me. And guess what? You'll still be my agent so you'll get a shit ton of money too."

I felt the room spin as my vision dimmed. I couldn't ask Rory to do that. Or could I? Maybe if I explained the situation to him, he'd understand.

"Technically," I said, "what you want to tell everyone isn't true, Axel."

"What do you mean?"

"Rory *can* read. He's been working really hard. We both have been."

"What? You think fucking Dr. Seuss books count as reading?"

"It's a start."

"Yeah, for a ree-tard."

I closed my eyes, trying to calm the fury raging inside me at his derogatory comment. I hated that word, especially when it was used as a description of my boyfriend.

Axel stepped closer. "So, the way I see it, you have two choices, sweetheart. Either meet me in room 810 in thirty minutes, or tell your boy to slip and fall and bust his ass in the finals at the X Games."

I stared at his repulsive face. There was no trace of teasing anywhere.

"Your choice, doll."

I swallowed hard, willing my chin not to quiver. I could not show him weakness no matter how fragile I felt.

A victorious smirk spread across his face. "I have a hard time believing your boy would throw the games for me, so I'll expect you in my room in thirty minutes."

I felt the blood drain from my face and I blinked several times, willing myself to wake from this nightmare.

"Want me to get you a refill on your drink, lover?" He brushed a strand of hair from my face, and tucked it behind my ear.

I shivered, my body going numb as tears pooled in my eyes.

He leaned closer and I could smell his putrid breath. "Save the water-works for someone who gives a shit, Hindley, because that person sure as hell ain't me."

"Please, Axel," I whimpered.

He slipped off the stool and threw a fifty-dollar bill across the bar.

"Oh, how I love a woman who begs," he whispered in my ear. "Thirty minutes, lover. Room 810." He ran his hand up my leg, cupping one hip. "Fuck, I can't wait to get inside you."

I slammed my eyes shut as the last spear from the matador pierced my skin. Axel waved his scarlet red cape high above his head in victory, his assault now complete. I was down for the count. Again.

Devasted.

Obliterated.

Destroyed.

CHAPTER 28

HINDLEY

MY HAND SHOOK as I reached out and knocked on his hotel door. I could barely hear myself think over the pounding of my heart. What was I doing here? How would I explain myself?

Sweat rolled down my back, I was so nervous. This waiting was killing me. Lifting my hand to knock again, I pulled back when I heard the click of a lock. The door slowly opened.

He stood in the doorway, rumpled and half asleep.

"I'm sorry," I said, "did I wake you?"

"Hindley?" His deep voice was thick with sleep as he peered out at me, eyes squinting.

"May I come in?"

"You have a key, gorgeous." He laughed. "No need to knock."

The sound of his laughter shook something deep in my core. This was why I was here. I needed him.

Rory swung the door open wide, revealing his gloriously naked chest and the detailed tattoo I'd grown to love.

I couldn't remember seeing a more welcomed sight in all my life. Before the door closed, I threw myself at him, molding my body against his as tears spilled down my face.

"Hey." He tried to push me back, to see me, but I held on. I never wanted to let my Skater Boy go. "Hindley, what's wrong?"

I didn't answer, I couldn't. I clutched him tighter. My meeting with Axel had weakened my resolve and I needed his strength. I couldn't lose him. I'd do whatever it took to keep him with me.

His hands slid up my arms and over my shoulders, cradling my cheeks before leaning me back. I finally met his gaze, not surprised to see worry etched across his face. "Baby, what's wrong? What happened to you?"

I shook my head. I had no words. I couldn't tell him. I needed him too much.

He placed feather-light kisses all over my face, his soft lips finally finding mine. Before I could deepen the kiss, he pulled away. "Have you been drinking?"

"Yes," I whispered.

"Why?"

I couldn't tell him everything, but I had to tell him something.

"I had a meeting with Axel."

He pulled back further. "And you drank?"

"It was the only way I could stomach him, Rory."

His eyes searched mine, and he clutched my shoulders. "Did that fucker touch you?"

What words did I have that could remotely begin to explain the situation? Yes, he hurt me. Not physically. And now he wanted me to go to his room and screw him senseless in about twenty minutes—which would destroy the one man I'd ever loved. There was only one answer I could give Rory.

"No, he didn't hurt me." Not yet.

"I'll kill that motherfucker if he lays one goddamn finger on you, you know that, right?"

I nodded, silently laughing at the absurdity of it all. That's exactly why I *couldn't* tell him the truth. I drew in a heavy breath. "I just want to lay down with you. I'm so tired," I sighed. At least that was the truth.

Without another word, he scooped me off my feet and walked across the vast suite, into the bedroom.

"How'd you rank up high enough to get a suite?" I asked.

"I have a good agent." He smirked.

"Well, I'll have to check her out."

"No, I think you should leave that to me."

His sexy smile made every erogenous zone tingle.

"Were you sleeping?" I asked.

"Yeah. Luis gave me some herbal shit to calm me down earlier. I don't know what the fuck was in it, but the shit knocked me out cold."

Luis was a vegetarian, a firm believer in the holistic approach to health. He never put anything in his body that wasn't organic or natural. I could only imagine what he'd given Rory. It broke my heart to know I was the cause of his anxiety.

"I'm sorry," I whispered against his neck.

"Why?" He gently laid me on top of the silky sheets.

They were cool against my skin and soothed my heated body. I knew I should respond but I was lost in him, his scent enveloping me, doing strange things to my best parts.

Rory Gregor was my drug.

His huge hands moved down my legs, gently removing my sandals as if I were a porcelain doll and he feared I might break. Lifting the covers, he quietly slid in beside me. He brushed my hair over my shoulder and pressed warm kisses against my neck.

I felt like a prized possession. His prized possession.

"Sleep, baby," he whispered into my hair.

As with most of Rory's commands, I willingly obeyed.

"Wake up, sleepy head." Rory's gentle voice echoed through my head as his soft lips scattered kisses across my face.

I knew I needed to get up but his bed felt like heaven. Reaching to stretch my hands over my head, I gave a huge yawn. I had no idea how long I'd been asleep but I felt like I could use another twelve hours, especially in this delicious bed.

"Come on, baby," he rubbed my leg, "let's eat some breakfast before you have to go."

Breakfast?

"What if I don't want to go?" I pouted. I lifted the covers and peered down at myself, surprised that I was still fully clothed.

Rory slid in beside me, his long lean body molding into mine.

He smelled so delicious, like expensive body wash, cologne, and toothpaste. I wanted to wrap my arms around him and never let go. So, I did.

He smoothed my hair back, brushing it with his hands as he gazed lovingly into my eyes. "Then don't go. You never have to leave me, Hindley. I want you with me always."

Unwelcome tears sprung to my eyes and my heart ripped apart as I realized what I had to do for him. No matter which path I took, he would be hurt, and may never forgive me.

He sat up, pulling me into his lap. "Okay, Hindley, you're starting to scare me."

Oh, shit. I needed to learn how to hide my emotions better.

"What's going on with you?" he asked. "You tossed and turned all night."

"I love you," I whispered into his chest.

"I love you too, baby." His large hands caressed my back. "What's going on with you?"

"Nothing. I'm just tired."

"And hungry?"

As if on cue, my stomach rumbled. "Sounds like it."

He gave me a quick peck on the lips and helped me stand. "Come on, I've got a tray of food in the living room. I need to feed you."

I followed him out of his bedroom into the huge sitting area, still surprised that he'd scored such a luxurious suite. "I really do have to talk to your agent." I giggled. "This hotel room is entirely too extravagant."

"I hate it," he said, his lip curled in disgust.

"Are you crazy? Why?" I couldn't imagine anyone not falling in love with this beautiful suite, especially that bedroom. "That bed was amazing."

"Yeah, the bed's great, especially because you were in it." He waggled his brows and I actually blushed.

I sat down and devoured a croissant with butter and strawberry jam. "So why don't you like the suite?"

"Because it doesn't have a Magic Door."

I laughed at his revelation.

"God, I love your laugh," he whispered against my neck, sending chills all over my body.

I was thankful to see the concern from earlier fade.

"Are you worried about the competition?" I asked, shifting his attention away from me.

"No."

"Then why did you look like the weight of the world had been lifted off your shoulders?"

"Because anytime I hear you laugh, I know that everything will be okay. With you," he paused, "with us."

I lost my appetite, listening to his declaration, and set the roll back on my plate. I wish I shared his optimism.

"What time is it?"

He glanced at the wall behind me. "Seven fifteen."

"What time do you have to be at the park?"

"Not until eight thirty. And you?"

"I'm supposed to meet Luis downstairs at eight." I raised an eyebrow, hoping he'd understand my unspoken desire.

"Oh, Miss Hagen, I believe I owe you an orgasm, don't I?"

"Why, yes, Mr. Gregor, I believe you do." I tossed my napkin on the table.

"I think we may have time for two or three before you leave."

My stomach did flips at the thought of what Rory could do with me in the next thirty minutes.

"You doubt me?" he asked.

Before I could answer, he lunged for me, flipping me over his shoulder and confidently strolling toward the bedroom.

The last thing I saw before he flipped me on the massive bed was the bedroom door slamming shut. I knew without a doubt we'd need the additional barricade to drown out my screams.

For the first time since I'd landed in Miami, a genuine smile spread across my face, all thanks to one man. My man. My Skater Boy.

CHAPTER 29

HINDLEY

I sᴀᴛ in the restaurant at the hotel, talking to one of the National Football League's most up and coming athletes. We were discussing Humberto's multi-million-dollar endorsement deal that I'd painstakingly drafted. I should feel golden, on top of the world, but I couldn't shake the uneasy sense of foreboding that had followed me all day.

Someone nudged my arm. I glanced over to see Luis's eyes staring at me.

Shit. I was being a complete space cadet, and this meeting was huge.

"So, Humberto, what do you think?" I asked, inserting myself in the conversation again. "I know you've tried the water and read about the company. We've gone over the contract and the stipulations, but tonight is all about you getting to know the company on a more personal level."

Humberto turned toward Matt. I could tell from the look on his face that he had some reservations.

"It's all right," Matt assured him. "If you have concerns please ask me."

"I'm half Latino," Humberto said. "I've done some research and read that Sonora uses illegal immigrants in some of their factories."

They did? That was news to me.

"Sonora received some bad press in the past," Matt said, "but trust me, we're a company that values human resources above all else. Of course, we believe in saving money, but not at the expense of humanity. Those claims were never legitimized. It's Sonora's policy to only hire legal, documented workers in all our factories. And to provide them all with adequate health insurance."

Humberto smiled as if relieved, slumping back in his chair. I was surprised that this had been his pivotal issue for him. Why hadn't I known it would be?

Suddenly the hairs on my neck stood on end. I sensed Rory somewhere in the room. Instead of being excited like I normally was, this time I was scared shitless. Something was wrong. I sensed it. Was he hurt? Had his mother called again?

I scanned the restaurant, searching for him. A scuffle at the front of the restaurant caught my attention.

It was Rory, arguing with a man and trying to push past him into the restaurant. His face was covered with a mask of anger so intense, it scared me. He was barely recognizable.

Something was wrong. Very wrong.

His eyes locked onto mine. This was dark Rory, the man who'd appeared in California after he'd talked to his mother. Tonight, it appeared all his fury was focused on me.

Holy shit.

I thought back to the events of the day. The tournament had gone extremely well. Rory had taken first place and Sonora Water and River City Skateboards couldn't have been happier. There'd been tons of photographers who'd taken some great shots of him wearing all the sponsor logos. Luis and I felt confident they'd appear in several magazines before the X Games, which would bring in even more bonuses.

But then I remembered Axel and the look on his face when he'd seen me earlier this morning. He was dark and sullen and almost as evil looking as Rory was right now.

Surely Axel hadn't said anything to the media, not yet. He promised to give me until the X Games before doing anything. But I knew I'd hurt Axel's ego last night by not showing up at his hotel room, and I was pretty sure he knew I'd spent the night with Rory instead of him. Before I could recall any other events of the day, Rory was standing behind Matt, glaring down at me.

"I'm sorry to interrupt you fine gentlemen tonight," Rory said.

I could tell by the tone of his voice and the dark circles under his eyes that this was going to be bad. Even worse than when he'd talked to his mother.

"You must be Hummm-bear-toe," he said, glaring at Humberto.

Oh, no, was he drunk? Please, God, don't let him be drunk.

Humberto's eyes darted from me to Luis.

I sat, completely dumbfounded, unsure what to do or say.

"Hey, Matt-oh-boy," Rory said, slapping Matt on the back.

He was drunk, he had to be. I clutched the arms of my chair to keep them from shaking.

"You better be careful, Bear-toe." Rory stared at Humberto then nodded toward Matt. "This one wants to get his dick inside her too."

Everyone at the table gasped. Luis and Matt flew to their feet but Rory sidestepped them, coming to stand directly over me.

"Ya gonna give him the starrrr treatment like you did me, sweetheart?"

I didn't even recognize this person standing in front of me.

"Rory, have you been drinking?" I whispered.

"Just be careful, Humm-bear-toe," he continued. "Once you fuck her, she may tell all your secrets."

My eyes went wide and I felt light-headed. Obviously Axel had betrayed me and disclosed Rory's secret to someone.

"Rory, please. I can explain." I pushed back in my chair, trying to stand, fighting back the tears.

Rory held me in place. "Oh, yeah, Bear-Toe, she'll beg for it. Beg you to fuck her. But it's worth it, trust me. She'll do some crazy shit in the sack." He threw his head back and roared with laughter.

Blood roared in my ears. My stomach rolled and I fought back my urge to vomit, or pass out, or both. Why was he doing this?

"That's enough, Rory!" Luis moved toward him at the same time Matt lunged after him.

Rory side-stepped them both, evading their attempts to stop him.

He was either drunk or high, or both. The rage inside me built to a fever pitch. He'd broken my confidence, ruined everything we'd had by admitting everything.

He leaned down and placed both hands on either side of my chair, his face mere inches away of mine. "What's wrong, wildcat?"

I'd never seen his eyes so demented, so dark, so crazed. I drew in a breath to retaliate but he continued his tirade.

"What were you doing, Hinny Bin, trying to get a few more bucks by selling all my secrets? Was I too much of a reee-tard for you?"

"Rory," I cried, tears streaming down my face. "Please."

He straightened and stared at Humberto.

Matt and Luis moved for him again but he skirted their efforts.

I blinked several times, my vision growing dim. I was going to pass out.

"Be careful what you say in the sack with her though, football boy, or it may be spread *all* over the Internet one day." Rory dug in his pocket and pulled out his phone, trying to show Humberto something.

Humberto wasn't interested. Instead, the six-foot-four mammoth football player grabbed Rory by the shoulders and physically pushed him aside with ease. Then he wrapped his arm around my waist, escorting me out of the restaurant with Matt and Luis in tow.

"Fuck you, Hindley!" Rory shouted from our table.

I died a thousand deaths as the words echoed off the walls in the restaurant.

"I know how to write that, you motherfuckers! F-U-C-K-Y-O-U." He chased after us. "Not so fuckin' stupid now, am I, you cock suckers. Maybe I'll put that in my fuckin' journal, Hindley!"

Hotel guests gathered in the lobby, gawking at the scene unfolding before them.

My shoulders heaved with deep sobs and I gasped for air.

Axel had revealed Rory's story. No, he'd probably *sold* Rory's story, and now Rory thought it was me who had betrayed him.

My chest burned and my heart broke into a million pieces. I thought I might actually die. I wanted to die. Anything to stop the guilt and anger suffocating me.

"What's going on?" Humberto asked as we made our way toward the front of the hotel.

I hiccupped through muffled sobs. "It's a long story."

Daring a peek, I glanced over my shoulder and saw Rory stalking toward us. Security guards rounded the corner on him.

I turned back to face forward as Humberto and Luis led me outside. Matt was holding open a cab door. That's when I noticed all the photographers outside, snapping photos and calling my name.

Oh, God, no. Please, no.

Before I slipped into the cab, I turned one last time to look at Rory through the glass wall. This wasn't Rory, this wasn't my Skater Boy. This was a man I didn't recognize. Gone was the tender, loving man who had taken care of me last night, holding me until I'd fallen asleep.

Suddenly Rory reared his back, about to throw something through the glass wall.

Anticipating his action, Matt covered me with his body and turned us around.

An explosion that sounded like a bomb detonating resounded behind me. Shattered glass pelted the ground at my feet. I tried to turn around, but someone pushed me into the waiting cab.

As the car sped off, I slumped against Luis as anger, sorrow and regret filled my heart.

"What on earth happened to him, Hindley?" Luis asked softly.

I glanced around the interior, surprised to find it was just the two of us. I felt safe in the cocoon of the cab, and for the first time ever, I broke down and told Luis everything.

CHAPTER 30
HINDLEY

I ROLLED over in bed and glanced at the clock on the nightstand. It glowed 5:57 a.m.

Even after Luis had fallen asleep in the bed next to mine, I'd tossed and turned and turned all night, sleep evading me.

Luis thought it best to stay away from the hotel for a few hours after Rory's outburst, hoping the press would die down. Three hours of aimlessly roaming around Miami, it had become obvious the press was camped for the night. Somehow Luis had found a way in through the back entrance shortly before midnight and snuck me into his room.

We spent the next hour searching the Internet, reading all the websites that had leaked Rory's story. Some sites were kind, quoting statistics on how many people in America are functionally illiterate and how it's a crime for the government not to fix the problem within our schools. The majority of the sites though were cruel in their comments and jokes, some including horrible pictures and cartoons.

My stomach knotted tighter with every word I read, good or bad, and I couldn't help but feel responsible for the barrage of rumors and innuendos.

The one thing I thought particularly odd though was the fact that none of the sites revealed their source. Axel was nothing if not sneaky, and I knew no one would probably ever find out it was him who'd leaked the story. Maybe I should tell the press, maybe that would help Rory's reputation. Doubtful.

In addition to breaking the news of Rory's illiteracy, many of the sites also revealed that Rory and I were having an affair. That little fact made an already impossible situation even worse. I had no idea how I would ever recover.

Without asking, I knew I'd probably lost my job...and Rory. He would never forgive me after this. A heavy blanket of depression wrapped around me, smothering me with images from my past.

Even though Rory had been a complete asshole last night—embarrassing the shit out of me in front of clients, colleagues, and half the hotel patrons—I knew where his anger and rage came from. It was his own fear and self-loathing personified.

His illiteracy had been a secret he'd held on to for years, perpetuating his own feelings that he didn't deserve the good things in life. He'd been abused, physically and emotionally, betrayed by people who were supposed to love him unconditionally. And now he felt as if I'd deceived him too. In the back of my mind I couldn't help but wonder if somehow I had without knowing.

I slipped out of bed, still dressed from the night before, and pulled on my shoes, trying not to wake Luis. I had to find Rory. I had to talk to him. Even if this thing between us was over, I had to let him know the truth, what I had been willing to risk to protect him. Maybe if he knew the truth, the whole truth, he'd understand.

I left the room and waited by the elevators, rubbing my palms so hard on my pants, they heated enough to start a fire. What would I say? What would he say? What if this really was the end for us? As cruel as he'd been earlier, I didn't want that for us. I was furious with him, but I loved him and I was willing to work through our issues.

I needed to see him, face-to-face, and find out why he'd been so cruel. The Rory I knew would never have lashed out at me like that. Something else had happened. If the lost boy inside him needed me, I would be there.

I walked down the hallway toward his room, each step feeling heavier than the last. The corridor was beginning to close in on me, making it difficult to breathe.

I stood outside his door, my hand trembling. A thought suddenly popped into my mind. Rory was a player. What if he wasn't alone? What if he'd reached out to one of those skater groupie bimbos who feasted on the athletes like piranhas? Oh, God. What would I do then?

No. He would never do that. I knew him, I trusted him. He may be mad at me, he may even hate me, but he'd never hurt me like that.

I held my breath and knocked on the door, standing back, waiting for him to answer. I remained stock still for several seconds but no one came to the door. I knocked again, this time louder. Maybe he was asleep. I waited for what felt like a lifetime and fought the urge to leave. I needed to see him face-to-face. Good, bad, or ugly, I had to know if we still had a future.

Then I remembered, I still had his key card. Slipping it from my back pocket, I placed it in the lock, holding my breath until the green light finally flashed. I opened the door, my heart pounding as I scanned the room. Everything seemed intact, no broken lamps or glasses. That had to be a good sign.

My shoe caught on something on the floor and I glanced down. "Oh my God," I gasped, fisting my hand and stuffing it in my mouth to keep from yelling.

Strewn about the floor were Rory's blue jeans and T-shirt, along with a woman's skirt and tank top. They didn't belong to me.

Fuck.

Bile burned in my stomach and I bit down on my hand to keep from becoming physically sick.

I walked further into the suite on shaky legs, my head pounding. Tears burned my eyes when I saw a pink satin bra lying across the back of the couch. I turned toward the bedroom. It was shut. Something tiny and pink hung on the handle.

Stumbling back, I bumped into the wall behind me, the room spinning. I drew in a ragged breath to steady myself but the air burned my lungs, the scent of cheap perfume making my stomach lurch. My entire body began to tremble uncontrollably. I wrapped my arms around my waist to settle my nerves. This couldn't be happening.

Images of Rory kissing another woman, touching her intimately, having sex with her, being inside her, flooded my mind. I moved toward the trashcan, knowing I was going to be sick.

Suddenly, movement in the corner of the room caught my eye. A woman.

Oh, God. No.

She stalked toward me, wearing a thick terry cloth robe that I recognized. It was from the hotel, similar to the one I'd worn yesterday morning—probably the same one.

As she moved closer toward the light of the lamp I narrowed my gaze to focus beyond the tears.

My eyes went wide and my body burned from the inside out.

It was Geneva.

My knees buckled and I clutched the wall for balance, willing myself to stand tall.

Her mouth curled into a malicious, evil grin. She was proud of what she'd done. Sleeping with Rory was a fatal wound to my soul, she'd known this would destroy me, and she was happy with herself. Her smug expression made it abundantly clear that she'd done this intentionally.

"He's probably still in the shower," she said, walking toward me.

I recoiled, shaking my head. This wasn't real, this was a nightmare. I turned to leave.

The bedroom door creaked open and I glanced over my shoulder.

Rory stood in the doorway, wearing a robe, his eyes heavy and half-lidded.

Had they just showered after spending the night fucking like monkeys? Oh, God. I'd never felt pain like this in my life. Not even when the police had told me I'd been raped.

Rory's eyes narrowed as he stared at Geneva. "What's going on?"

Geneva smiled like a cat who'd eaten the canary. "You don't remember?"

His gaze swung to me and he held his head like he might pass out.

I was paralyzed. I wanted to run, I wanted to scream, I wanted to be swallowed up by the black abyss of emptiness, but my body wouldn't move.

Rory glanced around the room, his eyes taking in the trail of clothing. Suddenly dawning lit his face. His eyes went wide, and wild.

I'm sure memories of their night together were flooding his mind, like they were mine. Images of him thrusting deep inside her, Geneva's legs wrapped around his body. Them in the shower, doing God only knew what.

In that moment, staring at the man I had once loved, there was no doubt in my mind now. Rory had fucked my stepsister, probably more than once.

I fumbled with the door handle, finally opening it, trying to escape before I puked.

Rory pressed behind me, pushing the door closed.

I wanted to cry, but I refused to give Geneva Barton the satisfaction of seeing that she'd completely destroyed me. I had to get out of this room before I passed out. Or killed someone.

I turned and stared up at Rory's eyes. They were bloodshot, the whites tinged with yellow. He was toxic.

He swallowed hard, raking his hand through his hair, his eyes darting between mine.

"Let me go," I growled.

"Hindley, it's not what you think," he said. "I don't even know what to think. I don't know what the fuck is going on here."

I peered over his shoulder.

Geneva smiled, pulling the belt of her robe tighter.

I nodded toward her. "She knows."

She knew *exactly* what happened last night, and if I stuck around, she'd tell me every last detail.

"Fuck this!" I yelled.

Rory flinched.

"Let me go, Rory, or I swear to God, I will kick you so goddamn hard in the fuckin' nuts, you'll never be able to screw another woman again, least of all my stepsister." The last word came out on a hiss.

His eyes shot wide, knowing I would.

I yanked the door open and stepped into the hallway, disoriented and sick to my stomach. Where did I go from here? Breaking into a run, I was almost to the elevator before someone caught my arm and jerked me around.

"Hindley, wait. I don't know what's going on. I'm sorry, it's…" He fumbled with his words, scratching his head. "Please, don't go."

Obviously, the reality of what he'd done was hitting home.

"Why her, Rory?" I choked through my tears. "Of all the women you could have fucked last night, why her?" I slapped my hand over my mouth to quiet the sobs that threatened to escape. I hated that he was seeing me totally breaking down.

"Hindley, it's not like that." His hands trembled and his eyes darted back and forth, silently begging me for something. He looked like a caged animal fighting for his life.

This time, I wouldn't save him.

"Just for the record, I *never* told anyone about your secret. It was Axel who leaked your story."

His eyes narrowed as he studied me like I was insane. "What?"

"Axel has known about your illiteracy for a while. He was threatening to go public with the information. He gave me an ultimatum— sleep with him or he would go to the media with the story."

Rory clenched his jaw, as he stepped closer.

I held up a hand. "Stop. Don't touch me."

He swallowed hard but obeyed my request. "I'm confused."

"I'll make it clear then. Your story went viral, which means I didn't sleep with him. Do you know why?"

He stood silently, just as paralyzed as I'd been in his room.

"I never slept with Axel," I said. "I never would. I would never do that to you."

His eyes darted over my shoulder and I turned my head, following his gaze.

Geneva stood in the doorway, arms crossed over her chest, wearing a shit-eating grin.

I jerked my head, unable to look at the bitch. I stared up at Rory, tears now streaming down my face. Gasping for breath, I clenched my trembling hands by my sides to ease the shaking. "But I guess I can't say the same for you," I choked out. "It's pretty obvious you fucked my stepsister," I spat the words at him.

I studied his face, committing every detail to memory so I would never forget how much I hated him at this very minute.

"I loved you, Rory." I hiccupped on a sob. "I would have done *anything* for you. You have no idea what I've already done for you. To protect you. To protect us."

He reached for me but I swatted his hands away.

"Don't you dare touch me."

He stumbled back, eyes wide as if I'd shocked him.

"You've completely destroyed me," I whispered. "Shattered me."

He shook his head, his eyes welling with tears. "No, Hindley. I didn't do this."

I laughed sarcastically, pointing back to my stepsister. "You did."

I wanted to hurt him, make him feel the agony consuming me, and I knew exactly how to do it. I could scream out, *'You're right, Rory, you do fuck up everything you touch! You're a fucking idiot!'* That would crush him. But I couldn't do it.

As much as I wanted to hurt him, I didn't believe those words. Despite his betrayal, I still loved him, more than I hated him. I cursed myself for being so weak.

Without another word, I shoved past him and walked toward the elevators, not surprised when he didn't come after me, but relieved that he didn't.

As the elevator doors closed, I sunk to the floor and curled into a tight ball, sobbing hysterically, wondering how on earth I would ever survive without my Skater Boy.

CHAPTER 31

RORY

A COOL BREEZE blew over my face as I reclined in the rocker on Jack and Kara's front porch.

Their house was nestled in a wooded area not far from Denver. The scenery was picturesque, with giant trees surrounding the property and the snow-covered mountains dotting the horizon.

Even in this serene environment though, I couldn't find peace. My heart and head were a mess. I spent long hours wondering if I would ever be able to function normally again.

Thankfully their home was void of cameras and reporters, for now. It was the escape I needed to lick my wounds. But I knew it was just a matter of time before someone discovered my hideout.

Ten days. Ten fucking days. That was how long it'd been since I'd stood in the restaurant at the swanky hotel in Miami and cursed Hindley out in front of God Almighty and two hundred plus customers and guests.

I'd tried a hundred times to relive the memories, but for the life of me, I couldn't. I had no recollection of the evening whatsoever.

One thing I knew with certainty, there was absolutely no way I'd drank alcohol that evening, so I couldn't blame it on a blackout. The only change in my routine had been the herbal supplements Luis had given me the day before to calm my anxiety. I'd taken two capsules that evening before dinner, hoping to settle down.

The supplements had to be it. But Luis assured me the herbs would never have produced such a profound effect on me. Sleepy, yes, blackout and belligerent, no.

Turns out, I didn't need my memory after all. Plenty of people had captured the entire event on video, and had been kind enough to publish it on every social media site known to man. The rag mags and talk shows had labeled me the "Illiterate Bully," an ignorant monster who intimidates women and children. That one hurt most of all.

I hadn't skated in over a week, and with the X Games only six days away, I knew I needed to do something. My legs felt like lead and my heart was even heavier, making it nearly impossible to do anything, let alone fly through the air on my board with any real passion.

And to top it all off, Hindley had found me semi-naked and alone with her stepsister. How could I have done this to Hindley? The guilt was crushing me.

I'd tried to call her a hundred times since then, but as expected, she never answered. Eventually, Luis told me to stop trying, so I did. He said she needed time to cool off and I needed to give her the time and space to do so. At this point, I had no choice but to take his advice. He was my only link to her, and I wasn't going to lose that.

Luis also shared with me Hindley's dire situation with Axel and all she'd endured on my behalf during his reign of terror. He explained how Axel blackmailed her with my secret, even going so far as to demand sex from her to keep him quiet. It made me want to smash his 'pretty boy' face in every time I thought about it.

What had I been thinking? Even blacked out in a fit of rage, I still should have known Hindley would never betray me.

Watching the videos of my verbal assault on her in the restaurant was surreal. I didn't even recognize the man who stood in the middle of the space, shouting obscenities at her. Even in my darkest days of drinking and drugging, I'd never acted so horribly, especially to someone I claimed to love.

The most devastating part of it all was the fact that I couldn't undo what had already been done. I'd hurt her so tragically, I was convinced

I'd never get a second chance. No excuse in the world would ever justify my actions.

Every day that passed meant Hindley was a little further away from me than the day before. The chances of getting her back dwindled with each passing minute.

Sometimes, the physical pain of that realization was too excruciating to bear and I found solace in the woods, releasing my tears, screaming my frustrations within the safety of the trees.

I'd always known from the start that I didn't deserve her. Now, it seemed I never would.

"Hey." Jack's deep voice called out.

I turned and saw him walk out from behind the screen door. "Hey," I said.

"I just got off the phone with Luis."

I sat up straight. "Did you talk to Hindley?"

He shook his head.

And just like that, my hopes were dashed. I leaned back in my rocking chair and exhaled a heavy sigh, wondering how on earth I was going to survive without my Drunk Girl. She was my rock, my anchor, my best friend. As usual, I had totally fucked it up.

Jack walked closer. "He wants you to do some television interviews."

I jumped up from the chair, hands clenched. "No way, Jack. There is no way I'm letting some jackass TV host make a fool out of me on national television."

"It's not going to be like that."

"What's it going to be like then?"

"They want to come here, to Denver, to get your story."

"Why? Who the fuck cares about my story?"

"Apparently, a lot of people do. Illiteracy is a big deal around the world."

I braced my hands on the railing, staring down at the ground. Kara had planted brightly colored wildflowers at the bottom of the porch. The vivid colors made me think of Hindley. Everything made me think of her. Suddenly, I felt his hand on my back.

"Maybe she'll see it, see the interview," he said.

His statement was the first glimmer of hope I'd had in over a week. I whipped around, staring at him wide-eyed. "Do you really think so? You think Hindley will watch it?"

"I don't know. But we have to do some damage control, and Luis thinks this is the best way."

"I don't give a shit about what people think," I said more defensively than I should have.

"I'm not talking about people, Rory. I'm talking about you. You have to do something, find a way to move on."

"From what?"

"From this." He waved his hand up and down my body. "You're isolated, you're depressed, you're distraught. You're not eating, you're not reading, and you certainly aren't skating."

He was right, I wasn't doing any of those things. But how could I? Without Hindley in my life or in my future, everything else seemed pointless.

"Do you still want to compete at the X Games?" he asked.

I drew in a deep breath of cool mountain air and focused on the woods in front of me. Did I want to compete? Of course I did. But could I? "Yes," I finally answered.

"Then you need to pull out of this funk and get back on the track. Soon. Figure out a way to throw all of this anger and hostility into your practice sessions."

I tightened my fingers around the railing and glanced at Jack. "What do you mean, they'll come here?"

"Paloma Monroe wants an exclusive."

Paloma Monroe was a nationally syndicated television talk show host with a loyal viewing audience in the hundreds of millions. If Paloma liked something or someone, the whole world loved it too. But she was also notorious for cutthroat questions that weren't always approved ahead of taping and had the potential to make the guest look like an A-number-one asshole.

"Who else?" I asked.

"Several of the prime-time news programs also want to interview you, but they want an exclusive as well. Luis thinks if we commit to one and it airs with high ratings, then the others will probably approach you to do additional interviews."

"I thought it would be an exclusive interview."

"Luis said there are ways to work around that."

I laughed, knowing full well Luis had many tricks up his sleeve.

"It's your call, son."

Son.

Did I even deserve that title anymore after the way I'd disappointed Jack and Kara?

I listened to the leaves blowing in the wind, the sound like feather-light kisses. Images of Hindley's body brushing against mine as we made love flashed through my mind. I wondered if she missed me half as much as I missed her.

"So, what do you think I should do?" I asked Jack.

"I think you should do it," he answered with no hesitation. "You have an amazing story to tell, Rory. There are a lot of kids out there in your exact shoes. You could give them hope."

"What if they rip me to shreds?"

"I don't think it could be worse than what's already out there, do you?"

He was right. At least if I did an interview, they would get the truth. "Who do you think I should go with?"

"Kara thinks Paloma would be your safest choice."

"You've talked to Kara about this?"

"Yes."

I was surprised Kara had weighed in on the subject. She'd barely said two words since I'd arrived. I knew she was furious with me for the way I'd treated Hindley. But it was so out of character for Kara to stay distant from me, and it only added to the self-hatred raging inside me.

"Kara will come around." Jack broke through my thoughts.

"I don't know. She hasn't spoken to me in days. She seems pretty pissed."

"She really cares for Hindley."

"So do I, Jack. I love her. I want to spend the rest of my life with her."

"Well, you have a funny way of showing it."

I closed my eyes, letting my head fall back. How could I have fucked things up so badly? "Please, don't remind me. I do enough of that on my own."

"Sorry," he said.

I lifted my head and stared at him. "Why Paloma?"

"She has a massive audience and she produces her own show."

"Why does that matter?"

"It means nothing will get by her unless she says so," he said. "We wouldn't have to deal with a bunch of execs from the networks, only her."

"But isn't she known for being pretty vicious with her line of questioning?"

"I think she reserves that kind of stuff for the more dramatic interviews, with people who don't want to right their wrongs. That's not you."

"What does Luis think?"

"He agrees. He said he could draft a document that will only allow Paloma to ask certain questions and assures us that we get to see the final copy and give our approval before it airs."

"We have that kind of power?"

"You do."

"What do you mean?"

"People want to hear from you, Rory." Jack seemed unfazed by my self-doubt. "You've been holed up here in the middle of nowhere for almost two weeks. All the public has to go on are the fabricated, sensationalized stories dreamed up by the rag mags and smutty TV talk shows. It's time you let everyone see the real you, the Rory who Hindley fell in love with."

"You think I should talk about everything?"

"It's your call."

"Yes, you should," a female voice said behind us.

I turned and saw Kara standing in the doorway. I wondered how long she'd been listening.

"Walk with me, Rory," she said, never looking back as she descended the front porch steps.

Next to Hindley, Jack and Kara were my lifelines, my lighthouse in the storm. I'd follow Kara anywhere if it meant she would talk to me again.

I glanced at Jack.

He shrugged.

Well, shit. I jogged to catch up with Kara. She was walking along the path she and Jack had built through the woods years ago.

I fell in step with her, a difficult feat given how small she was. We walked in silence for several yards, and my body broke out in a cold sweat. If I lost Kara in all of this too, I didn't think I would ever recover.

"Why did you do it?" Her voice echoed through the woods.

What was she talking about? The verbal assault on Hindley? The one-night stand with Geneva? How could I respond?

"I don't remember any of it, Kara."

"Please, Rory, I'm tired of that excuse."

I grabbed her arm and pulled her around to face me. Her eyes were wide with surprise but I didn't care, I had to make her understand. "Kara," I said, my voice nearly breaking, "you have to believe me. I swear to God, I don't remember any of it."

She studied me, her eyes narrowed. "Were you drunk?"

I shook my head. "No. I swear."

"Then what happened? How could you verbally assault and humiliate Hindley then sleep with her sister, and yet have no recollection at all?"

I shuddered from the contempt in her voice. She didn't believe me, and to be honest, I was doubting myself. I fell against one of the large trees, fearing I might pass out. "I don't know, Kara. I've tried to remember a thousand times, but I just can't."

"What's your last memory?"

I closed my eyes, thinking back to that awful night when my life changed forever. "I knew Hindley was in a dinner meeting that would probably run late so I called room service to get something to eat."

"What did you have?"

I opened my eyes and stared at her. "Why is that important?"

"Every detail of that night is important."

"Kara, I love Hindley. There is no way even drunk or in a drug-induced high that I would ever seek out Geneva, you have to know that. I can't stand that bitch."

"I know that. But the fact remains that she was found in your hotel room, both of you naked, with your clothes scattered around the room."

"We weren't naked," I yelled, pounding the tree.

She rolled her eyes.

I racked my brain, trying to think of every detail, no matter how minute. "I think I had chicken breast with gravy and brown rice, steamed broccoli. Oh, and vanilla pudding."

"Did you drink anything?"

"Sonora water." I laughed.

"Was it sealed?"

"Yes. It was in the fridge in my suite."

"Hmm." Her eyes narrowed and she tapped her chin.

"What?"

"I think you were drugged."

"How?"

"There's all sorts of ways. It could have been in your food, your water, anything." She stared off behind me. I knew better than to interrupt her. "What happened after you ate?"

"I kicked back on the sofa and started to watch a movie. Then someone knocked on the door. I went to open it and that's when I saw the envelope shoved under my door."

"Who was at the door?"

"No one," I said. "Just the note."

"What did it say?"

"Nothing. It just had a web address written on it."

"Did you go look at the site?"

"I didn't have my laptop, and the computer in my room didn't work, so I went downstairs and used the business center. The last thing I remember was pushing the button for the elevator on my way down to the lobby."

"You don't remember anything after that?"

I shook my head.

"You don't remember looking at the website that first leaked your secret?"

"No."

"You don't remember talking to a reporter about it either?"

"No. Did I?"

"According to witnesses, you did. You shoved the reporter and stormed into the restaurant."

I raked my hands through my hair, disgusted at the memory, or rather the images of the videos on the Internet of actions I didn't remember.

"The next thing I remember was waking up completely nude in my bed," I said.

"Were you alone?"

"Yes."

"Where was Geneva?"

"I don't know. I heard someone talking in the living room so I got up to see if it was Hindley. There was a robe next to the bed so I put it on and opened the door. I remember my head hurt so bad but I didn't feel hungover. That's how I know I didn't drink." I stood in silence, trying to replay every second. Suddenly a clear memory popped in my head.

"What is it, Rory?" Kara's hand wrapped around my arm—the first physical contact she'd given me since I'd arrived.

"My bedroom door was locked. I remember having to unlock it to open it. That's weird."

"Why?"

"If it was locked, there is no way Geneva could have been inside with me." I puzzled over that for a moment. "I remember Hindley telling me off at the elevators then going back to my room. Geneva tried to throw herself at me, but I pushed her off and told her to get the fuck out of my room."

"What did the bed look like?"

"What?"

"Your bed. Was it all messed up?"

"Why?"

"If you and Geneva were in bed together, it would have been a mess, right?"

"I guess." I scanned through the memories of that night but couldn't remember anything about the bed. I'd been too traumatized by the scene with Hindley and Geneva. "Even if it wasn't messed up and I slept alone in my bed, it doesn't mean that Geneva and I didn't have sex out in the living room."

"True," Kara sighed.

"But I know myself, Kara. I would never do that to Hindley. Ever."

"I know, Rory."

"You do?"

She nodded.

I felt like a massive weight had been lifted from my chest. "Oh, God, thank you, Kara, thank you so much." I yanked her into an embrace, crushing her against my body, certain she probably couldn't breathe. I didn't care. I needed her to believe in me again.

Her small arms wrapped around my waist and she squeezed me tight, pressing her cheek into my chest.

"I think you should do Paloma's show." She released me and stepped back, her big blue eyes holding a glimmer of hope. "And I think you need to tell her your story. Your whole story."

"Why?"

"Imagine back when you were a kid. Wouldn't it have meant the world to you to see a successful athlete share his story and know he understood your pain? Wouldn't that have given you hope?"

She was right. Knowing another person in the world had shared my experiences and come out on the other side, alive and strong, would have definitely given me hope. It might not have stopped my own abuse but it would have given me hope for a better future.

"Will you be there?" I asked. "For the taping?"

She smiled wide. "Of course I will be."

"Thanks. I need you there."

"I'm sorry, Rory." She grasped me tight and hugged me, her shoulders shaking.

I pushed her back so I could see her face. Her cheeks were lined with tears. "Kara, what's wrong?"

"I'm so sorry for how I've treated you, sweetheart. A mother should never act like that toward her child."

What was she saying? She thought I was her child? I'd always considered Kara a mother, the mother I'd always wanted, but knowing she'd considered me her son brought tears to my own eyes.

"Of course you're mine, Rory. I knew from the first minute I saw you in that skate park that you needed someone to believe in you. And now, when you needed me the most, I..." She buried her face in my chest and cried.

"Hey," I said, rubbing soothing circles on her back. "It's all right."

"No, it's not." She stepped back and wiped her face. "I've been awful."

"The only reason you doubted me is because you love Hindley as much as you love me. You were torn."

She nodded.

"I know that about you, Kara."

She slipped her arms around me again and held me tight.

I rested my chin on her head. "I won't lie. Not having you to lean on has sucked this last week, but I get it."

"Get what?"

"I don't have the cleanest track record."

She laughed.

"But I didn't drink, Kara, I swear. And despite what it looks like, I know I didn't sleep with Geneva, even if I can't prove it."

She stepped back and cupped my face. "I believe you, sweetheart. I always have. Come on." She tugged on me. "Let's go have some lunch and call Luis to schedule the interview. Then, I want to see your ass on that course, practicing today."

I smiled at her bossiness.

"I want to see The Helly at the X Games."

"No way." I shook my head.

"Yes, way," she said, poking my stomach.

"Owe!" I hollered.

"There's more where that came from, mister, if you don't get your butt in gear. I want you in tip-top form at the games. I want you to wipe the floor with that little prick."

My laughter echoed through the forest. Kara never got emotional about competitions, but I knew the Momma Bear in her was pissed, and I was thanking God with every step that her wrath was no longer directed at me.

CHAPTER 32

RORY

"ARE YOU NERVOUS?" Luis asked as I sat in Jack and Kara's kitchen.

The makeup artist was putting the finishing touches on my face. The production crew was doing the final installation of equipment on the front porch where my interview with Paloma would take place. Who knew that so much was involved in doing a sixty-minute interview?

"I'm a little nervous. But mostly, I'm relieved." I rubbed my palms up and down my jeans in anticipation.

"Really?"

"Yeah."

"Why?" Luis tilted his head and stared at me.

"I feel like this is my one and only chance to tell Hindley what really happened that night," I said.

"I thought you didn't remember anything."

"I don't. I'm hoping she'll believe me when she sees me say it over and over again."

Luis shrugged his shoulders.

"How is she?" I asked. I knew I shouldn't, but I couldn't help it. I missed her so much my body ached.

"About the same as you."

"Really?" Knowing she was miserable should have made me feel bad but it didn't. If she was hurting, it meant that maybe there was still a chance to redeem myself. I would take it.

"She quit you know."

"The law firm?"

He nodded.

I was shocked. I'd sent her tons of emails but they'd all been returned. I'd assumed she was ignoring me. Obviously something bigger was going on. "Why did she quit?"

"They tried to force her to still work with Axel."

"You're kidding."

"Wish I was."

I shook my head. "Fucking pricks."

"Pretty much," he said. "Also, turns out, Michael was the one who tipped off the media about your illiteracy."

My mouth fell open and I jerked my head to stare at him. "Are you serious?"

"Hey," the makeup artist groaned.

"Oh, sorry." I smiled at the woman, but inside I was fuming.

Fucking Michael.

I'd always been thankful that Luis never judged the fact that I couldn't read. In fact, after Hindley dropped out of my life, Luis had taken over her role as my mentor, making sure I was writing and reading and learning every day.

"Why'd he do it?" I asked.

"He was worried the story about you and Hindley being involved would break soon and ruin the reputation of the firm. Basically, he threw you under the bus to save the firm." He chuckled. "Turns out the joke was on him though. Your secret relationship came out anyway."

"Do you think she still loves me?"

"She'll always love you," Luis said.

"But?"

"But, this interview may not be enough to win her back."

As much as I didn't want to believe Luis, I knew he was right. This interview may be too little, too late. "I have to try, Luis. I love her."

"I know, man." He bumped my arm.

I felt a sense of strength and friendship. Luis was here. If I couldn't have Hindley by my side today, at least he was willing to stand with me.

"Let's go over the questions," he said. "I don't think Paloma will surprise you, but I want to make sure you'll be prepared for whatever comes."

"Thanks, man."

"For what?" he asked.

"For believing me, for believing *in* me."

"Look, Rory, it's not my place to judge. I'm sick that Hindley is hurting so badly, but I'm not convinced it's totally your fault."

"Have you told her that?"

"No."

I sagged in disappointment.

"It's not my place, Rory. I won't jeopardize my friendship with her, not now."

"I know, and I understand. I'm thankful she has you."

Luis opened his mouth to ask the first question.

"Don't." I raised my hand to stop him.

"Rory, you need to be prepared for Paloma's questions."

"I already am. I don't want my answers to be rehearsed. I want them to come from my heart. I know what the truth is and that's the story I intend to tell."

"Are you sure?"

"Look, Luis, I have nothing to hide. Losing Hindley has been the worst possible thing that could ever happen to me. There's no question Paloma can throw at me that I won't answer honestly and truthfully if it means we might have a chance at reconciliation."

"Okay, man, but don't say I didn't warn you."

"I won't." I laughed. "So, Michael leaked my story?"

Luis nodded, snorting in irritation.

"I didn't even know he knew I couldn't read. Did Hindley tell him?"

"Hindley didn't say shit to anyone. Not even to me until the night you went off the deep end. I confronted Axel and he confirmed that he'd had a conversation with Michael a few weeks prior. Axel threatened Michael as well about going public with your story if he didn't get a deal like you did."

"God, I feel awful for what Hindley went through for me. I'm such an asshole."

"Yeah, you kind of are."

"You ready, Rory?" A woman wearing a headset and carrying a clipboard stuck her head around the corner.

"Ready as I'll ever be." I pushed out of the chair.

"You'll be fine, man." Luis shook my hand and hit my arm with a fist, giving me his own brand of confidence.

"Maybe one day," I said.

He nodded, but the truth no one seemed to understand was that without Hindley in my life, I would never be fine again.

CHAPTER 33

RORY

I'D BEEN to the X Games six times since I'd gone pro so you'd think I'd be used to the media frenzy and drama, especially because I was going for gold medal number eleven. But the crowd today was different, borderline insane. Reporters and TV crews from around the world were packed in the press area, all vying for an opportunity to speak with me.

Since my interview with Paloma had aired two days ago, I'd become somewhat of an overnight sensation, in a good way. But it was all stress I didn't need right now.

I'd hoped to hear from Hindley after the airing of the show but no such luck. I even tried to call her once but wasn't surprised when I heard the number was no longer in service. It took every ounce of strength I had in me not to beg Luis for her new phone number. I refused to put him in the middle. He'd become too good of a friend to jeopardize our relationship.

"Holy shit, man, look at all these crazy bastards." Leif shouted over the roar of the crowd.

I was so thankful he'd come with me, even if it was to promote his own business. Having him near always settled my nerves. Not nearly as much as having Hindley, but it helped.

"So what's the story, morning glory?"

"What do you mean?" I asked.

"You doing The Helly today or what?"

"I don't know if I'm feeling it."

"Feeling it? Since when do you have to feel it? Just go out there and do it."

I smiled as one word came to mind. Tactile. God, I missed Hindley. Every fuckin' day.

"This crowd is insane," my fellow competitor and friend, Buzz Dahlke, shouted above the noise as he slapped my back. "You going for it today or what?"

"Going for what?"

"For what?" He laughed, nudging Leif. "The president's daughter, you moron. The Helly, dumbass. Are you going to do The Helly?"

"Why is everyone so obsessed with my move?"

"Um, because it's bad ass and if you stick it, you're all but assured a medal, golden boy."

"This is just the preliminaries," I said.

"All the better reason to try it out," Leif added. "No pressure to get it right."

"There's always pressure. I never want to try a trick unless I'm one hundred percent convinced I can stick it."

"Oh, shit," Buzz shouted. "Hold me back."

I didn't have to ask who. Hell, I didn't even have to look to know he was talking about Axel.

Since the show had aired, it had come out that Axel was part of the leak as well as my own law firm. Unfortunately, I was tied to Stedwick and Nigh for another nine months, but Luis assured me he was trying to work his legal-eeze to get me out of the contract. Even though it went against all of Luis's principles, he'd promised to stay with the firm until he got me through this crazy time. I was truly in his debt.

Luis planned to base my contract renegotiation on the premise of defamation of character, although technically, it had helped my public image.

My fans and the world in general were in love with the illiterate, abused underdog from the rough streets of Denver, Colorado. I'd received emails, letters, cards, and Internet posts out the wazoo in support. I'd even had offers from illiteracy groups and educational entities, asking for my backing and support.

I never thought in a million years anyone would ever want me to be the spokesperson who encouraged adults and kids alike to read. There was only one person responsible for my overnight success, and I missed her more than words could ever convey.

Now, here I stood on the platform of the X Games, trying to make a comeback and win my eleventh gold medal. I was more nervous than a whore in church, my hands wringing with sweat. I couldn't tell if the nerves were for the competition, my desire to kick Axel's ass, or the thrill of knowing that maybe, just maybe, Hindley would be watching me.

"She's out of the country." Luis interrupted my thoughts.

"Who?"

"The girl you just had on your mind."

"What do you mean, she's out of the country?"

"Dana took her down to some tropical island to get her mind off of everything. I think she chose a location so remote, they wouldn't get Internet, television, or phone signal, so Hindley wouldn't be tempted to watch you."

Well, fuck. "Are you serious?" I'd hoped that Hindley had seen my interview with Paloma, but if what Luis had said was true, she hadn't seen a thing. And now she wasn't even going to see me skate. I was more defeated than ever.

"Yeah, I'm sorry, man." Luis shrugged, his disappointment just as evident as mine. "I did try to talk to her though."

"You did?" I sounded like a twelve-year-old schoolgirl. "What did you say?"

"She's not ready to talk yet."

"Do you think she'll ever be?"

He rolled his eyes.

I knew the answer. No. She was well on her way to hating me forever and the thought had my stomach twisted in knots. I had no idea how in the hell I was ever going to compete in this state.

"You've got to pull yourself together, man. Seriously," Leif said, obviously frustrated by my attitude.

I sucked in a deep breath to steady my emotions. Leif was right. If this truly was over with Hindley, I had to get my shit together and carry on, even though I knew in my heart I would never skate the same without her. Hell, I wouldn't even be able to walk, talk, or breathe the same without her.

I turned to Leif and Buzz who'd been hanging on my every word. They'd been in my corner and supporting me in my fight to win Hindley back from the beginning, just as much as Luis had.

Fuck it. I had to take the first step toward life without Hindley Hagen, no matter how terrifying and painful it was. "I'm gonna do it, man!"

"Fuck, yeah." Buzz hollered. "Woo-hoo. He's back."

"I don't know if I'll ever be completely back."

Leif grinned, slapping me on the back. "We'll take whatever part of you we can get, man." He reached in his pocket and pulled out his phone.

"How the fuck did you hear that thing ring over this crowd, man?" Buzz laughed.

"Vibrate," Leif said, as if Buzz was a moron. "Hello!" he shouted into the phone, shoving his finger in his other ear. "What?" His brows furrowed. "What happened?"

His face washed ashen and my stomach dropped. Was it Jack? Was it Kara? Instinctively, I knew something terrible had happened.

"We'll be there as soon as we can." Leif ended the call.

"What is it? What's wrong?"

He stared at me blankly, eyes wide, fear etched across his face.

"Just tell me, Leif."

"It's Hindley."

Fuck.

CHAPTER 34

HINDLEY

"A FUCKING HURRICANE!" Dana yelled, banging the ticket counter.

"Ma'am, please, mind your language," the airline lady politely scolded. Her eyes darted around the gate area. Hundreds of other passengers sat about, anxiously waiting for the departure of a nonexistent plane.

I rolled my eyes at the woman. If she only knew Dana, she'd realize this was tame for her. And she'd be thanking the stars above and kissing those silver wings on her shirt that Dana didn't burst out in a song full of expletives that would have a sailor turning red with embarrassment.

This was just our luck. Leave it to Dana to book a trip to the Cayman Islands smack dab in the middle of hurricane season. I loved her to death, but she wasn't the brightest bulb on the tree. Hurricane Ethan was making his fury known up and down the Caribbean and was headed straight for the Gulf of Mexico, promising to be one of the largest storms in recent years.

"Hey." I pulled on Dana's arm, trying to get her away from the glaring eyes of all the moms with small children who were silently burning her at the stake. "Come on, let's take a walk."

"I can't believe this, Hindley. Of all the days. That stuck-up airline bitch pretty much guaranteed all the flights would be canceled."

"Dana, I don't want to get on an airplane heading toward a tropical island that's smack dab in the eye of a hurricane, I don't care how fruity the drinks are."

The tiniest promise of a smile swept across her face. "I'm really sorry."

"Why?"

"Because. This was supposed to be…" She waved a hand in the air then dropped it with a huff.

I knew exactly what she had been about to say and I didn't want to hear it. "Look, I'm fine. I wish you and my mom and Paul would get that."

"How the fuck can you be fine, Hindley? That prick cussed you out in front of like a zillion people and put it on display on every social media site for the whole goddamn world to see. And if that wasn't bad enough, then the scumbag goes and fucks your stepsister. Hello? Am I the only one here who's getting this? I can't believe you're not more upset."

"I am upset, Dana. I've cried so much, I don't have anymore tears left. What do you want me to do? Lay down and die?"

"No, I'm just worried about you." Her eyes brimmed with tears.

Her feelings had nothing to do with Rory and everything to do with the way I normally handled stressful events in my life. "I'll be fine. I'm a big girl. Look, it's late and we've been at the airport for like five hours. Let's go home."

"No. I refuse to give up. We're going somewhere."

"Really, Dana, you don't have to do this. I'll be fine, I swear."

"Look, go have a drink at the bar. I'm going to head back to the ticket counter and see if we can cash our tickets in and head somewhere north. Maybe New York City?"

I knew better than to argue with her when she made her mind up to do something. Instead, I nodded, picked up my carry-on bag, and headed toward the bar.

I pitched my bag under the counter and slid up on one of the wooden stools.

"What's your pleasure, little lady?" the bartender asked with a warm smile.

"To get out of this airport. And soon."

"I hear you." He laughed, wiping down the bar in front of me. "Until then, how about something to wet your whistle?"

I wasn't in the mood to drink, not today anyway. "Do you have lemonade?"

"Nope. No lemonade. Sorry. How about some cranberry juice mixed with seltzer water? It's one of my trade secrets." He cupped one hand around his mouth as if to hide the words from onlookers. "Then I throw in a little extra ingredient, but no one knows what it is." He winked.

I was already in his trusted circle. I smiled, a genuine expression, for the first time in days. "That sounds perfect."

"Coming right up then, little lady." He knocked on the bar with his knuckles then slid a square paper napkin in front of me and headed away to prepare my drink. I dug around in my carry-on for my iPad. Now I could finish reading the article on fashion merchandising I'd started when we'd been waiting in the gate area for our plane. The one that never arrived. And probably never would.

Since I'd left the firm, I'd floundered around, trying to figure out what to do with my life. Ideas popped in my head all the time, but it was fashion design I always came back to. I also thought of the joy I experienced helping Rory learn to read. Maybe I should be a teacher.

I shook my head. No. No thoughts of Rory Gregor, it was my new mantra. One I wasn't always good at keeping.

I took in a deep breath and set the iPad up on the bar, frustrated to see my battery was almost out. "Excuse me," I asked the bartender, holding up my power cord. "Do you have a power outlet?"

"Not at the bar." He pointed to a row of booths against one wall. "But there's one at every booth over there."

I stared around the restaurant area and suddenly my skin prickled. Staring back at me on at least ten different television screens was the man who'd once captured my heart. There was no place to escape from his face.

Glancing down at my napkin I noticed this wasn't just any bar, it was a sports bar. How could I not have noticed that before?

The X Games logo flashed behind him on every television. Well, hell. So much for my mantra.

I stood paralyzed, staring at his gorgeous face. Rory was just as beautiful as ever and looked no worse for the wear, unlike me. The only indication that he may feel as shitty as me were the dark circles underneath his eyes. He must not be sleeping either.

I stumbled toward a booth and slowly sunk into the bench seat. The volume was muted and I thanked God I didn't have to hear his voice.

Rory had left so many voice mail messages over the last two weeks, they'd filled up my entire inbox. I wanted to listen to every single message, to savor his voice, but I knew better. Or, at least I thought I did.

One rainy afternoon, against all my best intentions, I'd sat on my back porch all alone and played a few of them. It had been a mistake and I'd paid the price, spending the rest of the day and most of the night, curled up in a ball on my sofa, crying my eyes out as each message played over and over again in my mind, each one sounding more panicked than the one before.

His desperation echoed in every word. The old me wanted to call him, make sure he was all right, comfort him, care for him. But images of his body wrapped around Geneva's as they rolled around in his hotel bed always ripped through my mind just as I was about to dial.

"Here's your drink, little lady." The bartender broke into my thoughts as he set the glass down.

The multitude of flat screen televisions closed in on me like an angry mob.

"Big skateboarding fan?" He nodded toward the screen.

"You could say that."

"So's my son. He loves that guy."

I stared at one of the screens, Rory's face filling every inch. After zooming in, I could see he did look just as bad as I did. He'd lost weight, and there were no mischievous laugh lines around his lips when he smiled.

"I can't remember his name," the bartender said.

"Rory Gregor," I whispered.

"That's right." The bartender nodded. "Rory. My boy has posters galore of that guy up all over his room. Even has some of Rory's fancy skateboards too."

I laughed to myself. That was the target demographic we'd aimed for.

"I don't get it, personally." He leaned against the side of the booth, obviously preparing himself for a long stay. "It's a shame about what all he's been through though."

A shame? For Rory? I wanted to jump up and scream, "What about me, man?"

I slid to the edge of the booth to exit. "Umm, excuse me."

"I saw his interview with that famous Paloma woman the other night," he said, never moving. His attention remained glued to one of the televisions. "My boy can't seem to get enough of him."

I nodded my head, completely understanding his son's affliction. I couldn't blame him. I'd been caught in Rory's web too.

"But after I saw what he did to that poor lady on the videos out on the internet, I pretty much told him 'Chris, you can't worship a guy like that, not when he treats women the way he did.'"

I wanted to vomit, or shove my iPad in his mouth to shut him up.

"But then my son forced me to watch that interview, and I tell you…" he paused.

Suddenly I found myself oddly engrossed in his story. I leaned forward. "And what?"

"Well, he's had a really hard life that Rory fella. And the rumor is he was drugged."

"Drugged?" I hadn't heard that. Of course I'd purposely kept myself hidden away for several weeks to avoid anything to do with our story, so how would I have known.

"Yeah, drugged. Paloma said her producers talked to some employees at the hotel who worked that night. They pretty much ratted out another employee. Supposedly the kid told the cops that someone paid him to put some kind of drug in Rory's food. The doctor Paloma had on her show said that particular drug would cause people to act out and do things they wouldn't normally do."

Oh my God, could this really be true?

"Did the doctor say if it would make a person not remember what they'd done that night?" I said. "The drug, I mean?" Could this be true? Had Rory really been drugged?

"Oh, yeah." The man nodded. "The doc said people who've taken this drug have killed people and woken up the next morning never remembering a thing about it."

My mouth fell open and I slumped back into the bench.

"Well, shit!" Dana shouted from the front of the bar. "Leave it to your dumbass to come to a sports bar during the X Games."

I stood up from the booth and pushed past the bartender.

Dana snagged my bag from me and wheeled it toward the exit.

"Hope y'all have a good time wherever it is you're headed," the bartender shouted at us.

I secured my purse over my shoulder, yanking it tight as I stumbled through the bar.

"Hey!" he shouted at me.

I whipped around, wondering if I'd forgotten something. "Yes?"

"You're the girl from the story, aren't you? That skater's girl." He nodded toward the television screen.

Dana's hand gripped my arm and yanked on me, nearly pulling me over. "Thanks for the drink, Tex. We gotta go," she said, yanking me out of the bar.

My feet stumbled underneath me as Dana hauled me down the long terminal, refusing to stop until we'd reached the bathroom entryway.

"What are you doing?" I yanked my arm out of her superhuman hold.

She glanced around the area as if looking for an escape. "We need to get the fuck out of here."

"Why?"

"I wanted you somewhere far away from this shit, Hindley, not smack dab in the middle of it. The last thing you need is to watch his smug fucking face on television." Her chin quivered and tears welled in her blue eyes.

"Hey," I said, moving closer. Obviously she'd taken this ordeal with Rory much more serious than I'd realized. "It's okay, Dana." I put my arm around her shoulders and squeezed her tight, which was ironic given the fact that I was the one who'd been utterly destroyed.

Her ocean blue eyes rolled up to meet mine, not at all convinced I was telling the truth.

"Let's go home, okay?" I said.

"But I wanted to get away from all this shit." Dana waved her hand in the air. "You know, get you out of town, out of the country, off the planet."

"I don't think NASA allows civilians on the Space Shuttle yet." I laughed.

Dana smiled. "Good to know."

"I can't run away forever, Dana. This whole story will still be here when I get back. And obviously, someone is trying to tell us to stay home. So, let's appease the travel gods and go home. Okay? We'll take a fresh look at it tomorrow and maybe find a place to escape to then, all right?"

She nodded.

We left the airport with little fanfare. As we rolled down the highway, my thoughts went back to the bartender's comment. Had Rory really been drugged?

"Did you see his interview?" I asked.

"What interview?"

She was obviously trying to play dumb, but it *so* wasn't working.

"You know what interview, Dana." I rolled my eyes.

"I saw some of it."

"Did you watch the part about Rory being drugged?"

"I didn't watch that part, but I saw a story about it on the Internet."

"What did it say?"

"Do you really want to hear this, Hindley?" I could hear the fear in her voice.

"I wouldn't have asked you if I didn't."

"I'm sorry. It's just—"

"I'm fine. I swear." I wasn't but she didn't need to know that. "Just tell me what you read."

Dana held her breath for several seconds before sighing. "It said the police investigated the accusations that one of the employees from the hotel had put drugs in his food that night."

"And?"

"And, what?"

"What did the police find out?"

"One of the employees of the hotel said he overhead someone talking about putting something in Rory's food."

My stomach sank. "What was it?"

"They wouldn't say for sure because they said the boy may be a minor. The police said he's only seventeen, but the hotel isn't confirming it because the guy is an undocumented worker."

I sat silent, trying to process the fact that perhaps Rory had been drugged. Did that mean he hadn't really slept with Geneva?

"Look, Hindley, why are you doing this to yourself? It doesn't matter."

"What the hell did they give him, Dana?"

"They think it was either Rohypnol." She hesitated.

"Or?" I asked, my heart hammering in my chest.

She glanced over at me, her eyes anxious and fearful.

Images of Donald Lee Westbank flashed in my mind.

"It was GHB," I said, "the date rape drug, the same thing that scum bag gave to me, wasn't it?" I didn't need to see her face to know the truth. She was terrified what this information would do to my mental state.

"Hindley, don't," she said, squeezing my leg.

I fought the sobs threatening to break free as tears streamed down my face.

"Goddammit, Hindley, this is exactly why I wanted to get you the fuck out of here."

I heard her voice but didn't comprehend the words. All I could see were the videos of Donald Lee Westbank raping my comatose body relentlessly in every room of my apartment.

"I'm taking you home with me tonight."

I didn't fight her. I no longer had anything left inside me.

History had taught us both that I had no business being alone with my memories. And there was no way Dana would ever leave me in this state. Not after everything I'd just learned. That's why I loved her. She always protected me, especially from myself.

CHAPTER 35

HINDLEY

I TOSSED and turned all night. Going to bed with Donald Lee Westbank on my mind always meant sleep would be impossible.

Since it was obvious I'd never get any rest, I wrapped myself in a robe and walked down the hall to the living room. Dana's condo was rather large but I tried to walk quietly. I didn't want to wake her and make her worry anymore about me than she already had.

I searched for the remote, hoping some mindless show or movie would lull me to sleep. Clicking on the massive television, I tucked my legs underneath me and surfed the endless channels Dana subscribed to.

Then I remembered, she was addicted to those baby-daddy talk shows. The wild ones where the host would order a DNA test for a woman who was sleeping with at least three guys at the same time—two usually being cousins. Then the host would yell out the results and everyone would gasp in horror, and fighting would ensue. I laughed to myself. It was staged but who cared. That was exactly the kind of mindless television I needed tonight.

I positioned the pillows behind me and waited for the cable box to boot up, wondering if I should get some ice cream or popcorn. Before I could move, the list of recorded shows popped up on the screen and my heart stopped.

Paloma Monroe.

The show's description revealed it was Rory's interview and my stomach dropped. Should I watch it? Should I listen to his side of the story? My heart was already ripped to shreds. Why not totally destroy it with the truth?

I noticed two shows with Paloma's name. One was marked part one and the other part two. He must have had a lot to say, I thought.

Assuming part one was just a retelling of his youth, I chose to start with the second show. If he was lying I'd be able to tell within a few minutes.

As I pushed play and listened to Paloma go through her recap of part one of her interview with Rory, his face flashed on the screen and my breath caught, choking me. He was dressed casually but still looked devilishly handsome like he always did. His bright blue eyes held me in a trance. Suddenly I wondered if this had been a good idea.

I noticed they were sitting outside on the porch at someone's house, large trees dotting the landscape behind them. I couldn't help but wonder where they were filming. And who he was with. And if he was thinking about me as much as I was thinking about him.

"Let's go back to the night when you lost control," Paloma said.

Rory's bright blue eyes grew darker. "I'd love to talk about that night, Paloma, I really would, but I honestly don't remember anything."

"You've maintained that version of your story for weeks now," she said, "never wavering from it once."

"That's because it's the truth."

I watched him intently, looking for any signs he wasn't being honest, but sank back into the couch when I saw none.

Paloma pulled a paper up and glanced down at it before staring at Rory. "Would you be relieved to know our producers have discovered that a hotel employee *did* in fact drug you?"

I gasped. No way.

"I'd be surprised that someone would do that. But no, it doesn't surprise me that it happened. It's a scenario I've thought of recently in the past few days."

"Why?"

"People who really know me, people who know my character, understand I would never intentionally act out like that toward them. And the fact that I have no memory of the outburst would definitely indicate someone gave me drugs."

Did that mean I didn't know him at all if I'd questioned his actions that night?

"Well, you're exactly right," Paloma said. "The police have confirmed through witnesses that someone did put a drug called Rohypnol in your food that evening. Are you familiar with that drug?"

"I've heard of it, but no, I'm not aware of what it is and what it does to people."

"According to our medical sources, the drug would cause the exact symptoms that you experienced, including aggressive behavior, impaired judgment, reduced inhibitions, and memory loss."

Rory nodded in understanding, as if not at all shocked.

"You don't seem surprised by our findings."

He leaned in. "Look, Paloma, I know myself. People who love me know me. It's not a shock to find out that I ingested something that would make me behave in a manner that was so out of character for me. I'm devastated I hurt the woman I love. I promised her she would always be safe with me, that I'd protect her from harm, and yet I didn't."

My eyes stung with tears and I swallowed hard. Part of me considered turning off the television right then. I couldn't afford another breakdown. I reached for the remote but stopped when Paloma continued.

"You sound heartbroken," she said.

"I am. Completely." His voice cracked and I noticed his chin quivering.

"Oh, God," I whispered. He was totally telling the truth.

"You're talking about Hindley Hagen, your attorney and sports agent." It was a statement not a question.

He swallowed hard and nodded, unable to speak. He was hurting just as much as I was, maybe even more if that were possible.

"Are you still in love with her?" Paloma asked.

My heart stopped and I held my breath, anxiously awaiting his answer.

He never hesitated. "Of course I love her." He smiled, his expression changing into what looked like true joy. "I'll always love Hindley Hagen."

Oh, God. He'd said he loved me, said my name out loud. His declaration on national television may be my undoing.

"What about Hindley?" Paloma asked. "Does she feel the same way?"

"I hope so."

"You haven't talked to her though, since your outburst in Miami?"

"No." He turned and glanced into the monitor, and there he was. Staring right at me. My lost boy. My love. I ached for him in that moment, ached for both of us. "But I have faith."

"So what gives you hope?" she asked. "What makes you think she'll forgive you?"

"I won't give up on us."

I bit my lip, not sure if I wanted him to or not. He sounded so sure of himself, sure of my forgiveness. And wasn't that my Skater Boy.

"That's pretty confident thinking, isn't it?" Paloma asked.

"Actually it's a song, by Jason Mraz. *I Won't Give Up on Us.* I sing it every day, over and over, trying to psyche myself up."

"You have to admit that might sound completely insane to some people."

He shrugged and laughed. "Have you ever seen me skate? To be an extreme sport athlete, you have to be insane."

Paloma joined in his laughter.

Rory smiled, his shoulders easing down as he visibly relaxed.

I grabbed the remote and paused the show, staring at his image for a good minute. I hadn't realized until that moment how much I'd missed him, and how much my soul ached at the thought of never being with him again.

But, he'd slept with Geneva, I reminded myself.

Paloma said he was drugged.

Did that matter? Was that enough of an excuse to forgive him? I had no idea at this point and suddenly I was too tired to care.

I tugged at the pillow behind me and placed it under my head as I stretched out on the sofa. My eyes fluttered closed, and Rory's beautiful face floated through my mind. There was a lot I wasn't sure of but one thing was clear after watching him on TV. I still loved him. I just wasn't sure I could forgive him.

CHAPTER 36

HINDLEY

I sat at the head of the conference table, staring at those sitting around me. My mother and Paul were on one side while Dana and Luis sat across from them. Why were we all here?

I jumped when the intercom buzzed.

"Your guests are here," a woman said, her tone clipped.

Everyone turned and stared at me.

I realized they were waiting for my response. "Um, okay, show them in I guess."

The group seemed relieved, as if they thought I would say no to our visitors. Now I was really curious about our surprise visitors. Maybe they could shed some light on why we were all here.

The door opened and Geneva and Rory waltzed through the door, hand in hand.

What the hell?

They walked around the table, greeting everyone but me.

My heart nearly beat out of my chest and I felt light-headed. I was grateful I was sitting down, feeling like I might have passed out.

"Well," Geneva said, addressing everyone but me, "as most of you know, Rory and I—" She glanced up at him, her eyes alight with what looked like adoration.

Rory lifted their joined hands and kissed her knuckles.

I seriously thought I was going to vomit all over the conference table.

All eyes remained transfixed on the happy couple

I couldn't stand the silence. "What?" I yelled.

Every head jerked toward me, eyes wide with surprise.

Rory dropped Geneva's hand and walked around the table, stopping just in front of me. He leaned down wrapping his fingers around the arms of my chair.

I held my breath, staring into eyes that had once held so much love for me but were now cold and dark. I recognized the man in front of me. This was dark Rory.

"What is it, Rory?" I whispered, willing him to put an end to my misery. This couldn't be real.

A cruel, perverse smile spread across his face as he lifted one hand, letting his finger stroke my jawline.

I shivered from his touch and I hated myself for being so damn weak when it came to this man. "Just tell me," I pleaded.

He bent even lower, putting us at eye level, his nose nearly touching mine.

He smiled, a genuine expression of joy changing his once dark face.

I breathed a sigh of relief. Maybe he'd come to his senses and realized it was me.

"Geneva and I got married," he said casually as if the words wouldn't destroy me.

I struggled to breathe, my mouth going dry.

The room erupted in cheers as everyone congratulated the happy couple.

Dana hugged and kissed Geneva like they were best friends. Luis took Rory into a huge hug that had them both laughing.

What was happening? Why were the people I loved most in the world celebrating?

"Wait!" I screamed, but no one heard me, or if they did, they ignored me. As I slumped back in my chair, an idle observer to the chaos surrounding me, a cold hand wrapped around my shoulder.

"Ready, baby?"

I recognized the voice. It was Rory. Maybe all of this had just been a horrible nightmare. A sense of calm enveloped me.

The grip on my shoulder turned painful. Gazing in front of me, I realized Rory wasn't beside me, he was standing next to Geneva, showing off their new wedding bands.

Fear struck through me, leaving me chilled to the bone. The voice I'd heard wasn't Rory's. It belonged to someone much more sinister. Closing my eyes, I slowly turned in my chair, gripping the arms to brace myself for what I would find.

"Come on, Hindley," he snarled.

I blinked my eyes open, paralyzed, unable to make a sound. There standing before me with a sinister grin was the most evil man I'd ever known.

Donald Lee Westbank.

"No!" I screamed. Pulling my knees to my chest, I held on to the arms of the chair, preparing to kick him in the groin.

Before I could strike, his hands wrapped around my ankles and he pulled me to him, his face only inches from mine. "You'll never get away from me this time, Hindley," he said in a low tone. "Not ever."

I searched the room, looking for anyone who would help me.

He smiled, his teeth stained brown. I could smell his putrid breath as he spoke. "We'll be together. Forever."

I fought against his hold, beating any part of him I could reach.

He laughed. "I like a girl who fights."

"No!" I screamed, my head twisting as I searched for someone, anyone to help me.

"Rory!" I shouted. "Rory!"

He glanced over his shoulder, unaffected by my attack. "Bye, Hindley." He smiled and waved as if nothing were going amiss.

I watched helplessly as he and Geneva slipped out of the door, along with everyone else I loved. The door slammed shut with an ominous thud.

Donald Lee Westbank shoved my chair across the small room and into a corner.

I screamed until my throat was raw as I fought against him with all my might. This time I would not lay back and do nothing. I swung at him, putting everything I had into each blow as if I were fighting for my life. This time I was.

He laughed with the same wicked rumble I recognized from the tapes he'd recorded of us.

"No!" I screamed, punching his face. "No! No!"

"Hindley, wake up. Hindley."

I flailed about, kicking and swinging, trying to save myself from this mad man's attack.

"Hindley, stop!"

I quit fighting, recognizing a new voice, a safe voice.

Dana.

Oh, thank God, she'd come back to save me.

I shot straight up, willing my eyes to open but afraid of what I might find. What if it was a trick? What if Donald's voice now sounded like my best friend's?

"Hindley. It's me, Dana. You're safe. You're in my house, you're safe."

My lids fluttered open and I focused on the face staring back at me, one riddled with pain and worry, all because of me. I reached out and drew her into my embrace, clutching her body to mine like the lifeline she was.

"It's okay," she said, stroking my back.

"Oh, God, Dana," I cried. "It was awful."

Dana pushed me away to survey the damage as she softly and lovingly brushed away pieces of drenched hair from my face.

I felt mildly better, until I saw the fear in her eyes. "What? What is it?" I asked.

"Your parents. They're here."

"Here? As in, your condo?"

She nodded.

"Why?" As soon as I'd asked the question, I wish I hadn't. "What is it, Dana?" I whispered.

"They're down in the lobby. I haven't let them up yet. Why don't you get dressed and I'll go down and bring them up so they can talk to you?"

"Dana, what's going on?"

"I'm not a hundred percent sure, but I don't think it's good."

"Oh my God, Dana, what is it?"

She shrugged, feigning innocence, but experience told me she knew exactly why they were here. She was waiting for them to deliver the bad news so she wouldn't have to.

"Come on." She hauled me off the sofa. "So," she nodded at the television that was still on but thankfully not filled with Rory's face, "a little late night with Paloma, huh?"

I hung my head to avoid her question, and realized I was still wearing the same clothes I'd had on yesterday.

"You didn't even change into pajamas last night?" she asked, somewhat amused with my rumpled appearance.

I smiled at her light-heartedness but I couldn't shake the foreboding feeling burning deep in my stomach.

"Oh, well, come on," she said. "You look fine."

It was a lie. I was a mess. I always was after a nightmare about Donald Lee Westbank. But I didn't have time to care this morning. I had to find out what was going on with my parents.

"Go brush your teeth and hair and I'll be back in a few minutes."

"What time is it?" I rubbed my eyes.

"Almost twelve-thirty."

"Are you serious? Why didn't you wake me up earlier?"

"I knew you needed the rest." She walked toward the front door. At the edge of the living room, she glanced back at me, motioning to go get ready.

"Dana, you know, don't you?"

She avoided my gaze, but I saw the slight movement of her head in acknowledgment.

"Will you come back up with them, to be with me while they're here?" I pleaded.

"Oh, Hindley, why would you ever have to ask me that?" She rushed toward me, wrapping me in her small arms. She pulled back and stared up at me. Her normally sea blue eyes were bloodshot today and filled with tears. This was going to be bad, very bad, and I had to prepare myself.

"Did he get out?" I whispered. Donald wasn't up for parole for several more years, but after my nightmare, I knew it may be a foretelling of things to come.

"Just go get ready." Dana pushed me toward the hallway. She was refusing to be the bearer of bad news and I couldn't say I blamed her.

CHAPTER 37

HINDLEY

WHEN I RETURNED to the living room, Paul was pacing in front of the floor-to-ceiling windows that overlooked downtown Austin. One hand gripped the back of his neck, the other was clenched by his side.

My mother sat on the large sofa, her head in her hands as her shoulders shook.

Shit. This was really bad.

"What's going on?" I asked.

Their heads turned and they stared at me, eyes wide, and worried.

My mother stood and raced toward me, yanking me into a tight embrace. "Oh, God, Hindley," she moaned.

Before I could ask anymore questions, Paul was on top of us, his arms wrapped around both me and my mother.

"What's going on?" I asked, my breathing labored from the pressure of their embrace. "Did someone die?"

They both backed away, shaking their heads, neither one returning my gaze.

"Just tell me already," I said. "I'm sick with worry."

"Sit." Paul extended his hand toward the sofa.

"I think I'd rather stand."

Paul returned to the window, staring out aimlessly as Dana came to stand beside me. She wrapped a supportive arm around my waist and tugged tight. I knew in that moment that what they had to tell me could very well destroy me.

"Paul," I whispered.

He turned to face me, his expression weary and forlorn. "You may have heard that the authorities believe Rory was drugged the night he berated you."

I nodded. "Yes. And?"

"The police suspected someone within the hotel, an employee."

"Yes, I know already. Dana told me."

"It was Rohypnol," he said.

"I know that too."

My mother's head jerked up and she stared at me. "You do?"

I nodded.

"Rohypnol has different effects on different people," Paul said. "It's also intensified when ingested with other drugs."

My chest seized with pain. "Is Rory using drugs again?" If he was, then all hope for us being together again truly was lost.

"No, he's not using drugs," Paul said. "Not to my knowledge, anyway."

Oh, thank God.

"But he did take the herbal supplements from Luis," Paul continued, "and medical experts think those heightened the effect of the Rohypnol."

"So you're saying his actions really weren't his own?" After watching Paloma's show late last night, this was no surprise, but still I was thankful Paul and my mother were trying to clear Rory's name.

"That's right." Paul nodded. "He was literally out of his mind that night, Hindley."

"Why do you care? I thought you didn't like him, that he was beneath you."

"Why would you ever say that, Hindley?" my mother asked.

I stared down at her, surprised to see her brows furrowed in confusion.

"That night at dinner," I said, "you went on and on about how important college was, and—"

"That's really what you thought?" Paul interrupted, his eyes wide, mouth turned down in a grimace.

My mother stood and placed her hands on my shoulders, her green eyes searching mine. "Oh, Hindley," she cried, squeezing her eyes shut and pulling me in tight.

The hairs on my neck stood up. This was bad. Really bad.

"What is going on?" I said with more agitation than I'd meant. I pushed her away, needing to know the truth. "What are you guys saying?"

My mother's eyes fluttered open, her expression softening. "What we're saying is," she paused and I wanted to slap the answer out of her.

"Just say it, please."

"Rory has no recollection of the night," she said. "He truly doesn't remember because that's the effect the drug has on people."

I remembered my own experience with a similar drug Donald Lee Westbank had given me. The drug had rendered me helpless to his attacks, and wiped away any memories I might have had of the awful assaults.

"So why are you telling me all of this?" I asked. "You want me to forgive Rory, excuse his behavior?" My breathing grew shallow as I searched around the room.

My mother stepped forward. "That's not—"

"He fucked Geneva, for God's sake."

My mother winced.

"Please don't tell me you're taking his side too." I stormed around the sofa to the window on the opposite side of the condo.

Downtown Austin was quiet for a Saturday afternoon. The weekday buzz of the worker bees had been replaced with a handful of young, rich hipsters seeking an afternoon of music and mayhem. I envied them.

"Geneva came to us last night," my mother said.

I turned, garnering all my inner strength. "And I care because?" I asked.

"Stan brought her to our house last night and forced her to talk to us," Paul said, tears welling in his eyes.

"You haven't talked to her since Miami?"

"No," Paul said in a clipped tone.

"She tried to call, but Paul and I refused. Until yesterday." My mother had drawn a line and for once, she appeared to be on my side.

"So what did she say?"

My mother drew in a deep breath.

"No, please. Forget it." I waved my hand in the air. "I don't want to hear anymore." It was one thing to know Geneva and Rory had had sex, I didn't need to hear the sordid details from my mother.

"It's not like that, Hindley," she said, walking toward me and cupping my face. "Not at all."

I stared into her beautiful green eyes that were now filled with fear and remorse. For the first time in my life, my mother looked less than perfect. She looked…broken and destroyed. Like me.

"I love you, Hindley," she whispered. "I'll always love you. It's not about taking sides, it's about being there for one another."

"So, let me guess." I jerked my head from her grasp. "Geneva came over to cry on your shoulder about how she fucked my boyfriend, and you and Paul gave her the benefit of the doubt and welcomed her back with open arms."

She shook her head, her expression blank. "No, Hindley. That's not it."

"Then what is it?"

"Please, come sit down." She motioned toward the couch.

Feeling light-headed and nauseous, I decided sitting sounded like a good idea. I fell into one of the oversized chairs, needing distance.

My mother sat down on the sofa, reaching out to take hold of my hand.

Realizing I may need her support, I didn't fight her. Instead I clutched at her hand like a small child.

"Geneva has always been jealous of you, Hindley," my mother said. "I thought it would fade and you two would become sisters, but as the years progressed, her loathing of you grew stronger."

That was an understatement, I wanted to say.

She scooted closer. "I was naive, never wanting to believe Geneva could be so nasty and vindictive toward you. For that, I'm truly sorry. I thought if I just showed her enough motherly affection and love, one day she'd come around and we could all get along and be one happy family like we'd always dreamed of."

"But?"

"But this time, she's gone too far."

I cocked a brow. "You think? Sleeping with my boyfriend definitely upped her game?"

"It's worse than that, Hindley," she said.

"How could it be worse?" I snorted. "Is she pregnant?"

"That would be impossible. Well, at least not with Rory's baby," she added.

"Yes, I know. Rory's quite the little Boy Scout when it comes to contraception. Always prepared." I laughed sarcastically.

"They never had sex, Hindley," she said quietly.

My head lurched back and I stared at her like she had two heads. "Of course they had sex. I saw them."

"You didn't actually *see* them," she said.

"I didn't have to. Their clothes were scattered everywhere and they were nearly naked when I walked in."

"That's why Geneva came over last night," she said, ignoring my statement.

"Why?"

"To tell us."

I jerked my hand from hers. "And let me guess, you believed her over me? Even though you know she's a lying, manipulative little bitch, you're still taking her side."

My mother folded her hands in her lap, watching me with eyes filled with sorrow.

I sat back into the chair, deciding to play along. I'd never seen that look on my mother's face before. "So, what happened?"

My mother stared down at her lap, toying with the hem of her shirt. "Geneva was the one who provided the drugs to the hotel employee with instructions to give it to Rory."

What the—

I blew out a heavy breath, unable to process what my mother had just said. I knew she was evil but this went beyond anything I ever thought she was capable of.

"She knew Rory didn't drink and she wanted to seduce him," my mother said. "Apparently, he'd brushed off her advances several times that day and it pissed her off. She's used to getting any man she wants, especially if that man wants you." She lifted her head and stared at me. "When Rory denied her, her hatred for you escalated, and she put her plan into motion."

This could not be happening. This couldn't be true. Not even Geneva could be this malicious, could she?

"She thought if she gave him the drug, he'd have no choice but to sleep with her," my mother continued. "She bribed the boy from the hotel with money to have him put the drug in Rory's pudding. Then she said she gave the boy more money to let her into Rory's room. She was waiting for Rory when he got back from his tirade with you." My mother's chin quivered.

I glanced over at Paul. He was gripping the glass wall with both hands, his head hung low, shoulders slumped. I'd never seen him look so devastated.

My mother swallowed hard, steeling herself. "She said Rory didn't even know she was in the room when he came in and stripped down in the entryway. She tried to get his attention but he brushed by her, making a beeline to the bedroom. She tried to stop him, putting herself between him and the bedroom door. Apparently, she was totally nude."

A hiccup of a sob echoed in the room. I stared over at Paul again. One hand covered his mouth as his shoulders shook.

"When Rory finally realized who she was and that she was in his room, he became belligerent, like a crazy person. She said she feared for her own safety." My mother sat ramrod straight, all emotion from her usually animated face wiped away. There was no way she would condone Geneva's behavior, ever again. The thought pleased me more than I realized it would.

"Shit," I said on a heavy exhale, my head falling back onto the chair. Of all the things I thought Geneva was capable of, I'd never seen this one coming. I was too shocked to even be pissed.

Since I'd caught the two of them together in Rory's hotel room, it had never once occurred to me that he *hadn't* slept with her. He was a known player of the worst kind. Of course I'd believed he'd screwed her. But now? For the first time in over two weeks, there was hope.

I raised my head and stared at my mother. "What happened next?"

"She said Rory cried and moaned about hurting you, about losing you, about pushing you away. It only pissed her off more to see how much he loved you. She said it was obvious he would never sleep with her. But, she still tried."

Damn, the girl was brazen. Way more manipulative than I'd ever given her credit for.

"Instead, he pushed her off and told her to get out of his room before he called security. She said he went into his bedroom and locked the door, and that was the last time she saw him until he came out the next morning when you showed up."

"So he never slept with her?" The desperation in my voice was embarrassing.

My mother shook her head.

"And he never wanted to?" I searched her face.

"He never wanted to, sweetheart. Never would."

Could all this be true? Had Geneva told my mother and Paul the truth? Suddenly I was filled with hope.

"How could he be with anyone else, Hindley?" she asked. "He's so in love with you."

My mother loved Paul with everything inside her. They were soul mates. If anyone would recognize true love, it would be Caroline Hagen-Barton.

"Do you really think so, Mom? I mean, that he would never want to be with anyone else?" The idea astounded me.

"Hindley, I know so. Paul and I adore Rory. He's the best thing that's ever happened to you. You've come alive since you've met him. He's given you courage to be the real you. You have purpose again when you're with him."

My emotions were all over the map. I'd gone from depressed and desperate an hour ago to elated and euphoric.

Rory hadn't slept with Geneva. He had been drugged and was out of his mind and really didn't remember anything.

I had to call him. I had to see him. Now.

I jumped up from the chair, bolting for the phone.

"Wait!" Paul called out.

I stopped dead in my tracks.

"There's more," he said.

Oh, God. My body trembled at his words. He'd delivered the same sentence years ago just before telling me about the videos of me and Donald Lee Westbank. It seemed that my life would never end with a happily ever after.

"Sit back down," he said.

I stared at him in disbelief, wrapping my arms around me for support.

"Please, Hindley," he whispered.

I surveyed the three pairs of eyes locked on me. They were wide and filled with fear. For me. I sat back in the chair and tried, as best I could, to prepare myself for the worst.

"What is it, Paul?" I asked quietly, not really sure if I wanted to know.

He glanced at my mother and she nodded.

Shit.

"It's about your tapes," Paul said flatly.

I swallowed hard. "What tapes?" I asked, praying he wasn't talking about the tapes no one except me and the Dallas police detectives had seen.

Paul stared at my mother as if she held the answer.

"Paul," I repeated. "What tapes?"

He cleared his throat. "The tapes from your apartment."

My heart beat wildly in my chest, a sharp buzzing noise ringing in my ears. I steadied my breath, willing my heartbeat to slow. "The tapes of me showering and dressing and sleeping?" I asked. I prayed he didn't know about the other videos, but something inside me warned me.

He stared at me for a long moment before his head fell.

How had they found them? Had Rory told them? Why would he do that? Questions flew through my head. Any hope I'd had of Rory and me reconciling suddenly evaporated into thin air.

Dana came and knelt at my feet, placing a reassuring hand on my knee.

I stared straight at Paul whose head was still bent. "What videos, Paul?" I asked again.

He lifted his head and stared straight at me, his eyes bloodshot and red-rimmed. "No, sweetheart. Not those."

I wrapped my arms around my waist and fought for breath. All my worst fears had come true. The three people I loved most in the world knew that Donald Lee Westbank had raped me. I just prayed none of them had seen the tapes.

My mother choked out a sob, bending over and burying her face in her hands.

Paul's eyes brimmed with tears and his chin quivered. He stared at me with such fatherly love and concern that it nearly broke my heart.

"Why didn't you tell us, Hindley?" Dana asked.

I stared down at her, still not comprehending what they were telling me.

Tears streamed down her cheeks, her face flushed red. "Why didn't you tell us what that bastard had done to you?"

"I couldn't," I whispered. Tears warmed my cheeks. "I just… couldn't."

My mother surged toward me and took me in her arms.

Suddenly, I realized how much I needed her.

"Oh, darling," she cried. "I'm so sorry, so very, very sorry," she stuttered, her hands roaming up and down my back. "You've dealt with this all these years, all alone and we…"

"There's more, Hindley." Paul's voice broke through the room.

My blood ran ice cold, chilling me to the bone.

My mother scooted me over and sat beside me, her arm still clutched around my waist.

I stared at Paul, bracing myself for what was about to come next. As if knowing I'd need more strength, Dana clutched my leg, resting her cheek on my leg.

I squeezed my mother's hand. "What is it?" I asked quietly.

He walked to the coffee table directly across from me and sat down. He rested his elbows on his legs, his head falling into his hands.

Bile rose in my throat, choking me. I couldn't take much more.

"Tell me, Paul!"

He lifted his head, his eyes hollowed and dark as he held my gaze. "The tapes got out." His words were like knives to my soul.

My body felt like I'd been electrocuted, hit with a thousand volts of electricity. I shook uncontrollably, unable to breathe. This must be exactly what a fish out of water felt like when faced with its own impending death.

"What do you mean, *got out*?" I asked, pain coursing through my body.

"Someone found the tapes and they've published them," he said so quietly I almost didn't hear him.

"Published them where?" I shook my head, not understanding. "What do you mean?"

"They're on the Internet, Hindley," he said.

The Internet?

I gasped, slapping my hand over my mouth. "No," I choked out, shaking my head.

My mind raced through all kinds of scenarios. Maybe it wasn't as bad as they suspected. Maybe it was only on a few sites. Maybe we could have the websites taken down.

Paul remained stoic but I saw the anguish in his face. There was more.

"What else, Paul?"

My mother clutched me, squeezing me so hard I could barely breathe as she worked to silence her own sobs.

"Someone's taken the videos and spliced them together," he said.

I glanced around at everyone. "I don't understand."

Tears streamed down Paul's face and he reached for me.

Dana's muffled sobs echoed beside me.

I was going to be sick.

Paul wiped at his face with his palms. "They've taken the videos and reworked them, dubbing in music and sounds."

"And?" I still wasn't comprehending what he was saying. My mind was racing, trying to piece together what was going on.

Paul clenched and unclenched his jaw several times. "They've made it look like a porno movie, Hindley."

The room began to spin and my stomach lurched in protest. I slammed my eyes shut, trying to stave off vomiting. "I have to get up." I tugged myself free of my mother and Dana's death grip.

Reluctantly they released me.

I bolted down the hallway, slamming the bathroom door behind me, locking it for some unconscious reason. I sunk down to my knees in front of the toilet, expelling everything inside me. After several minutes of dry heaving, I sat back on my heels, wiping my mouth, trying to catch my breath.

I wanted to scream, wanted to cry, wanted to run, but I was paralyzed, glued to the floor. What was I going to do? The videos were on public display, available twenty-four seven to the entire world via the Internet. Not only that, but now someone had made me look like I was a willing participant.

Images of the disgusting videos ran through my mind.

Me, lying on the bed without pants on, my shirt pushed up to expose my naked breasts as he pumped into me over and over.

Me, face down on the sofa, completely naked as he covered my body with his own, grinding into my backside.

Me, on the floor of my living room, semi-conscious as his penis rubbed over my face, my neck, my breasts.

Oh, God.

I crawled back to the toilet and heaved more, nothing coming.

Everyone in the world was going to see the sordid images of me and Donald Lee Westbank. My heart beat so hard I feared I may actually have a heart attack right here on the bathroom floor.

I slumped back against the wall, trying to collect my thoughts. I needed a game plan, an attack, a way out of this hell I was in.

"Hindley," my mom called through the door.

I stood, grabbing the edge of the sink for stability, and stared at the image in the mirror.

Well, well, well, who do we have here?

I recognized the voice in my head. Rory wasn't the only one with a dark side.

If it isn't little miss perfect. Long time no see, Hinny Bin.

My image morphed into a person I rarely saw anymore. Her skin was paler, her eyes darker. To most we were one in the same. But I knew the difference.

This was the persona I'd created to protect myself during the darkest times of my life.

This was dark Hindley.

The girl who would take care of me when I was too weak.

I knew better than to let her take control anymore but today I couldn't fight her. I needed her. My world was spinning out of control and she was the only person who could save me now.

I told you you couldn't keep ignoring me forever without something bad happening. I'll take care of you, don't worry.

"No," I whispered, trying to fight her off.

"Hindley, open the door," my mother begged.

You don't really think they give a shit about you, do you? All they care about is their own image. Caroline Hagen-Barton, mother of a porn star? Please. No one cares about you. Only I do. I'm the only one who can protect you. Don't you trust me anymore?

I stared at dark Hindley, trying to break the spell she'd cast over me. I was weak though. My need to escape everything was stronger than ever.

I gazed down at a large candle encased in a glass container sitting on the vanity.

Pick it up. Go ahead.

I lifted the candle and stared at it for several seconds. "Go away," I shouted before squeezing my eyes shut and hurling the candle at my reflection.

"Hindley," my mother screamed.

My arm burned with pain. I opened my eyes and followed the warm trail of blood. A large piece of mirror was lodged in my forearm.

The throbbing ache in my arm reminded me that emotional pain could always be masked with physical pain. Like it always had been in the past.

Doesn't it feel good, Hindley? Doesn't the pain feel so intense and intoxicating? Don't you miss it?

I nodded.

Forget everything except the pain.

"Okay," I whispered.

I won't ever leave you. I'll never hurt you. I'll always be here. And you know it's only a matter of time before I take complete control.

I shook my head. "No," I whispered, pulling the piece of glass free. The blood trickled down to my fingertips. "You'll never take over again."

"Hindley!" Paul banged on the door.

I held the shiny piece of mirror in my hand, stained crimson with my blood, observing it as if it were a foreign object. But it was familiar, so familiar, and so welcomed. I pressed the sharp edge against the skin of my arm, pushing it in just enough to leave an indentation, but not enough to break the skin.

Push harder. It will feel so good. I promise you'll forget all your troubles, all your worries, all your fears, just like before. Maybe forever this time.

Suddenly the image of millions of people sitting in front of their computer screens watching that video of me and Donald Lee Westbank rolled through my mind. People thinking I was a willing participant as he raped me repeatedly.

Rory's face appeared. Him, sitting in front of his laptop, watching me, loathing me, hating me. He'd never want to be with a girl like me once he saw those tapes.

I drew in a deep breath and pushed the shard through the protective barrier of my skin. The emotional agony fled as the familiar pain enveloped me.

Warm, soothing blood trickled down my arm and dripped off my fingertips into a pool of crimson, staining the snowy white countertop.

Doesn't it feel good?

It did, better than it ever had before, better than I'd remembered.

I told you, Hindley. Trust me. Trust me. Trust me.

I pushed harder, dragging the shard of glass down my arm when images of Donald raping me filled my mind.

"No," I said. Only this time I wasn't talking to dark Hindley. "No more."

That a girl, Hindley. Deeper. Harder.

I pressed harder, the pain intensifying as I ran more trails down my arm.

Forever.

Finally the pain subsided, my vision growing darker.

No more Donald Lee Westbank, no more videos, no more Geneva, no more Rory, no more anything.

I slashed my arm over and over. The blood wrapped around me like a protective blanket, keeping me safe. The physical pain quickly eclipsed the emotional as my body floated higher.

You're almost there, Hindley, just a little closer. Forever. All your worries and your fears will be gone. Forever.

The door crashed open. Screaming echoed through the room but I barely heard it as the lights faded and darkness closed in.

I smiled. Heaven had finally reached me. The pain of cutting was the only thing that had ever brought me real peace in my life, even if for a little while.

All thoughts and reason faded away into nothingness as the darkness consumed me.

Forever.

"Forever," I repeated.

Oh, shit. Had those tapes gotten out?

"The guy apparently drugged Hindley, raped her, and recorded all of it," Leif said.

"That motherfucker." I searched for a bag. I was going to be sick.

"Shit." Matt sagged back in his chair.

"I know," Leif said. "Did you know about them, Rory?"

"Yes."

"Seriously?" Matt asked.

"Well, apparently you and the Dallas Police were the only ones who knew about them until sometime this week," Leif said.

Then it hit me like a bat between the eyes. "Oh, fuck!" I jumped to my feet. "They're out there, the videos. They're out on the Internet, aren't they?" I raked my hands viciously through my hair.

Leif dropped his head to his hands and nodded.

"What the fuck are we going to do now?" My heart raced and my palms broke out with sweat as I thought about Hindley discovering the videos out on the Internet, her sitting at home all alone with no one to console her because I'd been a complete douche. I knew her. She was strong, but she would never recover from this. Not alone. "What is taking this plane so goddamn long?" I paced the small cabin. "Can't this motherfucker fly any faster!"

"It's worse than that, Rory," Leif said.

"What?" I shouted. "How the fuck could it get worse?"

He stared past me at nothing in particular.

"Just say it," I demanded.

Leif took in a deep breath and turned to face me. "Someone took the footage, cut it up, and turned it into what looks a lot like a porno movie, including music and sounds."

Oh. Fuck.

I collapsed into the seat and I covered my face with my hands, trying to block out all the images.

This was beyond bad. There were no words for how horrible this situation was.

I drew in deep breaths, trying to slow my breathing to keep from hyperventilating. "Who the fuck would do that?" I shouted. "Who in the fuck would do something so sick and perverted?"

"The police are investigating the leak," Leif answered. "They may never find out though."

"How did she find out?" My thoughts were reeling from the discovery. "Did she see the video out on the Internet? Please God, tell me no."

"No," Leif assured me. "Dana said Hindley's parents came over to her condo earlier today and broke the news to her."

I slammed the arm of the seat with my fist. "Damn it. I should have been there."

"Dude, don't be so hard on yourself," Leif said. "None of us could have known this would happen."

"Yeah, but I should have been there with her when they broke the news. None of this shit would have happened. She wouldn't be sitting in a hospital room cut up and bleeding right now if I had been there to protect her."

"Look, Dana and Hindley's parents already feel awful."

"Well, fuck, they should. How could they have let her just walk away after dumping that kind of news on her if they knew she'd cut herself before? They should have seen this coming. I mean, it doesn't take a—"

"Stop, Rory!"

I flinched at the sound of Leif's booming voice still echoing through the plane.

Then he was in front of me, his finger waving frantically in my face. "I don't want to hear you say a fucking word to Dana or to Hindley's parents about this when we get there, you got it? They already feel like shit and they don't need your sorry ass dumping on them too."

I sat back at his reprimand. He was right. I was the last person to judge anyone's actions, least of all Hindley's best friend and parents. "Look, I'm sorry, man. I don't know what to do." I threw my hands up. "I feel like shit."

"Why?" Matt asked.

"Because I love her, more than anything. More than my own life. When she hurts, I hurt. It's excruciating not being there with her." I rubbed my eyes at the sting of the tears welling up.

"We'll be there soon, man, it will be all right." Matt reached out and patted my knee.

For the first time since I'd known Matt, I saw in him what Hindley had all along. He was a good man. All this time I'd been too blinded by fear, self-loathing, and jealousy to allow myself to really get to know him as a person. I needed good friends in my life. People like Matt Davis.

"Thanks, man." I gave him a half smile. "I'm sorry."

"For what?" He reclined in his seat.

"For being such a douche bag in the beginning. For calling your product douche water."

He laughed. "It's all good, Rory."

The atmosphere in the plane shifted, becoming lighter. I could finally breathe again.

"Hey, dude." Leif shook my shoulder.

I turned to find a grave expression marring his face.

"What is it, Leif?" I was right back in panic mode again.

"You know they're investigating that employee from the hotel for drugging your food, right?"

"Yeah, Paloma told me. Actually, it was her research team that found out the truth."

"Well, that wasn't the end of the story."

I sat up. "What else is there?"

"Someone paid him to give you the drugs."

"Who?"

"Geneva."

"I knew it!" I jumped out of my seat. "I knew that fucking bitch had done something. She hates Hindley so much. All this shit is her fault. God, if I saw her right now..." I clenched my fists trying to control my fury as I brooded around the small space, fighting off the urge to punch something, or someone.

"Calm down, dude," Leif said. "Getting upset isn't going to help anything."

"How the fuck can you say that? That little bitch is the sole reason I'm not with Hindley. She and I have been apart for two weeks because that psycho bitch hates her so much. And now, Hindley hates me and probably won't even let me into her fucking hospital room."

"That's not true," Leif said.

"How the fuck do you know?"

"Dana said her parents told Hindley earlier today that it was Geneva who gave you the drugs. Apparently, Geneva confessed everything to them last night."

"And so what, Geneva's cleared of all wrongdoing?"

"No, not that."

"Then what?"

"Hindley gets it."

"Hindley gets what?"

"She understands now that the guy who cussed her out in front of God and half the hotel, and supposedly slept with her sister, wasn't really you."

"What are you saying? She believes me?"

"I don't know if she believes you, but Dana said she at least wanted to talk to you after her parents told her that it was Geneva who drugged you."

I stormed toward Leif, placing my hands on the arms of his recliner. "Are you fucking with me, man? Because if you are, I swear to God, I will beat the shit out of you right here, right now."

"No, I'm not fucking with you." He chuckled. "Dana said Hindley realized that the drug had made you act so crazy. Geneva admitted that you two had never slept together."

"I knew it!" I shouted again. "There is no fucking way I would have ever slept with that skank." I fell back into my seat, scrubbing my face with my hands, feeling a fraction of relief from the guilt and shame that had been running rampant through me for the past two weeks.

I hadn't slept with Geneva. In the back of my mind, I'd always known that, but now Hindley knew it too. I couldn't remember feeling happier in all my life.

"So what made Geneva cave and tell the truth?"

"Dana wasn't sure, but she thinks her husband made her. Dana said he kicked her out of their house."

"Good. She deserves a hell of a lot worse than that. Did Hindley's parents take her in?"

"Hell, no," Leif said. "They're super pissed at Geneva. Especially now. Caroline told Dana that Geneva had crossed a line and she wasn't entirely sure she'd ever forgive her. Especially after what's happened with Hindley."

I was happy to hear that news. At least Hindley wouldn't have to put up with her parents acting like assholes too.

"So, Dana said she's done this before, Hindley, I mean?" I asked.

"Yeah, apparently after the guy's trial years ago, when she saw all the videos in court, it kind of started this whole cutting thing into motion."

"God, that's sick," Matt choked out.

I'd forgotten he was even with us.

"How could anyone do that to another human being?" he mumbled, obviously picturing Hindley's torture like the rest of us.

"So, you knew about the rape?" Leif looked over at me.

I nodded.

"I guess you're the only person she told. She must really love you, man."

"Do you think she'll forgive me though?"

"I think, right now, you need to focus on her health and safety and well-being. If you can do that, I think it would be a good start for her."

And that right there was why I loved Leif. He could break it down in simple terms, terms I could understand and follow.

"You're right," I agreed. "It's about Hindley. I'll do whatever I can to make sure she's taken care of."

"Even if that means she doesn't want to see you?"

I held up my hand. "Don't. I can't go there right now, man."

"I understand." He wrapped his hand around my shoulder and gave me a reassuring squeeze.

A voice boomed over the PA system of the plane. "Gentlemen, we'll be touching down in Austin in twenty minutes. Please find your way back to your seats and buckle in, if you haven't already."

My heart raced with the anticipation of seeing Hindley again. I didn't care what she looked like or what state she was in, as long as I could see her, maybe even hold her, I knew we'd be all right.

CHAPTER 39

RORY

THE SMELL of antiseptic and illness assaulted me as we burst through the sliding doors of the hospital. We stepped up to the reception desk.

"May I help you?" An older woman with shiny white hair gave us a glowering stare, as if she knew we were intruders.

"Um, yes," Matt said. "We're here to see Hindley Hagen."

The woman turned toward the computer, hitting keys like she was writing a best-selling manuscript.

Time ticked by like hours. I thought I'd jump out of my skin and straight through the plexiglass window dividing us if she didn't find the information we wanted soon.

Leif covered my fist with his. I'd been unconsciously banging it on the counter like a rhythmic drum. "Calm down, man. Dana said she's safe."

His words sounded hollow even though I knew they were true. As far as I was concerned, Hindley would be in harm's way until I saw her again.

"Oh, yes," the lady answered, her eyes narrowing. "She's on the fourth floor. I'm afraid that's a secure area."

Secure? Shit, this was really bad.

"Only family is allowed," she said.

What the fuck was I going to do now?

"Yeah, we're her brothers." Leif nudged his way in front of me.

"Really?" the lady cocked a brow and tilted her head. We were not going to pull one over this old lady.

"Yes," Matt said. "We're her brothers."

It sounded totally insane. None of us looked anything alike but somehow he held his ground, daring the woman to question him further.

She studied each of us individually, looking like a protective grandma bear, guarding one of her own.

I liked the fact that she was protecting Hindley from visitors who might bring her harm. I shook in my sneakers, knowing she probably thought that was me.

"Do you have ID?" she asked, her gaze landing on each of us with a questioning glare.

Shit, this was going to go south real quick. We pulled out our wallets and tossed our IDs on the counter. I held my breath, praying she'd let us by.

Grandma Bear surveyed each ID, holding it up to our individual faces like she was a bouncer at a nightclub. When she came to mine, she froze.

Ah, shit. She recognized me as the bastard who'd put Hindley in the hospital. Well, fuck Grandma Bear, no one was going to stop me from seeing the woman I loved. No one. I bullied my way past Leif, ready to do battle.

"Oh, Mr. Gregor, I'm so sorry." Her tone was now friendly, her attitude completely different.

Matt, Leif, and I exchanged questioning glances. "Why are you sorry?" I asked.

"They've been expecting you."

"Who's been expecting me?"

"The family. Mr. and Mrs. Barton. Hindley's parents. They've been asking about you."

"Are you shitting me?" Leif and I asked in unison. Why would Hindley's parents be expecting me?

Probably because they wanted to take my ass out in the parking lot and kick me into next week.

The receptionist cleared her throat. "Apparently, Ms. Hagen has been asking for you."

My heart burst with joy, warmth spreading through my body. Hindley still wanted to see me. I'd never received a better gift in my life.

"You'll need to check in at the nurses' station on the fourth floor," Grandma Bear instructed. "I'll call up there now and let them know you're on your way. You'll need to show your ID again. And here." She handed us tags.

"What are these for?" Leif asked.

"Who the fuck cares?" I shouted. "Just take it."

Grandma Bear cut her eyes at me. "It shows the staff that you've been cleared to be on the floor. I don't want you boys to be surprised when you get there. It's…a little bit different than our other floors in the hospital."

What the hell did that mean?

"Some of the patients will be restrained," she said. Her voice remained passive but I could see the concern in her eyes.

"Restrained how?" I asked.

"You may find that their arms and or legs will be strapped down to the bed."

"Are Hindley's?" The thought of seeing Hindley tied down brought tears to my eyes. I knew I'd restrained her before, but that was for much different reasons, and it was consensual. But this was—bad.

"I'm not sure of Ms. Hagen's current medical condition," she said. "I only know that she was recently brought out of surgery and is still under close observation. I wanted to warn you so you won't be surprised when you get to the floor."

"Thank you," Matt said.

"The elevators are around the corner to the right." She pointed beyond us.

We fled toward the bank of elevators. My only thought was of getting to Hindley as quickly as my legs could carry me.

～

I stepped off the elevator, my legs weak and wobbly, afraid of what state I might find Hindley in. An icy chill ran down my spine as we stepped into the hallway. The floor felt dark and heavy. I had to get Hindley out of this place as soon as possible if she was ever going to recover.

My eyes darted up and down the hall. "Did she tell you what room number?" I asked Matt and Leif.

"No, but there's a nurse. We'll ask her." Matt led the way toward a woman in dark blue scrubs. "Excuse me," he said quietly, "we're looking for Hindley Hagen."

The middle-aged woman with sandy blonde hair turned around and surveyed each of us as if we were the Russian Mafia here to execute a hit. "Are you family?"

"Yes, we're her brothers," Matt said with no hesitation.

Her eyes scoured the three of us but came to rest on me, looking me up and down in the same protective way Grandma Bear had. At least someone had been protecting her in my absence.

A cold sweat broke out across my forehead and I felt dizzy thinking about what had happened to my Drunk Girl.

"You gonna be all right?" she asked.

I nodded, swallowing hard.

"I know who you are." Her lips pursed as a brow arched high above her blue eyes.

Why did my shitty reputation have to precede me?

"You're definitely *not* her brother. But Hindley's been asking for you, so follow me."

"Is she conscious?" I followed her down the hallway.

"No, she's still pretty drugged up from surgery. Or she could still be in a comatose state."

"What?" Coma?

She turned and glared at me.

I had to stay cool or they would kick my ass out of this place.

"Her family can explain it."

I caught up with her so I could see her face. "Is she really in a coma?"

"It's not a coma in the medical sense," she said. "It's more of a psychotic coma, the body's way of protecting itself when it encounters too much emotional trauma."

"Will she come out of it?" Matt asked.

I was happy for his concern because suddenly, I had lost my voice.

"Usually, yes, but I've seen some people stay in a catatonic state for months."

Oh, God. Had I lost my Drunk Girl?

"Hindley seems resilient though," the nurse said, "and she's surrounded by a lot of people who love her. I suspect it's only temporary." She stopped and turned so abruptly, her ponytail slapped her in the face. "She cannot, and I repeat *cannot* become upset or agitated in the least. Do you understand?" Her menacing stare was directed at me.

"I understand," I answered quietly, trying to reel in my emotions. I knew I had to be strong. And calm. I couldn't lose my shit no matter how close I was.

"She is in a very delicate state right now, both physically and mentally. She is here to recover, not get worse. Understand?"

"We understand," Matt said.

"Good." She turned and continued down the hall.

Paul appeared in the hallway talking to someone in a white coat. The doctor maybe? He turned and our eyes locked. I was paralyzed with fear. Why did he want me here? Would he punch me in the face and tell me never to see his daughter again?

The hallway grew darker and closed in on me as I fought to catch my next breath. A look of relief washed across his worried face and I was finally able to exhale.

"It's all right, man." Leif rested his arm across my shoulders. "Remember, Dana said they wanted you here."

I turned to my best friend, silently thanking him for always being there for me, no matter the personal price to his own life.

The corner of his mouth curled up in a small smile and he nodded in acknowledgment of my gratitude.

"Doctor, this is Rory Gregor." Paul came to stand by my side. The doctor and I shook hands then his gaze traveled between Leif, Matt, and me.

"These are my friends," I said. The doctor's concerned look prompted me to add. "And Hindley's." I gestured to them. "This is Leif Jennings and Matt Davis."

I caught Matt's look of surprise at being introduced as a friend of mine. But, it was true. Anyone who would come this far and go through all of this with me and my girl was definitely someone I admired and wanted in my life.

"Nice to meet you all." The doctor shook hands with Leif and Matt.

"Dr. Saunders was just giving us an update," Paul said.

The doctor gave Paul a questioning glance.

"It's fine, you can share with them," Paul said, nodding.

"Hindley's condition is stable but still critical," Dr. Saunders said.

All I heard was *critical*. My sweet girl was *critical* and there wasn't a damn thing I could do.

"She sustained some pretty severe cuts to her forearm, cutting deep into the muscle. But thankfully, there's no permanent nerve damage, at least as far as we can tell. Some of the lacerations were so deep we had to do internal stitches as well, hence the need for surgery. We didn't want to put her body under more undue stress."

Fuck.

She had cut herself so fucking deep they had to do surgery?

The walls around me closed in and I couldn't breathe. I braced myself on the wall, praying I wouldn't pass out. I had to be strong, for Hindley.

"How is she now?" I asked.

"She's still unconscious from the surgery and not back in her room yet. We're having a hard time waking her up. I'm not sure if it's from the anesthesia or her protective comatose state she was in when she arrived at the hospital."

"Can I see her?"

"She should be back in her room soon," the doctor said. "It all just depends on her condition."

Suddenly, I felt her, her presence was all around me.

I jerked my head, searching for her, my heart thumping so hard, I feared it would beat out of my chest. I sucked in a breath, my lungs burning like they were on fire.

What would I find? What state would she be in? Would she recognize me? Would my presence send her back over the edge?

The doctor glanced over his shoulder. "Oh, here she comes now. Good. I'll be able to observe her before I leave."

Leave? Where the fuck was this guy going? My baby needed him. He couldn't leave.

My gaze followed his.

A hospital bed rolled down the hallway, containing a small body that lay motionless under the sheets and blankets. It was Hindley.

The only part of her visible was her beautiful face. Tears stung my eyes and my stomach plummeted. My Drunk Girl was suffering and there wasn't shit I could do.

Paul leaned into the doorway of the hospital room. "She's here," he said to someone.

Caroline and Dana rushed out to the hallway, shrouding Hindley's bed and gripping the railing as the attendant wheeled it toward the room. The grief and remorse on their faces told me they were blaming themselves for Hindley's situation just as much as I was.

The attendant shooed them away at the door and reluctantly they left Hindley's side.

Caroline turned toward me, her eyes red-rimmed and shadowed with worry. "Rory," she sighed, making her way toward me. "Oh, thank God, you're here."

Thank God?

Was what Grandma Bear said true? Had they really wanted me here?

Caroline threw her arms around my neck and squeezed me tight.

"You're really glad I'm here, Caroline?" I whispered, slipping my arms around her.

She abruptly released me, stepping back to inspect me.

"Of course we are. Hindley's been asking for you non-stop."

"But I thought they said she was comatose."

"She's been unconscious the entire time. Every time she asks for you, we all think she's coming to, but she never does. The doctors don't understand it. It's like she's stuck in a dream, or maybe a nightmare. I feel like you may be the only one who can reach her."

No words had ever brought me more relief. These past two weeks had been the worst of my life, second only to the death of my sister. I'd hurt Hindley, inflicting unimaginable pain when I'd promised to protect her. Now, her mother was telling me I may be her saving grace? I pulled Caroline back into my arms.

"Thank you," I whispered, as tears rolled down my face. "Thank you so much. I'm so sorry, I never meant to hurt her, I swear, Caroline, I love her so much."

"Rory, I know," she soothed. "We're the ones who are sorry. I'm so sorry for what Geneva did to you." Her voice was controlled but her body was shaking. She broke our embrace but kept her hands firmly wrapped around my upper arms.

Her words of apology were so surprising.

"Rory, you have to know," she said, shaking her head. "We had no idea what Geneva had did, not until last night, I swear."

I almost laughed out loud. I'd come here, expecting to be given the boot by her parents. Instead, Hindley's mother was apologizing to *me*, and saying I might be the only one who could save her daughter.

"Caroline, nothing matters anymore, only Hindley."

"Yes." She nodded, tears rolling down her cheeks. "You're right. Only Hindley."

Paul slipped in next to Caroline, wrapping her protectively against him like I'd done to Hindley so many times.

"Thank you for coming," Paul said, as if I'd done him the biggest favor of his life.

"Thanks for letting me come," I said.

His brows furrowed. "What do you mean?"

"I fully expected to get my ass kicked then promptly thrown out of here when I showed up, so you thanking me for being here comes as quite a shock."

"I think it's us who should be receiving the ass kicking from you," Paul said.

We both laughed and just like that, I knew Paul Barton was on my side.

"There'll be no ass kicking today," Caroline said, patting Paul's chest.

I glanced over Caroline's shoulder and noticed Dana wrapped in Leif's arms. I was so glad she had him. They were good for each other.

"She feels awful." Paul nodded toward Dana. "I can't seem to say anything to console her. She feels solely responsible for Hindley's break-down, and I can't seem to reach her."

"If anyone can, Leif can," I said. "Can we go in?" I asked the doctor.

"Just give them a few more minutes to set up her IV bags and let me assess her, then you can," he said.

It wasn't the answer I wanted, but I accepted it. There was absolutely no way I was giving anyone grief. Not today. But I was overwhelmed by all the questions flying through my head while waiting to see the woman I loved.

What had happened? How had it happened? Had she done this during the time I had known her? When I thought my head might explode from all the questions racing through my mind, I approached the delicate subject apprehensively. "So, what happened?"

Caroline shook her head and I knew there was no way she could relive the day, so I turned to Paul for answers.

"Last night, Geneva came to our house with Stan and explained everything to us," he said. "How she'd paid the waiter to drug you at the hotel so she could seduce you and try to get you to sleep with her." Paul took in a calming breath.

I realized that even though this was his daughter, he was furious with Geneva. What Leif said was right. Geneva had crossed a line and it may cost her everything—her stepmother, her father, maybe even her own husband. As far as I was concerned, that bitch deserved everything she got.

"Rory, you have to know," Paul said, "we had no idea what she'd done." He repeated Caroline's words.

"I know, Paul, I'm not upset with either of you."

"But you should be. I was furious with you," he said. "I would have killed you with my bare hands if I could have found you."

I laughed to myself, realizing that my decision to escape to Colorado after my incident in Miami may very well have saved my life.

"It's all in the past, Paul, okay? I just want to know what happened to Hindley, and how we can help her heal from this."

Caroline let out a sob, covering her mouth as she nodded her head in agreement.

"Do you know about the videos?" he asked.

"Yes." I tried to remain unaffected, for their benefit, but it was hard not to punch something.

"So you know what we're dealing with?"

I nodded, unable to say more.

"Well, anyway," he said, "we thought it best to tell Hindley about the videos in person, so we went to Dana's to meet her. Hindley was so relieved to learn that you hadn't slept with Geneva, she wanted to speak to you. She wanted to call you right then and there."

My gaze darted to Caroline.

She smiled and nodded in agreement. "She did."

I couldn't contain the smile inside me at the thought that my girl wanted to talk to me.

"But we had to tell her about the videos first," Paul said.

"How did you find out about them?" I asked. "The videos, I mean."

"I have an investor who has a large computer systems company. They constantly troll the Internet for all sorts of things to help them service their clients, although I'm not sure how these videos qualify. Anyway, that's how I first discovered them. By the time my client found the videos, they'd already gone viral."

"Fuck." I scraped my fingers through my hair, pulling at the strands. "I'm sorry."

"It's all right." Caroline smiled. "I said some pretty harsh words myself when I found out."

I couldn't picture Caroline Hagen-Barton cussing, but I reminded myself, she was more like me than I'd realized in the beginning.

I looked between the two of them. "Any idea who leaked them? I thought the police had all the tapes locked away."

"So you did know about them? All the videos?" Caroline asked me in a clipped tone. It was clear she was talking about the videos of Hindley being raped, not just the surveillance ones.

"Yes."

"For how long?" she asked.

The disappointment and hurt in her eyes at the realization her daughter had shared this news with someone other than her was palpable. I couldn't say that I blamed her.

"When she told me about the stripping, she also told me about the surveillance videos and being raped."

"Stripping?" Paul flinched.

Oh, shit. Apparently they didn't know about that one either.

Dana scooted in beside me. "Paul, calm down."

"How the hell can I calm down? Rory just told me my daughter was a stripper."

I looked over at Caroline who wasn't nearly as shocked as her husband. She knew.

"Caroline, did you know about this?" Paul asked.

Her eyes were wide, like a deer in the headlights and I knew she needed help.

"She was never a stripper, Paul," I said. "Not that that should matter."

"The hell it should matter," he said with contained fury.

"She only designed the outfits for the strippers," Dana said.

"You knew about this too?" He glared at Dana as if he was going to strangle her. "When did you find out, Caroline?" He narrowed his eyes, his lips pursed.

There was no doubt in anyone's mind, Paul Barton was pissed.

"Didn't you ever wonder how she paid for law school without your help?" Caroline asked with a mocking tone.

I wasn't sure that was safe, given Paul's current state of mind.

"I assumed it was grants, scholarships, and loans like she told us," he said. "I never dreamed she paid for it by stripping."

"First of all," I broke in defensively, "even if she had been a stripper, that would have been her choice, and it's a legitimate profession. If men are dumb enough to pay for something they can see for free, then why should we blame the women who provide them that service? Hell, those girls are geniuses if you asked me." Every head jerked, their eyes trained on me as they stood in stunned silence.

"You can't be serious?" Paul said through gritted teeth.

"I'm completely serious."

"So, if Hindley had been a stripper, you would have been all right with that?" Paul asked in disgust.

"It wouldn't be my desired profession for her, but yes, if that's how she had paid for school, I would eventually have come to terms with it. She's a smart, bright, intelligent woman. She would never do anything that didn't make sense."

Until now, I thought.

The doctor stepped into the hallway. "All right, you can go in now. Only two at a time though, please."

"Is she awake?" I asked, rubbing the back of my neck with worry.

He shook his head. "Not yet."

I knew what the silent prognosis was. She was unconscious, and he didn't know how long it would last.

I stepped aside, making way for Paul and Caroline to enter, but instead they moved back and motioned for me.

"It's you she wants to see, Rory," Caroline said softly.

"But you're her mother." The words came out choked on my tears.

"Yes, but it's you she's been asking for, sweetheart. It's been you in her thoughts and dreams. And I'm willing to bet it will be *you* who brings her back."

I caught Caroline up in my arms and buried my face in her neck, bawling like a small child. I'm sure I looked like a complete pussy, but I couldn't give a shit less. "I'm sorry, Caroline," I whispered. "I never meant to hurt her, I swear."

"Rory," she rubbed my back, "we know, sweetheart. We know."

I squeezed her tighter, absorbing her words.

"You would never hurt her," she whispered. "I should have known that from the start. I'm sorry Geneva did this to you. To Hindley."

We stood in the hallway, surrounded by family and friends, unaffected by their presence. I felt safe in Caroline's arms, like I did in Kara's. I knew if I was going to get through this, if *we* were going to get through this, we'd need to rely on one another's strength and love.

She pulled back from my embrace and cupped my jaw. "Go," she said, wiping away tears with her thumbs. "Bring my baby back home." She pulled me down and pressed a kiss to my cheek. "Please, Rory."

I stared into her beautiful emerald eyes, unable to believe that she needed me, that anyone would need me. I nodded once, vowing that this time I wouldn't let them down.

She gently released me and I turned to Paul. He wore the same pleading look in his dark blue eyes. I needed to be strong for them.

I turned to Dana. If I was going to be in Hindley's life again, I needed her by my side to guide me. There was no other way. I had to gain her forgiveness.

"It wasn't your fault, Rory," she said as if reading my thoughts. "Hindley knows that."

"It wasn't yours either, Dana," I said.

Her eyes welled with tears as she stepped closer.

Gazing down at her petite body, knowing full well she could kick my ass, I flinched. Was she gonna punch me in the gut or kick me in the nuts like I deserved?

Instead, she grabbed my face with her petite hands and yanked me down to meet her gaze. Bringing her mouth close to my ear, she pulled me in even further. "Fuck this up and I *will* kill you though. I'm Italian and I know how to hide bodies. Got it, One Nighter?" She released my face and took a step back, a perfectly manicured brow raised high over one blue eye.

I stared at her for several seconds before we both burst out in laughter. And just like that, I was back in her good graces.

I pulled her in tight, holding her close as her body sagged against me and began to shake, her tears flowing freely. In many ways, Dana reminded me of my sister Shelly, and I was happy to have her with me, to guide me and encourage me as we worked together to bring Hindley back.

"I promise not to fuck this up again," I said quietly. "But if I do," I leaned back and stared down at her, "I give you permission to kill me."

"Good." She smiled, knocking my arm with her fist as she wiped at her eyes.

"Just make it quick and painless."

She smiled, two huge dimples emerging on each cheek. "Not on your life."

I walked toward Hindley's room but glanced over my shoulder just before I entered. These people loved Hindley as much as I did. They were counting on me to bring her back. I nodded once in silent acknowledgment.

I would bring my Drunk Girl home.

CHAPTER 40

RORY

As I ENTERED Hindley's room, I saw her sleeping peacefully. The only reminder she was in a hospital were the railings on either side of her bed and two IV bags hanging from a stand next to her.

"One's an antibiotic so her wounds won't become infected," the nurse said as I investigated the bags. "The other is for fluids."

"Can she hear me?"

"Some people don't think so, but I believe she can. If there's something you want to tell her, it's all right. Even if she doesn't remember as soon as she wakes up, your words will always be tucked away somewhere in the back of her mind."

"How long will she be like this?" I waved my hand up and down her body.

"Unconscious, you mean?"

I nodded.

"It's hard to say. Part of it's the anesthesia, but most of it is her trying to keep her mind out of harm's way."

"From what?"

"Herself," she said.

I surveyed Hindley's motionless body and flinched at the thought of her hurting herself. I glanced up at the nurse and saw an expression that conveyed a wealth of empathy. She was connected personally in some way. As soon as the look came, it retreated, and her expression turned professional again as she continued to work around Hindley's body. She plugged in machines and took her temperature before checking her blood pressure.

"When Hindley feels safe again, safe enough to handle the trauma she's endured, she'll wake up." She paused in her efforts and came to stand in front of me. "But when she does wake up, you need to make sure you're here for the right reasons. If you can't handle this, her emotional trauma and the road she will have to travel to recover, then you need to leave. Now. Before she wakes up. She can't afford more stress or turmoil, like you leaving her, not in the state she's in."

I nodded. "I'm here for the long haul."

"I figured as much." She nodded once then busied herself again, taking care of Hindley's needs. "I saw your interview."

I looked up and saw her tending to Hindley's IV bags. I wasn't surprised she'd seen the show. It was on national television. And it had been broadcast over the Internet for the world to watch.

"Do you know if she saw it?" I asked.

"No, I don't know. Sorry."

My heart sank.

"It would be a shame if she didn't see it though."

"Why?"

"Because anyone who saw it knows how much you love her."

"Really?" Hope surged through me. If this stranger saw it, maybe Hindley had too.

"That's the only reason Pam let you up here."

"Who?"

"Pam, down at the front desk."

Grandma Bear.

"She's the gate-keeper of the fourth floor. She only lets up the good ones." She turned toward me and winked. "Take care of her, Rory." She stared at Hindley's motionless body.

"It's my mission in life," I whispered, my eyes glued to the woman I loved.

"Good. Press the red button there on the bed if you need anything."

I sat down in the chair next to the bed. "Can I touch her?"

The nurse came around and withdrew Hindley's left arm from the sheets.

I gasped when I saw it was wrapped in gauze and an Ace bandage from her wrist just past her elbow. Fuck. What had she done to herself?

"Just be mindful of her arm," she said. "Her right hand also has stitches."

My stomach contracted in pain and my body trembled at the thought of how bad her injuries were, how much pain she was in.

"Just avoid those two places. Anywhere else on her body should be fine." The nurse walked around to the other side of Hindley's bed and slid out her other arm and I noticed Hindley's right hand was completely covered with gauze.

I stared at Hindley's injuries, having no clue how to help her.

"No one's told you, have they?" she asked.

I shook my head. "They called it cutting, but I still don't understand," I admitted with a level of defeat in my voice that disappointed me.

"Sometimes, we go through situations in our life that are so traumatic, our minds can't handle it," she explained. "We all cope with it differently. Some people turn to religion. Some people, like you, turn to drugs and alcohol."

I flinched at the reminder of how much she knew about my personal life, thanks to Paloma Monroe. I'd spilled it all out during my interview, my childhood, my partying, my womanizing, and my drugs and boozing. I'd promised myself from the very beginning of the show that I'd hold nothing back, and I hadn't. I wondered if that decision had been a mistake, but the nurse didn't seem fazed by my past.

"For others," she continued, nodding toward Hindley, "they cut themselves."

I shook my head, unable to wrap my mind around the idea that cutting yourself could help you feel better, numb the pain. "I just don't get it."

"When you're in so much pain, emotionally, you'll do almost anything to numb it, right?"

I thought about my own past, trying to relate it to Hindley's situation.

"Why did you drink and do drugs, Rory?"

I shrugged, not wanting to analyze my own past, afraid of what I might find.

"You drank because you couldn't handle the shame and guilt of your sister's passing. In many ways, you blamed yourself, even though you couldn't have stopped it if you wanted to."

She was right, completely right. How had this woman been able to sum up my life by watching one interview?

"I'm a psychiatric nurse, Rory," she said. "I don't just take care of the physical needs of my patients, I take care of their mental and emotional needs as well. It's just as important to their recovery. Maybe even more so than the physical injuries they've endured. Plus, I get it." She pulled up her shirt sleeve to reveal tiny scars littered across the underside of her forearm.

She was a cutter too.

"For cutters," she said, "the physical pain is an escape from our mental anguish, like drugs were for you. Even better than drinking and drugs though, cutting is free and available twenty-four hours a day, seven days a week. Sharp objects are easily accessible, and if done right, no one even sees our injuries. That's the blessing and the curse of cutting. We often go for years without anyone knowing how much we hurt inside, or out."

I watched her speak but it was like an out of body experience.

"I lost you, didn't I?" she asked with a hint of a smile.

"No." I shook my head. "I get it, I think. It's just hard to believe."

"What?" She straightened Hindley's IV bag.

"Knowing Hindley was in so much pain, enough pain to harm herself, and there wasn't a damn thing I could do about it. It kills me."

"Don't you think your friends and family felt the same way when you were drinking and drugging?"

I froze at her revelation. I had never stopped to think about how my substance abuse had affected anyone else but me. Had they really been this worried and concerned for me?

"Anyone who loved you was just as worried as you are now," she said.

"So what can I do to help her?"

"Just be there for her. Don't judge her. Try to empathize." The nurse stared at me.

I felt like she was judging me, trying to determine if she thought I was up for the task.

"Do you think you can do that, Rory?"

"Yes," I whispered, reaching through the railing to stroke her upper arm.

"Reassure her that you'll be there for her, especially when things get bad again. And they will." She hesitated and I glanced up at her. "But I'm not kidding, Rory. You have the potential to take this girl over the edge."

I felt sick to my stomach, knowing I had done this to her. Hindley had always been so strong and brave. I'd never considered how much power I could have over her recovery.

"If you don't want to do this, if you can't do this, then say goodbye to her, now."

"No way." I clenched my fists to keep from shouting. "I can't exist without her. She's my whole world. I love her."

A smile spread across her face. "That's what I hoped you'd say."

I breathed a sigh of relief at her words. She understood Hindley better than any of us. And she believed in me.

"I'll bring you in some books and brochures to read about cutting." Her eyes went wide.

I understood why. She'd assumed I could read. My illiteracy was now public knowledge, but surprisingly enough, it didn't bother me anymore.

"I'll go over them with you," she said. "We can read through them together. Then we can talk about any questions you have."

"Thanks. I'd really appreciate that." I sagged back in the chair, thankful for her willingness to help me. I wondered how many other people would have withheld judgment and offered me help if I would have let them.

"No problem," she said.

"Are you better now? You know, with the…" I nodded toward her arm.

She gave me a blank stare, obviously unaware of what I was referring to.

"With the cutting," I said.

She looked down at her arm, rubbing it. "Oh, this? Yes, I'm better." She paused and I felt like shit for bringing it up. "It doesn't mean I don't think about cutting."

Fuck. Would Hindley have to deal with this the rest of her life? Probably. I had to keep my own shit in check to keep from drinking and drugging again.

"I have better coping skills now," she said, "like you do with your addiction. When Hindley realizes *she* has the power to act differently, and learns better behaviors, she'll come around too."

She walked around Hindley's bed, grasping the railing and staring down at my girl. "She'll probably always fight the urge to harm herself. But it won't be in a suicidal sense like some people think when they hear about cutters."

My heart stopped and my world went dark as I thought about Hindley taking her own life. That wasn't an option. I couldn't exist without my Drunk Girl.

"We all have triggers, Rory, things that set off our self-destructive behaviors. If Hindley can figure out what those triggers are, if you can help her, then that will be half the battle."

"You're amazing, you know that, right?" I said in complete awe of the way she was so eloquently, yet so easily explaining such a complex disease.

"So I've been told." She laughed, shrugging her shoulders.

I smiled, a real smile for the first time since Leif had received the call that Hindley was in trouble.

"She'll be fine, Rory. Just let her get some rest, stay with her, talk to her, assure her you'll be here when she wakes up, and eventually, she will." She poured water into a small cup and inserted a straw into the lid. "She'll probably be thirsty when she wakes up, so give her this."

I nodded, setting the cup on the tray beside me.

"My phone number is there on the board." She pointed up to a large white board on the wall. "Or push the red button like I showed you. I'll leave you two alone for a while, but I'll be back in a bit." She tucked in a string from Hindley's gown that had come loose, then patted her shoulder.

My heart settled into a steady beat as I realized Hindley was in good hands.

"She's been asking for you, you know." Her gaze swept over to me and she smiled. "Just let her know you're here and that you're not going anywhere." She turned to leave but stopped dead in her tracks, turning to face me. "Oh, no."

"What's wrong?" I asked, jumping up and scanning Hindley's body. "What's happened to her?"

"What about the X Games?" she asked. "You're supposed to be competing today."

My body sagged in relief. That was all she was worried about? "I don't give a flying fuck about the X Games," I said. "The only thing I even remotely give a shit about is the woman lying in this bed, who's had my heart ever since the first night I met her."

She laughed and nodded. "Good answer. Call if you need me."

I slid back in my chair and reached through the railing to caress Hindley's arm. She was my Drunk Girl, my everything, and I wouldn't rest until I brought her back to me.

CHAPTER 41

HINDLEY

I TRIED to speak but my mouth was so dry, my tongue was stuck. My throat felt like someone had scrubbed it with sandpaper. I turned my head and a stabbing pain shot through my temples. It felt like the worst hangover of my life.

Where the hell was I? I pried my eyes open, searching my surroundings, unable to focus on anything. I smiled, thinking of the first morning I'd woken up next to Rory.

Rory.

I reached out to push my body up but searing pain shot through my arm. I glanced down and saw my left arm was wrapped in some kind of bandage.

"Ow," I moaned, falling back into the mattress.

"Hindley." Someone lunged toward me from the corner of the room.

"No," I yelled, recoiling. Pain shot up both arms but I ignored it. I tucked my knees to my chest, preparing to fight back. He wouldn't hurt me again. I wouldn't let him. "No more," I screamed.

"Shhh," the voice said. "It's all right. You're safe, it's me, Rory." His gorgeous face emerged from the shadows.

"Rory," I whispered in disbelief.

"Yeah, babe. It's me."

My Skater Boy.

He smiled, his blue eyes shining.

I was safe. And he was here.

Stubble littered his jaw and his hair stood on end, as if he'd been yanking on it. My eyes drifted lower and I noticed his shirt was wrinkled, like he'd been sleeping in it. All in all, he looked like a hot mess, but he was still the most gorgeous man I'd ever seen. He took my breath away, just like the first morning I saw him lying in my bed.

He wiped a stray hair from my face, leaning in close as his lips pressed gently against mine.

I drew in a deep breath, reveling in the familiar scent of the man I loved.

He pulled away, staring down at me. "Welcome back, Drunk Girl."

"You came," I whispered.

"I did," he said, stroking my jaw. "And I'll never leave you again."

I smiled and closed my eyes, feeling safe for the first time in my life.

"Check!" Paul shouted triumphantly.

I studied the chessboard, smiling.

"What?" He searched the pieces, looking for my game ending move.

I slid my queen into position, unable to hold back my laughter. "Check mate." I giggled.

"Ah, shit, Hindley. How the hell do you do that every time?"

I shrugged. "I had a good teacher."

Paul laughed as he gathered the pieces and put them in the box. "Obviously, too good of a teacher."

I studied the man sitting before me. He was perfect in every way that mattered. And he'd always considered me his own daughter. Why hadn't I ever treated him like the father he was to me?

I folded up the board and passed it to him. Moving my arm still hurt like crap, but I was tired of everyone doing everything for me.

Working with a psychotherapist and a psychiatrist while I'd been in the hospital made me realize just how poorly I'd been handling the relationships in my life, or rather *avoiding* the relationships in my life. I pushed away everyone who dared get close. If I was ever going to survive long-term, I needed to make some changes. Starting now.

"Hey, Paul. I need to talk to you. If you have time."

"For you, Hinny Bin, I have all the time in the world." And that was why I loved Paul Barton. He would do anything for me. He deserved the same, and more from me.

"Will you come sit back down?" I patted the spot beside me on the bed.

He gently sat beside me, his brows furrowed. "Did I do something?"

"No." I chuckled. "It's me. I've done something, or rather it's something I haven't done."

His eyes narrowed as he studied me.

How could I start this conversation?

With honesty and love, from the beginning.

"I've been talking to a therapist since I've been here," I said quietly. "I just wanted to tell you I'm sorry."

He tilted his head and stared at me in confusion. "Why?"

"Ever since I've known you, Paul, you've done nothing but support me, love me, and nurture me, as if I were your own flesh and blood." I took a deep breath and pushed on. "And in all that time, I've held you at arm's length, never letting you in."

"Hindley, that's not—"

I held up my hand. "Let me finish." My voice quivered, but it was important—for me and for him—that I tell Paul everything. "I think in the beginning, when you first married my mom, I thought you were too good to be true. I held my breath those first few years, waiting for you to leave, waiting for you to realize how messed up my mom and I were."

He opened his mouth to speak again.

I narrowed my eyes in warning.

He snapped it shut.

"All these years you've always introduced me as your daughter, but I was quick to correct people, wanting them to know you were my stepfather, not my biological father. I don't know why I did that. I'm sure it has something to do with the fact that I never met my real father, but I'm working on figuring it all out."

"It's okay, sweetheart. You know that," he said, tears welling up in his eyes.

My own eyes burned. "I want you to know that even though I kept you at arm's length, you've always been here," I patted my chest, "in my heart." Tears slid down my cheeks despite my protests. "You've always been a father to me, Paul." I punched out the words through the emotion welling up inside. "And I know that no matter what happens between you and my mom, you'll always be there for me."

"Hindley." His voice cracked. "You know I will."

"I know that now. I've probably always known it, but I tried to be three steps ahead of every situation in life so I could protect myself. I didn't want anyone to hurt me, and I thought the way to do that was to distance myself, even though all I really craved was unconditional love."

I glanced down at my interwoven fingers. My heart beat out of my chest. I was learning that trust and unconditional love went hand in hand. I had to trust Paul if I truly wanted to experience both in my life.

Dragging in a ragged breath, I lifted my head and stared into his bright blue eyes. "You've always given that to me, Paul. Unconditional love. You've always made me feel safe, secure, and special, like I could do anything. And all I've done is kept you guessing about how I really feel about you."

"Hindley, that's not true. I've always felt your love." His eyes darted between mine as if fearing I may break.

"I love you, Paul, more than you know, more than I knew. Well, actually, I knew it, I was just afraid to admit it, afraid to let you in. Afraid you would leave me," I whispered on a sob.

He grasped my shoulders as if he were trying to keep me from floating away. "I would *never* leave you, Hindley. You *have* to know that."

I nodded. "I do, I always have. I just wouldn't let myself believe it."

He pulled back and stared at me. "And now?"

"Now?" I repeated. "Now I do, Paul. I don't want to push you away anymore."

"Hindley, I've honestly never felt you push me away. I've known from the start you were afraid to be hurt. You've put distance between everyone you've loved, even your mother."

I nodded. He was right and I would have to have a long talk with my mother next.

"The only person I've ever seen you let *all* the way in was Rory," Paul said. "You've told him everything."

"Except about the cutting."

"And you would have told him about that eventually, I'm sure. But you let him into your heart, and you were happy for the first time, ever. I mean, truly happy. And that's why it hurt so much when you thought he betrayed you, right?"

I nodded as tears rolled down my face.

He pulled me close against his chest, allowing me the freedom and comfort to release all my guilt and shame.

My chest heaved with uncontrollable sobs. It was the first time I'd ever let him truly comfort me, let anyone. The weight of unburdening my soul, of being taken care of by him was surreal. I fought the urge to chastise myself for not letting him do it all along.

When my weeping subsided, I slowly pushed away. I dabbed at my eyes with the sheet and dragged it across my nose, trying to muster the courage for what I wanted to ask him. "There's something else," I said. "Something I want to ask you."

"Anything, Hindley, you can ask me anything, you know that."

I studied his face, relieved to see that familiar expression of unconditional love staring back at me.

"In all these years, you've been a real father to me, in my heart, even if I didn't acknowledge that to you or anyone else. That's what I'm most sorry for, for not letting you know how I really felt about our relationship."

"Hindley, you don't—"

I held up my hand.

He nodded in understanding. "Sorry."

"Paul, you *are* my father, in every way a man can be. You've supported me financially, physically, and emotionally. You've encouraged me to do more than I ever dreamed I could." My voice wavered but I willed myself the strength to continue. "Your faith and confidence in me has helped make me the person I am today. Every good thing in my life started with you."

Tears welled in his eyes and spilled down his face. Mine came soon after. We reached for each other, clinging to one another for dear life.

This was the relief I needed, the respite from my pain, being here in Paul's arms. This felt better than cutting, better than anything that I once thought might alleviate my emotional pain. I smiled, realizing I was already finding new ways to cope with my issues. Tears were good. Honesty was important.

We finally pulled away and I drew in a ragged breath to steady my voice.

"You've taken care of me and my mom all these years," I said. "You've spent thousands of dollars to keep the news of those videos hidden. And you've spent thousands more on plastic surgery to hide the scars of my past. You've given me so much, I could never repay you."

"Hindley, you don't have to repay—"

I held up my hand again and cocked a brow.

"Sorry."

I smiled, grasping his hands and pulling them into my lap. "What I want to ask you is…" Why was I suddenly so nervous?

"Go ahead." He smiled.

"I want to call you Dad from now on. Not Paul. Just Dad. Because that's what you are to me, and what you'll always be. I know you'll never leave me and that's what I want. That's what I need. I need a Dad. I need you."

He released my hands and wrapped his arms around my shoulders, squeezing so tight I could barely breathe. But I didn't care. I needed him, and I wanted him to know just how much.

"Hindley," he sobbed. "God, I love you so much, sweetheart. I've *always* been your father, you have to know that."

I nodded against his shoulder. "I know, I just wanted *you* to know that I know it now."

"I have known, Hindley," he whispered, rubbing my back, soothing me like only a father could. "I've always felt your love."

"Guess what!" My mother's voice sang out as she rounded the corner of my room. "Oh, dear God. What's happened?"

My eyes flew open and I saw the panic in hers. "Nothing, Mom. It's all good," I said, never leaving Paul's embrace. My *dad's* embrace.

My mother tiptoed over to the bed as if her every move might disturb a sleeping baby. "Is everything all right?"

I lifted an arm, motioning for her to join us and she happily leaned over the bed, taking my father and me into her grip. The three of us remained locked in one another's arms for what seemed like an eternity, making up for lost time, supporting each other in our silence.

"I love you, Mom," I whispered against her hair.

"Oh, Hindley, darling, I love you too, sweetheart." She turned her head and kissed my cheek.

We all drew back from one another, our faces stained with tears.

She clutched my chin in her hand. "You know there's nothing I wouldn't do for you. Nothing."

"I know, Mom, and I'm sorry."

"For what, darling?" She brushed away the tears from my face.

"For not treating you better. For making you feel like you were a nuisance in my life."

She laughed, rolling her eyes. "You're a woman."

"I guess, somewhere along the way, I felt pushed out of your life by Paul, then by Geneva," I said.

"Hindley," she scolded.

"I know, I know. It wasn't true, but it felt that way. I convinced myself over the years that I didn't care. I didn't care that we were growing apart, that Geneva needed you more than I did. I let you go. And I'm sorry."

"Oh, God, Hindley, no. I've always loved you so much, baby." She pulled me in close. "It's been me and you from the start, you know that. You mean so much to me and I'm so proud of you." She rocked us back and forth.

I smiled against her shoulder. She was proud of me.

"I've always been intimidated by you," she said, pushing me away to look at me. "You're so smart and beautiful and brave. All the things I'm not. It seemed like after I married Paul, you didn't need me."

I stared at her in shock.

"It's true." She nodded. "When a baby grows up and doesn't need her mother anymore, something breaks inside." She tapped her chest. "Something broke inside of me, but I knew I had to let you go."

"I know," I whispered. "I didn't let you see how hurt I was. I acted brave, like it didn't matter, and that was my fault. But I do, I do need you, Mom. Now more than ever. And I need Dad."

She reared back, her brows knitting together. "Dad?"

I nodded toward Paul.

His face lit up like a Christmas tree as he nodded in confirmation.

"Dad," she repeated with a grin, winking at Paul.

She slid her arms around both of us and we returned her hug. Our group embrace was filled with something I'd longed for my whole life but never realized I had the entire time. Unconditional love.

"Did I come at a bad time?" The doctor stood in the doorway.

"No, no." I broke our embrace, and my mom and *dad* stepped aside.

Wow. *Dad*. It sounded so… right—more than right. It sounded perfect.

The doctor stared between the three of us, his once jovial mood evaporating.

"What is it?" I asked.

"I've talked to the attending psychiatrist and your psychotherapist and it sounds like you're making remarkable progress, Hindley."

I nodded. I did feel better, better than I had in a long time.

"And, judging by the scenario I just saw in front of me, I'd say you're well on your way to finding coping skills that work for you."

I looked between my mom and dad and nodded again.

"Your wounds are healing nicely and you seem to be on track with your therapy. I don't see why we can't release you tomorrow morning."

"Really?" I asked. "Oh, Dr. Saunders, that would be so great."

"As long as you schedule follow-up appointments with all your doctors, including your wound care specialist. I don't want those wounds to get infected."

Instinctively, I touched the bandage still covering my forearm.

Don't go there. I reminded myself.

I nodded my head. "Yes, absolutely, I can do that."

"I'll make sure of it," a deep voice rang through the room.

Rory stood in the doorway, his arms full of flowers and his hands holding two giant Hello Kitty balloons.

I burst into a fit of laughter.

"Looks like someone bought out the whole gift shop." The doctor chuckled.

"Oh, these aren't in the gift shop, Doc. These are specialty items." Rory's beautiful blue eyes swept over me as he winked and gave me a mischievous smile.

I waggled both brows and silently mouthed, "very special." His face lit up with the biggest panty-dropping smile I'd ever seen on his beautiful face. God, I loved this man. And I needed him.

He came over and deposited all the flowers on the bedside table.

My breath caught at the sight of him.

Although worn and weary, he was still the most handsome man I'd ever seen.

His smile lit me on fire.

He tied the balloons to the bed railing before leaning down to brush his lips against my cheek.

The connection sent shivers down to my toes.

"These are to remind you that I want to see *your* hello kitty soon," he whispered in my ear.

I closed my eyes, pressing my legs together for relief, hoping no one would see the desire coursing through my body at his words. Slowly, I lifted my lashes to find his smoldering gaze on me.

Those sky blue eyes said more in that moment than a million words could have. In Rory I'd also found the unconditional love I'd longed for my whole life. He silently reassured me that despite my past, he would always take care of me. We would take care of each other.

We still hadn't talked about everything that had happened between us. Part of me feared I'd pushed him too far and we'd never get back what we'd had before. But judging by his expression now, I'd say he was just as in love with me as ever before, maybe even more so.

"I mean it, Hindley," the doctor cautioned. "Every appointment."

"I'll make sure, Doc," Rory answered, never taking his eyes off mine.

I looked at him like he'd sprouted a third eye. "How? You'll be in California."

He nudged my hip, and I scooted over so his large frame could squeeze in beside me. He reached out and stroked my face.

I held my breath, afraid of what he was going to say.

"Hindley Hagen, if you think I'm ever leaving you again, you are sorely mistaken," he said.

My gaze moved from Rory over to my mom and dad.

They were standing arm in arm with shit-eating grins on their faces.

Something had happened between the three of them when I'd been unconscious. I wasn't sure what it was, but without a doubt, my parents were totally okay with me being left in Rory's care. The realization made every cell in my body sing with joy. The shackles that had once kept me prisoner to my past were breaking free, one by one.

"Well, all right then." The doctor looked from me back to Rory. "I'll be back in the morning to fill out the paperwork. In the meantime, I'd like to get you off these sleeping pills. Do you want to try on your own tonight?"

Fear gripped me. What if I sunk into the dark abyss all over again?

Rory twisted around, taking me into his arms. "I'll be right here with you," he whispered in my ear.

"You don't have to. I can do it on my own."

He raised an eyebrow.

He was right. I needed him and there was no shame in admitting it. "You don't mind?"

"What part of 'I'm not leaving you again' did you not understand, baby?"

I was overcome with joy and adoration. It was freeing to admit I needed help, especially when someone as beautiful and loving as Rory Gregor was the one offering it.

"I love you, Rory," I admitted shamelessly to all those present in the room. It was the first time I'd told him in weeks, and the only time I'd said it in front of others.

He leaned back ever so slightly as if he couldn't believe my words.

"What? I do love you." I didn't care who was around. I wanted everyone in the entire hospital to know it. "I love you, Rory Gregor!" I shouted at the top of my lungs. "And I need you."

The room erupted in thunderous laughter and I couldn't help but join in.

The doctor patted my leg. "Normally, I might be concerned by that type of outburst, Hindley. But for you, I think it speaks volumes. Literally," he added.

We all laughed even louder.

God, it felt good. Good to laugh, good to love, good to *be* loved. Especially by myself.

CHAPTER 42

HINDLEY

I LEANED my head against Rory's chest as we cuddled on my couch. He tucked me into his side as we stared at the television, watching nothing in particular. "Thank you for taking me to my appointments today."

"My pleasure, Miss Hagen." He stroked my upper arm.

"You know, you don't have to take me to every one of them. Dana and my mom are available too." I cut my eyes up at him.

His head cocked to one side with a raised brow, silently telling me I needed to accept his help and not push him away.

"Sorry. I meant to say, thank you."

He kissed the top of my head and lifted the remote to change the channel.

This felt so right, just being with him, doing nothing at all.

"And thank you for my Hello Kitty house shoes." I wiggled my feet that were propped on the coffee table. The little kitten's whiskers fluttered.

"My pleasure," he said in a low tone.

God, the way he said 'pleasure' made my knees weak. It had been over a month since we'd made love and I was about to explode with need.

Rory was living with me in Austin as I recovered, putting his own tour on hold to take care of me. He drove me to every doctor's and wound care appointment, cooked for me, and even cleaned my entire house.

It was hard to accept his help, really hard, but it had been a good challenge for me. His support forced me to question the thoughts in my head that said, "You're not good enough. You're not smart enough. You don't deserve to be happy and you never will be." Slowly but surely, with the help of those I loved, I was beginning to believe I did deserve better. The only thing I missed was his intimate touch.

"And thank you for the Hello Kitty pajamas, and the Hello Kitty watch." I held up my wrist, trying to ignore the wounds on my forearm that were healing nicely.

The surgeon on call at the ER the day I was admitted was a plastic surgeon and had done an amazing job. He felt like the scarring would be minimal. But, I didn't care. Any scars left behind would always be a reminder that it was okay to lean on other people, that I couldn't control my future, and that I always had to be honest with those I loved, no matter how much I thought it would hurt them—or me.

"What about your Hello Kitty panties?" He waggled his brows.

Rory had given me a box full of Hello Kitty paraphernalia when I'd gotten home from the hospital, including socks, a watch, slippers, pajamas, even oven mitts. But the most creative item had been the Hello Kitty days-of-the-week panties.

"Where in the world did you find them?"

"I'll never tell." He laughed.

God, that laugh. A spark ran through my mid-section and I was pretty sure I'd have to go change into my Friday panties soon if he kept it up. I turned to him, pushing onto my knees.

"You know," I whispered, "you may have forgotten what day of the week it is. Would you like to look at my panties and see?" I was going for sexy, hoping he'd take the bait. I tried to forget the fact that I'd basically been throwing myself at him for the last week, to no avail.

"Hindley," he stroked my jaw, "not until the doctor says you're one hundred percent healed."

I swung my leg over his lap and straddled his hips, brushing my fingertips up and down his strong arms. "Please," I said in my most pathetic voice. I rolled my bottom lip out, pouting for effect, like an errant child. I wasn't above begging.

He wrapped his hands around my waist, trying to move me, but I pressed my thighs against his hips, stopping him.

"How in the hell are you so strong?" He chuckled.

The vibration from his laughter did me in. I leaned down and pressed my lips against his, hard, not caring if he wanted me or not. I wanted him, and I wasn't going to take no for an answer, not tonight.

"I need you," I whispered against his mouth.

He protested, not opening his mouth to my probing.

I slipped my hands through his thick hair, massaging his scalp as I pressed my hips into his.

Slowly his hands roamed up and down my back as he submitted. His mouth opened and he tilted his head, deepening the kiss.

I moaned, working my hands down his chest and tugging at the hem of his shirt. I needed to feel his skin.

He grasped my hips, lifting me with ease as he flipped me onto my back, his body looming over me.

He lowered his body weight against me but somehow my arm had been trapped between us

Searing pain shot through my arm. I winced, biting back a groan. I refused to let him see the pain I was in. I didn't care how much it hurt. Tonight, I wasn't going to stop, not now that I had him on top of me.

He pulled back, his brow creased as he studied me.

Shit.

"What is it?" he asked.

I smiled. "Nothing, baby." I slipped my free hand around his neck, pulling him down.

He stopped only inches away. "Hindley," he scolded.

"Please." This time my voice wasn't coy, it wasn't sultry, it was pleading. My physical need for him had eclipsed any pain I felt in the moment. He was essential to my survival, like air. "I need you, Rory."

Those four words moved him into action. He snaked one hand in my hair, bringing my head up to meet his as our lips connected, tongues fighting, teeth bashing.

We were like teenagers making out for the first time. It was awkward as hell, but perfect. Neither of us cared that there was no finesse to our movements. We were desperate for one another.

His free hand found its way underneath my pajama top and he splayed his fingers on my bare abdomen, working his way up until he found my naked breast.

"Oh, God," I moaned as his fingers caressed my nipple. "Rory," I panted in his ear, wrapping my legs around his waist, grinding my hips into his for relief.

"You're so wet for me," he whispered against my lips. It wasn't a question.

"Yes," I whispered. "How did you know?" He was nowhere near my good parts.

He ran his nose along my jawline, planting kisses under my ear. "I can smell you."

I froze. What was he saying? My crotch *smelled*? That was disgusting.

He pulled away and stared down at me. "What?"

"No girl wants to hear that you can *smell* her. That's gross," I said, pushing away from him.

"What are you talking about?" He laughed, ignoring my humiliation as his hips held me firmly in place.

Shit! His laugh. The deep vibrations against my body was intoxicating. Suddenly I forgot why I'd been upset.

He leaned in, our lips a breath apart. His eyes were crystal clear, as blue as a cloudless sky.

I closed my eyes, not wanting to think about smelling.

Rory caught my jaw with one of his large hands, holding my face so I couldn't turn away. "Look at me."

This was dominant Rory. I hadn't seen or heard him in so long I was practically begging for him to take control. I opened my eyes. His eyes were narrowed, all trace of teasing gone.

"Hindley, the scent of your arousal is the most intoxicating perfume I've ever smelled. If I could, I would bottle the aroma and carry it with me everywhere I went."

Okay, that sounded kind of creepy. But kind of hot too. "Seriously?" I asked, still a little weirded out.

"God, yes," he hummed against my neck. He trailed his lips behind my ear, licking and sucking on the lobe. He had me on the verge of an orgasm before we'd even gotten to the good stuff.

I wanted to unzip his jeans and pull him free, but we were mashed together so tightly, there was no room for me to move without causing more pain. If he discovered my arm was hurting, he'd stop, and there was absolutely no way I was going to let him do that. Not now that I had him on top of me.

I slipped one hand around his back and dragged my nails down his soft skin. He moaned and arched into me, which only fueled me on.

"Rory," I panted.

"What, baby?" He pressed kisses all over my face.

"Please."

"Please, what?" He smiled against my lips. He would never tire of making me ask for *exactly* what I wanted. I was stronger now and this time I would ask for exactly what I wanted.

"I need you to take me to bed, strip me naked, tie me down, and fuck the shit out of me until I scream your name at the top of my lungs. Are we clear?"

He leaned back, his howling laughter echoing through my small living room.

I grabbed his neck and jerked him back down. "I'm totally serious. Right. Now." I punctuated each word with a thrust of my hips.

"Yes, ma'am." He chuckled, pushing off me to stand. He yanked on my good hand, bringing me up to a sitting position and I noticed his midsection was right in my face.

Hmm. Maybe sex could wait for a few minutes. I was suddenly feeling hungry for Rory Gregor.

I slipped my fingers into his belt loops and tugged him toward me.

"Hindley," he whispered.

"What, baby?" I mocked as I undid his button and lowered his zipper. I raised my lids, staring up at him as I batted my lashes.

His blue eyes pierced through me. He was conflicted. I could see he wanted this but he didn't want to hurt me.

I continued on, slipping my hand inside. He was rock hard. I wanted him inside me so badly. Maybe I wasn't going to be able to do this after all. I glanced up, not surprised to see an expectant grin on his face. He wanted this, and so did I.

I tugged at his waistband, sliding his jeans and underwear down in one fell swoop. I stared in awe at the massive dick standing at attention before me. I could never get enough of his beauty. Was it possible to *miss* a penis? I had. I had missed his.

Suddenly, the doorbell rang.

Shit.

"Who could that be?" he asked, glancing at the door.

"Just ignore it," I said, grasping him fully in my hand.

He tried to pull away but I grasped his leg. "No, Hindley. It could be your parents. Or Dana." He stepped back, out of my reach, and pulled up his briefs and jeans. And just like that, my seduction of Rory Gregor was over.

I was going to kill whoever was at the door. I'd waited over a month to get Rory's dick inside any part of my body, and I didn't know how long it would take to get this opportunity again. He'd had a moment of weakness and I'd played on it. Now I may be screwed, or actually *not* screwed, for another week. Whoever was at my front door was as good as dead.

I pushed off the sofa, glaring at him. "This isn't over, Rory Gregor."

He smirked and tilted his head.

Desire surged through me, my body buzzing with need.

"Really?" He raised his brows.

"Not by a long shot." I cupped his mid-section and squeezed, pecking him on the lips.

"Promise?" He laughed, pressing into my hand.

"Guaranteed, Mr. Gregor."

I straightened my clothing and ran a hand through my hair, trying to make myself presentable. I walked to the door and stared out of the peephole. My jaw dropped. I couldn't have been more surprised if the Pope were standing in front of me. Actually, the Pope would have been safer. He was a man of God and I probably would have thought twice before killing him.

Standing on my porch was the one person I despised more than anyone. The blue eyes staring back at me had tormented me over half my life, and had nearly cost me the love of my life—not to mention, my own life. I stood paralyzed, having no idea what to do next.

"May I come in?"

"Who is it?" Rory asked.

I glanced over my shoulder. "My worst nightmare."

"Hindley," she called, knocking again. "It's Geneva."

CHAPTER 43

HINDLEY

As I stood and stared slack-jawed, staring through the peephole, I saw emotions etched on Geneva's face I'd never seen before.

Remorse.

Regret.

Shame.

I opened the door, surprised to see an expression of humbleness as well.

"May I come in?" she asked, her voice shaking, hands wrapped around each other. The usually confident Geneva was gone, replaced by this meek, humbled woman.

"What the fuck is she doing here?" Rory exclaimed.

I ignored his comment. My therapist had helped me realize that, for better or for worse, Geneva and I were related. She was my stepsister, my father's daughter, and escaping her entirely was not an option, not if I wanted my dad in my life.

I stared at Rory, legitimately fearing he may tackle and strangle her.

I turned back to Geneva.

Her head hung low, every part of her body emanating regret, guilt, and grief. Despite how she'd treated me since we'd known each other, in that moment I couldn't help but feel there may be something deep inside her, something dark that had caused her to act out all her life. I owed it to myself and my father to listen.

"What do you want, Geneva?" I held my own anger in check, barely.

She stood silent for a long time, her fingers twisting together. Slowly she lifted her head and stared at me, her eyes hollowed with deep circles. She looked like shit.

Good.

"I was wondering if I could talk to you for a minute," she said.

Rory stepped beside me. "Hindley isn't supposed to be upset. And I'll be damned if you will walk in here and fuck her over again."

"Rory." I held up my hand.

"I'm serious, Hindley. I want her the fuck out of here. Now."

Geneva stared at me, eyes wide and pooling with tears.

"It's okay, Rory. I'd like to speak to Geneva." When he remained silent I glanced over at him.

Fury burned in his darkened eyes. He shook his head emphatically. "No," he seethed.

I gave him a reassuring nod and squeezed his arm. "Yes. Please."

He glared at Geneva, his jaw clenched. "Do. Not. Fuck with her." He punctuated each word with a finger. "I'll be down the hall. If you say one word that upsets Hindley…" he trailed off and I knew I didn't want to know what he'd do.

"Go." I pushed at his shoulder. "I'll be fine."

He cut his eyes to me, raising a brow.

"Go," I mouthed.

He nodded once and pushed past Geneva, stalking down the hall like a raging bull.

"Wait!" Geneva shouted.

Oh, honey, I thought. You do not want to mess with the beast.

Rory stopped but never turned around.

His shoulders were bunched, anger radiating from his body like heat from the sun.

"Rory, I wanted to talk to you too," Geneva said.

He stood stark still.

He wasn't ready.

"Now's not a good time, Geneva," I said, hoping she'd understand.

She nodded, her gaze fixed on Rory's back. "I just wanted to tell you that I'm sorry," she said quietly. "I'm sorry, Rory. For everything."

Rory spun on his heel, glaring at Geneva like she was the devil, which she kind of was. I could see the vicious words rattling around in his mind. God only knew what he'd say.

I held up my hand, hoping he'd understand. I need to hear what Geneva had to say and I didn't want her to be on the defensive.

His eyes darted from Geneva to me. "I'll be in the bedroom if you need me, Hindley." Glaring at Geneva again, he drew in a deep breath. "I mean it, Geneva," he pointed a finger, "if you say one thing, one fucking thing to upset her, I'll kick your ass out of here so hard you won't be able to fucking walk through the mall without sucking on your own shit."

I bit back a laugh, having no idea what he was talking about. "Go," I motioned toward the hall. "I'll call you if I need you."

He stared at me, seemingly unconvinced.

"I promise."

He nodded before turning and disappearing down the hallway.

I wasn't dumb enough to believe he had gone far. I knew he wanted to hear what Geneva had to say as badly as I did. Rory was my protector, my hero, and I loved him for that.

"May I sit down?" Geneva asked, her voice actually sounding different.

I motioned for her to sit on the sofa then took a seat in the chair next to her.

She leaned forward, her forearms resting on her thighs as she nervously twisted her fingers. She closed her eyes and drew in a deep breath. Slowly she released an audible sigh and turned to face me. Tears streamed down her face.

I'd never seen Geneva Barton cry. Ever.

"I'm sorry, Hindley," she whispered.

I'd also never, ever heard Geneva Barton apologize, for anything, even when she was blatantly wrong. I remained silent, waiting for her to continue.

"I'm sorry for hurting you, for trying to destroy your relationship with Rory, for drugging him." A moan escaped from her throat and she cradled her head in her hands as her shoulders convulsed with quiet sobs.

I felt awkward and uncomfortable. Should I console her or let her continue? I voted for silence. She didn't deserve my pity.

Her crying slowed as she dabbed at her eyes with her sleeves. I reached to the end table for a box of tissues, holding it out to her.

She grabbed several, wiping at her eyes. "I'm sorry about this. I didn't mean to cry, I was trying so hard not to. This isn't about me, it's about you and Rory."

Not about her? Did I hear that right? Everything for the past twelve years had been about Geneva Barton. This was beyond weird.

"Why, Geneva?" I asked. "Why did you do it? Did you really hate me that much?"

"I fucked up, Hindley." She lifted her head, silently asking me for something I couldn't give her. "I fucked up bad."

"Yeah, you did." Normally, I thought watching someone like Geneva grovel and beg for forgiveness would be so satisfying, but it wasn't. It didn't mean I was going to let her off the hook though. "Why do you hate me so much, Geneva? What did I ever do to you?"

"After my mom died, it was just me and my dad," she said softly.

Shit, she was going way back. She'd hated me from the day she'd laid eyes on me. That was no surprise.

"My dad and me," she paused, "we were each other's world." She stared at the crumpled tissues in her hand, smiling. "I was his princess, I was his everything. And he was everything to me. We took care of one another, supported one another."

In that moment, I understood Geneva Barton. What I'd assumed all along was true. She missed the tight relationship she'd once had with her dad. I got that.

She closed her eyes as a small smile emerged. It was obvious she was enjoying the memories of her youth. Slowly, her blue eyes opened and she stared at me.

Shit, what was she going to say? I braced myself.

"Then he met you and your mother," she said, "and everything changed. I wasn't his world anymore." She shook her head and I could see the sadness in her expression. "Before I could even blink, they were married, and I became third in line."

Third in line? "What does that mean?" I asked.

"There was your mom, you…and then me."

She really felt that way? I mean, shit, Paul loved my mom and me, but Geneva was his daughter, his own flesh and blood. Then I remembered Paul's words. He'd always considered me his daughter too, no questions asked. Maybe unknowingly he *had* pushed Geneva away, or at the very least, asked her to make room for two other people in their tight circle.

"I loved your mom." She smiled. "I mean, it was nice to have a female in the house again. And your mom seemed completely over the moon to have another daughter."

Of course Geneva loved my mom. It was me she hated.

"But then there was you." She stared at me, her face void of the contemptuous glare I normally saw when she mentioned me. "You were beautiful, and smart, and ambitious, all the things I knew my dad wished I was."

Beautiful? Geneva thought I was beautiful? And ambitious? I must be hearing things.

"Geneva, what the hell are you talking about? You've always thought I was the dumbest, ugliest person on the face of the earth, and you never had a problem letting me know it. Every day."

"Actually, I didn't think that at all, Hindley. I thought you were beautiful. So did everyone else."

"Who?"

"All the boys in school."

"You have *got* to be kidding me."

"What?" She shook her head. "You didn't know it?"

"Uh, no, I didn't know it because it wasn't true."

"Hindley," she said with amusement, "you were beautiful. You still are. You may have thought you were chunky, but trust me, the guys loved your curves."

"How do you know?"

"They told me. The only reason they wanted to go out with me was to get to you."

"What?" I laughed at her absurd comment.

"It's true. I never told you because I didn't want you to know. My beauty was the one and only thing I had on my side. I didn't have the brains or drive or creativity like you did. Well, like you still do."

Was I hearing these words correctly? Was Geneva complimenting me? This was not the Geneva I'd known for the past twelve years. Maybe she had changed.

"I started sleeping with the guys in high school so they'd quit asking me about you," she said. "Eventually, they knew I'd put out so they stopped chasing you and started coming after me." Her chin dropped to her chest. "I wasn't proud of it."

"Geneva."

She lifted her head and peeked at me through her long lashes.

"Are you serious?"

"I didn't start out hating you, Hindley, but somewhere along the way, yes, I hated you. I hated that everyone thought you were so smart and pretty and kind. I hated that your mother doted on you so much and you didn't even realize it. But mostly, I hated you because I felt like you took my father away from me. I felt like I'd lost the only friend I had in this world, my best friend. He loved you more than me and it was so obvious."

"That's not true, Geneva."

She rolled her eyes.

"He loved me for different reasons," I said. "But he never stopped loving you. He still does."

She shook her head. "And now," her voice broke, "now he won't even talk to me." Suddenly, the controlled Geneva of the past was gone. She completely broke down in front of me and sobbed openly.

I ached for her. I knew I had every right to hate her as much as she had me, but it didn't feel right. It wouldn't solve anything. Not anymore.

"But you know what really made my hatred for you grow?" she asked.

I sat completely still, not entirely convinced I wanted to know.

"I hated you because you just brushed him off, like he didn't even matter to you. All my father did was show you love, the kind of love he'd reserved only for me for so many years. But you never accepted it. I would have killed for him to show me that kind of attention again. Just once."

I fell back into the chair, expelling a sigh. Well, fuck. Apparently, I wasn't the only one who'd seen how shitty I'd treated Paul, and that made me feel like a real jerk.

"And then I was so jealous of you," she continued. "You had the best mother in the world and you just crapped on her too. It hurt her so much to watch you walk away from her like you didn't need her."

Okay, if this was an apology, it was the worst one in history. It felt more like an attack on me, not an act of contrition. My hands fisted in anger. I was getting pissed and I wondered how much longer it would be until Rory rushed out to save me.

"I'm sorry, Hindley, I'm not trying to upset you at all, I swear. I'm just trying to explain how I got to this point. To the point where I was willing to risk it all to hurt you."

"Geneva, you didn't just hurt me, you destroyed me."

She nodded. "I know, Hindley."

"Do you? Do you really get it?" I held up my arm so she could see my scars.

She exploded into tears again. "I'm so sorry, Hindley, I just…"

"Just what, Geneva?" The fury bubbled up inside me and I had no desire to let her off the hook. She'd nearly cost me everything.

"There is no excuse for what I did," she whispered. "I know that. I destroyed you, Rory, Stan, your mom, and my father. I don't know how or when I became this person," she said, waving her hand along her body. "My hatred for you consumed me."

Geneva hating me was no surprise, but to hear her say it out loud was not nearly as gratifying as I thought it would be. It actually hurt me, a lot.

"What do you want from me, Geneva?"

She shrugged her shoulders.

"Forgiveness?"

She shook her head. "No. I know I won't get that from you, and I don't expect it, ever."

"Then what?"

"I love Stan, more than I ever realized. My actions have completely destroyed him. He kicked me out."

I was blown away to hear her mention Stan in her apology. I never thought she cared for him that much, just his money. And now, to hear her confirm that he not only left her but kicked her out. No one left Geneva Barton. Ever.

"And I hate that I hurt my dad and your mom too, to know that I disappointed them, again. They're worried about you, and rightly so. I know we all are."

"Yeah, you're concerned," I said mockingly.

She scooted over on the sofa so our legs were almost touching.

"I am, Hindley, I'm worried about you, you have to know that. I never, ever wanted this." She pointed at my arms. "I didn't have anything to do with those videos and I didn't tell the media about Rory. I swear."

She was desperate for me to believe her. And I did. I just wasn't ready to admit that to her. Not yet.

"I'm not asking for forgiveness, Hindley. Well, I mean, I am. I want to beg for your forgiveness." Her eyes were wide, bloodshot, and genuine. "I know it won't come anytime soon. Hell, it may never come at all. But for the sake of our parents, I hope you'll at least find a way to tolerate me."

"Did you just call them *our* parents?"

She nodded. "My dad has been your father since day one. I've known that, he's known that, and your mother has known that too. It was you who had to figure it out. And it was me who had to step back to make room for you." She placed her hand on my knee.

I stared down, surprised her touch didn't burn a hole in my leg.

"Don't get me wrong," she said, "this isn't easy. I'm not asking for you to feel sorry for me. I started therapy shortly after I got back from Miami, and I'm starting to sort out all of these issues I have surrounding my relationship with my father. I regret hurting you and Rory more than anything. I've broken the circle of trust within our family, and for that I will always be sorry."

"We were never a family, Geneva."

"I know, and that was my fault, completely."

"Well, I don't know completely. You're right. I never did let your dad into my life, not all the way. And I did push my mom away."

"I love my father *and* your mother," Geneva said. "They're my parents and I hate that I've hurt them, and disappointed them in all of this. I haven't just broken their trust, I've broken their family." She choked on her own tears and gasped for her next breath.

I stared at her in disbelief. This was not the same woman I'd grown up with. Maybe she truly was remorseful.

"Whether or not you and I ever saw the four of us as a family, they did," she said. "Or, at least they dreamed of it. My actions basically destroyed that dream for them. They don't expect you to forgive me. Ever. I hope and pray that you will one day, but they believe it may never happen. They may never get the family they've longed for because of me and my actions." She started sobbing again.

I couldn't take seeing her suffer, hearing her own insecurities, watching and listening to the struggles she'd gone through with her own demons. I gently laid my hand on her back.

Her gaze snapped to mine as if I'd electrocuted her. Her eyes darted between mine, her face riddled with fear like a caged animal awaiting slaughter.

"What?" I asked.

"I, I…" she stuttered. "I just never expected you to accept me, in any form."

"Look, Geneva, I'm not saying I'm magically over what happened. What you did was horrible and you have to know that."

"I do." She nodded, her face completely pained.

"But, you're right. Our parents deserve to be happy and I don't want what's happened between us to make it hard on them. They've been through enough having to take care of the two of us."

We both smiled and the mood shifted, ever so slightly.

"I'm not forgiving and forgetting," I said. "Let's say, you coming here, it's a start."

Her face lit up and her shoulders slumped as if a weight had been lifted.

A new Geneva I'd never seen before appeared before me. She looked lighter, brighter, even more beautiful, and for once, I wasn't jealous. I felt like I'd contributed to her beauty and that made me happy.

"It's not *all* your fault, Geneva. I'm no saint," I said. "I haven't made things between us easy either."

"Hindley." She scooted even closer. "None of this is your fault, not one piece. That's not why I came here."

"I know." I removed my hand from her back.

"I wanted to give you some insight as to how I ended up here." She waved her hand along her body again. "I mean, I don't understand it all myself. How could I have been so cruel and evil, jeopardizing every relationship, even breaking the law?"

"How did you break the law?"

"The employee at the hotel, the one I gave the drugs to, the police in Miami are saying he's only seventeen, but the guy isn't talking to them. Apparently, he's an undocumented worker so they can't prove his age. And the hotel is protecting him. The police are considering charging me with contributing to the delinquency of a minor, or a misdemeanor coercion of a minor if they can prove his age. I just don't know yet. They still haven't figured it all out. I'm definitely looking at some criminal charges though. And that's okay, I deserve them. I fucked up. Bad."

"Wow. I had no idea."

"Hindley, it's nothing compared to what I did to you and to Rory. Seriously, if I could spend time in the Dade County Jail and be assured you and Rory, my parents, and Stan would forgive me when I got out, I'd plead guilty to every charge right now and start serving my time."

I searched Geneva's face, looking for some sign that she was kidding, but instead I saw that she was telling the truth, the absolute truth. It was amazing to see this side of her. "Geneva, I don't know what to say."

"You don't have to say anything, Hindley. I didn't want this to be about me, I really didn't." She laughed. "I know, that's a first, right?"

I joined in her laughter until she sobered.

"Stan's left me, my father and your mother aren't speaking to me, and I completely understand. I deserve it all. I wanted you to know I am sorry. I'm sorry for letting my hatred build up so much that I could do something so awful to you and Rory." Tears welled up in her eyes again, but I could see she was working hard to keep them at bay. "I know today isn't the day, but I truly hope that one day in the future you can forgive me. Or, maybe at the very least, stand to be in the same room as me so I can swing by for a few minutes at Christmas." She laughed, but it was a nervous amusement.

I knew the thought of losing her relationship with our parents terrified her most of all. No one wanted to feel abandoned and alone, no matter how much of a bitch they were. "I appreciate you coming over, Geneva, I really do. I have to admit, it took some balls. But I've always known you've had them."

We both laughed.

I straightened in the chair. "I'm not saying I won't forgive you because I know I need to in order to process my own feelings and heal myself. I do know it will take me a while though. You have to understand."

"I completely understand," she said with such relief in her voice. "That's more than I could have ever dreamt for, and so much more than I deserve. Thank you, Hindley." In a surprising gesture, Geneva reached across and hugged me.

I stiffened. She'd never shown me physical endearments. But eventually, I softened and wrapped my arms around her. If she could make the effort, I could too. The road before us wouldn't be easy, but it was a start.

"Well, I better go." She released me and stood. "Thanks for letting me in." She walked to the door, but before opening it, she called down the hallway. "I'm sorry, Rory. I hope one day you'll allow me to say it face-to-face. Even though I never expect your forgiveness and I don't deserve it, it is something I'll always wish for." She slipped through the door and gently closed it behind her.

I stood in silence, forgiveness already seeping into my heart. Two words raced through my mind—words that had both haunted and inspired me my entire life. Unconditional love. That's what we all deserved.

CHAPTER 44

HINDLEY

I WALKED into the living room, staring at the front door in bewilderment. "Well, blow my dick with a rubber hose. What the fuck was that?"

"Geneva apologized." Hindley shook her head, looking as if she were in a daze.

"You're not seriously thinking of forgiving that bitch, are you?"

She remained quiet.

"Hindley."

"Rory."

"That bitch drugged me."

"I know." She moved closer, sliding her arms around my waist.

God, she felt good against my body. My dick sprung to life, but I chose to ignore it until we got this shit with Geneva straight. "I refuse to let anyone hurt you again."

"You're in for a very long life with me, Mr. Gregor." She grinned. "Hurting people and being hurt can't be prevented, I'm afraid."

I ran my palms over her shiny mane of golden hair. "I'll never hurt you again, Hindley," I whispered, trying hard not to remember what all I'd put her through over the last month.

"Rory, we'll both hurt each other. Maybe not intentionally."

"I swear, Hindley, I won't." And I meant it.

"You're hurting me right now," she whispered.

I dropped my hands and stepped back. "Oh my God, is it your arm? I'm so sorry."

"No." She giggled. "Here." She took my hands in hers and placed one on her breast and the other between her legs.

"Hindley!" I shrieked like a little girl, pulling away.

She laughed.

Her amusement made my heart swell. And my dick. This sexual predator blossoming inside of her was arousing, but I didn't want to hurt her.

"I'm serious, Rory. I haven't had sex with you in weeks and I'm aching for your touch."

Oh, shit. Aching?

I'd slept next to her every night for a week since she'd come home from the hospital and every night, I'd had to take an ice-cold shower. Being within two inches of Hindley Hagen always made my dick rock hard, but I'd been holding back on doctor's orders. Now, with her mocha eyes staring back at me, I couldn't resist.

I cupped her face and drew her in for a gentle kiss before stepping back. Her eyes were still closed but her pouty lips parted in a smile. My dick nearly broke through my jeans just thinking about our earlier encounter.

"Rory," she whispered.

I held my breath.

"Please," she sighed, her eyes still closed.

I skimmed my hands across her collarbone and down toward her chest, watching for any sign this was too much. Seeing nothing but a pleasure-filled smile, I moved lower, massaging both nipples through her thin top. I twisted and tugged on them just the way she loved, and smiled at her light moans.

"Do you know what day it is, Hindley?" I breathed against her lips.

"No. What day is it?" She swayed, her face glowing with desire.

"I asked, do you know what day it is?"

"Uh uh," she whimpered.

My hands roamed down her sides and my thumbs hooked into the elastic of her pajama bottoms. I knelt in front of her, sliding them down with me.

Her hands rested on my shoulders for balance as she raised each foot in turn to allow me to remove the pants completely.

I gently stroked one hand up the back of her thigh to cup her ass as I let the other trail over her Hello Kitty panties.

"Ah, Rory." Her body convulsed as her nails dug into my shoulders.

There would be marks tomorrow, and I was totally okay with that.

"It's Thursday, baby," I whispered against her inner thigh. "T," I said, tracing along the embroidered letter on her underwear with just enough pressure to drive her crazy. I kissed the soft material before pulling away. "H." I continued with the same motion.

She panted with desire.

"U. R." I breathed against her skin, tracing the letters as they moved dangerously close to the spot I knew would drive her insane. "S." I licked the letter with my tongue.

"Oh, God, Rory," she whimpered. "You're killing me."

"D-A-Y," I ended quickly before gently kissing the familiar face of the Hello Kitty character sitting in the center of the panties. "That spells Thursday, Hindley."

"I don't give a flying fuck how you spell Thursday, just get your face down in *my* hello kitty before I pass out."

My head fell back as I bellowed with laughter. That was the funniest thing I'd ever heard in my life, and coming from a woman as rich and refined as Hindley Hagen made it even more hilarious. God, she was so sexually charged, and I couldn't say I blamed her. So was I.

"Are you sure?" I chuckled.

"Rory!" she shouted, pounding my shoulder with her fist.

"Ow!" I cried out in real pain.

She grabbed the sides of my head and tilted it up so I had no choice but to stare at her. Her hair fell forward, framing her angelic face. Her cheeks were flushed with desire, and her eyes were glazed over with longing and need.

It was all over. If I didn't take care of her, and soon, she might kill me. But I waited patiently, allowing her to take control this time.

She sat on the arm of the couch, tugging my hips until they nestled into the crook of her spread thighs.

My dick was throbbing. I wanted to take her so bad, but this was about Hindley. I sank down to my knees and spread her legs even further apart. As I positioned my mouth directly in front of *her* hello kitty, I blew warm air over her exposed flesh.

Her body wobbled and she nearly rolled off the sofa.

"Hold on to me, baby," I whispered.

Her fingers slid into my hair as she gently massaged my head.

Fuck! I was supposed to be bringing *her* pleasure, taking care of *her* needs. Instead, her gentle caress was about to make me shoot off a load in my damn pants.

I curled one finger around her panties and tugged them to the side, exposing the most delicious part of her body. My tongue ran across her once, twice, three times, applying the perfect pressure. Before I could stroke her a fourth, she cried out in release, her body quivering from her climax. I'd wanted it to last longer, but obviously she was more pent up with desire than I'd realized.

Wanting to draw out her release, I remained in position, my hands and mouth constantly in motion as her orgasm rolled on. She'd been craving this for weeks, and honestly, so had I. But I'd denied her, much to my own pain and suffering. For once, someone else's needs had been above my own. I'd been more concerned about Hindley's recovery than my need to be inside her.

When she finally stilled, I dragged her into my arms, satisfied with my efforts as her body went limp. She was completely wasted and worn out. "Thursday." I smiled against her ear.

"Thursday." She giggled. "The best day of the week."

Her light laughter was my undoing.

I scooped her up and carried her into the bedroom, gently laying her on the bed. Her drooping eyes and limp body warned me she was ready for sleep, not sex. Shit. Now I'd have to spend the next two hours in a freezing shower. Again.

She sat up, her face within inches of my mid-section. Her hand rubbed against the bulging denim.

Stars exploded in the back of my head.

She slowly undid the button and slid down the zipper.

I wanted her lips around me, but I needed to be inside of her more. Gently taking her wrists in my hand, I pulled them away from my pants.

Her dark brown eyes peered up at me, her thick lashes fanning out over her lids.

God, she was beautiful.

Her brow creased and her delicious lips curled down in a frown.

"Not like this," I said. "I have to be inside of you right now. I need to show you how much I love you."

A wanton smile spread across her face. She understood this wasn't about sex. It was about my need to become part of her.

She pushed back onto the bed, making room for me as she slid off her panties. "Thursday." She giggled, throwing them at me.

"Oh, you're bad, Miss Hagen."

"You made me bad, Mr. Gregor."

"That I did. And now I plan to take full advantage of you."

"Promise?" She laughed.

I worked double time to rid myself of my clothes, jumping on top of her, wedging my knees between her thighs. She was still soaking wet from earlier and I knew no matter how hard I tried, this wasn't going to last long.

"Do we need a condom?" I asked. A month had passed since I'd made love to her, and in that time, I had no idea what she'd done. My mind filled with horrific images of her having sex with other men, them touching her and fondling her.

"Come back to me," she whispered, tapping my temple.

I shook my head, focusing on the sex goddess lying underneath me, a place she was born to be. "I'm here." I laughed.

"No condom, baby," she answered.

Shit, this was gonna be over before it even started. Skin on skin with Hindley would be like heaven.

"I'm sorry," I whispered as I nestled between her legs, my dick rubbing against her.

"Why?"

"This isn't going to take long," I confessed, hoping she'd understand.

"That's okay. You've got the rest of your life to make it up to me."

Before she said another word, I slid inside her, trying to control my own desire.

She cupped my ass, pulling me in deeper. "More, Rory," she pleaded.

I thrust in deeper as our bodies took one another to an unworldly place of unconditional love that shook me to my core. It was the place where the lost boy inside me hid.

Our bodies rocked against one another in perfect rhythm, pushing us higher to release.

"I love you, Rory," she shouted as we came together.

"I love you, baby," I whispered into her neck.

Blinking back tears, I was overtaken by emotions that I'd held inside for years. No matter what happened to either of us, I vowed to never let Hindley go. I was hers, she was mine, and I would love her, unconditionally, for the rest of our lives.

CHAPTER 45

RORY

"Wow," Hindley whispered breathlessly as she fell onto my chest.

I loved watching her body writhe in unbridled passion as she completely let go. According to her, I was the only man who'd ever offered her such an explosive release. And for that, I thanked fuck's sake. The thought that another man bringing her more pleasure made me see stars.

I brushed back a strand of hair from her face. "For such an articulate person, that's the only word you can come up with?" I rubbed her back, silently thanking God she was still here with me, to hold in my arms.

"Articulate? Well, excuse me, Mr. SAT Word of the Day."

"I knew I shouldn't have told you Luis bought me that calendar."

She lifted her head and rested her chin on my chest. "I'm glad to hear you're using it. Can you spell articulate?"

"No, but I can spell love. L-O-V-E," I said. "And that's what I do for you. I love you, Hindley."

Her face went red with an emotion that I wasn't familiar with. Was it embarrassment? God, I hoped not.

"I love you too, Rory." She pushed up to plant a soft kiss on my cheek. "So, how many orgasms do you think a person *can* have in one night?" She giggled, her body quivering on top of mine as she ran her fingers over my chest.

I flipped her over so she was on her back, hovering inches above her. "I don't know, but I'm willing to go through the grueling process to find out."

"Well, let's see, we're up to..." she paused, counting silently in her head. "Five. Are you kidding me, five orgasms and, what time is it?" She glanced over her shoulder at the clock.

"It's still early." I grinned, rubbing my nose against her jaw. "We're making up for lost time."

"Well, in that case..." She wrapped her hands around my neck and leaned down so our lips were nearly touching. "Thank you."

"For what?"

"For not giving up on me."

I stared at her like she was crazy. "What are you talking about?"

"I'm kind of a high maintenance girl."

I laughed out loud at the lunacy of her words. "Hindley, I've been with high maintenance girls."

She scowled. "Girls don't want to hear about your exploits with other women while still in bed."

"Duly noted." I smiled.

She pecked me on the lips and pulled away.

"Trust me though, you're not high maintenance, at all." I lifted my head and brought her mouth down in silent reassurance, but as I fell back onto the mattress, I sensed my words still hadn't appeased her. "Hindley, you're the only girl for me. You know that."

Her blank expression said she still wasn't satisfied.

I gently rolled her off me and rose from the bed, walking to my duffle bag in the corner. I pulled out my journal. "I want to read you something." I sat back down on the bed, my journal in hand.

"Ooo, this sounds serious." She smiled.

I shrugged my shoulders. "It's just a poem."

Her eyes danced with excitement. "Did you write it?"

I nodded.

Her grin widened.

"Do you want to hear it?" I asked.

"Of course I do. Does it have a title?"

"Um, no. No title. I wrote it while you were in the hospital." I opened the journal to the page I'd marked earlier and tried to avoid her gaze.

She pushed up. Sitting cross-legged and gloriously naked, her knees pressed against mine.

"Are you ready?"

"Yes." She nestled herself against me for what seemed like story time at the library.

Her excitement spurred me on. "Okay, here goes. Don't laugh."

"I'd never laugh at you, Rory." She brushed my cheek with her hand.

"Yeah, right," I snorted, leaning into her touch.

"Not for this." She placed a reassuring hand on my thigh.

My dick twitched.

Shit. Not now One-Eyed Willie.

I drew in a deep breath, preparing myself, fearful of what she would think. I couldn't allow my anxiety to stop me from revealing how I *truly* felt about her. I'd almost lost her, and I wasn't going to waste anymore time on self-doubt, not when I knew how much she truly loved me.

"All the words are mine, but Luis helped me write them down in the beginning. Eventually, I've been able to go back and learn all the words. So, what I'm reading to you really is something *I* wrote."

She nodded her head, smiling as she latched on to my arm. Her touch gave me the confidence I needed to read my poem aloud.

"I awoke to her voice, the sound so serene,
    That she instantly drew me in,
    Her heart was so pure, her face so bright,
    True beauty shined from within."

I paused, trying to steady my racing heart. I couldn't fuck up the words or start crying like the pussy-ass punk I was. I didn't want to stutter and sound like a *complete* fool. Not tonight. This was important.

"It's all right, Rory." Hindley squeezed me. "I love it. I love you.

Take your time. I want to hear every word, no matter how long it takes you, because every word was written by you."

She stared up at me, her face glowing with a kind of love I'd never known before.

I cleared my throat and smoothed out the page, reading the next line.

"How could I explain from the depths of my soul,
Just how lost and lonely I felt.
Knowing that one day she'd have to reject me,
To protect her heart from myself.

Now watching her pain and hearing her cries,
I realize we're both just alike.
Maybe together is where we're destined to be,
Despite all the tragedy in life.

They say love isn't yours 'til you give it away,
But I will never let her go.
Because sometimes it takes a broken person,
To truly make you whole."

I sagged in relief, glad I'd made it all the way through without stumbling. I closed my journal and stared at her, surprised to see tears streaming down her cheeks. Oh, shit, she hated it.

"Was it that bad?" I asked.

"Oh, God, Rory, no. It was beautiful," she said. "You wrote that?"

I nodded. "Luis helped me spell some of the words. We added them to my sight list."

"You still have your list?" she asked, seeming surprised that I'd kept up with my lessons.

"Of course I do. I mean, no offense, Hindley, but with or without you, I wasn't going to give up on reading."

She threw herself into my arms, toppling us both over. "I'm so proud of you, Skater Boy."

"I'm glad you like it. It's for you, Drunk Girl. It's about you."

"God, it better be." She smiled, wiping her eyes with the sheets. "Can I ask you something though?"

Her body sunk into mine as she lay naked atop me. I was finding it harder and harder to resist her as my dick grew firm with desire.

"Anything. You can ask me anything, you know that."

"You said you'd never let me go."

Her face was adorably contorted and I tried not to laugh out loud at her confused expression. She was falling right into my trap.

"Yes," I said flatly, as if I didn't understand.

Her eyes narrowed and I knew she might kill me if I didn't come clean.

"Hold on." I shoved off the bed and walked toward my duffle bag again, bending down and rummaging through until I found the package at the bottom. I pulled out the thin oblong box wrapped in Hello Kitty paper and made my way back to the bed. I'd gone shopping for her when she was still in the hospital and had been *completely* surprised at how much Hello Kitty shit there was out in the world. Tonight though, I was thankful for it.

"Here." I held out the package to her.

"Another Hello Kitty present?" She giggled.

God, I loved her laugh. I loved her, period.

"Of course, you know I'm addicted to your *hello kitty*?" I rubbed her thigh.

She swatted at my hand. "Not yet." She winked with a side grin. There was hopefulness in her eyes of things yet to come.

I watched with anticipation as she ripped off the paper. I loved that she wasn't one of those kind of girls who was so careful with wrapping paper. I panicked, wondering what her reaction to my gift would be. My heart beat wildly out of my chest and my hands broke out with sweat. What if this *wasn't* what she wanted?

"Come back to me," she whispered, caressing my face with her fingers. Her voice instantly set my mind at ease. I knew her better than anyone in the world. This was *exactly* what she wanted.

"Oo. Nordstrom's," she admired, showing me the box.

"What, were you expecting, Tiffany's?" I snorted.

She smirked and hit my arm. "No," she said, but I saw a spark of disappointment.

After listening to my poem, I knew she expected to see a ring-sized box, but that's not what I had in mind for her. Tiffany's would never be my style.

"Open it," I coaxed.

Slowly, she removed the lid. Her eyes were bright with wonder as she tried to figure out what was inside.

"What? You don't like it?" I tried to sound disappointed.

"It's a Hello Kitty bracelet." She admired it with about as much enthusiasm as someone preparing for a root canal.

I was afraid I was going to bust out laughing. "You don't want it?"

"No, no," she tried to assure me, "I love it, it's beautiful."

God, she was such a crappy liar, but I guess I should be thankful for that.

"Do you want me to put it on you?" I was surprised she hadn't noticed the shit-eating grin on my face.

"Sure." She held the box out.

"Take it out first."

Her brows furrowed, but she complied. As she lifted the bracelet out of the box, the ring dangled from the last link on the chain and swung in the air. Her eyes grew wider than I'd ever seen when she realized this was no ordinary Hello Kitty bracelet. The box fell to the floor as her free hand clasped over her mouth.

I slipped off the bed and came to kneel in front of her gloriously naked body. Removing the ring, I held it in my hand as I fastened the bracelet around her wrist. I lifted my eyes, focusing on her beautiful face, her eyes now overflowing with tears.

"Rory," she whispered.

"Hindley, I lost you once and barely survived. I don't ever want to lose you again. I can't exist in this world without you. Marry me."

She remained stock still and I feared what she was thinking. Was it joy or panic, maybe fear? I mean seriously, if I stopped to think about it, what did I have to offer this girl?

She tilted her head and stared at me for a long moment. "What you said sounded an awful lot like a command, not a question."

I sat back on my heels to gauge her reaction. The sparkle in her eyes and the devious smile lighting up her face assured me she was screwing with me. I guess I deserved it.

"It wasn't a question, Miss Hagen, it was a demand. Marry me."

Her eyes searched my face and again, I was overcome with a vulnerability I'd never experienced before.

"Okay," she whispered, nearly bouncing off the bed. "I'll marry you."

"Well, thank fuck for that!" I shouted, pushing off the floor and crashing into her as our bodies fell onto the bed.

"So, can I get the ring now?" She giggled.

I held it out to her.

"Oh my God, Rory, it's beautiful."

It was a two-carat square cut diamond in an antique setting, surrounded by a shit-ton of smaller diamonds and positioned atop a diamond-covered band. I'd taken Kara with me to choose the ring when Hindley was still in the hospital. As soon as I'd seen it in the local jewelry store in downtown Austin, I'd known it was Hindley through and through. The look of adoration in her eyes proved I was right.

"You like it?"

"Like it?" She extended her arm into the air, twisting her hand back and forth, watching the diamond catch the light. "It is the most beautiful ring I've ever seen. How did you know? It's perfect."

"Because I know you." I ran my finger over her jaw, down her neck, making my way to one of her breasts. Leaning down, I took one pert nipple into my mouth, sucking hard.

"Oh, Rory," she moaned.

I peered up and saw her attention was still stuck on the ring.

"Hindley," I growled, flicking her nipple with my tongue.

"Hmm," she buzzed.

"Do you want to make it six?"

She wrapped both hands around my cheeks and lifted my head. Her eyes were bright with joy…and love. For me.

I'd never felt so cherished or admired in all my life.

"I want to make it forever, Mr. Gregor." She smiled, her thumbs caressing my cheeks.

"Your wish is my command, Miss Hagen." I leaned down and worked my mouth lower on her body.

"It won't be Miss Hagen much longer," she corrected.

I smiled against her smooth, soft skin. "I can hardly wait, Mrs. Gregor. I can hardly wait."

CHAPTER 46

RORY

I took a small sip from the steaming cup of coffee as I stared at Hindley, sitting beside me at the dining room table.

We'd barely slept the night before but she had an early doctor's appointment this morning, which meant the alarm clock had rung entirely too soon for either of us.

I stared at my plate of pancakes and bacon, my mouth watering.

She'd awoken early and made breakfast, knowing the smell of bacon would be the quickest way to get me out of bed. She'd been right. I could never resist her pancakes.

"Promise me something," she said, handing me the syrup.

"Anything." I shoved another fork full of pancakes in my mouth.

"Please promise me that you won't treat me like I'm some delicate flower, like you think I'm going to break or hurt myself again."

I swallowed the contents in my mouth. "I can't promise you that, Hindley. You are delicate to me, and I will always protect you, even from yourself if I have to."

"Good God, you're so overprotective." She fell back in her chair. "Is this how you're going to be with our kids?" She laughed.

Kids? Holy shit.

I'd never wanted kids, had never even thought about having them.

"What's wrong?" Her brow furrowed.

I shook my head, not knowing how to respond. I pushed my plate away, my appetite suddenly gone.

"You don't want kids, do you?"

I swallowed hard, praying this wouldn't be a deal breaker for us.

"Tell me the truth, Rory. You *never* want children?"

I didn't want kids, but I didn't want to lose her either. We'd agreed that we would never lie to one another again, about anything. Basically, I was fucked.

"Honestly, I've never thought about kids," I said.

She sat up straight in her chair, crossing her arms on the table. "Well, now I'm asking you to think about them."

I shrugged, trying to figure a way out of this mess. "Do we have to talk about this now?"

"Yes, we do."

Fuck.

I raked a hand through my hair. "I don't know, Hindley. I mean…"

"What?" she asked, her voice soft and reassuring.

"It's just," I stumbled to articulate my feelings. "I didn't have any role models growing up."

"What about Jack?"

Jack was a good man, a wonderful husband and father. But he'd come along later in my life, after my bad habits had already been formed. I didn't know how to express that in a way she could understand.

She reached across the table, her hand covering mine. "Just say it. I won't judge."

"I don't want to fuck up a kid, especially *your* kid. Not the way I was."

"Rory, how can you ever think you would fuck up your own child?"

"Look at me, Hindley." I waved a hand up and down my body. "I fuck up everything I touch."

I pushed the chair back from the table, screwing my eyes shut. Visions of the countless times I'd fucked up in the past—with people I loved, with Hindley—swirled around in my head. I knew I'd do the same thing with a kid, only that would be worse, way worse.

My eyes opened when I felt her press into my lap.

She gently placed her hands on either side of my face and stroked my cheeks. She spread feather-light kisses across my face and down my jaw. Hindley made it nearly impossible to concentrate on anything but her love for me.

"You are *my* Skater Boy. You are *not* a fuck up. And you don't fuck up everything you touch."

I stared at the pale skin of her neck, trying to let her words soak in.

"Look at me, Rory," she commanded.

I lifted my gaze, staring into her dark chocolate eyes.

"You saved me," she said.

"What?" I laughed.

"I was lost without you."

"When?"

"The two weeks we were apart, it was like I was missing my other half. Then, I opened my eyes in the hospital and there you were, and I knew. I just knew."

"Knew what?"

"That no matter what, you'd *always* be there for me."

"God, Hindley, you know I will." I pulled her against my chest. "You know I'll do anything for you."

"And you will for our babies too."

"What?" I half shouted. "Babies?"

"Umm hum," she whispered in my ear. "Babies. As in more than one."

"Hindley," I shook my head, "I don't know." My breathing became shallow as I fought back a full-blown panic attack.

She leaned back, her eyes searching mine. "Rory, do you love me?"

"Of course I do. You know that."

"And you'd do anything for me, right?"

"Yes."

"That's how I know you'll be an amazing father." She smiled as if it were that simple.

"What do you mean?"

"This baby will be half you and half me."

"What the fuck? Are you pregnant?" I grasped her waist, about to toss her off me.

"No." She laughed. "I meant in the future tense." She covered her mouth to stifle her amusement. "I'm sorry."

I clutched my chest like I'd had a heart attack. "Fuck, Hindley, that wasn't even funny." I lifted her from my lap and paced the small room, trying to think of anything other than Hindley being pregnant.

"Hey." She circled her hands around my waist. "Stop."

"Stop what?" I asked, covering her hands with mine, my heart beating like a stampede of elephants.

"We're gonna screw up, Rory, with each other, with our kids, in life. It's all part of living. It's how we deal with it that matters."

I stared down at her. She looked…peaceful, and that steadied my pulse.

She squeezed me hard. "Before I met you, I never allowed myself to need other people, and look where it got me." She raised her arm to show me the bandage still wrapped tightly around her forearm.

I winced in pain.

"But you know what?" she said. "I wouldn't change it, any of it, because it's taught me a better way to deal with my life. It's taught me to lean on people and ask for help. And it's forced you to look at some of your demons too."

I dug my fingers into her hair to hold her steady. I wondered, not for the first time, how in the fuck I'd ever been lucky enough to convince a woman like Hindley Hagen to marry me.

"I'm lucky to have you, too," she said.

I smiled, realizing she'd read my thoughts. We were joined together, in every way, physically, mentally, emotionally. How could I not give this girl everything she wanted.

"How much longer do we have until my appointment?" she asked, glancing at my watch.

"We need to leave here in about forty-five minutes."

"I can get dressed in fifteen." She smirked, lifting her brows. I understood her silent request.

"Oh, Miss Hagen, I believe I can do something with you in thirty minutes." I scooped her up and traipsed down the hallway toward the bedroom. "Many things."

"God, I hope so, Mr. Gregor. Otherwise, I might have to return your ring."

"Never!"

"No, never." She laughed. "I'm yours. Forever, Skater Boy."

I leaned down and pressed a kiss against her temple. "Forever, Drunk Girl."

EPILOGUE
HINDLEY

ONE YEAR LATER

"Max, Miguel!" I shouted from the front of the classroom. "Shut the computers down, it's time to go."

The boys groaned.

I smiled. Knowing these boys wanted to stay at our facility longer was a dream come true.

Six months ago, Rory secured an abandoned warehouse on the Southeast side of Austin, an area known for drugs, violence, and gangs. It was the ideal spot for his passion project. He'd told me of his dream shortly after he'd proposed a year ago.

Rory wanted to open a facility for at-risk youths. A place where they could come after school and during the summer for help with their schoolwork and a chance to play.

He wanted the kids to have the opportunity for productive downtime while keeping them safe from the rough and often seductive streets of their neighborhood.

It'd taken considerable work and planning, but six months after he'd told me about his dream, we broke ground on the facility—thanks to sizable donations from all seven of Rory's sponsors, as well as other pro extreme sports athletes on the tour.

Thankfully, the warehouse had been donated by the city and Leif had offered his planning services for the indoor skate park attached to the main part of the campus.

The building included four large open-air style classrooms that could be subdivided if more rooms were needed. It also housed three offices, one for the director of the facility, Dora Rodriguez, a long-time educator and high school math teacher. The other two offices were for our part-time counselors and the volunteers.

Rory named the facility Shelly's Hangout, after his sister. He'd felt that if he and Shelly had had a place like this to hang out at after school, perhaps they could have escaped their troubled youth. And maybe they would have had a safe person with whom they could have shared the stories of their abuse.

"Come on, guys, I'm serious," I said. "It's late and you both need your beauty rest." Plus, I was dog-tired.

They grumbled but powered down the computers.

"Bring your folders up front so I can check your progress report if you want your star stickers."

We'd come up with a reward system for the kids that seemed to work. For each positive action they performed, they received a sticker. After they'd accumulated enough, they could purchase things from our inhouse 'store'. Things as simple as extra time on the computer, all the way up to new skateboards donated by River City Skateboards.

We'd even talked some of the pro extreme sports athletes into stopping by from time to time, and we'd sell what we called 'Star Tickets'. The kids would accumulate their stars and buy a ticket to come watch the athletes perform or maybe even get a one-on-one lesson with the pro. It was something for the kids to strive for, help them to learn better habits than they'd learned on the streets.

Teachers in the community raved about our program, saying not only had their schools seen improved test scores, but student behavior had improved as well. The city was starting to take notice of our program and was talking to us about starting up other facilities around town. For now, we were happy with Shelly's Hangout.

Miguel set his red folder on my desk, opening it up to his Star Bar as we called it.

"How many so far?" I asked.

"Ninety-four."

"That's a lot of stars," I said. "What are you saving up for?"

His eyes lit up as a huge grin spread across his face.

"Could it possibly be the new board I saw River City deliver last week? The one with the orange and red sunburst, signed by Rory?"

He nodded his head like a child waiting for Christmas morning, which I guess, really, he was.

It broke my heart to know an item as simple as a skateboard, something I'd taken for granted my entire childhood, would be enough to motivate this boy to do better, to *be* better. It was during moments like these that I was proudest of Rory and his vision.

"Well," I said, "you know you get five stars if you get your parents to come to the English class on Friday, right?"

He nodded.

We'd discovered over the last few months that children whose first language in the home was something other than English performed lower in the classroom and on standardized tests. With the help of the schools, we'd gone to the homes of the children to talk to their parents and relatives and realized they did, in fact, want to learn English, they just didn't have the means or the time.

That's when we developed the Kick Flip to English program, or Kick as we referred to it. It was Rory's idea to name it Kick Flip, telling everyone that even though it seemed like the easiest trick in skateboarding, the kick flip had been one of the hardest for him to learn as a kid.

The program was in its fourth week and already our numbers were growing. The parents were receptive to the classes and to their own education once they found out how much it motivated their children. Plus, it was fun to watch the parents play around in the adjoining skate park with their kids after their own classes were over in the evenings.

Miguel cast his eyes down to the floor as he knocked his feet together, fisting his T-shirt. Something else was going on with him.

"What is it?" I asked.

"My dad says he won't come."

"Why?"

He shrugged his shoulders.

"What about your mom?" I asked.

"She doesn't drive."

The despair in his voice seized my heart with pain. I couldn't let him lose hope. I understood better than anyone what could happen if you did. You were in danger of losing everything.

"What if someone from the center came to pick her up? Do you think she'd come then?"

His smile was back. "You'd do that?"

My heart hummed with joy. I'd given this boy hope.

"Of course," I said, barely able to contain my own excitement.

"Maybe," he said. "I could ask."

"Okay, stop by Mrs. Rodriguez's office before you leave and tell her your mom may need a ride. Tell Mrs. R to call me if she has questions. We'll make sure your mom gets here if she truly wants to, Miguel, don't worry."

"Thank you, Mrs. Gregor." He ran around my desk and grasped me in his arms. "Thank you so much."

Tears burned the back of my eyes. I knew in that moment I was exactly where I was meant be.

Miguel released me and I turned toward Max. "How did you do on your math exam?"

His down-turned face told me the news wasn't good. I felt so bad. Max had studied so hard for that test. One of our volunteers, a college student who was majoring in math, had even come in to help. But like a lot of kids in the center, Algebra didn't click with Max. I understood that all too well.

Slowly, he pulled a thick packet from his folder. Good, bad, or anything in between, we encouraged the kids to share their schoolwork with us. We had taught them there was no shame in failing, only in not trying.

He held it out with his long slender fingers.

As I took it from him, I noticed a small smile emerge across his face.

I flipped it over. Blazing across the top in bright red ink it read eighty-three and had the words 'Amazing job Max' with four exclamation points from his teacher.

"Oh my goodness, Max!" I jumped up. "This is awesome. We have to go put this up on the wall."

He nodded, his smile growing wider.

Rory had created what he called a 'Sick Wall' in the main hall of the facility. Apparently, the word 'sick' was a complimentary term in the extreme sports world, meaning something was completely insane and amazing. I wasn't a big fan of the term, but the kids seemed to understand its significance and that's all that mattered.

The wall was painted bright purple, Rory's favorite color, and located between the classrooms and the skate park.

Anyone who entered the building walked by the Sick Wall, which was a way for the kids to acknowledge their accomplishments and learn how to be proud of their hard work. The display was also a lesson in humility, a way for the kids to learn how to be happy for one another, not just themselves. The wall helped ward off jealousy, an emotion that had almost cost me everything.

"Miguel, will you grab a tack from the cabinet over there?" I pointed toward the supply closet then waited patiently for Miguel to join us. I knew displaying Max's accomplishment would be as much an honor for his best friend as it would be for Max.

"What's going on?" A familiar deep voice echoed through the classroom. My eyes went to the source of the sound, and my knees went weak just thinking about how much I loved him.

Rory stood in the doorway, beads of perspiration dripping from his face. He'd obviously been skating.

He often helped with tutoring when we were in town, but most of his time was spent with the kids in the skate park, helping them learn their tricks and talking to them about life and their problems. It always blew me away that a man so accomplished would humble himself so kids could learn the greater life lesson—anything was possible, with hard work and perseverance.

"Max made an eighty on his Algebra test," Miguel shouted.

I was thrilled to see him being so supportive of his best friend.

"Eighty-three," Max corrected.

Miguel rolled his eyes but I knew there was no animosity.

"All right, Max." Rory fisted his hand and bumped Max's knuckles. "Way to go. That calls for a celebration."

"Mrs. Gregor said I can hang it on the Sick Wall," Max said.

"Well, get after it then." Rory motioned toward the front of the facility.

I turned off my own computer and put away my supplies then approached my sweaty, hot husband.

"What's all the commotion about?" Geneva asked, walking up behind Rory.

Geneva had been charged with drug possession and food tampering last year in Miami. But thanks to her high-profile attorney, the charges against her had been dropped in exchange for her serving a shit ton of community service.

She spent a lot of time working with the Austin Police Department in their D.A.R.E. program, speaking to kids about drug use in schools. But after Shelly's Hangout opened, she'd logged most of her hours here. She'd completed her mandated volunteer hours months ago, but she enjoyed the kids so much that she'd stayed on to help.

Rory and I were both appreciative of the time she spent here. But more than that, I was happy that we were finally growing closer.

"Oh, um, Max got an eighty-three on his Algebra test," I said.

"Max, that's incredible. I'm so proud of you," she said. "You've been working hard with Patrick and Joe. Why didn't you tell me earlier?"

He shrugged, staring down at the floor.

I could sense she wanted to hug him, but we'd made a rule that there be limited physical contact with the kids. Some had been sexually abused or assaulted and their lines between appropriate and inappropriate touch were skewed.

"We're gonna hang it on the wall." Miguel smiled wide. It was wonderful to see how proud he was of his best friend's hard work.

"Well, let's go." Geneva motioned toward the front with her hand.

"Are you coming with us, Mrs. Gregor?" Max looked back at me.

"We'll be there in a minute, Max," Rory said.

He seemed appeased and they continued toward the front of the building without us.

I stared at Rory, his mischievous grin warning me that he was up to something. I smiled just thinking about all the amazing things he'd done for me since I'd met him.

"What are you thinking about, Mrs. Gregor?" He laughed.

"You, Mr. Gregor."

"Why do you make them call you Mrs. Gregor, instead of Hindley?"

"It's a sign of courtesy and respect."

Rory rolled his eyes then grinned.

"What?"

"I just think you like being reminded every day that you're my wife." He wrapped one arm around my waist and leaned me back. Supporting my neck with his other hand, he bent down and placed kisses along my neck.

"Rory, stop."

"Admit it, Mrs. Gregor," he whispered against my neck.

I forgot where I was, sliding my fingers in his hair and pulling his face toward mine as we locked lips in a passionate kiss that took me to another galaxy. Kissing my husband would never get old.

When we surfaced for air, he planted me on my feet, but my equilibrium was off and I had to grab onto his shoulders for support.

"Whoa." He steadied me. "You all right?"

"Yeah, just a little woozy."

"Probably from all my passion." He chuckled.

"Probably." It was a half-truth. I needed to share my news with him, but I was terrified about how he would react.

"What's in the box?" I changed the subject. I wasn't quite brave enough, not yet.

"This is one of my X Games medals." He held it up with pride.

I rubbed the scars on my arm, remembering how he'd left the games last year to be with me in the hospital after my breakdown.

He lifted my arm to his lips and lightly brushed my scars with kisses.

It had become his way of reminding me that he'd always be there for me. Always, he'd say emphatically.

We'd just returned from Los Angeles, where he'd won not one but three gold medals in this year's games, sweeping the events he'd entered. No one had been prouder than the kids at the center.

"You're going to hang it up here, on the Sick Wall?" I asked.

"Yeah, I figured the kids would get a kick out of it. It's as much theirs as it is mine."

He never ceased to amaze me with his humbleness.

"Why, what's wrong with that?" he asked.

"Well, I don't want to sound mean, but I'm afraid someone may take it."

"I ordered a special case for it," he said. "It's here, in the box. I'm going to install it this weekend."

"Oh," I sighed. "Was that wrong of me to say?" I felt bad for assuming the worst of the kids.

"Not wrong," he said. "Realistic. They're a product of their environment. But we're working to change that, right?"

I nodded as I stared up into his beautiful blue eyes, watching as the golden flecks danced around his pupils.

"What?" he asked.

"Just admiring my husband."

"Admire away, Mrs. Gregor." He wrapped his hand around my neck and pulled me in so his lips were pressed to mine.

What started as a slow kiss soon turned passionate, too passionate for the center, but I was helpless when it came to Rory.

Someone cleared their throat behind us.

Oh, shit.

I pushed Rory away, watching helplessly as he nearly tumbled backward over another box I hadn't noticed.

"Shit, Hindley, you damn near knocked me on my ass."

"Rory, language." I turned, thankful to find it was just Geneva.

"Oh, God, I'm so sorry, Geneva," I said.

"You two never stop, do you?" She laughed.

"She may be the death of me." Rory rubbed a spot on his calf that he'd hit on the large box behind us.

"What's in that thing?" Geneva asked.

"A surprise." Rory smirked.

"I thought it was the display box for your medal," I said.

"Oh my gosh, you have your medal?" Geneva asked.

She was definitely not the same girl from a year ago. The Geneva I'd grown up with would never have been excited for anyone else's achievements and successes, least of all Rory Gregor.

"May I see it?" she begged.

Rory took it out of the pouch and held it out for her perusal.

"Rory, this is amazing," Her mouth hung open as she admired it from every angle.

His eyes lit up with pride as he watched her appreciation for his accomplishment.

"The kids were so excited for you when you competed." She carefully passed the medal back to him. "Kids from all over the city came to watch you."

"From all over the city?" He shook his head slowly. "But, how?"

"Jeremy set up a huge blow-up screen in the middle of the skating area," Geneva said.

Jeremy Phillips was another volunteer who was pursuing a graduate degree at the University of Texas in psychology with an emphasis on family and marriage counseling. As with most men, he'd been smitten with Geneva from the start, but she had no desire to pursue a relationship. She'd been working on her own education, gaining a teaching certificate three months ago shortly before our wedding in May.

"You really didn't know that?" Geneva asked.

"No, I didn't." Rory looked at me. "Did you?"

"Nope." I shook my head.

"Geneva organized it." I heard another voice chime in.

I looked over Geneva's shoulder and saw Jeremy standing in the shadows, his face totally enamored by the woman he was talking about.

The old Geneva would have had this kid in her back pocket and in her bed by now. But this new, more mature version of my stepsister had forced her once overgrown ego to take a back seat. She'd made real progress, working hard to right her wrongs, and I was happy for that. It made life with our parents much more enjoyable.

Unfortunately, Rory was not convinced of Geneva's new persona. I couldn't blame him or force him. After all, the woman had drugged him, seduced him, and almost cost him the love of his life.

But Geneva had come clean, and she was making changes in her life that were in line with her words of apology. In time, Rory would come around too. He was protecting me and felt like he needed to stand guard in case the old wicked stepsister decided to emerge.

"I'm leaving for the night. Unless you guys need anything else," Geneva said.

"No, we're good," I said.

"I'll see you Saturday?"

"Saturday?" I furrowed my brow as I tried to remember what was on Saturday.

"Your mom's birthday dinner," she reminded me.

"Oh, crap, I forgot. Must be the fuzzy brain." I tapped my temple.

"The what?" Rory asked.

Crap. "Um, nothing, I'm just tired."

"You're always tired, Hindley," Rory said. "Are you sure you're not coming down with something?" He lifted his hand to my forehead. "Maybe it's mono?"

I laughed nervously, swatting his hand away from my head. "We'll see you Saturday," I said.

Geneva leaned in closer. "Is it all right if I invite Jeremy?"

My face lit with excitement as my brows shot straight in the air. "Really?" I quietly squealed.

For weeks, I'd thought Jeremy would be the perfect match for her, but Geneva needed to recognize that for herself. She'd been divorced for almost six months. Stan hadn't been able to forgive her for what she'd done in Miami. She hadn't dated anyone during that time, which shocked the shit out of everyone, especially her.

A small smile spread across her face as she nodded like an eager child.

"That would be awesome," I said.

"Do you think your mom would mind?" she asked.

"Are you serious?" Rory broke in. "That woman has been trying to hook the two of you up since your divorce was final six months ago."

Geneva and I stared at Rory with blank expressions. I had no idea he was even remotely aware of anything Geneva did. Maybe he was coming around after all. The thought warmed me.

"Thanks, Rory." She reached out and touched his hand. "And congratulations on the medals. You were amazing."

"Thanks for organizing a viewing party," he said. The look in his eyes was one of genuine gratitude.

"Okay, well, I'll see y'all Saturday." She waved as she headed toward the lobby.

"Hold up, Geneva, I'll walk you out," Jeremy shouted, giving both Rory and me a wink when Geneva's back was turned.

Rory laughed. "There may be hope for her yet if she snags a guy like Jeremy."

I stared up at my handsome husband. "Thank you," I whispered, standing up on my toes to brush his cheek with my lips.

"For what?"

"For giving Geneva a second chance when no one would have blamed you for writing her out of your life forever."

"She's your family, Hindley."

"I know, but still."

"Look, I love Caroline and Paul."

"And me?" I asked, batting my eyes.

"Well…" He laughed.

I hit his arm.

"Damn, Hindley, quit hitting me and shoving me. That shit hurts. You're a fucking dynamo."

I giggled when he winced in pain.

"Yes, I love you too." He rubbed his arm where I'd hit him. "I don't want things to be weird for you guys. I'm not saying I'm completely over what she did, and sometimes, I still wait for the old bitchy Geneva to surface. But I have to admit she's changed and that deserves something."

The moment suddenly turned serious. Maybe this was the time to share my news. Instead, I chickened out. "What's in the other box?" I pointed to the one on the floor.

"Oh, this." He smiled. "This is for you."

"Really," I squealed. I loved surprises and Rory was the best at giving them. "Can I open it?"

"I don't know. *Can* you?" he mocked my incorrect use of the verb.

"You've become such a grammar snob, I swear. I'm sorry, good sir. I meant, *may* I open it?"

"Yes, you *may*." He laughed, holding the box up for my scrutiny.

It was huge and I had no idea what could be inside. I was surprised that he hadn't wrapped it, but judging by the sheer size of it, that may not have been possible. "What is it?"

"Open it and find out."

I tugged on one end, trying to pry loose the industrial strength adhesive. "I can't get it," I moaned like a pathetic child.

"God, Hindley, for someone who punches like Floyd Mayweather, sometimes you're the biggest baby."

"Who?"

"Never mind." He ripped the end open with ease. "Here," he sighed, shoving the box toward me.

I peeked inside but it was completely dark. I had no idea what it could be.

"Oh, for God's sake." He took the box from me, stuck his hand inside, and pulled out a brand-new skateboard.

"Oh my God, it's a skateboard," I cried. "For me?" I'd never skated before and the thought was really rather ridiculous when you stopped and thought about who I was married to.

"Yes, for you. You think I'm going to ride this ridiculous board." He rotated the board to show me the bottom.

I busted out laughing. It was black lacquered with a huge emblem of Hello Kitty on one end and hot pink letters on the other that spelled out "DRNK GRL," in graffiti type font.

"Oh, Rory." I took it from him, holding it up in front of me like it was a precious child. I spun all the hot pink wheels.

"Here." He held out a black helmet.

"For me?" I squealed.

"Well, it sure as hell isn't for me." He rotated the helmet.

I laughed again when I saw the sides.

"God, I love your laugh," he said in a wanton voice.

I heard him speak but his words didn't register, I was too entranced by the shiny, black helmet with a Hello Kitty face and her signature bow along with the letters "DRNK GRL" written in cursive.

It reminded me of our wedding bands. We'd each had them engraved before the wedding. His read, 'MY SK8R BOY 4EVR' and mine read, 'MY DRNK GRL 4EVR.' No one else would understand the deeper meaning behind our expressions for each other, and I was completely okay with that. In fact, I counted on it.

"As I seem to recall, Mrs. Gregor, there was a time when you sat in my home in California and told me the only way I would ever be able to get you on a skateboard was if I married you. Do you remember that conversation?"

I closed my eyes, trying to think back, but my brain was fried. I could barely remember what I did ten minutes ago, let alone a year ago.

"You wanted to help me learn to read." He smiled. "I said only if I could teach you how to skate. I believe your words were something along the lines of, 'I would have to marry you to teach you'."

I let my mind wander back in time as I relived the memories in California. Now, I remembered vividly. It was the night I'd given him the journal and set us both on this amazing journey. It was the catalyst that had led us here, to this magnificent facility that offered so much to the kids of the community. And to us.

"Sound familiar now?" He lifted his brows.

I nodded. He was right. "I believe the marriage part of the equation came from you though, Mr. Gregor."

"Those are just semantics, my darling wife."

"Semantics," I repeated. "Ooo. Word of the Day calendar?"

"Courtesy of Mr. Luis Marquez." He grinned. "My attorney slash sports agent. My last one fired me."

I laughed. We'd both agreed that me being Rory's agent after we were married wasn't the best thing for wedded bliss.

He stared at me as he stuck out his hand.

"What?" I asked, looking at his muscular arm. God, he was gorgeous. I always called him sex-on-a-board.

"I believe we have a date with that skateboard." He gestured at my hand. "You've been my wife for several months and you've gotten away with this long enough. It's time your spazzy little ass gets out there on the course and at least tries." He swatted my butt.

I yelped in surprise and anticipation. It was still a wonder how he could excite me by slapping my ass.

"Later for that, Mrs. Gregor, I promise."

God, the erotic tone of his voice was positively unbearable. My legs pressed together in anticipation.

"I can smell you," he whispered against my neck.

"Shut up!" I hit him on the arm.

He grabbed my wrist and his entire demeanor changed. "You hit me again, Mrs. Gregor, and I will take you into that office, tie you to the desk, and spank your ass until it's red, then thoroughly fuck you until you beg for mercy."

His words went straight to my lady parts. I flexed my hips with anticipation, thinking I might just hit him again.

Scanning his face, I wasn't surprised to see a hint of fear in his expression. He was afraid his threat had gone too far, worried perhaps I might consider his threats on the verge of abuse, which would bring back unwanted memories. It pained me that he still felt the need to worry so much about my past and protect me from it. I had to reassure him that was not how I felt.

"Promise?" I whispered in my most sultry voice, my eyes wide with anticipation.

His eyes danced with relief and his lips curled into a wicked smile. Any concern he'd had was wiped away. "Oh, I more than promise," he growled. "I guarantee it."

"I might have to hit you again then." Mockingly, I raised a fist, not surprised when he grasped my neck with his free hand, bringing me in for a forceful yet intoxicating kiss. It lasted forever as we sought our escape in one another's embrace.

I knew it sounded corny and completely unbelievable, but every time we kissed, it took me back to the first one, when he'd totally consumed me at Geneva's wedding. Even then, he'd been protecting me from an old boyfriend. And now, over a year later, he was still ravishing me in the midst of protecting me. There was no bigger turn-on. I had to tell him before he threw me down and had his way with me.

I tried to end our embrace, but he pulled me in tighter, and I knew I would have to ride out this kiss. Not that I minded. I'd been more ramped up with sexual desire for weeks.

"Rory," I moaned against his mouth.

"Hmm." He buzzed his lips against mine, sending a wave of desire through my body.

It took every ounce of effort I had but finally I was able to drag my mouth away. We both stood, panting like dogs in heat, which we kind of were. God, I loved him. I just prayed he would understand when I broke the news.

"What's wrong?" His eyes darted between mine. "Are you all right, are you sick?"

"No." I laughed, thinking of the irony.

"Then, let's go skate." He pulled on my hand.

"Wait." I stopped him.

"What?"

"I don't think it's a good idea."

"Why? Are you scared? I won't let you get hurt, Hindley, you know that."

"I know that," I whispered, looking down at the board, unable to meet his gaze.

What if he was pissed at me, enough to walk away? This hadn't been our game plan. If he left me now, I didn't know how I would ever recover.

His hand slid under my chin as he lifted my face to his. "You're starting to scare me, Hindley. What is it? You know you can talk to me."

Here goes, I had to do it. "Well," I stumbled for words, "I can't skate right now because…"

"Because?" He drew out the word.

"It's just, the doctor doesn't want me doing anything strenuous or dangerous. Not right now."

"Oh, fuck, what's wrong with you, Hindley?" He dropped the board and helmet and took me into his arms.

"It's nothing like that, Rory." Shit, this was going all wrong. I meant to go for humorous, but this was anything but.

"Then what is it?" He leaned back, searching my eyes for the truth.

I nodded down to the board on the floor. "Did Bucky and Pena from River City make my skateboard?"

"Don't, Hindley."

"Don't what?"

"Don't change the subject. You do that all the time. Why did you go to the doctor? What's going on with you?"

"Do you think Bucky and Pena could make another board? A smaller one?" I tilted my head and winced, praying he'd understand what I was trying to say.

"This one is custom made to fit your height, Hindley. It's perfect, you don't need another one."

"Well, we'll probably need another one, a smaller one."

"Why?"

I gazed up at him, trying to gauge his mood by his expression.

"Do they make skateboards for babies?"

"You mean kids? Yeah, they make them for kids, you know that. They supply all our boards for everyone here at the center."

"No." I winced. "I mean, smaller."

His expression went stone cold. "What are you saying, Hindley?"

My stomach twisted in fear. Please, God, don't let him be mad. Don't let him leave me. I drew in a deep breath, hoping beyond all hope that he'd understand I hadn't done this on purpose.

"I'm saying," I released a heavy sigh, "that in about seven months, we're going to need a new board for someone who'll only be about eighteen inches high." I closed my eyes, my entire body tense as I waited for his fury. Instead, there was silence. Deafening silence. This was bad.

I lifted one eyelid, surprised at the man standing before me.

He was smiling, his face innocent and joyous and…happy?

"Say something, Rory," I whispered, staring up at him.

"Are you telling me that you're pregnant, Hindley?" His flat tone was in direct opposition to the smile he still wore.

"Yes." I winced. "I'm pregnant." Tears rolled down my face. "I'm sorry, Rory, I didn't do this on purpose, I swear. The doctor doesn't know how it happened with the IUD. He said maybe—"

My words were cut off as his lips pressed against mine. It wasn't an aggressive kiss, but it wasn't sexual either. It was reverent.

Rory finally pulled away and I was terrified of what I might see. He'd kissed me, so I was pretty sure that was a good sign, but with Rory I never knew.

"Hindley, did you honestly think I would be mad to find out you're going to have our baby?"

I couldn't believe what I was hearing. Was he okay with this? "Well, yeah."

"Why?"

"You don't remember our conversation the day after you proposed?"

"I remember it," he said.

"You said you were scared shitless to be a father, remember? You said you hadn't even thought about kids."

"What I remember is you explaining the fact that I would love anything that was a part of you." He put his hand over my stomach that was already beginning to protrude. "Yes, I'll fuck it up sometimes." He smiled. "We both will. But I think love will overcome it all, don't you?"

Tears streamed down my face. I wasn't sure if it was the hormones, his loving words, or just the intensity of the moment.

"Hindley," he whispered in my ear. "I love you. I'll always love you, no matter what. I'm never letting you go again. I'll love our baby just as much."

"Probably more." I laughed.

"Never." He backed away so I could see his beautiful face. "I could never love anything or anyone as much as I love you, Drunk Girl."

"Me either, Skater Boy. My Skater Boy." I smiled. "I love you *so* much, Rory."

"I know, baby. And we'll love our little nugget even more."

"Maybe it's a Baby Skater Boy." I placed my hand on my stomach. "Or a Baby Drunk Girl."

His eyes flew open. "Oh, shit. What if it's a girl, Hindley?"

"What?"

"Oh my God. I won't be able to sleep ever again."

I laughed at the protective nature he'd already discovered for his unborn baby. He was so amazing.

"I think this baby will be loved and protected its entire life, whether it's a boy or girl, or both."

"Both!" His hands flew up to his head. "Are you having fucking twins, Hindley?"

"No." I laughed. "The doctor only heard one heartbeat."

"That shit's not funny, at all."

"Actually, it was pretty funny." I giggled.

"God, I love the sound of your laughter," he sighed.

"What about me? Do you love me?"

"Always." His blue eyes focused on mine. "I'll always love you, Hindley."

"Forever?" I asked.

He leaned in and pressed his mouth to my ear. "F-O-R-E-V-E-R," he spelled out.

I nodded. "Forever."

Thank you for reading
Extreme Devotion

The first two books in the X-Treme Love Series deal with serious real-life issues. If you or someone you know needs help, please click the **Resources** section of this book to find additional information.

Be sure to turn the page for a sneak peek at
Dana and Peter's love story

Extreme Sacrifice

Dana Di Grazio is fearless and feisty, but struggling to find her purpose in life. Hiding behind a hardened exterior, she's erected walls to protect herself from the devastating losses of her past. When thrust into the role of caretaker for pro motocross rider, Peter Fontenot, she must sacrifice her own boundaries in order to care for him. Fear soon sets in when Dana realizes Peter may be the first man capable of breaking down her walls.

When a motorcycle accident forces extreme sports champion, Peter Fontenot to rely on a foul-mouthed, Italian spitfire, he's surprised to find himself drawn to someone so crass and ill-suited. Suddenly, Peter must rethink the expectations of his well-planned life. Dana is the one thing he doesn't want, but the only thing he can't live without.
Can the spark between two opposites create a lasting fire? Or will it detonate an explosion that leaves them both alone...forever.

Extreme Sacrifice
X-Treme Love Series, Book 3
Available now

BONUS CHAPTER

Can't get enough of Hindley and Rory? Me neither. So I wrote a bonus chapter. Visit my website to read it.

Link to the bonus chapter
www.kaymanis.com/pages/extreme-devotion-bonus-chapter

WANT TO RECEIVE A FREE EBOOK?

Join my email list and I'll send you *Extreme Beginning*, the X-Treme Love Prequel for free. It's the story of Caroline Hagen and Paul Barton. Just visit the website below and join today.

I also give away free things all the time, including ebooks and signed paperbacks (my own and from best-selling authors) and more.

You'll also receive exclusive sneak peeks and teasers of upcoming books in my series.

Join now and receive your free ebook today!

www.kaymanis.com

IF YOU ENJOYED THIS BOOK

Please:

1. Write a review. It's so important to my work.

2. Tell your family and friends about my books.

3. Visit my website and sign up for my newsletter. You can also send me an email. I love to hear from my readers.

www.kaymanis.com

4. Follow me on social media.

Facebook: www.facebook.com/kaymanisauthor2

Twitter: www.twitter.com/kaymanis

Instagram: www.instagram.com/kaymanis

JOIN MY FACEBOOK GROUP
THE MANIS MOB SQUAD

We support and enable those diagnosed with **MOB Disease (Mania of Books)** - a rare and debilitating disease that causes sufferers to become unable and/or unwilling to stop reading and obsessing over all things book related.

Are you a book-aholic? Do you have a One-Click addiction? Then come join this support group. We're all about fun in here, no judgment.

EXTREME SACRIFICE EXCERPT

X TREME LOVE SERIES BOOK 3

DANA

I walked through the entrance of what had once been one of Austin's most dilapidated warehouses, astonished by its transformation. I barely recognized the space. The building had been transformed into a world-class skate park, all thanks to my good friend, Leif Jennings.

Our city was hosting the X Games, and people were coming out for the event like dollar bills at a titty bar. Most people were here for the events, the music and the cameras. My reasons to brave this crowd ran deeper than that.

As I walked down the ramp into the venue, someone shouted my name.

"Dana!"

I turned toward the familiar voice that had been a part of my life for over twenty years—ever since our gym teacher had paired us up as badminton partners in second grade.

As our gazes caught, Hindley and I were transported back to elementary school. We squealed in delight as I flew down the stairs.

"Hindley," I screamed, grasping her in my arms and hugging her tight.

Hindley Hagen was my best friend. Well, now she was Hindley

Gregor, having married professional skateboarder Rory Gregor. Her husband would be competing at this year's event.

Hindley and I had been inseparable since elementary school, done everything, shared everything. Well, almost everything.

"Oh my God, I can't believe you're here," I cried out, holding on to her like someone would steal her. "I've missed you so much."

"We've missed you too," she said.

"Ow." I yelped. The familiar tug on my hair was an instant reminder of the bundle of joy I'd *really* come here to see. I drew back from Hindley's embrace and gazed up into the most beautiful face I'd ever seen.

The toddler in Hindley's arms gave me a mischievous smile. I noted a few more teeth had popped up since the last time I'd seen her. A pang of sadness hit my heart, knowing I hadn't been present for all her milestones.

With her bright blue eyes, blonde ringlet hair and chubby cheeks, Hindley's daughter was a welcome sight. I didn't want to admit it, but she looked a lot like her daddy, and acted like him too.

"Hey, Squirt." I tickled Abbi's belly.

She arched back and giggled.

Hindley and I couldn't help but join in.

"No," Abbi said once she'd caught her breath, swatting my hand away.

Hindley pulled Abbi's hand back. "We don't hit people, Abigail."

"Ooo." I wiggled my fingers in the air. "Using her full name already."

"Ooo," Abbi mimicked, wiggling her pudgy hand.

Hindley shook her head. "Don't encourage her."

"Who, me?" I touched my chest. "Auntie Dana, encourage my niece's unruly behavior? What in the world would ever make you believe I would do such a thing?" I winked at Abbi.

Hindley stared at me, her brows raised. We both burst into laughter.

"Come here, Abbi Wabbi." I tugged her from Hindley's arms. "Who loves their Auntie Dana?" I asked in my best baby talk voice. Usually I made fun of idiots who talked like that, but when it came to Abbi, I willingly tossed out every ounce of self-respect.

"Me, me, me!" Abbi jumped in my arms.

I lifted the toddler high in the air and blew wet kisses on her exposed belly.

Her laughter echoed in the air. If there was a better sound on earth, I'd had yet to hear it.

God, I missed Hindley and Rory and their beautiful baby girl, Abigail Adele. She'd been named after me, both of us sharing the same middle name as my mother. But everyone had called her Abbi since the day she was born.

I clutched her to me and shook my head. "I can't believe how big you are." It always amazed me how much Abbi had changed every time I saw her.

"She's almost sixteen months now, and she has eight teeth," Hindley said proudly.

I'd always wondered why new moms gave the age of their kid in weeks and months instead of years like the rest of us. And why had milestones like how many teeth they had, how many hours they slept consistently through the night, or if they were peeing and pooping in a toilet, suddenly become major news stories?

Hindley was my best friend though and I loved every morsel of information she offered me about anything related to my precious Abbi.

"Show Aunt Dana all your teeth, big girl," Hindley said, staring at her daughter.

Abbi locked her lips and shook her head.

I laughed. If Abbi didn't want to do something, she wasn't going to do it. She was just as stubborn as her daddy, and her momma too, if truth be told.

"You don't want to show Auntie Dana your teeth?" I pouted, hoping to coax her.

She shook her head.

The little stinker. I'd have to try another approach if I wanted to see her new pearly whites.

"Well," I said, "if you had teeth, I was going to take you downstairs and get you some nachos, but—"

Abbi clapped her pudgy hands and squealed in delight.

"I guess we know what she's motivated by." Hindley laughed.

"Like mother, like daughter, apparently."

Hindley shook her head. "You know she can't eat nachos, right?"

"I'll let the cheese soak them until they're good and soggy, won't I, Abbi Wabbi?" I poked my finger in her belly.

She erupted into fits of laughter that warmed my heart. This was the medicine my aching heart needed.

Before Abbi had been born, I had no idea what "love at first sight" was. But as soon as Hindley had placed her in my arms, I'd worshiped the little squirt ever since. If Abbi wanted anything, I got it for her, no questions asked. That was what aunts were for, right?

I had to take every opportunity to spoil her that I could. Hindley and Rory were on the road so much with his skating, I didn't get to spend nearly enough time with Abbi. Thanks to webcams and mobile chatting, I never went more than a few days without seeing her precious face.

Rory and Hindley returned to Austin every few months. They'd opened a facility for at-risk youth a few years ago called Shelly's Hangout. The non-profit was named in memory of Rory's sister who'd died of a drug overdose as a teenager.

The center provided tutoring and counseling for local kids. And the skate park next door to the facility—which had also been designed by Leif—provided an escape from the dangerous streets they lived on. I even volunteered there from time to time.

Sometimes, it hurt me, knowing Hindley was moving on without me. But then other times, like these, when I could revel in my time with Abbi, spoiling her, I forgot about my own dismal future.

Thankfully, Leif lived in Austin so I wasn't all alone. Leif was my best friend, second only to Hindley, and I loved him dearly. Everyone wanted Leif and me to become romantically involved. That only made our decision to remain just friends even harder for people to understand as they tried to push us together.

Leif was everything to me, but it had never been like that for us. We tried to tell our family and friends but no one ever listened. Instead, they were insistent that one day we'd realize our friendship had blossomed into something much stronger. They were so fucking clueless I almost felt sorry for them. I could have assured them that day would never happen, but that was Leif's story to tell and was best kept close to my heart.

"Ready, Squirt?" I asked Abbi as I bounced her on my hip.

She nodded enthusiastically.

"Let's go. See ya, Momma," I shouted over my shoulder, giving Hindley no opportunity to resist the kidnapping of her daughter. I half walked, half jogged down the ramp toward the concession stand. Abbi and I laughed as her beautiful blonde ringlets bounced with every step.

I glanced at the lines. Since the X Games was an international event, people had come out in mass. Rory's first event wasn't scheduled for another few hours but the crowds were growing quickly.

Abbi would grow impatient if we had to wait long. She wasn't a patient kid. The situation had the potential to turn lethal, for me and those around us. I laughed silently.

"You're just like your daddy, you know that, Squirt?"

"Da-da." She clapped.

"That's right. He's your daddy, isn't he?"

She smiled wide, nodding enthusiastically.

Abbi adored Rory. And he worshiped his little girl. He was such a wonderful father.

"Dah-nah," Abbi called, stroking my face with her little hand.

"Oh my God, I can't believe you just said my name." I grinned like the smitten idiot I was.

She slid her arms around my neck and nestled into my shoulder.

I inhaled her delicious baby scent as I rubbed Abbi's back. "I love you so much, Squirt," I whispered in her ear.

One of her hands slowly slipped down my back as she began to rhythmically pat me.

This was exactly what I needed, unconditional love from the little girl who'd captured my heart the instant she was born.

I absently moved up the line, not really focusing on anything except my little squirt.

"What can I get you two pretty ladies?"

I started at the attendant's booming voice.

"Oh, um." I surveyed the menu.

"Nah-toes," Abbi yelled.

The man and I both laughed.

"One order of nachos then?" he asked.

"Yah," Abbi squealed and clapped.

"Looks like it," I said.

"Anything to drink, hun?"

I'm sure Hindley had packed some type of nutritious, kiddie fruit drink for Abbi, but it was my turn to spoil my niece. "Whatcha want, Squirt?"

Her brows knitted and her lips pursed as she tilted her head and stared at me with the most adorable frown.

I turned back to the attendant. "What do you have?"

"For the little lady there," he looked over at Abbi, "we've got Sprite, Coke, Dr. Pepper and Hi-C Fruit Punch."

"See, see, see," Abbi exclaimed.

The man smiled. "I like a lady who knows what she wants. Hi-C it is."

The middle-aged man filled a small cup and secured it with a lid, holding it out to Abbi. "Straws and napkins are right over there, ladies." He pointed toward the side of the counter.

I took a straw and unwrapped it, putting it in Abbi's cup.

She grabbed the drink and clutched it with both hands, shoving the straw in her mouth.

"And for you, Momma?" the man asked.

"Oh, I'm not her mom. I'm not anyone's mom, actually." A sense of longing pierced my heart at the admission. "I'm actually her aunt," I said, trying to cover up my pain. "Well, not by blood, but still." Oh God, why was I babbling to this man?

"Well, then, what will it be for you, sweet Auntie?" He winked.

"What do you have on tap?" I asked. My nerves were already frayed, and if the past had taught me anything it was that alcohol would cure what ailed me, even if it was only temporary.

"Let's see," he turned, "we've got Bud Light, Miller Lite, Coors Light."

I laughed to myself. All light beers. Gag. "Nothing local?"

"'Fraid not, sweetheart." He shrugged.

"All right, give me a Miller Lite, please."

"One Miller Lite, coming up. I'll just need to see some ID."

Oh, shit. I'd left my purse back with Hindley. I'd only shoved money in my pocket, not my ID. I looked back at the line. It was twenty people deep now.

"Nah-toe, nah-toe," Abbi yelled.

Well, fuck. There was no way I could hold up the line to run back to the grandstands. Abbi would have a shit-fit if she didn't get her nachos soon. I guess it was Hi-C for me too.

"She's cool." A deep voice rumbled beside me.

My arms prickled. That voice. Good Lord, it was sexy as hell.

I turned, not surprised to find a man whose very presence screamed Sex-on-a-Stick.

He was tall, but then who wasn't compared to my five-foot-two frame. His jet-black hair fell in waves, like mine, but was cut short. His natural curls were barely visible. Unless you gawked at him like I was now. He had a strong jaw littered with stubble that you knew he kept just for effect—and it was working.

The man's gray T-shirt was stretched taut across his broad chest, hanging loose around his narrow waist. His well-defined biceps stretched the sleeves to the point I thought the material might rip. Black jeans hugged his muscular thighs and I swallowed back a moan. He looked like a model who'd just stepped out of a *GQ* magazine photo shoot, despite the fact he probably hadn't put much effort into the outfit.

An aching throb pulsed low in my mid-section, making me realize it had been way too long since I'd had sex.

Finally, my perusal led me to his face and my breath caught. His eyes. They were mesmerizing, each a different color—and at that moment, locked on mine.

"Are you finished looking?" he asked.

My face flushed with heat. It was unlike me to embarrass so easily.

"Nah-toes! Nah-toes!" Abbi cried, jolting me from my lurid thoughts.

"All right already, Squirt." I turned back to the concession worker. "Um, forget the beer," I said.

"Too late," the man said.

I glanced down at the counter, surprised to see a plastic cup filled with amber liquid sitting next to Abbi's nachos. I stared at the cup then back to the attendant. "I thought you needed my ID?"

He nodded toward the mystery man next to me. "If Peter says you're good, you're good."

Peter?

Who the fuck was Peter? And why was his word golden?

I turned and stared at mystery man, Mr. Sex-on-a-Stick. He must have been Peter.

"Uh, thanks, I guess." I shrugged, staring just beyond him, avoiding his eyes. I bit my lip in an unusual display of shyness. God, what was wrong with me? Guys never made me nervous.

"Need a holder?" the attendant asked behind me.

Shit, I'd forgotten about our order. I was carrying Abbi. I only had one free arm. How the hell was I going to carry all of this crap and Abbi?

"I've got it," Mystery Man said. He reached over me, his huge hand grabbing the beer, his other the nachos.

I drew in a breath, about to argue, but his scent invaded my senses. I shook my head to clear my wayward thoughts.

"Don't you need to order?" I asked.

"Pee-tah, Pee-tah," Abbi cried, reaching for Mystery Man. She leaned so far, she nearly fell out of my arms.

He stared down at me, one brow arched. "Nachos or Abbi?" he asked.

I stood motionless, unable to think or answer him. God, his voice, it was too sexy to be legal.

He tilted his head, eyes narrowed, staring at me like I was a dumbass. "Well?"

"How do you know Abbi?" I finally asked.

"Pee-tah," Abbi squealed again, reaching for Mystery Man.

Without answering my question, he set down our food and drinks and slid his large man-hands under Abbi's arms. As if he'd done it a hundred times, he scooped Abbi from my grasp and shook her high above his head.

Her uproarious laughter echoed through the cavernous underground.

Mystery Man grinned, revealing teeth so white they could be in a toothpaste ad.

Holy fuck, this dude was hot. I couldn't remember being instantly attracted to anyone in a long time, if ever. Shit like this only happened in sappy-assed romance movies. Didn't they?

Suddenly it hit me like a ton of bricks. This was a stranger to me and he had my Abbi in his clutches.

The momma bear in me sprang into action. I reached up to grasp Abbi from his hands. Ah, who the fuck was I kidding? The man was a giant, and with Abbi held up so high in the air, it would have taken a six-foot ladder for me to reach her.

I put both hands on my hips. "Give her to me," I said, stomping my foot.

Mystery Man remained unfazed by what I thought was a death glare. He was enthralled by Abbi's squeals of laughter.

"Give her to me. Now," I shouted. My voice echoed through the area like a shotgun.

Everyone in line turned their heads and stared at us.

Mystery Man brought Abbi down to his chest, clutching her tight, but still didn't relinquish her. His mismatched eyes narrowed as he studied me like I was the crazy one.

Maybe I was.

I held out my hands to Abbi. "Come on, Squirt."

She shook her head and curled up in a tight ball, hiding her face into Mystery Man's neck.

I envied the little shit for being so close to this dude.

He smirked, as if he'd won some silent competition.

Now I was really good and pissed. "Abbi, come here now," I demanded in a firm voice. "Mommy will be very worried if we don't get back soon."

"Pee-tah go," Abbi demanded, pointing back to the arena.

"Looks like you're stuck with the nachos and drinks," Mr. Sex-on-a-Stick said. His smug laughter surprised me.

My body burned, and not with fury. Dammit, why was he affecting me so much?

Before I could say a word in protest, Mystery Man turned and walked toward the ramp leading back into the arena.

I ran to catch up with his long strides.

"Miss," the man from behind the concession stand called. "Don't forget your food."

Shit! Abbi's nachos.

"Wait," I shouted to the fleeting couple. Racing back to the concession stand, I scooped up the nachos and beer before turning to chase after Mystery Man. Instead of moving forward, I took one step and crashed into something hard. "Oh, shit," I shouted, raising my head.

Standing before me was a tall, well-built man, now covered in beer. My beer.

I lifted my gaze and our eyes locked. One dark blue, one hazel green.

Mystery Man.

"Well, shit," I muttered.

"Shit," Abbi repeated with perfect clarity.

Oh, double shit! Hindley was gonna kill me if she ever heard Abbi say that.

Wait, what the hell was I worried about? Her father's favorite word was fuck. It was probably the first word Abbi had ever learned.

I snorted at the image of Abbi screaming "Fuck, fuck, fuck," and Hindley having a field day, ripping Rory a new asshole.

"Is spilling beer all over me funny to you?" Mystery Man's low voice rumbled with irritation, all trace of the playfulness from earlier gone.

What? Was he serious?

I stepped back, eyes narrowed, and glared at him. "What the fuck are you talking about? This was all your fault. You're the asshole who stole my niece."

He jerked his head back, his upper lip curled in disgust as if I'd thrown dog shit all over him.

Was he shocked by my language? Oh well, welcome to the world of Dana Di Grazio.

Yes, I knew I should have chosen better language being in public, and in front of Abbi, but this a-hole deserved it. He was the one who'd stolen

Abbi from my arms. He was the one who planted his huge beast of a body in front of me.

Averting my eyes from his scrutiny and judgment, I stared in front of me at his chest. Wrong choice.

His T-shirt was soaking wet, and solidly stuck to his chest and abs. His body underneath was just as I'd envisioned, rock hard and all man. The dude lit my body on fire without even striking one match. Now I felt like the asshole.

"Sorry," I said quietly, trying to save my pride but failing.

"It's all right," he said. He tugged his shirt away from his body and fanned the material in the air to dry the stain.

I noticed my own chest felt unusually cool. Glancing down, I discovered my T-shirt was also soaked through. My eyes went wide with horror when I realized my nipples had tightened into hard pebbles.

I reached to cover my boobs with my hands but remembered they were full with nachos and a half-empty cup of beer. My massive breasts and pert nipples were now on prominent display like I was in a wet T-shirt contest. Shit! Maybe he wouldn't notice.

I slowly lifted my head, not surprised to find his gaze fixated on my chest. God, I wanted to die of embarrassment.

Suddenly his eyes darkened and his pupils dilated. Did he like what he saw?

I bit back a moan. What was wrong with me, lusting after this dude?

His eyes slowly lifted until his gaze met mine. He stared at me, his mismatched eyes holding me captive. His lips parted and his tongue licked at the corners of his mouth.

A hunger rolled through me that no meal would ever satisfy. I drew in a sharp breath, my body vibrating like a spring wound too tight.

No matter how disgusted he'd been by my earlier outburst, one thing was clear. He was just as turned on as I was.

Mystery Man blinked several times and turned back to Abbi. "We better get you back to Mommy," he said, tickling her belly.

Abbi giggled and just like that, the spell was broken.

Without another word, he turned and walked toward the arena entrance.

I stared at his delicious ass as he strutted in front of me. The view from behind was every bit as glorious as the one from the front. In that moment I knew I was in trouble. Deep trouble.

To read more of Dana and Peter's love story purchase
Extreme Sacrifice
X-Treme Love Series, Book 3
Available now

ALSO AVAILABLE BY KAY MANIS

X-Treme Love Series

Extreme Risk (Hindley and Rory)

Extreme Devotion (Hindley and Rory)

Extreme Sacrifice (Dana and Peter)

Extreme Trust (Dana and Peter)

Extreme Attraction (Geneva and Berk)

Extreme Courage (Geneva and Berk)

Extreme Promise (Hindley and Rory)

Extreme Gift: The New Arrival (Hindley and Rory)

Extreme Beginning: The Prequel (Caroline and Paul)

Baxter Bay

You Could Be Mine (Aiden and Olivia)

Sumner Brothers Series

Born to Be My Baby (Ben and Maggie)

Never Say Goodbye (Emmett and Elle)

Thank You for Loving Me (Max and Devlin)

With These Two Hands (Aaron and Kayleigh)

I'll Be There for You (Jake and Lina)

If That's What It Takes (Grant and Sophie)

Now and Forever (Max and Devlin)

Season of Love Short Story Series

Second Chance Heart

Dance with Me

Fall for Me

ACKNOWLEDGMENTS

I found out when you write a book, there are *a lot* of people to thank along the way. So here goes…

Kimberly, my daughter (a girl who's more like me than she'll ever admit) — You were the first person to believe in my abilities as a writer. My intense, late night therapy sessions with you really are the reason I'm still writing. I can't thank you enough for making me believe in myself. I love you, shoogie and wish you much success in your own life. I hope I can be there for you as much and as often as you have for me.

Tony, my husband — You've been my best friend since we met, and one of my biggest supporters throughout this process. Your belief in me boosted my confidence and made me take this crazy-ass journey into the unknown world called writing. Your support has allowed me the freedom to pursue a dream I never even knew existed. I love you.

Lorrie Anson, my editor — You've made me a better writer in spite of myself. You've also become one of my best friends. Words can't express how much your friendship means to me. I truly am blessed to know you. And equally as blessed that you put up with all my psycho bullshit.

Julie, Melody, Christina C. Stacy, Christina B., Jessica, Elisabeth and Jane, my Beautiful Beta Bitches — You girls helped me find the voice within me that I never knew existed. Thank you for giving up your spare time to help me make my series the best it could be.

RESOURCES

The first two books in the X-Treme Love Series deals with tough issues facing some of us today. I didn't want to leave you, the reader, hanging, especially if you or someone you know is going through the same situations as Hindley and Rory. Below is a list of resources to help guide you should you need it. And please feel free to contact me any time and I'll be happy to talk to you. Just visit my website for contact information.

wwww.kaymanis.com
Don't suffer alone!

CHILD ABUSE
National Child Sexual Abuse Helpline
Darkness to Light
www.d2l.org
1-866-FOR-LIGHT (1-800-367-5444)

National Child Abuse Hotline
www.childhelp.org
1-800-4-A-CHILD (1-800-422-4453)

DOMESTIC VIOLENCE
National Domestic Violence Hotline

www.thehotline.org
1-800-799-SAFE (7233)

National Coalition Against Domestic Violence
www.ncadv.org
1-800-799-SAFE (7233)

SEXUAL ASSAULT

National Sexual Assault Hotline
www.rainn.org
1-800-656-HOPE (4673)

SELF INJURY

S.A.F.E. Alternatives
Self Abuse Finally Ends
www.selfinjury.com
1-800-DONT-CUT (1-800-366-8288)

Safe Haven
www.self-injury.net

To Write Love On Her Arms
www.trloha.org

ADULT LITERACY

American Library Association
Adult Literacy Program
www.ala.org/advocacy/literacy/adultliteracy

America's Literacy Directory
www.literacydirectory.org

ABOUT THE AUTHOR

Kay Manis is a funny chick who's sprinkled with a little crazy on top. Okay, let's be honest. . . there's ALOTTA crazy up there.

She writes books filled with passion, promise and purpose (with laughter and a few tears, but always an HEA).

She is a native Texan and lives with her family in Florida. When not reading or writing, you'll find Kay eating out with friends or napping with her favorite pillow (stolen from an Inn in Vermont - true story).

Please feel free to contact her at: **www.kaymanis.com**

 facebook.com/kaymanisauthor2
X x.com/kaymanis
 instagram.com/kaymanis

.